The Edge of Sleep

And then she heard the boys. They were laughing out loud just as she was inside and the sound rang through the mall like birdsong in the spring.

Dee turned and saw them, angel boys, cherubs taken straight from Italian frescoes and put in baseball caps and jeans.

Perfect boys. Young and funny and sweet. As jolted with energy as young cubs frisking outside the den, as innocent as seraphim. Perhaps one of these wonderful boys was hers.

Dee put the pill back in her purse.

David Wiltse is a playwright and novelist. He is the author of *Home Again, The Fifth Angel, The Serpent, The Wedding Guest* and the three suspense thrillers featuring Becker – *Prayer for the Dead, Close to the Bone* and now *The Edge of Sleep. Prayer for the Dead* was chosen by *Time Out* as one of their books of the year.

David Wiltse

THE EDGE OF SLEEP

Mandarin

A Mandarin Paperback
THE EDGE OF SLEEP

First published in Great Britain 1994
by William Heinemann Ltd
This edition published 1994
by Mandarin Paperbacks
an imprint of Reed Consumer Books Ltd
Michelin House, 81 Fulham Road, London SW3 6RB
and Auckland, Melbourne, Singapore and Toronto

Reprinted 1994

A CIP catalogue record for this title
is available from the British Library
ISBN 0 7493 1788 4

Printed and bound in Great Britain
by Cox & Wyman Ltd, Reading, Berks

To Annie,
to Laura and Lisa,
and to Elisabeth,
with love to all.

1

Along the border between Virginia and West Virginia the mountain ranges of the Alleghanies and the Appalachians erupt like the edges of a worn molar through a jawbone, eroding cusps rising irregularly beyond the tree line and running roughly parallel through the dentition of the American south-eastern massif.

Thirty miles outside of Wytheville where the eruption is at its sharpest stands a jagged eructation of rock called Hatchetface. With movements as whimsical and random as bugs in water, a small team of climbers picked its way slowly up a face of stone, a facet of the mountain side that had sheered off as if from a hammer blow, shedding its burden of ages in a cataclysmic rending and leaving itself splinter straight and smooth. It was the most difficult ascent on the mountain and the climbers had chosen it for that reason. They were not after elevation – there is no oxygen-thin height in the east – but hardship.

The leader of the group reached a two-foot-wide ledge that jutted from the face like the serrated tooth of a saw. Carefully hauling himself up, he wedged a nut into a seam in the rock and secured a spring-loaded carabiner gate to it. The climbing rope went through the carabiner and anchored the safety line for those who followed him.

His arms were trembling with the stress of the climb

and he let them hang at his side as he looked down at those coming up the mountain to join him. The nearest was a young woman. Lithe and lean, she scrambled up like a spider, seeming to follow the leader's hard-earned path as if she were weightless, as if she could have come straight up without benefit of hand holds or rope, carried aloft by an updraft. Below her, however, the next climber was struggling. In the informal nomenclature of the sport the leader was known as Ace because he was the first on to the mountain. The young woman was Spidey and the middle-aged man below her was Rich. It was not his name; the others accused him of being wealthy.

Rich had made a wrong move. Out of boldness or over-confidence he had ignored the leader's carefully chosen route and struck out on his own. The two paths ran parallel to each other, did not deviate by more than a few feet, but the difference was crucial. The handholds that had lured him had turned out to be inadequate and Rich was caught now in mid-step without the ability to advance or retreat. Like a jumper who has learned in mid-air that the ground before him has opened into a pit, Rich had nowhere to go but down.

The leader shouted instructions, trying to direct Rich's blind feet to a position that would support his weight but the man was already too far gone. The young woman had reached the ledge and the leader pulled her alongside him.

"He's going to go," the leader said. "We'll have to pull him up."

Twenty feet below them, Rich had begun to buck violently, his whole body quivering.

"What's wrong with him?"

"Cramps," the leader said. He pulled the safety rope taut while Spidey chocked a secondary anchor into the seam of the rock. "He's been putting too much strain on his hands and feet for too long. He must have been frozen in that position for several minutes."

"I never realised," she said.

"Wasn't your job, it was mine," the leader said.

"It was *his*. Why didn't he call out, tell me he was in trouble?"

"Too proud," the leader said. "And pride goeth before a fall. Get ready."

A fourth climber was hurrying upwards towards Rich but he was too late to help. Rich's spasms bucked him off the mountain face and the leader and the young woman strained against the rope. Rich swung on the end of the lifeline like a human pendulum, his whole body shaking as if he were having a seizure. With the fourth climber assisting from below, the leader and the woman pulled Rich up to the ledge as he quivered and yelled in pain, powerless to help himself.

They stretched him flat on his stomach on the shelf of rock, his muscles fighting against them, trying to bend his body into the fetal position. The woman sat on his legs, the leader on Rich's back, pinning him so that his gyrations didn't jolt them all off the ledge. The fourth climber had secured himself just off the ledge, his feet standing on pitons as if on a ladder so he could help with his hands.

"What do I do, Ace?" the fourth climber asked. He had to yell to be heard over Rich's agonised cries.

"Take his arm, bend against the cramp," the leader said. "Then massage as deeply as you can."

The woman was bending Rich's toes towards his head, digging her knuckles into his calves where the muscle had bunched so violently it felt like a rock under skin. The muscles in the small of his back spasmed suddenly and he arched, bowing like a breaching dolphin, nearly hurling the leader's weight off the face.

Rich's cries and their own shouted communications were so loud that they didn't hear the helicopter until it was almost upon them. The whump of the rotors slammed off the mountain wall, drowning any human noise. The rescuers looked up to see the 'copter hovering a few hundred feet from the mountain. A signal light flashed insistently from the open door of the helicopter and the climbers could see two helmeted heads in the front of the machine. The letters F B I were written large in white on the side.

The occupants of the helicopter had not spotted the climbers. They continued to scour the area, still flashing the coded light message for the whole mountain to see.

After the leader managed to get the cramp in Rich's right arm to release, he turned to help the young woman work on the man's tortured legs.

The helicopter came back for another pass, farther away this time. Someone inside had swung the light around so that it was still aimed at the mountain. The flashes came in measured bursts.

"What the hell is that about?" the woman asked.

The leader studied the lights, his lips moving silently.

"It's Morse code," he said.

"What does it say?"

The leader spoke the letters as he saw them come in their longs and shorts.

"B ... E ... C ... K ... E ... R."

"Becker?" the woman said, puzzled. "What's a becker?"

The leader sighed heavily, then returned his attention to Rich's leg. "I'm afraid I am," he said.

2

Dee was looking for something to beat him with. Cursing, she thrashed angrily around the room, testing potential instruments against the furniture, then tossing them aside – sometimes hurling them at him in disgust at their inadequacy. Ash lay on the bed, waiting. He watched as she tugged furiously at the clothes hangers in the motel closet, but they were clunky wood and metal things, permanently secured to the rod. Their resistance only enraged her further. He thought of telling her that she had already tried the hangers, but decided against it. A wire clothes hanger had always been her favourite whip in the past but the current frugality of the motel chains had forced her to use whatever came to hand.

He lay on the bed, waiting. She would find something she liked eventually. Although it looked at the moment as if she were going to use all of her fury on the search itself, as if she might collapse, exhausted and spent, before she even got around to Ash, he knew that once she started the beating her vigour would be restored. She drew strength from the violence, just as her anger fed on itself to grow into rage.

She turned for the third time to her suitcase as if she expected a wire hanger to materialise suddenly. Ash did not remind her she had already looked in the suitcase. He had left the hanger behind in their previous motel when she told him to pack. He did not like the wire hanger, it was too thin and left ugly welts. She had been suffering one of her blinding headaches which was why she had entrusted him with the packing, and she had not noticed when he slipped the hanger under the bed. Ash was surprised that she hadn't caught him in the act of betrayal. She always seemed to notice everything. She had told him many times that she could read his mind and he believed her. Maybe the headache had affected her mind-reading ability.

She stopped abruptly, her back turned to Ash, and let the suitcase fall to the floor. Slowly she turned to face him and her voice was very calm.

She had read his mind after all.

"Where did you put the hanger?"

Ash did not even think of lying to her. It never worked, she saw through him like glass.

"I left it in Branford, he said. He thought Branford was the last town they had lived in. He wasn't sure, geography confused him.

"You did it on purpose," she said.

What was the point in denying it? She knew everything. Her face was very, very still as she looked at him. Her lips were taut and the skin around her mouth had turned a greenish-white. White patches showed on the wings of her nostrils where they flared out from the central ridge.

She was very dangerous when she got like this. It was at such times that she really hurt him.

"Take off your clothes," she said. Her voice was so low he could barely hear her.

"I'll get you another hanger," he said as he rose from the bed. "I'll get it right away." He yanked his shirt over his head without undoing the buttons. "I know where to get one."

6

"No, you don't" she said.

She was right. He did not know where to get another wire clothes hanger although he thought he might be able to steal one somewhere. He felt self-conscious as she continued to stare at him. It was so much better when there was anger in her eyes. Now there seemed to be nothing there at all, as if she had gone away and left her body frozen in place behind her.

Ash looked down at his chest where her gaze was fixed. He was a big man, massive through the upper torso without need of weights or exercise. Dark hair sprouted and curled from his belt up to the soft skin on his throat. He knew she hated the hair and at first she had made him shave it but she had abandoned that process since starting with the boys. The boys had changed many things.

"The pants," she said.

Ash stepped out of his pants and stood naked before her. He had stopped wearing underwear several months ago when she forgot to buy him a new pair.

"Give me the belt."

Ash pulled the belt from his trousers and handed it to her. He watched carefully to see how she wrapped it around her hand. If the buckle was in her palm, he would be all right. He did not mind so much when she used the belt because it was a broad strap of leather and the blows did not cause welts.

She put the tip of the belt in her palm and wrapped it once around her hand, leaving three feet of leather dangling down. The buckle was on the hitting end.

"We will see how much you prefer this to the hanger."

She made him ball his socks and put them in his mouth, then bent him over to clutch the back of the chair. In this position she could hit all of him, everywhere.

She beat him in silence punctuated only by the grunt of her exertion, the whoosh of the belt, the slap of leather on flesh, the duller sound of metal colliding against skin. Normally she would scold him, tell him what he had done wrong, revile him with his own failings. This time she was saving her energy for the job at hand.

Ash held on. There was comfort in knowing he deserved it. He always deserved it. There was not punishment enough in a lifetime to be more than he deserved.

When he came to, Ash could hear her steady breathing from the bed. He lay on the floor where he had collapsed, his face pressed against the musty, threadbare carpet. His balled socks were only inches from his face. He lay very still for a long time, knowing that when he moved the pain would overcome him again. He wished he could see her from where he lay on the floor; he loved to watch her sleep, knowing she was safely in the same room with him, at peace, so that he could watch over and protect her while she was swathed in what little calm and serenity she ever knew. He would watch her half the night, one eye on the television screen, the other noting her every shift and turn. The sweet tranquillity of her face in slumber restored Ash from the turmoil of her waking hours and he knew that he loved her then.

He pushed himself to his knees and the pain came at him from all sides. He gripped the chair to steady himself but could not keep from pitching forward again. For a long time he stayed on all fours, his head hanging down like a sick animal. He was careful not to moan too loudly and wake her. He did not want her to see him like this; she was used to thinking of him as powerful. Sometimes she called him her bear. Those were the good times, the very good and tender times. Ash worried that she would not continue to think of him as her bear if she saw him so bruised and swollen and sore that he could hardly move. He must get dressed and hide his condition. His

8

face was unmarked, she was always careful about his face, and with the boys as well. It was important to her that everyone should be able to go out in public the next day as if nothing had happened. That was especially important with the boys, of course. She didn't mind if Ash spent days at a time in the room, but she liked to have the boys with her in public. That was the whole point of taking them.

He must dress himself but first he must be sure that she was not in danger. Ash's beating had been very severe – that was unusual for her. It was a bad sign. He crawled to the bed and raised himself to look in the purse which was on the night stand. Ash rummaged through the purse until he found her medicine. Everything was all right. She still had it, the bottle was half full of pills. She wasn't in danger, she was still with him. The beating must have been especially severe only because her thoughts of what he had done overwhelmed her. That was all right, because he deserved it.

Ash found his own pills in her purse. At least a dozen remained in the plastic bottle. So he was not in danger, either. She was still taking care of him. He eased himself on the bed beside her and closed his eyes. He would pretend to be asleep because she preferred not have to deal with him immediately upon waking. Ash never really slept, he didn't allow himself to. He didn't dare to allow himself to sleep, even with the medication, but he was very good at pretending. He eased his breathing into the same steady rhythm as hers and let himself think of her and not the pain. He was so glad she lay beside him. He was so grateful to her.

Tomorrow he would go out and find a wire hanger for her, he didn't care what he had to do to get it. He would ask the motel people, they would help him.

"I love you, Dee," he whispered softly.

3

The helicopter landed on a private airstrip that normally handled only two single-engine planes and the gliders they towed aloft for rides at fifty dollars per trip. As most of the customers returned to earth disappointed by the noise and bumpiness of glider travel – if not actually airsick – there was little repeat business. The field was almost knee high with weeds and the shack that served as control tower/ reception area looked equally unkempt and neglected.

The owner of the airfield was overjoyed and a bit awed by the sudden arrival of a chopper filled with FBI agents. He entertained the pilot at the counter that served as ticket office and operations room while Becker and Karen Crist sat across the room at the magazine-littered wrought-iron table that had once served as garden furniture. The owner brought Karen and Becker styrofoam cups of instant coffee and, at a glance from her, retired to talk to the pilot. He tried to engage the pilot in flying stories but the other man only grunted, wishing the owner would shut up so that he could more effectively eavesdrop on his boss and her legendary guest.

Becker looked at the coffee with some distaste. Clots of white artificial cream floated on the surface.

They had not tried to fight the roar of the helicopter

engine and had ridden in silence. When he spoke, it was the first time he had addressed her since their initial meeting.

"Thanks for the ride," he said. "I've always wanted to come here."

"I thought we could talk better here than the side of a mountain," Karen said.

Becker sighed. "I thought I was retired."

"It probably just felt that way because you weren't working. Actually, you're on what's called 'indeterminate medical extension'. I looked it up in your file."

Karen looked at the surface of her coffee as she stirred it. It was hard to meet his eyes after all these years. But he still looked straight at her most of the time. She remembered that. She remembered most of it, maybe all. Which didn't necessarily mean that she was ready to deal with it again.

"I wanted to make sure," she continued.

"Of what?"

"That you were available."

"Silly me. I was actually convinced I was out of the business."

"Indeterminate medical ..."

"Who determines when it's determined? Me or the Bureau?"

"It's a mutual thing," she said. "You can come back to work whenever you think you're ready."

"Or?"

"Or the Bureau can reinstate you."

"They can, huh?"

"I mean, they can change your status."

He grinned. "Have you come to change my status, Karen? No one's touched it in such a long time, I didn't think I still had one."

"That's not what I heard," she said.

11

"Is that in my file, too?"

"There's also an unofficial file," she said. "You know that."

"I seem to remember."

"They say you were living with a woman during the Roger Dyce business."

"I was."

"And?"

He was looking squarely at her. Karen forced herself to keep her gaze on the bridge of his nose. It could give the impression that she was looking him in the eye, not that Becker would be fooled, of course.

"What happened with you and … ?"

"Cindi. With an i."

"Cindi." Karen squirmed in her seat, crossed her legs, looked away from him. She remembered clearly that he was wonderful to talk to when she was willing to be as honest as he was. It was only when she was being evasive or less than candid that it got uncomfortable. Becker had so little tolerance for doing things in a roundabout way. It always made him act as if he knew the joke and was just waiting for her to get to the punchline. It was the way he was acting now.

He was going to make her ask again.

"Are you still together?" she asked.

"The file is out of date?" He sounded amused. "She found it rather difficult to live with me. I'm sure you can sympathise with that."

"Actually, you and I never really lived together," Karen said.

"Not actually."

Karen sighed. "Look, do we have to go into it?"

"Not if you want to avoid it."

"I don't want to avoid it … I just don't want to go into it. It's very painful, all right?"

12

"Sorry." Becker changed the subject. "What are you now, second-in-command in Kidnapping?"

"How did you know?"

"I read your file."

"When?"

"Most recently? Six months ago."

"They let you do that? While you're on indeterminate?"

Becker laughed. The pilot glanced in their direction.

"They let me do all kinds of things, as long as I don't ask officially. No one wants Hatcher to find my name on any request memos."

"Hatcher has nothing to do with Kidnapping," Karen said.

"I know. He keeps getting kicked upstairs. All he has to do is screw up one more case, blame it on somebody else, and he'll make Deputy Director of the whole Bureau."

Karen let the Hatcher discussion die. It would only make her job more difficult if Becker got riled up about his former colleague.

Becker swept all the magazines into a pile and dropped them behind him on the sagging naugahyde sofa. The sofa frequently doubled as a bed for the owner and his form was permanently moulded into the cushions. Karen allowed herself to study Becker for the moment that he wasn't looking at her. He seemed so little changed by the intervening decade since she had last seen him. The unfairness of it almost made her laugh aloud. She was showing every one of her thirty-six years and probably a half dozen more thanks to stress and insufficient sleep. By all appearances Becker, whose internal life she knew to be as tormented as a self-flagellating anchorite's, seemed impervious to age. The jawline was still as firm, the stomach as flat, the eyes as unwrinkled as ever. There was a bit more grey in the hair, but that only served to add a touch of distinction. It was worse than unfair. She thought he had even improved with age.

"So you've been a hermit for all this time?" she asked.

"Hermit – or pariah ... let's just say I've been living alone and managing well enough."

"I'm glad to hear it. I mean, that you're managing well enough."

"Which is not to be confused with liking it." Becker said.

"So how often do you look at my file?" she asked.

Becker shrugged. "A couple of times a year."

"Why?"

He shrugged. "Going fishing? Why do you suppose I look at it?"

"I didn't want to suppose. I wanted to know. That's why I asked you."

"What makes you think I'll tell you?"

"Because I think you'd rather be honest than smart," she said. "You're completely without guile when it comes to women, aren't you?" She touched the back of his hand and he recoiled slightly in an involuntary moment.

"Have you been theorising about me for the last nine years?"

"It's been ten years and it wasn't a full-time preoccupation."

"And you concluded from my lack of guile that I'm a block of stone, is that it?"

"On the contrary. I think you're the most vulnerable man I've ever known."

After a moment, he said, "I'm not going to do it, Karen."

"Do what?"

"Whatever you've come to ask me to do."

"OK. I didn't think you would."

"I can't."

"I understand."

"I have everything under control now. I want to keep it that way."

"You no longer feel the urge ..."

Becker shook his head. She tried again.

"The compulsion ..."

"Desire," he said.

" ... to kill ..."

"More like lust than anything else. But stronger. Much stronger ... but it's gone now. There's no reason for it to arise in my new life."

"I understand," she said.

"I doubt it. The only people around who can really understand are in prison."

"You put them there," Karen said.

"Some of them. Some of them I killed."

"You were always justified," she said.

"So they tell me."

"Why don't you ever take it easy on yourself, John?"

"Because everyone else does, I suppose. Somebody's got to punish me." He grinned but she knew he was not joking.

"You're a lot more open about it than you used to be," she said.

"It's the AA twelve-step method. First you admit what you are to the group. Problem is, I can't seem to get a group together. Everytime I find somebody with the same problem, he ends up dead. We never seem to have conversations."

"You didn't kill Roger Dyce."

"No."

"He tried to kill you. You were alone with him, he was armed, he tried to kill you. The man had murdered at least a dozen people, he killed an agent, he was about to kill your friend, the cop ..."

15

"Chief of police. He's touchy on the subject. Tee Terhune."

"You had provocation, you had cause, you had opportunity. Maybe you wanted to, I don't know."

"I wanted to. The way an addict wants a fix."

"But you didn't. You brought him in."

"It was a very near thing," Becker said.

"We knew that. Everyone knew that. You battled with yourself and won."

"My file must be popular reading."

"It's not in your file."

"But the Bureau knows."

Karen shrugged. "They know you've caught people no one else could find. They know you've been in situations no one else would have survived. They know you're the best hunter in the FBI, with more skill, more courage, more intelligence, more ... what should I call it? More 'understanding' of the mind of a serial killer than anyone in the Bureau."

"Call it 'fellow feeling'. "

"I won't call it that and I don't see what good it does you to do so. You've never done a thing that wasn't in the line of duty and perfectly justified by the circumstances."

"Thank you. I feel so much better now. You've helped me to see that I've been beating myself for no reason at all."

"Gold thinks you're ready to work again," Karen said.

"Good of him. The alcoholic is sober so take him out and buy him a beer."

"He doesn't see it that way."

"Possibly because he has his head up his ass. Hard to see things my way from that position."

"I would think that is your position," Karen said.

Becker laughed. "But for me it's a normal posture." He

touched her hand with one finger, drawing it slowly from wrist to fingertip. "I'm sorry I jerked away from you a minute ago," he said. "I'm not used to being touched."

"You used to be very receptive," she said. She noticed that the pilot and owner had stopped talking. She did not look at them.

"That's when you were single," he said. He lightly pinched her ring-finger where a wedding band should have been. "Did you take it off just for me or don't you wear one for professional reasons?"

"The file is out of date," she said. "I've been divorced for four months and separated for three years before that."

"Sorry," he said.

"Not at all. But thanks."

She pulled her hand from his fingers, glancing towards the pilot. The pilot was staring too innocently out of the window.

"I'm really not here to stir up any old flames, John. I'm here to get your help."

"So tell me about it," he said.

"About what?"

"The case that was so important you needed a helicopter to find me. That's an expensive item compared to a phone call."

"Did you have phone on the mountain with you? Wish I'd known. Besides, I thought you weren't going to help me."

Becker shrugged. "I'll help you if I can. I'm not going to get involved. If I can do anything useful while I'm sitting here, I'm happy to help."

Karen placed a folder on the table in front of him. He abruptly put his hand on it.

"Don't start with pictures of the victims," he said.

"All right."

"That was always hard to take."

"I don't enjoy it either, but how do you know they're those kind of pictures? This is kidnapping."

Becker removed his hand from the folder. "Kidnapping ends up one of two ways," he said. "The victim is released or the victim is dead. You didn't come to see me about victims who have been released."

"There's a third alternative," Karen said. "Sometimes the victims stay missing."

"Those are kids who are taken by one of the parents in a custody dispute and packed off to a different State. You didn't come to me for that kind of thing, either."

"Why not?"

"It's not where my talents lie."

Karen nodded. "OK."

"And it cost you too much personally to seek me out and talk to me again," he continued.

"Did it?"

"You may not be as guileless as I am, Karen, but that doesn't mean that you're unreadable. Whatever this case is, you felt it was worth the price, which means it means a lot to you."

"Yes. It means a lot."

"Save the pictures. I'll look at them if I have to, but first just tell me about it. Let me get a feel for the case without the emotional load of the pictures."

Karen blew softly and silently through her lips before starting. "It's kids," she said, her voice barely above a whisper. "Some son-of-a-bitch is killing kids." Karen was surprised and embarrassed by the sudden flood of emotion. Her voice cracked and her eyes filled with tears. Becker reached out to comfort her but she pulled back from him and shot her chin up. When she spoke again she sounded angry but there was no sound of tears in her voice. "Kids – boys – have been going missing from New

York, New Jersey, Massachusetts, Connecticut. They're gone for a time, a month or two – the longest was eleven weeks – and then they are found dead."

"How many?"

"Six – that we know about. The first that suits the pattern was a nine-year-old boy named Arnell Wicker who disappeared from a shopping mall in Upper Saddle River, New Jersey. Eight months later it was a boy from Bethpage, Long Island. Last seen in another shopping mall. His mother let him go for a slice of pizza while she was buying some shoes. He never came back. They found his body in a garbage bag beside the highway thirty miles from Bethpage two months later."

"When was the next one missing?"

"Eight months later. Peabody, Massachusetts. Body discovered six weeks later."

"How long had he been dead when he was discovered?" Becker asked.

"Less than forty-eight hours. Again it was in a garbage bag, beside a highway."

"This one taken from a shopping mall, too?"

"Yes."

"You've checked all the employees to see if any of them worked in more than one of the malls." It was not a question; Becker knew the answer.

"One employee in common. Peter Steinholz was the manager of a cookie franchise in Upper Saddle River and in Stamford, Connecticut where the fifth boy was snatched. He's a family man, wife, two kids."

"Doesn't mean anything."

"No prior arrest record except one DWI three years ago. Reasonable alibi. He checks out pretty clean."

"Sales reps? Suppliers? Service people? Anybody who might have been at all the malls? The guy who fixes the cookie-maker's ovens, for instance."

"A few overlaps, six or seven, but the timing is wrong on all of them. You know it wouldn't be that easy or we would have found him already."

"I'm just asking out of habit. I know you've done all you could or you wouldn't be here. Tell me about the fourth one."

"Ricky Stine, Newburgh, New York. Disappeared from a schoolyard during recess. Went out to play with the rest of the kids, never came back. They thought maybe he'd just wandered off, had him listed as a runaway for a couple of weeks until they found his body."

"Why a runaway?"

"He was hyperactive, always into trouble of some kind. Not a bad kid, just hard to control. His parents said he'd had a history of running away from home, showing up again in a day or two. This time he didn't show up again."

"How long was that after the kid from Peabody was found?"

"Ricky went missing six months later."

Becker nodded. He kept his eyes fixed on the folder as if reading it through the cover.

"Significant?" she asked.

"Not yet. How long till number five?"

Karen looked at her notes. "Four and a half months."

"He's getting more frequent. There was an interval of eight months after the first two, then six months, then four and a half."

"Because he's getting away with it? More confident?"

Becker shot her a glance. "He's not thinking about getting away with it, not when he snatches them. Later, when he has to dispose of the body, he might think about details then."

"What is he thinking about when he snatches them?"

"He's not thinking at all. He's feeling."

"Feeling what?"

20

"I don't know yet. I don't know what he does with them."

"When I tell you what he does with them will you know what he's feeling?"

Becker heard the trace of contempt that Karen could not hide and looked up from the folder. He leaned back in his chair. "It's why you're here, isn't it?"

"Sorry."

"You don't approve, but you'll use it."

"I didn't mean anything, John. I know you don't like it."

"I don't know anything everybody else doesn't know. The only difference between you and me is that you censor it out. You don't allow yourself to think it, or feel it and so you tell yourself it's alien to you. My particular curse is that I can't censor it out. I know what those bastards are feeling because I can't keep it out. You can. Inside, you're just the same as I am."

Karen shook her head adamantly.

"You don't accept that about yourself? That you have the capacity to understand even the worst of the bastards if you'd allow yourself?"

"You wanted me to believe this before. I don't."

"You won't."

"No, John. I don't. I do not know what they're feeling when they do the things they do. I don't mean anything against you, but I just don't have the capacity."

"You don't want it."

"You're right. I don't want to get into their minds. I don't want to get into their hearts. I just want to catch them and put them behind bars. That's all."

"I'm not suggesting you would ever act on those feelings, Karen. I accept that those who do are different. But having the feelings in the first place ..."

"When you see the photos, you'll know what I mean. I could never empathise with this monster in any way ..."

"Empathise is not the same as sympathise. I'm not suggesting you feel sorry for him."

"I hate him," she said. She pushed the folder towards him. "Look at them. Look at the pictures and tell me I have anything in common with this beast. Look at them."

She spilled the photos on the table, spread them out with a push without looking at them herself.

Becker winced. The photos were taken in the morgue. He recognised the particular light and clarity, the coldly impersonal attention to detail. It was not as bad as seeing the bodies in person, but it was bad enough.

Becker knew he would have to study the pictures later, but alone, when he could allow himself to feel the complex mix of revulsion and sickened fascination without a witness. The photos were obscene, but he had seen worse. And so had Karen. At this moment the strength of her reaction concerned him as much as the cause of it.

Becker shuffled the photos together and put them back in the folder. "What were they beaten with?" he asked.

She looked neither at him nor the table. "A variety of instruments, apparently. Some of them wooden, they left splinters. Some metalic. They found paint chips under the skin. Some were caused by unknown objects."

"Lumber or wood?"

"What?"

"Were the splinters from processed, finished lumber, or was he using birch switches off trees."

"Birch switches? When was the last time anyone used a birch switch for anything? The wood was processed, lacquered, chemically preserved, rot retarded, commercial pine. Birch switches? You've been in the mountains a little too long. How can you look at those pictures and ask me if someone beat those kids with a switch?"

Becker sat quietly, waiting for her anger to pass. "I'm out of practice," he said at last.

Karen breathed deeply and placed her hands in her lap. "Sorry," she said softly.

"Tell me about number five."

"Stamford, Connecticut. A mall, a very big one called the Town Center."

"Where the cookie man – Steinholz? – worked."

"Correct. Larry Shapiro, shopping for a birthday present for his mother with his teenage sister, who met some friends, got talking, told Larry to amuse himself for a minute. She thought he had gone to the toy store ... They found his body on the divider of the Merritt Parkway six weeks later."

"On the divider? Not the side of the road?"

"On the divider. Is that significant?"

"Curious, anyway. The divider is on the driver's side of the car, in the passing lane. I know the Merritt Parkway, there's no way you could pull over and stop on the divider without drawing an awful lot of attention to yourself."

"Which means?"

"Which means either he stopped on the right-hand shoulder, which is not uncommon and wouldn't attract too much attention – but then he had to carry the body across the highway to the divider. Or he pushed the body out of the driver's side while driving, which makes him both very strong and very adroit. The boy was how old?"

"Nine."

"While driving he had to lift a corpse weighing what? Sixty? Sixty-five? Seventy pounds? This one was in a garbage bag, too?"

"The manufacturer calls them leaf bags. You can buy them in any grocery store by the dozen."

"So he had to manipulate a seventy-pound bag, even tougher because there's nothing to grab on to, no arms or legs for leverage."

"Christ, Becker."

"You want me to stop?"

"I don't like the image of this monster grabbing a nine-year-old boy by the arm and tossing him out the window."

"The boy was already dead."

"I'm not sure that makes it any easier to take."

"He was already dead, wasn't he?"

"Forensics said he'd been dead about three hours before he was thrown on to the divider."

"He was thrown then?"

"At some time after death, anyway. There was vast post-mortem trauma."

"Was the bag torn?"

"I don't know. But they're made not to tear."

"Find out."

Karen nodded.

"So, either we have this guy performing a considerable feat of strength while driving a car at some speed, or else we have him dashing across the highway with a body-bag in his arms. Either way he's taking a considerable risk. Why?"

"I don't know. Why?"

"Only one reason I can think of offhand. Were the others found on the side of the road?"

"Yes."

"So why is this one in the middle? What is there about the middle of the road that is different from the side – where it would be a lot easier and safer to put the body?"

"Don't play Socrates with me, John. If you know, tell me."

"If the body is on the middle divider, you can't tell which way the car was going when the body was dropped. If the body is on the right-hand side, you might as well place an arrow saying 'car going this way.' But if it's in the middle, the car could have been going in either direction."

"Which tells us the bastard is concerned about being followed. He knows, or thinks he knows, that we're after him."

"Maybe," Becker said.

"Which means he's left a pattern and is aware of it and thinks we are, too."

"Although you're not," Becker said.

"Yet," said Karen. "Which means he knows we're after him in the first place. Now, how would he know that? We weren't posting rewards, there was no publicity suggesting a connection between these cases."

"But the Bureau had in fact already linked these deaths?"

"I've been working on it since Ricky Stine in Newburgh. The computer alerted us of the similarities."

"You've been on the case for a year?"

"Seven months."

"Two kids killed in seven months' time?"

"Six months. We found the latest a month ago."

"He's accelerating very rapidly."

"That's part of the reason I'm here, John. This guy has started to need them so frequently he's practically in free fall. If he knows we're on to him, it hasn't slowed him down, it's only made him cagier."

"So how does he know you're on to him? Does he have a spy in the Bureau?"

"I'm not that paranoid."

"Maybe he knows someone has been asking questions."

"How?"

"Maybe he knew someone who was interrogated?"

Becker left it hanging for her.

"Or maybe we interrogated him? Christ, Becker, do you think we might have talked to this guy and let him go?"

"I don't know. He didn't change his pattern until after the fifth one was snatched – and before you knew he was dead. I'd go back over the interviews at Stamford, maybe you'll catch something you missed the first time."

Karen's face had turned grim, her jaw clenched. "If he's in the interviews, I'll find him," she said.

"There's another possibility for covering his tracks in Stamford, of course, that might not have anything to do with his knowing about your investigation. It might just be a special place for him. Maybe he's from Stamford originally. Maybe someone who knows him is there. Maybe there's a clue of some kind there that he knows about but can't change. Just an awareness of his increased vulnerability could cause him to act differently."

"Still another reason to go back to Stamford."

"I'd say so. It can't hurt to go over the ground again. And there's one other thing the body on the divider can tell us."

"Why do I have to ask?"

"I'm thinking it through. It's really a pretty clumsy way to put your pursuers off the track. A far better way would be to dump the body somewhere far away from the highway so there's no clue as to direction at all. Or better yet, hide the body completely, give yourself months to get away. Or simply drop the body on the right-hand side of the road, turn around and go the other way. He didn't do any of those things, and my guess is that he was in too much of a hurry. He'd been seen with the kid or something else happened to panic him. Check the incident reports with the Stamford police to see if anything unusual happened within a few hours of the estimated time of death. If he left fast, what did he leave behind? Did he leave owing rent, a mortgage? Most likely not, since he seems to be moving around so much. He's probably a transient. In a motel, not a hotel – you wouldn't want to walk through a lobby with a kidnapped child. Check all the motels in the area, see who left that day, particularly anyone who left either without paying or ahead of time ..." Becker paused and smiled at her. "You've done all of this already, haven't you?" he asked.

"Most of it," she said. "But you're right, it wouldn't hurt to check again."

"It's not what you need me for."

"In part. You're very good at it. I hadn't considered I might actually have interviewed the son-of-a-bitch and let him go. I can't tell you how that makes me feel."

"You conducted the interviews, Karen?"

"Some of them."

"The second in command of Kidnapping is in the field doing interviews in person?"

Karen shifted uncomfortably. "I haven't forgotten how. I'm pretty good at it."

"I don't doubt it. Normally."

"What do you mean, 'normally'?"

"If you're not too involved."

"Of course I'm involved. I've been working on the case for seven months. I want to hang the bastard by his balls."

"You were doing interviews in the field in Stamford after the fourth boy's disappearance. That was after you'd been on the case for only about five months."

"Five months is a long time."

"Not really. Certainly not long enough to drive most deputy directors out of the office and on to the street. Every one of them I've ever known has been more than happy to give up fieldwork. It doesn't look leader-like, poking around amongst the common folk, asking questions any agent could ask. It doesn't help someone with

27

ambitions to lay her reputation on the line by going back on the street. It's a dumb move, Karen, especially if it doesn't pay off. It makes you look like a poor agent and a lousy executive. That's why I say too involved."

"That's why I came to you."

"Maybe. Although I doubt that you'd come to me just to save your ass, even assuming I could do it. Or would do it ... How old were the victims, Karen?"

"Four of them were ten years old, two were nine."

"Your file says you have a child. A boy, isn't it?"

"Jack."

"About ten?"

"He turns ten in three weeks."

"Does that have anything to do with your extra involvement?"

"That's fairly simplistic reasoning, especially coming from you. I don't see that my son has anything to do with it."

"You have custody?"

"Of Jack?"

"Someone got custody after the divorce, right? Is it you? Or is it your ex-husband?"

"What the hell does the status of my custody arrangement have to do with anything?"

"I don't know. What is it?"

"I don't think you'd be asking a man this question. Would you need to know Hatcher's 'extra involvement'? No, you'd just treat him as a fellow professional and get on with it."

"I happen to know that Hatcher doesn't have enough creative imagination or sensitivity to get involved in anything other than his own career. You are very different, Karen, although you're still ambitious as hell. You have both the imagination and the emotional proclivity to get involved."

"Emotional proclivity? Come on, Becker. Speak English, you're among friends."

"You know what I'm talking about."

"No, I don't. And I never did. You wanted me to have some twisted involvement in the Bahoud case. I thought I understood why, back then. You were sleeping with me. We were about half in love, I guess. You wanted someone to share what you were feeling about the case because it frightened you and made you lonely, so you imagined I was the same way. But I wasn't. I almost wanted to be, just because of our relationship, but I'm not that way. I'm just not. Why you need to think I'm that way today is frankly beyond me."

Becker stood up and put his hands on the back of his chair. "Tell me about sixth victim," he said.

"Why do men always do that? The minute a problem comes out in the open, the very second you have a chance to discuss something, off you all go. Out of the room, out of the house. Don't want to talk about it, case closed."

"I don't remember you being quite so much fun to work with the last time," he said.

"That's because you were so busy humping me."

"Humping you? I thought we were 'half in love'."

"Maybe you were, maybe you weren't," she said. "I just said that."

"Were you?"

Karen shrugged. "Half, a quarter, an eighth. Some, John, OK? Some."

"So then what's with the humping?"

"That's what we did on the bed."

"I get the impression I'm being blamed for that part," Becker said. "For you it was being some fraction in love and for me it was humping, is that how you remember it?"

"To tell you the truth, John, I scarcely remember at all …

Oh, yeah, I nearly got killed and spent a month in hospital. I remember that part."

"Do you mean I tricked you into doing something that you didn't want to do? Is that what you mean? You'd already been married and divorced by twenty-six. How did I seduce you? Put drugs in your drink? Did I charm you out of your pants? I think we've already established that I don't have any charm."

"I believe we agree on that point, yes. The pilot is laughing at us, if that interests you."

Becker turned toward the pilot who was openly staring and trying unsuccessfully to assume a straight face.

"Can you imagine anyone seducing Deputy Assistant Director Crist?" Becker demanded.

The pilot coughed and turned back to the owner again. They suddenly became involved in a weather chart. In fact, the pilot had spent the better part of his trip to the mountains trying to figure a way to make a move on Deputy Assistant Director Crist without endangering his career. If Becker had ever seduced her, the pilot would have loved to know how. So would most of the men in the Bureau. If the Deputy Director had had any private life at all following her divorce, it was exceedingly private. Her brief affair with Becker ten years ago was well known, of course, because Deputy Director Hatcher had flirted briefly with the intention of making an issue of it. But, as with most things involving Agent Becker, this case had fallen into a special category. Becker, it was rumoured, literally got away with murder. Like most of the other agents, the pilot did not hold it against him.

Still fuming, Becker strode to the soft-drinks machine, kicked it, and returned to the table. The owner thought briefly of saying something but a glance from the pilot persuaded him otherwise. Becker sat abruptly.

Karen said, "I'm supposed to command these people,

John. It doesn't help if you have these little tantrums and involve me in them."

"Is that the voice you use to keep your son in line? Stern but reasonable?"

"Jack doesn't kick things," she said. "And he doesn't embarrass me in public."

"Sounds like a dull kid."

"Never say that to a parent," she said sharply. "Jack is a wonderful child, a bright and sensitive and creative boy who doesn't need to get violent to express himself."

Becker gave her a wan smile. "Sorry," he said.

"We seem to have drifted a bit from the point. The sixth victim," Karen continued, "was Craig Masoon who vanished from a school trip to the Natural History Museum in Quincy, Massachusetts."

"How soon after the previous victim?"

"Two and a half months."

"Christ. He's not just hungry any more. He's ravenous. How long did he keep this one?"

"A month."

"And how long ago did you find the body?"

"A week."

"He's about due to strike again."

"That's another reason I'm here."

"You expect me to stop him before he takes another kid? You don't need me, you need a miracle. Try prayer."

"I have," she said. "The Lord helps those who help themselves."

"Glad to hear He helps someone," Becker said. "What kind of profile do you have on the kids?"

"All boys, nine or ten years old. Caucasian, brown hair, eyes either blue or brown – four brown, two blue. All boys next door."

"Next door to whom, though? You've seen their pictures, I mean the ones from home, not the morgue shots,

31

what do they look like, Karen? Are they beautiful, male model types? Tall, short for their age; do they all wear glasses, were they all wearing baseball caps? Give me something to work with."

"They're white bread," she said. "Norman Rockwell kids, snub-nosed, freckled-faced – without the actual freckles, if you know what I mean. Nice looking, nothing extraordinary. None of these kids were living in a slum, they weren't runners for drug-dealers, they weren't gang members." A bitterness had crept into her tone. "They look wholesome, if you remember what that's like. Hell, John, they look sweet. They look innocent. They look the way you probably looked as a kid."

"At that age, I looked scared," Becker said.

Karen paused. Then, gently, "I know, John. I remember you told me. These kids must all have looked awfully scared for the last weeks of their lives, too."

Becker nodded, looking at the table.

"You survived it," Karen said, her voice still low and gentle. "They didn't. In a couple of weeks another one won't."

"Cause of death?" He was still looking at the table.

"Asphyxiation."

Becker came to himself abruptly. "Asphyxiation? Not the beatings?"

Karen shook her head. "Medical thinks the prolonged and repeated trauma must have brought them pretty close to death, but at the end he smothered them."

"Smothered, not strangled?"

"Medical thinks it was probably a pillow, blanket, something like that. There was no real sign of struggle at the end. But then there wouldn't have been any hair or skin or blood under the nails, anyway."

"Why not?"

"They were washed thoroughly after death. 'Cleansed'

is how Medical put it. Nails cleaned, hair combed, bodies scrubbed. Not a fingerprint on them, not a trace of anything."

"Hair combed?"

Karen nodded. "Parted and combed … And cut."

"Cut? He gave them a haircut after he killed them?"

"It looks that way."

Becker thought for a moment. "He may be saving the hair. We may be looking for someone with a bag full of trimmings."

"What does he want with them?"

"How the hell do I know. They were sexually abused, I assume."

Karen shook her head. "It puzzled all of us, but no. No sign of sexual abuse."

Becker was silent for a long time. "I assume the Investigative Support Unit is involved? Have they given you a profile of the guy?" he asked finally.

"Sort of. It isn't much help yet, they don't have a lot to work on and they seem to be thrown by the lack of sexual abuse."

"Did Gold have anything to offer?"

"Gold was a bit confused."

"Surprise, surprise."

"He's helped you, you've said so."

"Allow me my own twisted response to my shrink, if you don't mind. What was he confused about?"

"He thought it was very unclear, he was getting conflicting signals from this guy. At least Gold was frank enough to admit it."

"So the psychological profile isn't much use?"

"As usual. You can give us a better one."

Becker looked at her, smiled ruefully. "We know why that is, don't we?"

She chose to ignore his remark. "I'll let you see Gold's

33

profile, of course. I can put everything we have in your hands in less than a day."

"How much do you have on the man himself?"

Karen glanced at the pilot and owner, then back to the file on the table in front of her.

"Nothing," she said finally.

"Partial description?"

"No one has ever seen him."

"He took six kids away from public places, once from a schoolyard, once from a school outing at a museum – and no one saw him?"

"No."

"He just walked off with them? No protests from the kids, no foot dragging, no struggles, no tears. Nothing to make anyone notice? Nothing to even make someone imagine they saw something peculiar? There's always someone around who's willing to make up something in exchange for attention from us. No lonely clerk who likes having the FBI talk to him as long as he can fantasise what he thinks we want to hear?"

"Nobody, John."

"Who is this guy, the Invisible Man?"

"The agents are calling him Lamont Cranston. Apparently there was an old radio show called *The Shadow* about this man, Lamont Cranston, who could cloud men's minds and become invisible ..."

"I remember," said Becker.

"Before my time," said Karen.

"Your loss," said Becker. He fell into a deep announcer's baritone. " 'Who knows what evil lurks in the hearts of men? ... The Shadow knows'."

"Yeah, I've been hearing a lot of that one," Karen said.

"Orson Welles did the voice, I think," Becker said.

Karen waited impatiently, clearly not interested in nostalgia.

"How does he get them to leave so peacefully that no one sees anything?" Becker was musing aloud, not expecting an answer. "As if he had them hypnotised."

"We checked hypnosis, actually."

"I wasn't serious," Becker said.

"We weren't either, but we checked it anyway. None of them had ever been previously hypnotised, so there was no post-hypnotic suggestion at work."

"What physical evidence have the forensic people come up with."

Karen shook her head. "Nothing. I know it's hard to believe, but nothing. I told you the bodies had been cleansed. There was nothing in the bags except the bodies. No hair samples, no prints, no fibres ... Part of that is the nature of the plastic used in the bags, apparently. It's chemically inert and very smooth so it won't pick up fibres from a car's seat covers, for instance."

"No prints on the outside of the bags? That stuff will hold fingerprints."

"Only the prints of the people who found the bags along the highway. I don't know, John. It's like he killed and cleaned them in a scientific lab."

"You've checked that?"

"In every case we investigated every lab within a fifty mile radius of where the kids were taken. Every medical lab, every scientific research facility, every university with a science department, every place we could think of that keeps a sterile facility."

"Nothing?"

"Nothing. Hundreds of names of people who work there or have access to the facilities. But no connections to the victims, at least none that the computer could find. Maybe you could tell the computer what else to look for."

Becker fell into a deep silence. When Karen started to speak to him he lifted one hand, stopping her. After a moment she slid out of her chair and crossed the room to join the pilot and the airport owner. Instinctively, they all spoke in hushed tones.

"Is he going to help find Lamont?" the pilot asked.

Karen arched her eyebrows, cocked her head slightly. Becker was not a man to make predictions about.

"He's helped already," she said.

"Did he come up with something?"

"No. But he's confirmed that we've done all the right things."

The owner craned his head to look past Karen, studying Becker as if seeing him for the first time. "Is this guy really all that bright?" he asked.

Karen shot the pilot a hard glance. She did not like the idea of discussing Bureau business with a civilian.

"I just mentioned that he's someone special," the pilot said shamefacedly.

"Doesn't look it," said the owner.

"That depends what part of him you're looking at," Karen said.

The owner looked at the pilot, suppressing a smile. The woman wasn't his boss, after all. He had no reason to be afraid of her.

"What part are you looking at?" he asked.

"The part that's looking at you," she said.

Becker was still staring blankly at the table.

"He's not looking at me," the owner said, puzzled.

"Which ought to tell you something," Karen said. To the pilot she said, "We'll be leaving in fifteen minutes. Are you ready?"

"She's ready when you are."

The pilot looked at Becker. If one hadn't heard the stories they told about him, Becker would appear to be a fairly rugged man, no longer young but certainly not old, an ex-athlete perhaps, who still stayed in shape, still had his hair. Presentable but nothing remarkable. But if the viewer had heard the stories; if even half of what they said about him was true …

Karen sat down at the table again and waited for Becker to return from wherever he had gone. She remembered having found him in the middle of the night in the living room of the hotel suite they had shared in New York, while on the Bahoud case. He had been sitting in the dark and, when she asked him why, he had said because he was afraid of the dark. His face was wet with tears. She had thought him the strangest, most exciting man she had ever met. That night she had comforted him with her body and the next day he had killed the murderous Bahoud in a prolonged struggle in the pitch-black sub-basement of the apartment building where he had been hiding. Becker had killed the man – who was armed with two weapons – with his bare hands in utter blackness and Hatcher had said they had located Becker at last only by the screams he emitted. He had wept again when he sat beside her hospital bed and she knew that he was crying as much for himself as for her.

She had lied earlier when she told Becker she had been half in love with him. She had been totally in love with him, and frightened by what he represented and of the danger he posed to her control of herself. Ten years later, she still could not look at his hands without wanting to feel them on her body.

"This is going to hurt," he said, jolting her out of her reverie as he came out of his own.

She understood that he was talking about himself.

"I don't think I can do it without you," she said. "He'll keep on doing this until we get dumb lucky. We don't have much time."

"You don't have any," Becker said. "He's snatched another kid already."

"Are you sure?"

Becker shrugged. He wasn't certain but it made no difference. If Lamont hadn't struck again, he would at any moment. "Why shouldn't he? He's hungry, he'll eat." He looked directly at her for the first time in several minutes. "It's going to hurt a lot," he said.

"I know." She touched his hand with hers. "I do know, John."

"I have sole custody of my son," she said at last.

"Your husband fought it." It was not a question.

"Bitterly," she said.

"And?"

She knew he was way ahead of her already, but there was sometimes a necessity to go through the formalities.

"And I wasn't sure I should have custody at all. I'm not sure I deserve it … I'm not sure I want it …"

Becker waited, looking at her.

After a moment she said, "It scares me, John. Having complete control over him. I'm … I'm sometimes afraid of what I might do."

Becker nodded slowly. He gripped her hand with his own, squeezing briefly. "You won't," he said.

Becker pulled the file with the photographs towards himself. "I'll need to look at everything as soon as you can get it to me," he said. "But first I need to be alone with these."

4

Dee was feeling good, she couldn't remember when she'd been in such good spirits. She felt so good she didn't even object to the sight of Ash eating tacos.

She saw the man watching her from his solitary table in the corner where he sat nursing a cigarette and a cup of coffee. He couldn't take his eyes off her. She knew she was fascinating. A vibrant, attractive woman, full of energy and high spirits. Who wouldn't watch her? Who wouldn't want her?

She said something to Ash and then laughed, tossing her head back, filling the place with her ringing merriment. Dee loved her laugh, it was so free, so honest. She hated people who tittered behind their hands. Dee let the whole world know she was amused, God damn it, and if it was too loud for some people, then to hell with them. They didn't know how to have a good time. If there was anything Dee did know, it was how to have a good time. She was even having a good time right this minute, watching Ash spill taco and salsa on himself. She knew the secret of joy. Some book had come out with a title like that, *The Secret of Joy*, and Dee had read it to see if the author was someone like herself. But she hadn't known what she was talking about and after a few pages Dee had thrown the book across the room in disgust. The real secret, the only secret, was to just let yourself. If you wanted to laugh, then laugh, God damn it. Laugh as if you meant it and screw all the poker-faced killjoys like that toad of a cashier who was looking at Dee as if she had her tit caught in the cash register. The man in the corner knew what she was laughing about. She could see him smiling from the corner of her eye. She could tell he was caught and mesmerised by her.

"Dee," Ash said, sounding worried again. He looked at her with concern, bits of tomato and shredded lettuce spilling from the taco.

There was a bar at the restaurant just a few doors down. Dee had made note of it as soon as they entered the mall. "Ash, I want you to walk home," she said.

His eyes went wide.

"You work your face like a clown," she said lightly.

"Sorry," Ash said.

"Don't apologise. I like it, it makes you easy to read," she patted him on the cheek.

"Walk home?"

"Don't act like you've never done it before. You know how to do it. Go out of the mall and turn left."

"Left," he said, concentrating.

"Turn left and just keep walking until you get to the motel. You know the name of our motel, don't you?"

"OK," said Ash.

"OK nothing. What is it?"

Ash furrowed his brow and she laughed again. "You wouldn't even have to paint the creases and lines on the way clowns do," she said merrily. She glanced to see if the man in the corner was appreciating her good humour. He smiled and inclined his head slightly. Dee looked at him as if he had startled her with his familiarity, as if she had only now become aware of him and wasn't at all certain how to take such boldness.

Ash saw the exchange and knew why he was walking home. He would be spending another night outside the room, listening to Dee and some stranger. But mostly to Dee, her laughter, her shouts of exuberance, her ecstatic screams at the end. It hurt him so much to listen to her, to see her behaving this way for the benefit of the strange man in the corner, to know she was giving herself to someone else.

"What is it?" she was saying.

"Nothing," he said, thinking she was enquiring about his thoughts. She would figure it out on her own soon enough, she always did, but it hurt him even more to tell her how much it hurt.

"Nothing? That's a strange name for a motel."

"Oh." So she was not reading his mind. That happened sometimes when she was this happy. She seemed to lose her magical wisdom when she was this way.

"Day's Inn?" he guessed.

"Daybreak," she corrected him. "Daybreak Motel. Got it?"

Ash nodded.

"Say it."

"Daybreak Motel. Daybreak. I turn left and stay on the highway till I get to Daybreak Motel."

"That a boy. You'll do just fine. Now pop the rest of that muck into your mouth and off you go."

Ash rose dutifully and let her swipe once at his face with a napkin.

"Are you all right?" he asked.

"Never better," she said. "Don't worry about a thing, we've got the world by its ying-yang."

Ash smiled. He thought the word was funny even if her mood frightened him.

"Now scoot," she said.

"Daybreak?"

41

"Stop stalling and go on."

Ash shambled out the door, looking back at her once with the face of a mourner, and Dee waved goodbye to make sure the man in the corner understood that she was now alone.

She stayed at the table for a few minutes more to emphasise the separation. She opened her compact and checked her make-up, holding the mirror at an angle so that she could see the man's reflection. He was still studying her, of course. He couldn't keep his eyes off her. Now he raised his hand and wiggled his fingers in a greeting. The gesture looked silly in the mirror, weak, feminine. Dee hoped he wasn't one of those, but if he was, there were lots more fish in the sea and she was just about the best bait they were likely to come across.

Dee started out of the taco shop and paused once to look back at the man. She held his eyes fully and smiled. He smiled back. Dee saw no point in being too subtle about these matters. It just wasted time.

The bar portion of the restaurant was noisy and she could hear the music and the sound of voices spilling out as soon as she stepped from the Mexican place. At this time of night most of the shops were closed except for the food pavilion and the individual restaurants so a little more noise would get no complaint from neighbouring merchants.

Dee had time to order a white wine and study the men on either side of her before the man from the restaurant showed up. The other men looked passable enough, provided they were in proper working order – so many men were not these days – but she still preferred her friend from the restaurant. He was a little younger than the other two, a little cuter, and he did not sport a gold chain. Dee had long since despaired of men who wore gold chains as hopeless to talk to and useless in bed.

"Is your – uh – friend gone?" he asked.

Dee looked at him, then around the room, then back to him. "I like to think I have friends wherever I go," she said.

"I'll bet you do, too. I just didn't want to intrude if your friend was coming back. He's one big bruiser, I wouldn't want to get on the wrong side of him."

"He's gone home," she said.

"And left a pretty lady like yourself all alone?"

"He's never much company at the best of times," she said. "I like a man who can express himself. Can you express yourself, Lyle?"

"Edgar," he corrected her.

"You're not one of these strong, silent types, are you? Although you look strong, I like strength, but not silence. I like to know how a man is feeling. I like some noise."

"I thought you might. When I saw you in the restaurant, I said to myself, there's a very pretty woman who is not afraid of a little noise. I'll bet she's pretty noisy herself. Under the right circumstances."

"Are you the right circumstances, Lyle?"

He grinned, a lop-sided affair that dragged his face to the left and narrowed his eyes. Dee realised he thought it was his sexy look. "You better believe it," he said. He leaned closer to her. Dee grasped a hair from his chest and yanked it free from the skin. "Hey!"

"Just checking," said Dee. "You are going to be noisy, aren't you?"

Ash trudged along the highway, keeping his head down so the approaching headlights would not blind him. The gusts of wind created by passing trucks were strong enough to rock him and many of the motorists honked at him even though he was not on the road. He could hear their bleeps dropping downscale as they raced away, still angered and startled by his appearance in a night they had assumed was ordered just for them and the traffic.

It was always a bad sign when she sent him home alone. He knew she still had her pills, he had checked only two days ago. Maybe he should count them, he thought. Maybe she had them but wasn't taking them. She was feeling too good, she had too much energy and too much enthusiasm. Something was bound to disappoint her eventually. If nothing else, then Ash himself. And when she was disappointed she would crash from where she was now. She would fall as fast and as far as the eagles fell when they swooped down for a rabbit. Ash loved to watch them on the nature shows on television, the way the great birds just folded their wings and plummeted straight down from the clouds. Watching the birds was exhilarating, but watching Dee was terrifying. Like the birds which always rose up once more triumphantly clutching a fish or a hare, Dee would rise again with her prey in her talons.

Lights behind him flashed bright and dim, bright and dim, and he heard a horn blaring a tatoo of recognition. Dee's car flashed by and he caught a glimpse of her waving hand, her smiling face illuminated by the beams of the car behind her. She blew him a kiss, still honking as she sped away towards the motel.

The man from the restaurant was in the car behind Dee. Ash saw his puzzled look as he stared at Ash momentarily before he, too, raced away into the darkness towards the motel.

"See you later, Lyle," Ash said. His voice was drowned out by the whoosh of air, the squeal of tires on pavement.

Ash put his head down and trudged on.

Edgar decided she could call him Lyle – or Heathcliff or Geronimo if she wanted to. He certainly wasn't going to

44

keep correcting her and risk queering his luck. He worked as a sales representative for a sportswear firm and spent half of the year on the road, servicing accounts. Occasionally he got lucky and was able to service some of the ladies who worked in the stores as well – or women he would pick up like this one. When he did get lucky he often gave them free tennis shirts from his samples as a token of his affection. From the look of things so far with this lady, however, a tennis shirt would never suffice. He would bestow her with shirts, shoes, warm-up suit, the whole outfit. He hadn't just gotten lucky this time: he had won the lottery.

She had his shirt off him before the door was closed. She seemed game for anything and Edgar hoped he would have enough imagination to take advantage of the opportunity.

She threw her arms around his waist and pressed her face into his chest. The strength of her embrace surprised him. She was not small but she was no giant, either, yet when she squeezed him it took his breath away. Suddenly she was lifting him off the floor, her face still in his chest, and she twirled him with a few staggering steps. When she put him down she pulled her face away and looked up at him. She was smiling, grimacing really, with his chest hairs in her clenched teeth.

"Hey!"

"What are you, a baby?" she said. "Is um baby?"

"You're kind of hyper, aren't you? Let's take it slow."

"Is um baby?" she mocked. She stroked his chest. "Did I hurt ums? Did I hurt baby?"

"I guess I'll live," he said. "You just surprised me." It was his first opportunity to glance around the room. He half-hoped to see a trapeze or some other device of exotic erotica. Whatever it was, whatever she had in mind, he would try it. Edgar felt he had spent half a lifetime thinking about the more advanced and complicated techniques of sex that he was only dimly aware existed. He was never precise in his mind about the details and he had always lacked the confidence to experiment. The things he wanted to do seemed embarrassing, unreasonable – almost rude – and he could not bring himself to ask his normal bedmates to try them. Especially not his wife whom he would have to face again in the cold light of day. But with this woman, this Dee, he knew he would not have to ask permission for anything. In fact, it might be all he could do just to hang on.

"I know what baby needs," she said. She pulled her blouse over her head without undoing the buttons. She wore no bra. Her breasts were small and firm and she arched her back as if she were proud of them. He thought she should be. Her ribs showed against her skin and with her back bowed her belly sucked inward the way it did in statues. She was not small of bone, her shoulders were broad and her hips flared distinctly from her waist, but she was lean and strong. Edgar loved them lean. He liked to feel as if he could lift and move his women when he needed to; he liked to feel in control.

"Does um want some?"

"I do," he said and put his hands on her biceps as he lowered his head. The muscles were firm under his fingers.

She moaned loudly as he took the breast in his mouth. Edgar knew he was going to love this. He sucked her breast briefly, switched to the other one, heard her gasp with pleasure, and reached for the zipper of her skirt.

"I'm going to take good care of you," he murmured. He buried his face in her neck as he fumbled with her skirt.

"Shut up," she said. She took his head in her hands and

placed it back on her breast. "I'll tell you when you're done."

Ash reached the motel after an hour's walk. He saw the Daybreak sign, mouthed it aloud to himself, and turned into the courtyard. Their room was on the corner, Dee always took a corner room if possible. It cut their neighbours in half, she explained.

Ash had tried to visualise their neighbours being cut in two but the images always led to thoughts of violence and blood and he soon stopped trying to understand what she meant.

The curtains were only partially drawn and the lights within the room were on. Ash peered in and saw Dee on the floor on all fours. The Lyle was behind her, thrusting at her. Dee's teeth were bared as if she were snarling and he could hear her calling.

Ash did not want to watch. He sat on the hard concrete stoop in front of the motel-room door.

"Daddy, oh, Daddy!" he heard her call. "Yes, Daddy! Come on, Daddy!"

Ash covered his ears and squeezed his eyes shut. He tried to think about the last good time with Dee. It was just last night when she was beginning to be happy but she wasn't yet too happy the way she was today. He was watching one of his nature shows. A snake had encountered a frog that, instead of hopping for its life, had inflated itself to twice its size and risen on its legs. It seemed too large for the snake but the snake knew better. Ash was taken by the stupefied look on the frog's face as it was being swallowed. It showed no alarm, no fear, just a stupid wonderment.

"See that?" Dee had said. "It doesn't even care."

Ash had liked having her watch the show with him. She so often wasn't home or wasn't in the mood, but last night she had chosen to spend her time with him, just hanging around the room, watching television and commenting on things they saw. It was the kind of time they had together so seldom.

When the thoughts of last night could no longer drown out Dee's yells, Ash started to do push-ups. In the exercise yard many of the men had done push-ups to kill the time and Ash had become the best of all. He did them now, easing himself down until his nose touched the concrete before pushing up again, scrupulously avoiding any use of his legs, which he knew was cheating. He worked until sweat poured from his face and his arms trembled with the effort.

Dee had stopped screaming and now he heard the sound of voices in conversation.

Edgar lay back on the bed, convinced he was going to die, but, as the old saw had it, what a way to go. She was all he had hoped for, imaginative, indefatigable, multi-orgasmic – and loud as hell. He did not have to guess how matters were proceeding, she let him know at the top of her lungs.

And was he ever doing well. He'd always suspected he was pretty good at this sex business, but he now realised he was a champion. He had pleasured her until she could no longer move. She lay beside him, drenched in sweat, exhausted and satisfied deeply enough to last a normal woman a month. Edgar could not resist a smug smile of self-congratulation as he stared at the ceiling. He'd certainly given her more than she had bargained for.

He would have to get this woman's phone number. He would be back in the area in a month's time and she was certainly worth a repeat visit. There were a few variations he had been tempted to try and would certainly get around to them next time. He had also learned a few new wrinkles which he would use with his wife. They weren't apt to work, of course, because they relied on a certain level of enthusiasm and enthusiasm was a quality his wife lacked – in spades. But if he had ever entertained thoughts that her shy reserve – not to say torpor – was in any way his fault, he could certainly dismiss those suspicions now. He had just driven this woman crazy. And she was a bright, good-looking woman, too; the kind of woman who could have just about any man she wanted. She had wanted Edgar – and he had just proven that she had made the right choice.

Edgar could not remember when he had felt more gratified after a bout with a relative stranger – or less inclined to bolt out the door after the passion was gone. Still, it was late, he had to work in the morning and he had already lain beside her for several minutes. She could not reasonably take offence if he left now.

He made a show of looking at his watch. "My God, is it that late?" he said, sitting up abruptly.

She put her hand on his naked thigh.

"I had no idea,' he said.

"Where do you think you're going?" she asked. She had that edge to her voice that he had heard once or twice when they were hot at it. He had chosen to ignore it then, chalking it up to the heat of passion, but he had not liked it then and he liked it even less now.

"It's late," he said. He swung his legs over the edge of the bed, pulling away from the hand on his thigh. "I've got to go."

"You're not going anywhere," she said.

He understood the sentiment. Naturally she would want to hang on to him. That's how women were, they never knew when to let go. But damn, he didn't like that demanding tone. It made him angry.

"I've got to run," he said. "I didn't realise it was so late."

"You're not done," she said.

He chose to laugh even though he wanted to belt her one. So aggressive, so demanding.

"I'm done,' he said. He gave her a big smile and a wink. "For now. There's always next time."

"You may be done," she said, rising to her knees on the bed.

She really was a good-looking woman, Edgar thought, even though he found her nudity mildly embarrassing without the lust to justify it. Most women would not look all that good to him after sex, not in the harsh light of the motel room. Their breasts would sag or their tummies shake or their thighs would bulge. They had moles and veins and stretch marks, none of which fit the perfection of the women in magazines which had formed his notion of feminine beauty. Most women felt better to Edgar than they looked. But this woman really did look good. Her stomach went in, her breasts seemed almost boastfully upright. What a shame that she was turning into a bitch.

"You seemed pretty done to me," he said, hoping she would join his chuckle. He didn't want a scene.

"You may be done, but you're not finished," she said.

Edgar picked up his shirt from the floor. She scrambled off the bed and stood between him and the door.

"Are you kidding? I just gave you enough for six women. You ought to be grateful for what you got."

"I'll be the judge of what I got and it was precious little," she said. She yanked the shirt out of his hand.

"I've never had any complaints before," said Edgar.

"You got some now," she said. "Get back on the bed." She pushed him on the chest, the edge of the bed caught him on the back of the knees and he tumbled backward.

She was atop him, her hand between his legs, pulling impatiently at him.

50

"Get it up," she said.

"Christ, what's the matter with you?" he demanded, trying to twist away but being constrained by her forearm on his chest and the hand in his crotch.

"Get it up," she repeated. "Play with it."

"You play with it. That's not my job."

"You've done it often enough," she said. "Play with it, get it up."

He squirmed underneath her, afraid to make a maximum effort to get her off for fear that she was stronger than he was. "Cut it out. That's enough for one night. I'll come back tomorrow and we'll get it on again."

"Do it now!" she exclaimed. She took his hand and clapped it between his legs. "Do as you're told."

She lost her leverage when she moved and Edgar managed to roll to the side, pushing her off. "Christ!" He started to rise and was halfway up when she grabbed him from behind, pulling him back. He jerked forward and her nails ripped down his back.

"You stupid bitch!" He turned and slapped her hard across the face. Blood was already coming from her nose by the time she sat up again. The look on her face was so savage that he recoiled in anticipation of an assault but she stood without a word and walked into the bathroom.

Edgar hurried to get dressed. "You made me do that," he called over his shoulders towards the bathroom. He hopped on one foot, trying to draw his trousers on while holding his underwear, he could put on the underwear later. "I'm not the kind of guy who hits women," he said. "But Jesus, you've got to calm down. Enough is enough, you know?"

He heard her moving about in the bathroom. Her movements sounded as hurried as his own. The door of the medicine cabinet opened and closed.

"I'm willing to just forget this," he said, looking for his shoe.

She came out of the bathroom with the blood from her nose running past her chin and dripping on to her chest. She seemed completely unaware of it as she once more stood between him and the door.

"You thinking of going?" she asked.

He saw his shoe against the wall just behind her. Something told him not to bend over to get it and expose his back to her again. But what was he afraid of? A stark naked woman standing defencelessly between him and the door. She was armed with a slightly demented look in her eyes, but apart from that he should be able to get her out of his way with a well-placed kick.

"Yeah, I'm going," he said. "I'll call you in the morning."

"You're quite a disappointment," she said, not moving.

"Well, there you go,' he said. "I had a great time. You're a very sexy lady, but you never know how these things are going to work out."

He found it very disconcerting that she continued to ignore the blood that dripped from her nose. It trickled slowly down her torso towards her pubic patch. It was eerie that someone could so totally disregard an injury to herself.

"I tell you what," she said, "since you don't know how to use that thing of yours, you don't really need it, do you?"

"What?"

"Why don't you just leave it behind, here with me. You'll be better off without it. That way you won't be making any more promises you can't keep."

Edgar thought he might very well leave without his shoe. She was getting weirder by the moment. "What are you talking about?"

"You said you were going to take good care of me," she said. "You promised."

"Hey, I tried. You happen to have a little problem there."

"You disappointed me.' she said. "Everyone is always disappointing me, and frankly, I'm getting just a little tired of it."

She lifted her right hand to waist height. The thumb and forefinger were clasped around something.

"Come here, sweetie," she said. "We're going to relieve you of that thing that's causing you all that trouble, and then you can run home to your mother."

Edgar peered at her hand. She held a razor blade between her fingers.

"I told you to come here," she said, her voice suddenly stern. "Do as you're told. This instant.' Dee took a step towards him and Edgar kicked out in panic, aiming for her crotch. His toes struck her in the abdomen and she tumbled forward. The razor blade fell from her fingers and Edgar picked it up off the carpet. She was on all fours, gasping for breath. He had half a mind to slash her on her exposed back just to show her how it would feel.

"You're crazy!" he yelled at her. "You're out of your mind!"

She muttered something he did not understand. He leaned over her, his mouth close to her ear.

"You're crazy! You ought to be locked up!"

Her head hung down like a defeated animal and the blood dripped from her nose directly on to the carpet.

She muttered something again. Edgar bent closer, holding the razor blade as a weapon in case the crazy bitch tried to bite him or something else insane.

"What?"

She had caught her breath. "You think I'm crazy?" she said. She tilted her head up to look him in the face. She sounded amused. The blood ran over her lips but she still did not seem to notice.

"I know you're crazy," he said.

He grabbed the door and yanked it open. The huge man from the restaurant whom he had seen trudging along the highway sat on the stoop in front of the door like a dog awaiting its master.

"You think *I'm* crazy?" she said.

The man stood up, blocking Edgar's way.

Edgar looked from the man to Dee who had rolled into a sitting position. He wanted to suggest that things had gone far enough, that he had meant no harm, that there was no need to carry things farther. Edgar tried to grin at her, to demonstrate his good will, his certainty that she bore him no real hard feelings.

Dee looked at him and smiled beatifically. The blood was smudged across her stomach where he had kicked her and the entire lower half of her face now seemed to have been painted red. When she spoke her teeth were smeared.

"He hurt me, Ash," she said.

Ash grabbed Edgar by the throat and squeezed. Edgar managed to slash at him once with the razor blade before his body was hurled against the wall.

After Ash put the man in the trunk of his car he returned to the room to clean up the mess. Dee was curled up on the bed, still naked, her knees pressed to her chest, her face to the wall.

"We have to go, Dee," he said. He put all of her clothes into the suitcase, folding them carefully as she had taught him.

"I just want to sleep," she said. Her voice was so sad that Ash wanted to cry for her.

He put his extra shirt atop her clothes then went to the bathroom to add their toiletries to the suitcase.

"We have to go before they come," Ash said.

"I just want to sleep." Her voice was low and fading, as if she were already deep in slumber. He knew she would be like this for several days, immobilised by lethargy, too depressed to even dress or feed herself. He had to get her away from the motel before she sank too deeply to be roused.

He checked her purse and made sure that her pills and his were still there. He tried to remember how many capsules had been in her vial the last time he checked, but he could not. She must not have taken any in several days, he knew that much. There was no point in trying to make her take one now. He knew from experience he would have to trick one into her somehow, but not when she was this low, and not when she was too high, either. She was too clever then. It was only when she would come out of this depression of her own accord, when she was on the way up but not yet high, and ravenously hungry after days of starvation, that he could slip one of the capsules into her food. After that she would take them herself. For a while. Never for long enough, but at least for a while.

Until she did come out of her depression enough to find them a place to stay, they would have to live in the car. Ash could never check into a motel by himself, he knew that. They would all surely know about him immediately. They would be able to tell as soon as he opened his mouth that he was not competent, that he was not to be trusted. They would laugh at him, or worse, send for the authorities to take care of him.

So he would have to wait until Dee could take care of both of them. He would find a rest-stop on the highway where he could get food from the vending machines and water from the toilet facilities and he would stay there and protect her. It wouldn't matter to Dee where they were when she was in the worst of it. Any place with shelter would do until she returned to herself to take care of him.

Getting a washcloth to clean the blood from the carpet and the wall, he saw his reflection in the mirror and stared, surprised, at the cut that ran from his cheekbone to his jawline. It was shallow and hairline thin and the blood had already dried. He wasn't aware that the Lyle had cut him. He hadn't felt a thing.

He only managed to spread the smear on the wall and the carpet seemed to have absorbed Dee's blood like a sponge. Ash looked at the washcloth. His blood from the wall and Dee's from the floor were mixed together into a brownish stain on the cloth. He liked the idea that their blood was mingled.

"We're packed, Dee," he said, approaching the bed with the washcloth rinsed and wet again. He rolled her over and began to dab at the blood that had dried on her face. Ash tried not to look at her naked body. It aroused him and it also embarrassed him.

With a sob, Dee threw her arms around his neck and pulled him on to her. She nipped his ear with her teeth and then whispered directly into it so that Ash felt the effect in his groin, as if her warm breath were travelling all the way through him.

"Come on, Ash," she whispered. "Come on."

One hand held his neck and the other was already reaching between their bodies, fumbling with his belt.

Ash squeezed his eyes closed. He was so grateful. First that she was not as far gone as he had feared – although he knew it was just a matter of time – and second that she wanted him again. It was so seldom these days; there had been such a long succession of Lyles since last she had needed Ash.

He did not resist her in any way, but let her use him as

she desired. It was the way she preferred it, and he preferred whatever she wanted. With his eyes shut he imagined her as a bird, a large and beautiful and dangerous bird, graceful and effortless in flight, remorseless in pursuit. Lethal and lovely. She was an eagle.

He was a bear, lurking in a cave. Bears hid. They did terrible things, too, they killed, they clawed and bit, but they hid – because they were afraid. The eagles never hid, she was never afraid. There was nothing in the world that could hurt her. The eagle never hid, never stalked, never lay in wait. She circled overhead, seeking her prey with an eye that could see forever. She could see the terror in the rabbit's eye from afar and had but to fold her wings to be upon it before it could move.

She could even attack a bear, she could rip him apart with her talons, skewer his eyes, grab his heart. To Ash, a bear was helpless before an eagle, he could not hear her approach as she plummeted from on high, he could not see her before she was upon him with her terrible grace and beauty. He could do awful things with his strength, but never to the eagle. He was powerless under the eagle's attack.

He felt the eagle upon him, the flutter of the giant wings, the caress of feathers, the ripping of his fur and hide with beak so razor sharp it gave no pain. His flesh opened out to her as if in blossom and she fed upon him.

And then he heard the beauty of her song ringing out, filling the cave and reverberating off the walls with the richness of her joy. 'Oh, Daddy,' she sang. "Come on, Daddy. Daddy!"

5

Becker's home in Connecticut was forty-five minutes from the Town Center mall in Stamford. He drove there on the Merritt Parkway and studied the central divider. It was as he had remembered it when talking to Karen. A low guardrail made it impossible to pull a car on to the central strip without severe strip damage to both the railing and the automobile. There were occasional flowerbeds on the divider and so many trees there, as well as on both sides of the road, that the experience was one of driving at high speed through the deciduous forest which still held New England in its grasp. In summer the Parkway was a blur of green and in autumn it blazed with autumn colours, providing sudden vistas that made the road known for its beauty. As a highway for commuter traffic to New York, it served, although just barely, with four lanes and merely adequate engineering. But as an avenue through the forest, it was Connecticut's pride and joy, and the State devoted a good deal of effort to keeping the divider well trimmed and clean.

It was no place for pedestrians, however. Anyone walking there would be seen by dozens if not hundreds of drivers per minute. Becker made a note to investigate the state employees who tended the strip. Their uniforms would not make them invisible but somewhat less noteworthy.

Becker pulled into the passing lane and rolled down his window. On the passenger seat next to him lay a brown leaf bag that he had purchased that morning. Inside the bag, taped together, were three twenty-five pound sacks of cat litter. First he tried to lift the dead weight from the seat and across his body with his right hand while steering with his left. He made five attempts, stopping midway each time when it was apparent he was about to lose control of the car. Next he tried to steer with his knees while handling the heavy bag with both hands. He lost control almost immediately with the exertion necessary for the lift. Finally Becker dragged the litter-filled bag on to his lap and lifted it from there to the open window. Opening the door was out of the question, it would require him to be too far from the divider. After several failed attempts Becker managed to get the bag balanced on the window opening. The blast of a horn brought him back to the realisation of his position. He was swerving dangerously and his speed had dropped to less than forty miles an hour. Angry motorists were passing him on the inside and gesturing as they went past.

"And I haven't even gotten the thing out the window yet," he thought. Nine times out of ten he would have swerved into the guardrail or another car if he'd made the final effort of throwing the bag on to the divider. He knew that throwing was the wrong idea. There was no way he could throw anything this heavy and unwieldy from a sitting position behind a steering wheel, never mind the demands of driving a car at the same time. It would be all he could do to push it far enough away from the car not to fall under the wheels. Becker eased into the right-hand lane, still balancing the bag on the open window, until the line of cars that had built up behind him had passed. Middle of the night reduced traffic would make things somewhat easier, but not enough.

When the road was clearer, Becker pulled into the passing lane once more. Steadying the car with his knees, he pushed the bag as hard as he could with both hands, grabbing the wheel again immediately to avoid a crash. The bag hit the guardrail and split in two. The sacks of litter hit the highway and spilled on to the pavement. He looked at the mess behind him in his rear-view mirror. The first car had already reached the mess and was warily swinging wide to avoid the torn sacks and flapping plastic. Any worse push and he would have caused a traffic hazard within minutes. As it was, there would probably be a slow-down for several minutes until the wind of passing cars pulled the plastic free of the litter and sent it winging crazily away from the road. And that was the best I could do, Becker thought. He knew he was stronger than most men because of a lifetime of staying in shape. His arms were conditioned by the rigours of pulling himself up rock faces on a rope. If he had been higher and had more of an arc for the push, the bag might have cleared the rail. From the cab of a diesel semi-trailer truck, for instance. But this was the Merritt Parkway and commercial vehicles were prohibited. Driving such a truck here was an open invitation for arrest by the state police. Either the man who had successfully put the Shapiro boy's body on the divider had carried it across two lanes of traffic and dropped it there, or he was possessed of great strength. Becker wondered if he were chasing a man who was a monster in more than one sense.

The Town Center was five vertical layers of shops surrounding a central well with a courtyard, a fountain and tiers of steps for sitting. Both elevators and escalators gave access from the ground floor to the higher levels. There were exits on every floor to the parking garage which ascended parallel to the central shopping core, as well as three ground-level pedestrian entrances from the street. Security guards sat in glass booths at the parking lot exits but, as Becker noted upon entering, they paid only intermittent attention to the flow of people. If some-one tried to drive a mini-van through the exit and on to the elevator, they might notice that, Becker thought. Otherwise, their value as witnesses was limited. The guards had been positioned where they were for three reasons. One, the glass offices were out of the way of the shopping flow and would not be bothering customers with unpleasant thoughts of security. Two, their position next to the exits just might give shoplifters second thoughts – although experience had shown this was a very questionable premise. And three, the nook behind the elevators was a relatively secluded spot where trouble might be expected to spring up were it not for the prox-imity of the security guards.

Becker knew, however, that the occurrence he was most concerned with had taken place somewhere else. The man known as Lamont Cranston had snatched his quarry somewhere in the body of the building. By the time he passed through an exit, he already had the boy completely under his control. Anything else would have been far too risky. The boy could have shouted to the security guards, fallen to the floor and made a scene, anything to attract attention. Lamont had done it suc-cessfully six times, four times from places such as this. Whatever his method, it was not haphazard. It was effec-tive and had Becker baffled.

On the fourth level where he had entered from the garage, Becker stood at the railing and looked down at the activity below him. It was a Saturday and the mall

61

was crowded with customers, a Chamber of Commerce dream of joy. Exhausted husbands with low shopping tolerance, eyes glazed, grim expressions on their faces, stretched out on the seating areas around the fountain as if their feet were killing them. A few teenagers congregated there, too, but only briefly as they made their plans before sallying forth again. Otherwise the activity was in the shops and the food halls. From a distance Becker thought it looked rather like the apparently chaotic motions of a hill of ants that managed to get things done in such an efficient way. Becker's sympathies were with the groggy husbands, but then Becker was no shopper.

He was a hunter. He found his quarry on the second level, inside the video arcade where dozens of children ranging in age from six or seven to late teens stood mesmerised by the flashing images of dragons and heroes and karate choppers. It was a kindergarten of treasures for the predatory or perverted. While parents shopped, their children milled and mingled, waiting for their favourite game or moving to the next like Las Vegas patrons at the slot machines. It would be impossible for any but the most diligent and paranoid of observers to keep track constantly of any individual for long. It was like keeping one's eye on a single specimen among a shifting school of fish.

Lamont had not been distracted by the motions or the numbers, however, but then Lamont was very single-minded. He could look at such a group, make his pick, await his moment, then strike with the swiftness of a shark. What was it that set the victim apart? Did he fill a type the killer preferred? Did one seem more vulnerable than the others? More appealing to Lamont's peculiar aesthetic taste? Could Lamont tell at a glance that one of the many was more apt to lend himself to capture? Or simply better designed to slake his thirst? And was it at a glance, or did Lamont study his quarry at length? And how would he do that without drawing attention to himself?

Becker felt conspicuous even now, standing apart from the arcade and watching the children. He looked around him to see if he was being observed. Lamont would look like a shopper, or course. He would carry a shopping bag or packages. As Becker watched, a man walked into the arcade. He had the haircut and shoes of the wealthy middle class although his jeans and T-shirt were part of the nation's universal weekend uniform. The man approached one of the teenage boys and spoke his name aloud. After waiting long enough to assert his independence, the boy turned and glared at the man with the sullenness reserved at that age for one's own family. As they left together the man tried to put a paternal hand on the boy's shoulder but the boy dipped, slid away and walked in front of the man as if he were not really his father.

The man glanced at Becker and offered a fading smile as if knowing that any male of a certain age could sympathise. A transaction as common as humanity itself, Becker thought, repeated endlessly in all the malls and public places of the country. And yet a few weeks ago something similar had happened here that had ended in a child's death. Becker had noticed this meeting of father and son, but would anyone else have had any reason to note an occurrence so mundane? But if the man was not the father, if the boy was a little younger, at an age when parents still warned their children not to talk to strangers, what would the meeting have looked like then? And how would the man have convinced the child to accompany him?

Perhaps it was not that sort of selection process, Becker

thought. What if Lamont went after a target of opportunity, the one member of the group who distinguished himself in some way, not by appearance, but by movement. The first to move away from the crowd, perhaps.

Was Lamont that hungry? Would just any victim do? Did the man come to the mall, cruise until he saw one of the boys alone or in the position Lamont required, and then strike? It was possible, but the idea didn't sit well with Becker. For one thing, it was much too dangerous. It discounted the fact that so far no one had noticed anything unusual. If Lamont was making it up as he went along, if he was grabbing at the first opportunity, he would have been hurried, he would have made a mistake. And more important was the desire. Lamont kept the boys for a couple of months before he killed them. That implied care, lodging, food, a major investment of time and caution. The victim had to be watched over during that time, probably guarded. Certainly obsessed over. Lamont was no mad-dog sex fiend who dragged the boys into a dark corner and had his way. For two months at a time he lived with them. It made no sense – not even the twisted sense of a serial killer – to devote that much to a random choice.

And finally, Becker knew it just didn't work that way. Serial killing, like any passion, was a matter of the heart. Men do not fall in love randomly, they respond again and again to a template implanted early in life, perhaps by the mother, perhaps the first love, the nanny, the nurse. The objects of their passion could appear very different to others, but all shared some elements of the original intaglio. Often a mystery to the world, the traces of the pattern still shone brightly in the lover's heart.

However tortured and buckled the original template, or however tormented and bizarre life had made the killer's perception of it, the process was the same. Like any man in the throes of passion, the killer responded to those messages of the old pattern.

Becker rode the escalator to the ground floor, letting his eyes play over the youths around him. So many of them, so free, wandering alone and with others of their age, money in their pockets, no fear in their heads. Kids who once hung out on street corners or played kick-the-can on deserted evening suburban streets now congregated in the malls. It was not a new phenomenon, but one that Becker had formerly paid no attention to.

Some of the children were with their parents but even they drifted apart as each followed his own interests. Do you know where your children are, he thought? Precisely where they are? In the other end of the store? Just around the corner looking in the window of the neighbouring shop? How far away do you think danger lies? How long do you think it takes? He wanted to scream at them, protect your children, for God's sake! There are monsters loose!

Becker stopped beside a boy peering wide-eyed through plate-glass at a display of telescopes. Come with me, he thought. How do I get you to come with me?

Could he drug the boy? A swift but guarded jab with a hypodermic needle to send sodium pentathol pulsing through his veins, loosening his brain to a hyper-suggestive jelly. And the crucial seconds until the drug took effect? And the long walk out of the mall with a boy whose legs were as wobbly as his brain?

Becker rejected the idea. The killer Roger Dyce had drugged his victims, but always alone and late at night. He had missed Becker himself with the needle by the thickness of the cloth on his shirt before Becker had captured him. The method would never work in daylight in public.

Becker peered down at the boy. It had been so long since he had talked to children. What could he possibly say to induce the kid to walk away with him? What fantasy, what Pied Piper tune would tempt a boy to step into danger? And if the man next to him was the giant with enough strength to toss the boy's frame across his body while driving a car? How luring a melody would he have to pipe then?

The boy noticed Becker looking at him and eased away, sensing something creepy. Becker walked away. I hate this fucking job, he thought.

The men's room was on the ground floor around a corner from the third ice-cream/frozen yogurt stand that Becker had noticed in the building. There was a brief hallway, then the tiled foyer, then the lavatory itself. The cookie boutique that Steinholz had managed was two floors away. If Steinholz had worked at the ice-cream stand he might conceivably have seen the boy of his preference enter the lavatory and then reacted instinctively. But not from two floors away. If he took them from men's rooms, he would have to do as Becker was doing, enter and loiter and wait.

Becker stood in front of a sink, using the mirror to study those who entered the men's room. It was here that the victims could select themselves for Lamont. Unlike girls, boys did not necessarily go to the lavatory in groups. Some would come in singly, separating themselves from the crowd and Lamont would have them alone to himself for however long he needed. There had been cases of professionals kidnapping babies and infants who had acted in this way. Working in teams, they had wheeled away strollers from behind the backs of distracted mothers, dyed the child's hair in the sink and changed their clothes in less than a minute while a confederate kept people out of the restroom. When the kidnappers and their victim emerged into the mall proper minutes later, security guards – if they had even been alerted yet – were looking for a different coloured snow-suit, long blonde curls now shorn and blackened.

But that was with children too young to cry for help, children small enough to wheel or carry and to quiet with a rubber pacifier. It wouldn't work with ten-year-old boys. Becker stood at the sink, washing his hands again and again, trying to time the effort. If he took the boy next to him right now, slapped a sign on the door saying 'closed', how long would it be before a hurried stranger pushed his way into the room, ignoring the sign? How long before an employee came in to see what was wrong? It was impossible to predict, but he knew it wouldn't be long. Certainly not dependably long enough. And what would he be doing to the boys in the meantime? How did you get a ten-year-old to shut up and not call for help? Put a gun to his head? Maybe, it was possible, but seemed unlikely to Becker.

Lamont knew something about children he himself did not, Becker concluded. He left the mall feeling slightly soiled and seamy after the day's work. It seemed that he had accomplished little other than to prove that what had been done was not do-able.

Sitting behind the wheel of his car in the parking lot, he looked over the cement ramparts at the city below. Dusk was settling, he had been in the mall for hours, avoiding the real work he would have to do now. He had tried the easy way first because the hard way was so painful.

Becker rested his head against the steering wheel, his eyes fixed sightlessly on the control panel of the car. There was no escaping it. If he was to help beyond the marginal assistance he had already given, he would have to step into the problem completely. He could no longer feel it around the edges, trying to gauge its size and shape and substance from the fringe, like the blind man limning the elephant from the heft of its tail or trunk alone. He must embrace the problem fully. Worse, he must step inside it and learn how its heart beat. It was a task he dreaded, a task he knew Karen Crist fully expected him to take on. He was good at the other process, the basic police work that solved most cases. He was as good at it as anyone, better than most. But it was not his genius.

If Becker was to help, if he was to have any chance of stopping Lamont before he killed another boy, he would have to live with the photographs of the dead victims. Becker quailed at the prospect. The price was always too damned high.

The photographs of the dead boys were spread across the floor like so many miniature corpses, as if Becker's living room had become the scene of a slaughter. Before laying out the pictures Becker had turned on every light in the room and positioned his favourite chair so his back was against the wall. He was used to fear, but he did not welcome it. It had become a frequent visitor, but never a friend and when possible he did all he could to diminish its effects. Horror films caused him to react with the fright of a young child and he restricted his reading to the non-violent safety of non-fiction and history. Becker needed no goads to his imagination, it was already filled with real-life horrors. Where others delighted in the vicarious theatre thrills of being safely terrified by madmen with axes stalking babysitters, Becker winced and looked away. He knew it was all too true and possible.

With the room brilliantly lit, the colours of the wounds stood out starkly against the pallor of the boys' bodies. The original lividity of the contusions had waned after death, but the difference in colour that remained was enough to show the relative age of the bruises. The older ones had begun to fade, the latest, the ones caused by blows administered on the day of death, were still intense against the surrounding flesh. The boys had been beaten over a period of time. The scientifically dry forensic report had estimated the floggings took place over a relatively short period of time, perhaps three weeks. A short period of time, Becker thought derisively. Twenty-one days of torment were a lifetime in themselves.

He stared at the photographs for a long time, forcing himself to see every detail, to let the pain the boys had felt reach out and engulf him. Then, forcing himself to move against his own dread, he crossed the room and one by one turned out the lights.

Becker sat on the floor, surrounded by the pictures, and let the demons come. He was at home, but he was no longer in the safety of his own living room. His mind was once more in the pitch-black cellar of his youth.

He felt again the density of the darkness, an envelope heavy with menace that moved across his shoulders and down his back like a malevolent, living thing. It seemed to ripple over him like a giant serpent and even though the muscles in his back twitched with warning for him to move he knew that to turn was worse for he might have to see the creature face to face, its eyes glowing like fire in the dark. Becker did not know how long he had been banished to the cellar, there was no time there, no way to mark the minutes except to count the terrified throbbing of the blood in his veins. Nor did he understand what he had done to deserve the punishment of which the cellar was only the prelude. He thought wildly, trying to re-member what childish indiscretion had doomed him, what offence had merited this retribution. It was only much later in life that he would realise it was his punishment that mattered, not the crime.

They always left him alone in the dark so very long. Shivering with fright, fearing abandonment as much he feared the creatures that peopled his imagination in the blackness, he would be almost relieved to hear the door open at last. So alone and so scared that he almost welcomed the appearance of his tormentor.

And finally there he stood, the object of Becker's love and loathing all at once. The heavy tread upon the stairs. The sour smell of beer on his breath. The matter-of-fact tone that only gradually rose to anger.

The beatings often began as nothing more than a chore, dutifully but wearily tended to. "I hope you've had a chance to think about your behaviour," he would say.

Or, "Your mother tells me you were a bad boy."

Or, "Anything to say for yourself?" in a voice of such reason, as if there was room for discussion, a chance for repeal or pardon. It was often the cruellest hoax, giving young Becker the flash of hope, as if a chance to explain himself or plead for mercy would lessen his sentence by as much as a single blow.

Only later would the voice drop its veil of civilisation. Then it would be "bastard" and "little son-of-a-bitch" as the rain of blows grew into a torrent.

The boy Becker would cry, of course, and clutch his father's legs and promise to be good and promise to try harder and promise and promise and promise. As if anyone was listening. As if there were some way to avoid punishment at the hands of parents who took their delight from it. As if there was any offence so vile that a child would warrant such beatings at the hands of his loved ones.

Over time it was the "loved ones" part of the equation that injured him the most. The body could recover and grow strong. But the shock, the continually stunning revelation that his abusers, the ones to whose whim his body was held constant hostage, were the people he loved most in the world-was the part that hurt most of all and did the deepest damage.

For it was not always this way. There were times, many times, when they seemed to love him. There were times when his father would ruffle his hair with the same huge hand that delivered the blows, when the voice that growled abuse would cheer him for his athletic skills. Moments when they would laugh at the dinner table at young Becker's antics or congratulate him on his academic grades. There were times when his mother would caress him with her warm and gentle hands, soothe him with her smile, whisper in her urgent voice to "Never tell". Never. Anyone. To tell was to risk the loss of his family's love. To risk the loss of the very family itself. Young Becker learned the value of secrets and the deeper truth, that everyone possessed them.

There were also other moments when his father's furies would overtake him so swiftly that he would send the boy sprawling across the floor with a cuff or a kick. But these impromptu beatings were rare and quickly over. They seemed to frighten both his mother and father with their volatility and caprice.

His father, Becker knew, prided himself on being a rational man, a reasonable man, a man in control of himself. Spontaneous violence was contrary to his self-image. Both parents preferred ordered, predetermined, "rational" justice. They liked to have him beaten in a way that was in keeping with their middle-class persona.

Now in the darkness of his living room the adult Becker shrunk once more from the abrupt and shocking sting of the blows, clutched his father's leg, whined and moaned and cried and promised – and divined his own version of the truth of human nature – and his own. As he had over the years several decades earlier, Becker formed his own template of a starkly different kind than most. But not all. He knew he was not alone in his vision of the world, or in the bent and ugly pattern of passion that had gouged a space in his heart. There were others out there. He could recognise them. He wondered if they could recognise him before it was too late.

6

If it had been his choice, Edgar Rappaport would not have reported the incident with Dee to the police because he was afraid that word of it would get back to his wife. He could explain his broken nose to her in a number of ways. The multiple bruises could have been the result of a mugging. Mimi would probably accept even being locked in his own car as the cruel whim of thieves, although by the time he got home there would be no way for her to know about his hours in the trunk curled atop his sportswear samples. He had bled on two golf shirts and crushed and wrinkled a peach-and-cream coloured tennis skirt almost beyond recognition.

The police wouldn't accept a story of mugging, however; not after they had been summoned by the motel owner who had finally responded to his muffled cries for help and found him in full possession of his wallet, credit cards and cash. Edgar had no choice but to tell them the full story – or a slightly edited version that omitted his striking Dee in the face and allowed for a more spirited self-defence against Ash, of whom Edgar offered the speculation that he was probably a jealous husband.

Since the motel was located more than two miles outside of the city limits of Saugerties, New York, the State police answered the motel owner's call. They dutifully took notes, wrote down the descriptions given by both Edgar and the owner, photographed the room and the bloodstains. The owner, who had been paid a week's rent in advance, had come to like Dee, a bright, bouncy woman, but she was definitely uncomfortable around the man, a hulking brute whose name she never knew. However, since stains in her carpet were nothing new and she had three extra days of unearned rent in her pocket, the owner was indifferent to Dee's apprehension. After a time, when Edgar had made it clear that he would not press assault charges, the police released him.

One week following Edgar Rappaport's interview with the New York State police, Dee and Ash were in Connecticut.

Director Lewis tapped Dee's letters, sucking in his upper lip. He was a fat, sallow man who lived his life steeped in hypocrisy and exercised it without thought or hesitation.

"These certainly appear to be in order," he said, referring to the letters. "Naturally I'll have to check them out."

"Of course," said Dee. They both knew that he wouldn't check her references at all. It was hard enough to find anyone to do this work, much less a trained professional. The whole industry was chronically short of workers; she had the job when she entered the building, and both she and the Director knew it.

"Perhaps I should speak to you again when you've checked my references," she said, deliberately tweaking him. It was one of the few times she would have any power over him, so she might as well enjoy it. The truth was she needed the job as much as the man needed her. After a week living in the car, her cash was gone. Savings were impossible, she owned little of value. She needed work now.

"Well, I don't see any reason you couldn't start working first," the Director said. "I'm sure everything will be fine. How would tomorrow suit you?"

Dee smiled. "Tomorrow would be fine," she said. "I have a little shopping to do first."

"Of course, of course," said the Director. He rose with some difficulty because of his weight. "If there's any way I can be of assistance ..." He tried to suggest the wide range of assistance he would be willing to offer her without giving offence. Women were so touchy these days. But she looked like she'd be a hot number, there was something in the eyes that suggested abandon. The husband is probably a drunk, he thought. That was what usually brought them to this place, family problems, general unemployability, desperation. This one didn't look desperate, however. Nor unemployable. Which usually meant troubles at home, a recent separation. A woman like that was frequently amenable to extracurricular comforts. The Director wanted to let her know he had a very understanding nature.

"There is something," Dee said.

"Yes?"

"I wonder if there are any shopping malls close by," she said.

"These days, there's always a mall close by," he said, and then he told her how to find it.

With her purchases in a bag on her lap, Dee settled into a chair at the food pavilion. Her feet hurt and she had a mild headache. The day had been taxing, but filled with optimism. The first days of a new leaf always were. She would behave herself this time, she would devote herself to her work and to Ash and really sink some roots. Most of all she would stay on her medicine.

She took a pill from her purse and lifted her coffee to

75

wash it down. There was a twinge inside her as something leaped up. It felt like the first bubble of something just beginning to simmer. Dee savoured the feeling; she knew the pill would kill it. She waited to see if it was still there, the pill and coffee both suspended before her mouth.

It came again, a little tug like a distant voice calling for her to come and play. If she took the pill, it would go away. It wouldn't trouble her, she wouldn't be sad anymore. Nor happy, either. The feeling came again, bubbling up through sense and caution, something lighter than air that could not be suppressed. This time she thought of it as the first tentative pant of laughter of a schoolgirl trying not to giggle behind her hand. She wanted to laugh inside, she was just exploring the possibility, seeing if there was any interest in merriment in the rest of her. Dee knew that if she let it, the laughter would come full force. She would ring and peal and roar with laughter. And they wanted her to stifle it. Ash wanted her to, the doctors all wanted her to. But what did they know about it? They were grey, drab, dull people who had never known this kind of laughter. And they all wanted her to feel it, deep in their hypocritical hearts they did, because they loved it when she entertained them. They, too, were drawn up a bit by her levitation, she made the world better for all. And it was always her they expected to do it. Always Dee they waited on to infuse them with her energy and her enthusiasm. They never complained when she leaped to her feet to lead the dance. She was the dance, the music, the twirling lights, all the elements in herself. She always had been. Even when she was on their medicine she knew she was the life, not only of the party, but the world.

She continued to pause, pill suspended. The tickle inside her wanted so badly to expand.

And then she heard the boys. They were laughing out

76

loud just as she was inside and the sound rang through the mall like birdsong in the spring.

Dee turned and saw them, angel boys, cherubs taken straight from Italian frescoes and put in baseball caps and jeans.

Perfect boys. Young and funny and sweet. As jolted with energy as young cubs frisking outside the den, as innocent as seraphim. Perhaps one of these wonderful boys was hers.

Dee put the pill back in her purse.

Ash knew there was trouble as soon as he saw the box of plastic gloves on her bedside table. He held them up and looked at her in wordless reproach.

"I have to handle wastes at work," she said.

"You promised."

"You don't want me catching AIDS or hepatitis or something, do you? ... Well, do you?"

"No."

"All right then." Dee took the box from his hand and shoved it into the night-table drawer.

"You promised, " he repeated.

"I put them away. See? All gone."

Ash continued to look at her reproachfully.

"Case closed," she said. She dusted her hands and tried to look serious, but the merriment inside her could not be contained.

"You are such a worry wart," she said, laughing now. "Haven't I been good lately? Haven't I?"

Ash watched her narrowly. She had been good for several days. But several days was not long enough.

"Haven't I gone to work every day? Haven't I? Yoo-hoo, Ash, I'm talking to you? ... Haven't I gone to work every day?"

"Yes," said Ash.

"Haven't I been sitting home with you when I wasn't at work? Haven't I?"

"Yes."

She was moving ceaselessly around the room now. Ash stood in the middle and slowly pivoted to keep her in his view. She was not pacing, there was nothing frantic about her movements. Indeed, she seemed to have a purpose at all times, straightening the bed, adjusting the curtains, picking his socks from the floor and putting them into the laundry bag. But she never stopped moving.

"Well, then?" she demanded. She put her face close to his, grinning, shaking it in front of him. "We-ell?"

Ash looked down the front of her blouse. She caught him at it, of course. Dee waggled a finger at him, clasping a hand to her chest.

"Peeking? I am shocked. I am stunned. What kind of a man are you?" Dee pulled the coverlet from the bed and held it in front of her. "What sort of a man am I locked in this room with?" she declaimed in mock horror. "A peeping Tom? ... Or, gasp, worse?"

She tugged his arm, urging him to respond. Ash never understood what she wanted. He did not know the games.

"What sort of a man are you?" she cried.

"I don't know," Ash said.

She threw her forearm across her brow like a heroine in a melodrama. "What shall become of me now? Who will save me? Who? Oh, will no one take care of me? Will no one protect me from this monster of lust?"

"I'll protect you," Ash said.

"No, Ash, you're the villain. You can't protect me."

"Yes, I can. I always take good care of you."

"Alas, trapped with a sex fiend who will have his way with me! I am at your mercy, sir, I must submit."

"I'll protect you, I will," said Ash.

With a sigh, Dee dropped the coverlet and the game at

78

the same time. "Never mind, Ash," she said. She sounded weary, but not angry.

"I'll play," said Ash. "I'm playing, I am playing."

"Never mind." She pulled the bedclothes taut with brisk efficiency, squaring the hospital corners the maid could not match.

There was something Ash was going to ask her that he had forgotten now. The confusion of her role playing had driven it from his mind.

"Never mind," Dee said, touching his arm. "It will come to you."

Ash looked at her in wonder. How had she known he was trying to remember? As always, it gave him a creepy yet exciting feeling to know that she could see right inside his head.

Dee was at the door. "Come on, stud. It's time for dinner before I go to work."

"Can we have Chinese?" Ash asked.

"I don't know if there's a Chinese place there," she said. "I didn't notice."

"There's a Chinese," Ash said.

"Are you sure?"

"I think," Ash said. He wrinkled his brow in concentration. It was hard to tell one place from another since they moved so often.

"That's close enough," Dee said. "Bring the laundry. You'll have time to do it before I have to leave for work."

Laundry was Ash's chore. He enjoyed putting the quarters in the slots, he liked measuring out the soap. Dee said she couldn't stand the sitting around and waiting, but Ash didn't mind the waiting at all. It gave him a feeling of pride to bring home the laundry, still warm from the drier, carefully folded as she had taught him, smelling fresh from the fabric softener sheet. Because of the special handling they required, Dee took her dresses to be cleaned and starched at the cleaners, but Ash took care of the clothes they wore every day.

With the laundry bag cradled on his lap, Ash settled in for the ride. Dee drove the same route every time so he could be sure to learn the way in case he should have to come home alone. She hadn't made him walk home yet, which was good. But the appearance of the plastic gloves was bad. Ash remembered what he had forgotten. He was going to ask Dee if she had been taking her pills. She would probably get mad at him if he asked, she didn't like being treated like a child. He didn't want to ask her now, because she was singing. She sang better than the car radio, he thought. Such a high, sweet voice. She always sang softly, almost as if to herself, but the sound was so pure Ash could hear it no matter how far away she was. It made her face so peaceful. Sometimes she cried when she sang, tears would appear on her face, but her voice never quavered. Ash was never certain why she cried. The songs were so lovely. Lullabies, she called them. Songs you sing to babies, she said. Babies always made Dee weep; Ash never understood why.

Dee sang all the way to the mall. When they pulled to a stop in the parking garage, she continued to sing until she had finished the refrain, staring straight ahead as if she were still driving. She held the last note for a long time, not wanting to let it go because the melody and its comfort would be gone.

When she was finished, she turned to Ash and smiled sweetly. Her cheeks were wet, but she looked gently happy.

She patted his face. "Because you're not a woman," she said. "That's why you don't understand. Nobody loves like a mother."

Still carrying the laundry bag because he had forgotten to put it down, Ash followed her into the mall.

7

As soon as Becker pulled off the Merritt Parkway and on to the road network leading into his home town of Clamden, he was aware of the police car behind him. Driving up the long, steep hill that led into the Clamden city limits, Becker accelerated slowly but steadily to see if the cruiser would keep pace. Convinced that he was being followed, Becker turned left at the crest of the mile-long hill, picking up speed as he crossed the intersection. Just before his view of the police car was blocked by the intervening buildings, Becker saw the flashing lights come on atop the cruiser.

Becker turned right at the first intersection, then left at the next. The police car loomed ever larger in his rear-view mirror, closing the gap between them. The lights continued to flash but there was as yet no siren. Becker turned right and then immediately into the driveway. When the police car raced past, Becker pulled out of the driveway and went back the way he had come, turning the corner and just glimpsing the tail-lights of the cruiser come on as the driver slammed on his brakes.

Around the corner and temporarily out of sight of the police car, Becker parked and got out. He was leaning on the hood of his car as the cruiser came rapidly around the corner and sped past him. Forty yards away the police car came to a stop and began to back up, very slowly, towards Becker.

When the police car came abreast of Becker, the cop leaned out his window.

"Cute," he said.

"Thank you," said Becker.

"Make me run back and forth, spinning my wheels like something in a cartoon. I'm a role model, you know."

"I hadn't heard," said Becker.

"Lots of kids look up to me for clues on how to live their lives."

"I wasn't aware."

"It doesn't do for them to see me looking like a jerk. I'm the Chief of Police."

The policeman got out of the car. He was a large man, tall and strongly built, but with muscles now sagging and fat beginning to fill out his face and abdomen.

"How many kids look to you as a role model?" Becker asked. "Just offhand. If you know."

"Hundreds, maybe dozens. How about you?"

The policeman shifted his gun belt in a movement with which Becker was long familiar. The chief rode in the car with his holstered automatic nestled between his legs for comfort. Once standing, he twitched it into place again, a motion that looked at times as if he were preparing for a fast draw.

"Kids run screaming when they see me," said Becker.

"Funny reaction," said the policeman. "Personally, I find you rather attractive."

"I'll try to work on that," said Becker. "Nice driving, by the way."

"I took a course in that," the policeman said. "Taught by some sissy yob in the FBI." He leaned against the hood next to Becker. "I can go around a corner on two wheels and do a three-sixty just like the guys in the movies. I have all the skills."

"Which is why they made you chief, I imagine."

"That and my detective talents."

"Is that right? Good at sleuthing, too, are you?"

"Fucking A." The cop placed his hand on the centre of Becker's hood. "This car has been driven recently, just for instance."

"How can you tell?"

"He's still sweating. I know something else."

"Tell me everything you know, Tee. I've got five minutes."

Thomas Terence Terhune, know to everyone as Tee, hitched at his belt again, pulling it up so that it fitted tightly across his stomach. It would stay there until he inhaled again and then slip down to accommodate his paunch once more.

"I know that a young woman was in town looking for you a couple days ago. She was a seriously good-looking woman. Had a whole lot of body stuffed under her clothes."

"Probably trying to hide it from your eagle eye."

"She forgot my powers of detection. She had breasts and hips and other stuff."

"Face?"

"Also a face, yes. What a softer guy would call a lovely face. But she was trying real hard not to let on that she was such a looker. Flashed a very heavy badge at me. But I wasn't fooled."

"Because you have a badge of your own."

"I have a badge and a gun. I've got a car with lights on the roof. I have a radio on my belt."

"You are the chief, after all."

"Fucking A. So I wasn't fooled by this girl's badge. I still knew she was a very seriously attractive woman. Now why in hell would a good-looking woman be asking about the whereabouts of a guy like you, I wondered. Especially when she was looking square in the face of a guy like me."

"Bad eyesight?"

"Or too good. I think she spotted the wedding ring right away."

"You ought to remove it from your nose at times like that."

"I'll tell my wife you said that. Does Cindi know about this handsome babe who's asking about you?"

"Cindi and I are divorced," said Becker. "Just to remind you. You were my best man at the ceremony."

Tee shrugged. "Nothing unusual there. I'm the best man wherever I go."

"Because you're the chief."

"Fucking A ... She still asks about you," Tee said, his tone now more serious.

"Who?"

"Cindi. She asks how you're doing, like that."

"You see her?"

"In the course of my appointed rounds ... She still cares about you, John."

"I still care about her ... Is she – uh – OK?"

"No, she's not seeing anybody," Tee said. "Although I can't imagine why. I don't know if you ever noticed it during your marriage, John, but Cindi is one very fine female."

"I was aware ... I was lucky to be with her. I didn't deserve her."

"This is true."

"Unfortunately she finally realised it."

"That's not quite the way she tells it."

"Even eyewitness accounts vary," Becker said.

"You know why no one's asking her out, don't you?"

"They've all turned fashionably gay?"

"I'm serious, John."

"Why?"

"They don't ask her out because they're afraid of you."

"Bullshit."

"It's true."

"Nobody in Clamden has any reason to be afraid of me. I've never hurt a soul here."

"They hear the stories."

"How do they hear the stories? I don't tell them. Cindi doesn't tell them."

Tee held up his hands in innocence. "Don't look at me. Your past is private history as far as I'm concerned."

"So how do they hear 'the stories'?"

"I don't know. Word gets around. Rumours are hard to stop."

"Does Cindi think I'm trying to scare people off?"

Tee shrugged. "Not intentionally."

Becker studied his feet. "Jesus Christ, Tee, are people really scared of me?"

"Not those who know you, John."

"But others. Those who just hear about me? They think I'm – what – dangerous enough? Demented enough? Bloodthirsty enough to hurt them for trying to date my ex-wife? I've never hurt a soul except as part of my job."

"I know that, John. Most people know that."

"I live here, God damn it! I can't have people being afraid of me!"

"I'm probably exaggerating it. I shouldn't have brought it up."

"Start another rumour ..."

"I didn't start this one."

"Tell them I'm harmless. Tell them I'm a pussy-cat. Tell them I quit the FBI because I was afraid of the work ... That's the truth, anyway."

"You weren't afraid of the work in the sense of being

afraid of it, John. Give people a little credit, they're not going to believe that."

"I don't want to be a monster in my own home town, Tee. Jeesus."

They were quiet for a moment, both men studying a teenaged boy who was moving a lawn as if he held real interest for them. The boy glanced at them curiously.

"Do you suppose that youth with the mower is viewing me right this minute as a model and guide to his future?" Tee asked after a time.

"Why do they all wear baseball caps?" Becker said.

"Why do they all wear them backwards?"

"I don't want anybody to be afraid of me, Tee. Honest to God, that's terrible."

"I'll do what I can, all right? ... It'll pass."

Becker shook his head sadly. It always surprised Tee that his friend, whose career was a thing of courageous awe to every law enforcement officer who knew about it, was so vulnerable to the opinions of others. Particularly the opinions of people he did not know. The man would flail through a case, stepping on the toes of everyone who got in his way in the pursuit of his prey, but in civilian life he would worry about offending the sensibilities of the local grocer. Tee didn't pretend to understand him – he just liked him.

"I told the FBI woman you were proving your virility by jerking off on the side of a mountain," Tee said finally. "Did I do right?"

"You are a police officer, sworn to tell the truth."

"You didn't tell me not to tell anyone. You just said you wanted to be alone to jerk off for awhile."

"It's OK, Tee."

"I noticed in the course of my sleuthing that this FBI woman did not wear a wedding ring, by the way. Unlike myself. But very much like your good self."

"A second ago you were pushing Cindi on me, now you want me to mate with an agent?"

"Somebody ought to. And masturbation is an ugly thing to see in a man your age."

"You might stop watching."

"Hey, I'm the chief."

"And rank has its privileges," Becker said.

"I know something else you don't know," Tee offered.

"I suspect I'm about to. What?"

"The same lady is at your house now, waiting for you."

"You just happened to notice her?"

"In the pursuance of my duties I did notice a car in your driveway and, knowing that you were hanging by a thong around your dong from Mt. Kilimanjaro, I stopped to investigate further."

"Ever vigilant."

"She might have been a burglar come to heist your valuables."

"I have no valuables worth heisting."

"This I know, but a burglar might not, burglars being what they are. She was sitting on your porch, waiting, pretty as a … as a … what? What's particularly pretty?"

"A pretty woman?"

"There you go! She was sitting there, pretty as a pretty woman. Clever devil, you are, not having a car-phone so she could reach you … Do you often have gorgeous women paying you house calls?"

"We have a little business together. Just business. She wants to pick my brain."

"Have her do it through your pecker."

Becker returned to his car, shaking his head in mock disgust.

Tee closed the door and leaned against it.

"You're a great role model, but one hell of a bad influence."

"I thought you were out of the business," Tee said.

"I am. This is special."

"Because of her? Because of the babe waiting on your porch?"

Becker studied Tee for a moment as if seeking the answer in his friend's face. "You know, Tee, you've got all the natural instincts of a busybody, and a matchmaker. You may have missed your calling."

"Salaries for busybodies are so low, though. And besides, think what law enforcement would be missing without me."

"A chief?"

"Fucking A. So, is it because of her? And if not, why not?" Becker started the engine, then paused. "I wish it were that simple," he said.

"Yeah, it's complicated, sure, that's how you like to make things, I respect that. But you're really doing it for her, right?"

Becker sighed. "Right, Tee. Right."

He pulled away slowly because the big policeman was still holding on to the door.

"You dog," Tee said in gleeful approval. "Happy hunting." Tee slapped the side of the car as if it were a horse.

Becker drove away, still shaking his head in amused disdain at his friend's simple-minded analysis. But when he pulled into his driveway and saw Karen standing on the porch, balancing herself in that distinctive way she had, one foot behind the other like a dancer, he wondered how big a part of it was exactly what Tee suggested. He could not look at her without feeling a stirring of something that had nothing to do with official Bureau business.

Karen Crist stood when she saw Becker's car approaching. For a moment she longed to check her appearance in a mirror, but repressed the urge. In the first place, her appearance was irrelevant, she told herself. She was second-in-command of Kidnapping, she had hundreds of men under her authority. Becker was a consultant, nothing more. And in the second place, she had been compulsively looking at her image in the porch windowpane ever since she arrived. She looked as good as she was going to on this day ... although she wished her jawline were a little firmer. She always put weight on her face first, which was damned unfair. It didn't allow her the few extra pounds of leeway most women could add to the thighs and ass. Whatever she ate too much of showed up immediately and then went below her waist. And she had been eating too much, lately, she knew it. The stress of work and raising a child as a single parent and ...

Becker was out of the car. Karen stood by the porch railing, unconsciously arranging her legs in line with each other which thrust her pelvis forward and straightened her back. It was the pose she had adopted in primary school and incorporated so completely into her habits that she was unaware of both the unnaturalness of it and its effect on others. To men, she looked like a ship's figurehead, bracing into the wind, bold and inviting. Neither the sobriety of her expression nor the propriety of her demeanour – nor even the loftiness of her official position nor the seriousness of her career field – could ever completely overcome the impression of her body language. However much men might be impressed or even intimidated by her in other ways, they still reacted to Karen Crist as a woman. It was a situation she was aware of, and she used it when she needed to.

Becker was out of sight beyond the angle of the garage for a moment, and when he came into view again he was smiling. Karen loved his smile. He was normally of sober mien so that when he smiled it offered such a happy contrast. If he had been a man who practised charm, it would be a formidable weapon, Karen thought, for it made him look boyishly winning, shedding years and revealing a sweet and mischievous side to him.

"A pleasant surprise," Becker said.

Karen resisted her own impulse to smile. "I couldn't raise you on your phone," she said. "I was passing here, so I thought I'd try my luck in getting you at home ... And I got lucky."

"If you consider me good fortune."

"Your local Chief of Police apparently does. We had a little chat."

"Tee likes to chat."

"I noticed. He seems to think rather highly of you."

"We've been friends since high school."

"I got the impression he was trying to fix us up."

"Did you tell him we'd already been fixed up?"

"I didn't think that was for me to say," Karen said. "He's your friend, I don't know how much you want him to know."

"With Tee, it's probably better for him to know than to let his imagination go to work. I'm surprised he didn't try to pick you up himself."

"He does that, does he? He's a married man."

"It's not that he does it. He just can't seem to stop thinking about it."

"Men," she said.

"You're right. I can't argue."

"No wonder women are losing patience."

"I don't know why you've put up with us this long."

"It's a tribute to our good nature." Karen tilted her head slightly, hoping to firm her jawline. "But enough is enough." Becker sat on the railing and grinned at her. The directness of his attention summoned her back to the business that had brought her here. "Another boy is missing," she said.

"A snatch?"

"We don't know yet, it's too early. We have the State and local police in New Jersey, New York, Connecticut and Massachusetts reporting any disappearances that fit our profile immediately. It's a nine-year-old boy, physically he matches the others, he was last seen at a mall ..." Karen shrugged. "Maybe he'll show up by the time we get there. Maybe he fell asleep in the movies ..."

"Maybe. Where was it?"

"Bickford."

"That's about an hour from here."

"If we go in my car, we'll be able to talk. But I'll have to leave no later than five-thirty, so if you think you'll want to stay longer, maybe we'd better take both cars."

"Why do you have to go?" he asked.

"I have to be home by seven. That's when the babysitter leaves."

Becker blinked.

"I have a child, remember?"

"You do this every day?"

"Do what? Go home? Take care of my son? Act like a parent? Yes, I do it every day. That is what mothers do, isn't it? Or did I get that part wrong?"

"Sounding a little defensive there, Karen."

"Why do you people always act surprised when you hear that I'm a mother? I do mother things, I love my son, I make myself available for him."

" 'You people'?"

"I'm acting like a mother. If we could get more men to act like fathers, the world wouldn't be in the mess it's in."

"Why do I feel I have to justify myself?" Becker asked. "I don't have any children."

"Then I can't expect you to understand," she said. Karen was furious with herself. She had vowed to keep the meeting professional.

"Understand what?"

Karen started abruptly for her car. "Your car or mine," she said. "Suit yourself."

"Are you so sure I'm coming at all?" Becker asked, staying on the porch.

She turned to him angrily. "I don't have time for you to be coy," she said. "Of course you're coming."

Becker hesitated.

"Oh, Christ, don't make me woo you," she said. "We've already done that number. Let's get on with business."

She got into her car and buckled up, not looking at him any more.

Becker thought about telling her to go stuff herself. He thought about it all the way to the car.

They were already on the Merritt Parkway and heading east before he asked. "What made you so sure I was coming?"

"Because the trail is still warm and you know you have a better chance of people remembering something now than you will a day from now. You're smart enough to know that."

He looked at her curiously. She was concentrating on her driving, pushing the car to eighty miles per hour, flashing her headlights in annoyance at anyone who slowed her down. Presumably she was saving her siren until she hit ninety. Her jaw was clenched and thrust forward defiantly. Becker realised she was angry as hell about something and he just happened to be available.

It wasn't until they swept north on route eight that she seemed to relax. Traffic had cleared and she sped along in the left lane basically without interference.

"What made you so sure of me?" Becker asked again.

This time she turned from the road long enough to glance at him. The tension eased from her face and was replaced by sympathy.

"I knew you'd have to study the photographs," she said. Her eyes went back to the highway. "You told me something about your childhood once, John. Do you remember?"

"No."

She sniffed. "Men don't. They never remember anything."

"Women do," he added.

"Yes, we do. We labour under the delusion that the things you tell us are true."

"I never lied to you," he said.

"No."

After a pause he added, "And I do remember," although he was not certain that he did.

He briefed her on what he had learned – and not learned – during his visit to the Stamford mall. She spoke into her tape-recorder as she drove, taking notes on what he said. When he was finished she telephoned her office in New York and gave orders in a crisp, clipped tone.

"Fax me the results to …" she turned to Becker. "What's your fax number?"

"I don't have a fax," he said.

Karen sighed. "I'll have the Bureau get you one. It's time to enter the decade, John." Into the phone she said, "Malva, fax the results to my house. I want it waiting for me by the time I get home … Yes, seven o'clock, of course." She hung up and eased into the right lane as she saw the exit for Bickford approaching.

She was aware that Becker was studying her openly.

"What?"

"I'm remembering you ten years ago when you were still in Fingerprinting and looking desperately for a way to get out of there. Now you're in charge of how many people?"

"And I was nicer then, right? Sweeter, softer, more feminine? Something like that?"

"Younger."

"Oh, you smooth talking son-of-a-bitch. How did you know that was exactly what I wanted to hear?"

"I didn't mean you looked old," Becker said defensively. "I meant you seem very much in control."

"Do you ever say anything tactful to anyone?"

"Not if I'm interested in them."

Karen had started to say something, but stopped abruptly. She glanced at him, trying to read his meaning in his face, but he seemed to be studying the traffic with great curiosity.

"I didn't mean to be so short with you," she said. It was not what she wanted to say, but it seemed safer. She knew him well enough to know that she should never ask Becker a question unless she was prepared to deal with the truth. "I am a bit defensive about some things," she continued. "You have no idea how hard it is, being a mother as well as an agent."

"They're a pretty chauvinist bunch," Becker said. "I imagine they give you a lot of grief. At least behind your back."

"Having a woman tell them what to do shrivels their gonads right up," she said.

"It's not the gonads that shrivel, but I take your point," he said.

"I thought they did something like that."

"They sort of recede into the body cavity," Becker said. "If it's cold – or dangerous. It's the penis that shrivels."

"That I know about," she said, trying to keep the ridicule from her voice. It amazed her that her contempt for men had seemed to increase in direct proportion to the amount of time she had lived without one. She had expected it to work the other way around, absence making the heart grow fonder and so forth. Maybe her fellow agents were right in their muttered assessment of her, she thought. Maybe she really did need a good fuck.

"They call me dragon lady, I know that," she said.

Becker dismissed it. "They call any woman in authority dragon lady. Don't take it personally. Just think of all the things they call Hatcher."

"They mean those things personally," she pointed out.

"Only because Hatcher deserves them. You don't."

"You don't know that. Maybe I do deserve them. Maybe I am a stony bitch. You wouldn't know, you don't know me at all any more."

"I'm starting to."

"You've got no idea how hard it is. None of you men know. Just try it one time, just try being a hard-assed executive – but not too hard, don't want to threaten anyone's masculinity – and then turn into a loving mother every night at seven until you get him off to school the next morning. All those articles about single parents? They're not kidding, it's a bitch. Just try it for a month or two and see how sweet you are."

"You seem to be managing awfully well," he said drily.

She laughed. "Yeah, I'm a whiz. I'm acting, acting all the time. I feel like the world's biggest hypocrite."

"Which role is the hardest to sustain?" Becker asked. "The hard-assed exec or the loving mother?"

Karen did not answer immediately. She manoeuvred the car on to the exit ramp and stopped at the traffic light.

When she spoke her voice was deliberately contained. "I am a loving mother," she said.

Becker nodded.

"I am."

"OK," he said. He held her eyes for a moment, watching her jaw tighten again. A horn honked behind them as the light changed to green.

"You don't know anything about it at all," she said. Her eyes glared angrily.

"About what?"

"About parents and children, what that's all about."

The car behind them honked again. Karen turned and very slowly lifted her middle finger at the driver.

"I know half of it," Becker said.

Karen gunned her car through the intersection and followed the sign towards the mall. The driver behind her blared his horn in frustration.

"No you don't," Karen said. "You don't know any of it! Your childhood was not normal. You can't judge normal people by your experience. You have no frame of reference for me and my son, none. None!"

"OK," Becker said softly.

Karen could hear the pain in his voice. It only made her angrier. "Could we just dispense with the personal stuff? I won't dig into your life if you leave mine alone, all right?"

"All right."

She glanced at him. He looked so wounded. She wanted to comfort him but did not dare.

She said, "Let's just do the fucking work, John, OK?"

This time he didn't answer at all. Karen had not merely read his file, she had studied it. She knew in detail what he had done to other men, and how. How could he be so sensitive and still survive, she wondered. And if she found the combination of strength and vulnerability so dangerously attractive, why weren't women chasing this man down the street, clutching at his clothes? His ex-wife must have been a moron to let him go, she thought. And then she remembered that, she, too, had let him get away once. She had thought at the time that it was for her own good. It seemed instead that very little good had happened to her since, at least when it came to men.

She pulled into the vast parking lot and stopped the car next to a police car, slipping the FBI identification card under the windshield before the nearest cop could tell her to drive on. Flashing her badge, she led Becker past another huddle of cops and into the mall.

Just before they stepped into the elevator that would take them to the security office, Karen touched Becker's arm lightly.

"John, I'm an asshole," she said softly.

"I know," he said.

"Thank you."

"But you're probably right about me," he added.

They rode the elevator in silence.

When they reached the top she said, "Nobody taught me how to be a mother. My mother didn't know."

"I know," he said. "You told me once."

"And you remembered?"

He grinned at her with the kind of smile that could break hearts. "You told me a lot, one way or the other."

"It was a very busy few days," she said.

"Six," he said. "Six days. And I remember every minute of every one of them."

8

They had a sign burned into a chunk of maple on the counter in the motel office announcing them as 'The Lamperts', as if they were a pair of Siamese twins, not just an aging married couple, as if they were a team, yoked to a common cause – but in fact only Reggie thought of herself as a part of an indissoluble unit. George considered himself a free agent, always had, intended to continue to until they carted him away, no matter that he had been married to her for forty years and had never yet strayed in any significantly threatening way. He still might, he had it in him. He might decide tomorrow to just chuck it all, including his nagging wife and this burden of a business that was supposed to have been their retirement heaven, and hike on out to Utah or somewhere with a lot of sky and plenty of women to treat him with respect. He just might do that little thing, because, no matter how bad Reggie looked these days, he wasn't that old yet.

Reggie knew that George harboured these defiant little notions and she had purchased the "Lamperts" sign just to remind him that he was about as much a free agent as the back half of a jackass. The sign was on the counter to serve as a daily reminder – so she wouldn't have to.

Like the back half of the jackass, however, George did

need to swish his tail now and then, and Reggie was too smart by far to try to deny him that. She took his flirtations in her stride, regarding them as old habits that no longer had much meaning but were too comforting for him to discard. He looked about as much like a lover as the WWI vet saluting the flag on Memorial Day looked like a warrior. George was not capable of saluting anything these days – and who would know better than she who had tried, God knows, every trick she could think of to get some lead into his pencil. So she let him have his flirtations with the guests, confident that he had as much at stake in seeing to it they never took him up on it as she did. The humiliation would make him unbearable, and he was tough enough to get along with as it was. If she had believed in sainthood and all that Roman claptrap, Reggie would have figured someone should put her name on the Pope's waiting list just for having tolerated George Lampert for all these years.

He was flirting now, the damned old fool. She watched him from the office window as he patrolled the motel "cabins", supposedly checking to see that they all had fresh towels. He knew damned well they had fresh towels because Reggie had seen to it herself that very morning. It was just his flimsy excuse to talk to the woman in number six again. He hadn't shown any concern for the guests' towel situation earlier, she noticed. Only when he saw the woman's car bring her back from work. Then he was all of a sudden concerned about the linens.

The woman came out of the cabin as soon as he approached, closing the door behind her. Reggie could see her lift her head in laughter, hear the sound of it ringing across the grounds. She must have said something funny, Reggie thought. She certainly couldn't be responding to George who hadn't said anything original in a couple of decades at least. Reggie could tell what he was going to

99

say before he even opened his mouth, and, often as not, she could tell she didn't want to hear it. Which was one of the reasons they spent so much time in silence.

There was nothing silent about the woman in number six, however. She was one of the talkiest women Reggie had ever seen. And so good natured that Reggie sometimes had the urge to ask her what world she was living in. She was a pretty thing, if you liked that type with the shortish dirty-blonde hair. More brown than blonde, of course, but Reggie, whose own hair was a faded pink, did not hold the use of artifice against anyone. A girl did what she had to do. Still, the woman actually seemed like fun and if she weren't a guest, Reggie might have liked her.

She never allowed herself to really like any of the guests because she didn't trust them. They always wanted something more, more blankets, more towels, more channels on the TV. As if they had pulled off Route 78 and into the Ritz, not the Restawhile. And they treated the cabins as if they were kept clean by an army of Puerto Rican maids, not just Reggie herself. And George, of course, when he felt like catering to the fancies of pretty guests.

Look at him now, leaning against the post supporting the phony porch roof, arms folded in front of him so the towels flopped down like some sort of highwaisted breech cloth. As if he had anything to cover up. Leaning and smiling and chatting away like a teenager. She wished a gust of wind would come along and blow those carefully arranged remaining hairs atop his head into disarray. He was so vain about those silly, forlorn-looking white scraps that he composed so meticulously each morning. As if they hid any of his shiny scalp. As if they fooled anyone but him. Reggie was forgiving about cosmetic deception for women because that was how that particular game was played and you played the cards you were dealt, but in men it seemed nothing more than the last crow of the dying rooster. She wished she had a video camera so she could tape him and then make him watch himself acting like a foolish old man for the benefit of this young woman. No fool like an old fool, and none bigger than George Lampert.

Now he was returning to the office. Reggie busied herself behind the counter. She could have made it into the next room and settled herself in front of the television before he reached the office if she had wanted him to think she hadn't been watching. By staying behind the counter she could keep him in doubt. Maybe she'd watched him, maybe she hadn't. A little uncertainty would help keep him in line. The trick was to not let him think he was getting away with anything so he got cocky, but not to make him think he was spied upon so he got rebellious either. Being a good wife required a precise understanding of nuance.

"She's a pisser," he said approvingly as he entered, letting the screen door slam behind him as usual. She had told him a thousand times. Just as he had promised to fix it several hundred.

"Oh?" Reggie did not bother to look up.

"Got more juice running through her veins than a dozen women. You know who she reminds me of? That girl on television, the spunky one who's always getting herself into trouble then getting out again, you know the one I mean, she's on that show you like."

"Who?"

"I don't know her name, she's on that show you like, what do you call it."

"Who are you talking about?" Reggie asked, trying to conceal her annoyance. Just like him, to come in trying to cloud the issue with his very first breath, bringing in irrelevant people, television stars.

"Dee," he said. "Full of piss and vinegar, she is." He

chuckled as if just thinking of all that piss and vinegar made him happy all over again.

"Dee? Dee? What's a D?"

"The woman in six," he said, pretending he didn't notice the acid creeping not very subtly into her tone. "We just had a chat."

"Oh, is that right?"

As if you weren't watching every second of it, he thought. As if you didn't act like I was going to whip into one of the cabins and boff a guest everytime I stepped outside the door. Well, this guest I wouldn't mind, wouldn't mind at all. I'm not so certain she'd mind, either. She was cute and bright and friendly and had a way of talking to a man as if she'd known him for years, as if she knew him so well she knew what he was thinking all the time – and didn't disapprove of it, either.

"She seems like a nice person," he said. "And she's going to save us some work."

"Oh?" Reggie like the 'us'. As if he did any work that anyone could notice.

"We don't have to clean her room. She'll take care of the linens herself, so I told her to just let me know when she wanted towels or anything."

"What are you talking about?"

"Her husband's got a problem with his eyes. Opto, opto something or other, I didn't get the name. He can't take the light. It's all tied up with migraines and such. She doesn't want him disturbed. So she said she'll do the cleaning herself, we don't need to bother."

"He's sick?"

"Not sick. It's a condition, he's got a condition. It's not contagious or anything. It's just a temporary thing, it will clear up, you know how it is."

"I haven't got any idea how it is. She didn't say anything about a condition when she checked in."

"You're not going to catch it," he said, beginning to wish he hadn't brought it up, not so soon after he had been seen talking to Dee, anyway. Reggie was bound to think it was some kind of trick. As if he were being manipulated and duped in some way. She was the most distrusting woman he had ever seen. He should have left her when he had the chance, before they'd sunk all their savings in this motel, while he was still young ... Not that he wasn't still young enough. He might take a hike to Utah at any moment. And maybe he'd take Dee with him. She must be getting pretty weary of being saddled with a husband with a condition. Not that you could tell it by talking to her. Not a whisper of complaint. Unlike some women he knew.

"In other words, we're supposed to keep out," Reggie said.

"She's entitled to privacy, for Christ's sake! The man has got a condition, he needs to be left alone. What do you care? It's one less cabin to worry about."

"It's one cabin to worry more about, if you ask me. What's she up to?"

"Maybe she keeps him naked and tied to the bed with the sheets, that's why she doesn't want you to change them, because he'd get loose and ravage all the women in the neighbourhood."

Instead of dignifying his statement with a response, Reggie pulled aside the curtain and studied cabin six. The curtains were drawn, the door closed. It might as well have been empty for all the signs of life it revealed. Number six was the farthest from the office of any of the cabins and Reggie remembered now that the woman, 'Dee', had requested it especially. At the time she had said she thought it was the cutest, and in truth it did have rather better shrubbery in front than the others, the angle of its alignment had kept the sun at its back and

consequently it had weathered less than the others ...
Now, however, Reggie wondered if it wasn't simply that
it was the farthest away from scrutiny.

"I told her it was fine with us," George said.

Reggie looked at him. He was puffing out his chest,
preparing for a battle. Just like a rooster. All strut and
puff and bluster. "Oh, you did, did you?"

"I sure did." He lifted his hand, waving currency in her
face. "She's paying two weeks in advance. In cash. I
figure that entitles her to as much privacy as she wants."

Reggie took the money from his hand, counted it and
made an entry into the books. As if money had anything
to do with it, she thought. It was all about control, and
she knew that "Dee" knew it, too, even if George was too
charmed to realise it. Money had nothing to do with it.

He was still spoiling for a fight, nothing he'd like
better, Reggie saw, than to tangle with her in defence of
another woman. A rooster with his comb engorged and
flaming. Well, she wouldn't give him the satisfaction.

"Well, that's fine, then," she said. Closing the books as
if that put a period to the discussion. As if some woman
could keep her out of the cabins she owned and cared for
and depended on her livelihood from just because she was
full of piss and vinegar.

George was left with his fists balled for a fight and no
one to swing at. She watched him with amusement as he
tried to adjust. His relief almost outweighed his surprise.

"That show you like is coming on," he said, glancing
into their living room. "Come on and watch."

Strutting out of the office, as if he were personally
responsible for bringing her show on to the television.
Little banty-legged, bald-headed rooster, thinking he'd
cowed the world with his crow. Well, hens laid eggs with
or without a rooster. Everyone knew that – except maybe
the roosters.

*

Ash lay on the back seat of the car, hidden under the blanket. The blanket was coarse and cheap, stolen long ago from some motel or other, and it had been used for a dozen purposes over the years, every one of which Ash could smell when the itchy cloth covered his face and nose. There was the odour of grease and oil upon the blanket, the smell of the spare tyre against which the blanket was usually stored in the trunk of the car, the scent of grass and even of Dee herself who had often been wrapped in the blanket while she lay inert and mournful during her bad times. Ash could catch whiffs of himself, not only now but from the other times he had hidden under here, waiting for Dee to give the signal to come out. And he could smell the boys. Their young bodies, their fresh skins. Their fear.

On one of the nature shows Ash had seen a wolf spider that built itself a den, complete with a camouflaged opening. When the spider's prey approached too closely to the mouth of the den, the spider popped out and grabbed it, sucking it back into the lair in an instant. Ash had watched the show with fascination, wondering how the spider knew how to do what it did, how it knew that something edible would ever come by, how it knew the method to construct its elaborate web and den. He knew that he could never do anything that intricate himself. "It just does it by instinct," Dee had said. "It doesn't know what it's doing."

But that was no explanation for Ash. He would not have known what he was doing, either, and he was certain he had no instinct to guide him through anything so elaborate.

And why was it called a wolf spider? Ash had seen wolves on other shows and they didn't act at all like the spider. They hunted in packs and ran for miles and miles to catch their prey and only lived in holes when they had babies. There were always so many puzzles on the nature shows. Dee seemed to understand them all, even when she was attending only peripherally, dropping her comments in passing as she paced the room, but her explanations never helped Ash.

"They call it a wolf spider because of all that hair, it looks like fur," she had explained. "Didn't you hear him say that? I heard it and I wasn't even listening."

Ash hadn't heard because he was so busy watching, but even if he had he would not have understood. Rabbits had fur, too. So did mice. Why didn't they call it a rabbit spider? He loved to watch the shows, anyway.

Now, as he lay under the blanket in the back of the car, he thought of the wolf spider. Was this what it felt like as it waited for something to walk by close enough to grab? Was it a little bit scared, as Ash was? And excited, but sad, too, about what it would have to do? Did it get nervous?

Ash wanted to go to the bathroom, it seemed to be taking Dee so long. It always seemed to take her too long, but she said that was just because he was anxious. He knew he didn't dare to leave the car to find a toilet. He didn't even dare to sit up and look to see if Dee was coming.

"That's all we need," Dee had told him. "You lifting up from the backseat like a periscope. That wouldn't look funny, would it?" He knew she didn't mean funny to laugh at although Ash thought the vision of himself as a periscope was very comical.

There was to be no going to the bathroom, no peeking above the seat, no moving at all just in case someone happened to wander by and glance into the car.

Ash told himself he was the wolf spider. It wasn't twitching around in its den while it waited. He had seen it, it stood like a statue, all its legs bent and ready to spring, its huge eyes peering straight ahead. The camera must have been right on top of it but it didn't twitch a muscle, not a hair on its body moved. If it had to go to the bathroom, it just didn't, that's all.

He heard footsteps approaching and opened his hands under the blanket to be ready to grab. His fingers were just like all of those spider's legs, he thought, taut and poised.

He heard the door open, felt the weight of a body on the seat. Ash sprang like the wolf spider, engulfing the boy immediately, covering his body with the blanket as he shed it from himself. Ash's arms locked around the boy's body and his hand clamped over the boy's face, pressing the cloth on to his mouth.

The car was already in motion but Ash stayed below the windows, knowing he was not to be seen by anyone until they were safely away. He lay atop the boy, pinning him to the floor with the weight of his body but careful not to crush him.

After the first moment of attack Ash adjusted his hand, making sure it covered only the boy's mouth and not his nose, too. That was the only time when they really struggled, when he was inadvertently smothering them. Otherwise they lay very still. Ash thought of the insects captured by the wolf spider. They hardly seemed to struggle at all as the spider wrapped them in silk. He thought of the inflated frog being swallowed by the snake, only its enormous eyes registering protest.

Ash understood that the spider turned its victim into a mummy with the silk, not only immobilising it but preserving it for consumption at a later time. In a way that was what he was doing with the blanket. He wasn't just preventing the boy from struggling. He was wrapping him up for storage.

Not that they were going to eat him, exactly, Ash

107

thought. But Dee would drain the juices from him, in time. She would leave him dry and hollow.

"Don't you hurt my beautiful boy," Dee said. She sounded excited, merry, almost, as if it were Christmas and the package Ash held in his arms was the best one of all and just for her. And it was for her, of course. For her and Ash, too, but mostly for her.

The car was gathering speed, which meant they were away from the town centre and heading towards the highway. Soon, with the roar and speed of the throughway to mask all sounds, Ash would be able to get up and unwrap the package. It wouldn't matter if the boy yelled then; no one would hear him above the noise of traffic.

Then they would drive and drive, it didn't matter where as long as it was on the throughway. They would drive the twenty miles to home and past it, just keep going, then turn and come back the other way, killing time until it was dark and safe to return to the motel under cover of darkness. Ash would wrap the boy in the blanket once more and rush him into the privacy of their room in a matter of seconds, too quick for anyone to see, too fast for the boy to scream or kick his way free.

In the meantime Dee would explain to the boy what his duties and responsibilities were and what she expected of him. He wouldn't understand at first, they never did. He would complain and tell them to take him home. If he was very foolish, or very frightened, he would threaten to call the police. Dee would forgive him today. She always forgave everything at first, she was so happy about her new present that she didn't care if it had little imperfections. It was only with time that the imperfections would become apparent to her, and then they would seem to grow and grow until that was all she could see. The image of her beautiful boy would fade and she would see only ingratitude and disappointment.

But that would be a few weeks from now. In the meantime, Dee was his beautiful eagle again, soaring so gracefully above him. And the boy was her unfledged chick, confined by necessity and the surrounding dangers of hunters and lofty heights to the nest where she would care for him. And when she flew away to find food for her new hatchling, Ash would keep it company in the nest, like a big flightless bird himself, no more able to leave the eyrie than was the boy, but stronger, protective. Even instructive. Ash could teach the young bird things it must know to please its mother. He could never teach it quite enough, it seemed, for eventually it would fail to please. No matter how hard Ash tried, no matter how manfully the boy attempted to win her approval, ultimately he would fail.

And then the bits of flesh that the mother eagle carried back to the nest to feed her chick would change. They would turn into pieces torn from the chick itself. She would feed the chick itself to eat. And the young bird, so carefully schooled by then in gratitude and submission, would dine upon itself without complaint until it was all gone.

9

There were over two dozen witnesses to nothing. The police had gathered the many employees and shoppers who were, or might have been, present at a non-event.

Interest dulled by repetition, the local police dutifully took down the stories of people who had seen everything except the one thing that mattered. Karen and Becker moved among them, FBI identification displayed, eavesdropping and sometimes adding a question themselves.

It was like interviewing the neighbours after a Mafia murder, Karen whispered to Becker. Nobody knew nothing. In this case, however, they were not being uncooperative. They were like witnesses at a magic show who had seen but not seen, and did not know what the conjurer had done.

"What you got to realise is this place has always got crowds," said the manager of a doughnut stand whose open-fronted shop gave him a large view of the main floor of the mall. "I'm not saying business is all that great, I'm not saying people are buying much – but they're here, is what I'm saying." The man sucked on a toothpick, waggling it up and down when he paused.

Becker stood just behind the interviewing officer, watching the man whose name-plate identified him as Fred.

"They come in groups, they come in pairs, they come alone. Who can keep track, you know what I mean? This morning they brought people from the nursing homes. You never saw so many walkers and canes and wheelchairs. They bring them every two weeks as an outing. Just coming here is a treat for them, I guess. They certainly don't buy any big ticket items, you know. At that age, why bother?"

The man called Fred spoke with his teeth clamped together to hold the toothpick in place, giving him the look of a man with lockjaw, Becker thought.

"This afternoon there were the kids from the school. I saw them, sure, they trooped right by here on their way to the scientific toy shop, I guess, I didn't see where they went. Sometimes it's the pet store, they look at the tropical fish as part of their science projects, something like that, I don't know. I know they don't stop here."

"Kids don't like doughnuts?" Becker asked.

The police officer in charge shot Becker an annoyed glance until he noticed the FBI medallion on Becker's chest. He still looked annoyed but said nothing.

"Who doesn't like a doughnut? But these kids were supervised, you know what I mean? You got a teacher in front of the pack, another one alongside, a school nurse bringing up the rear to get the stragglers. It's like a cattle drive or something. They're not about to get loose to come over for a quick doughnut."

"Did you see any of the kids alone at any time?" the officer asked.

"How'm I supposed to know that? You see individual kids alone all the time. How do I know if they're from that group or with their friends or with their parents or just here to ride the escalators, they don't wear signs saying 'I am alone'. "

"Do you pass your shop to get to the men's room?" Becker asked.

The manager thought for a moment, striking the toothpick with his tongue so that it danced up and down. "You can, sure, but I'm not that close to the john, if that's what you mean. You can pass down the whole corridor to get to the john. Or you can get there from the other direction."

"Did you see any boys in the company of an adult during that time?" the officer asked.

"That time? What time?"

"The time we're talking about," the officer said wearily. This was his fifth interview in less than an hour. It was like asking people sitting on their lawn if they'd seen any grass. "Between three-thirty and four o'clock."

Fred snorted rudely as if the cop were an idiot. "Did I see any boys with adults between three-thirty and four o'clock? When do you think parents take their kids shopping?"

The cop tried to ignore the sarcasm by controlling his breathing. It made him sound more impatient than ever. 'Did you see anything unusual? Any sign that any of these adults was forcing the children in any way?"

"Forcing them? You got kids? You got to force them half the time."

"What do you mean?" Becker asked.

"Well, they're like wild animals, ain't they? You got to control them. So you give them a yank on the arm, a swat on the butt, you know what I mean."

"Yes," said Becker.

"Sometimes you grab them by the scruff of the neck and march them along. Is that what you mean by forcing them?" Fred was now addressing himself to Becker, attracted to the FBI initials like a moth to a light brighter than the ordinary policeman.

112

"Did you see any of that?"

"I see it all the time. Did I see it between three-thirty and four? How do I know? Probably. You see parents with kids, you're going to see some forcing. Nothing wrong with that, I do it myself. If I didn't give my kids a yank by the ear every now and then, we'd never get anywhere. Frankly, they need a swift kick every so often."

"Thank you for being so frank," said Becker. "Did you notice any men with boys? That's not as common, is it?"

"No, it's not. Except on the weekends. Then you see plenty of it, guys pushing strollers, guys with Cub Scouts, you name it."

"How about today? Between three-thirty and four."

"Look, I don't really keep that close track of what I'm seeing when, you know? It all just kind of passes in front of you, people, just lots of people. You notice the real strange ones, or the real good-looking ones, but otherwise ..." He shrugged. "I get paid to sell doughnuts, is what it is. I'm a people watcher, yeah, but I ain't a student, if you see what I'm saying. Now you, you guys in the FBI are trained observers, right?"

"How about weight lifters?"

"I mean, you're trained to look at a crowd and pick out the one guy you're after by the way he's walking, or something, right? Is it true you can look at a guy and see if he's carrying a gun?"

Becker looked directly at the policeman, his eyes holding on the holstered pistol on the man's belt. "He's carrying one, for instance," he said.

Fred laughed. "No, I mean ..."

"Did you see any weight lifters, any body builders, any men who were particularly pumped up?"

"That's not uncommon these days."

"Did you see anyone who looked particularly strong

with a nine-year-old boy? That ought to be something a little different that you'd notice, wouldn't it?"

Fred paused for a moment, his eyes falling from Becker to a point in the middle distance. He even took the toothpick from his mouth. "No," he said at last. "I don't think I saw that combination."

"Did you see any men who looked like that at all, with or without a kid? Did you see any men out of the ordinary, period?"

The manager shrugged again. "What's ordinary? We get all kinds in here. We get the whole world through here, eventually. But no, I know what you mean, and no, I didn't see anybody like that, I didn't see anybody I'd call suspicious at all."

Becker started to leave then pivoted on his heel and came back for one more question. This time the policeman made no attempt whatever to disguise his annoyance.

"Were the people from the nursing home gone by the time the kids from the school got here?"

Fred stared at him blankly for a moment before Becker continued. "You would have noticed that. Children mixing in with the walkers and wheelchairs. Did you see that?"

The cop turned to Becker and spoke to him for the first time. "You're thinking somebody put him in a wheelchair and took him out that way?"

"Seems possible."

But the manager was shaking his head. "Nah, the old people were long gone. They don't have that much attention span, you know. Or they get cranky, I don't know. They never stay more than a couple hours before their nurses wheel them out of here. They were gone before lunch."

"Are you certain?"

"Absolutely. I was hoping to sell them doughnuts at lunch time. They love sweets, you know." Fred spoke as if he were referring to a different species.

"Who does?"

"Old people."

"And children?" Becker asked.

"And children. And I didn't make any sales to either one of them, come to that. Too much supervision. Entirely too much supervision."

"It's like that every time," Karen said as they drove back towards Clamden. "That's why we call him Lamont, he seems to get around like The Shadow."

"He's not invisible," Becker said.

"Of course not," Karen said. "There's probably another word for someone who can come and go unseen."

"He's seen," Becker said. "He's just not remembered,"

"Because he clouds men's minds."

Becker put his head all the way back against the headrest and tried to ignore the speed at which Karen was driving. She used the car as an instrument of her anger, battering space with it.

"We don't know yet that this was even a snatch," Becker said.

"It was." She bit her words as if they hurt. Becker watched her warily.

"Maybe the boy is lost. Maybe he ran into his aunt and went home with her. Maybe ..."

"It's Lamont," Karen said with finality. "I know him by now. I can't see the son-of-a-bitch, but I know him. He was there this afternoon and somehow he managed to make off with Bobby Reynolds. And unless we get so lucky it defies all the laws of probability, in two months we'll find Bobby Reynolds in a garbage bag. And that cocksucker will be free to do it again."

"So then let's get lucky," Becker said.

"What the fuck does that mean?" she spat.

"Nothing," he said. "I'm just trying to calm you down."

"Don't. Anger is the only thing I've got working for me. I sure as shit don't have any clues."

"Maybe he doesn't walk out with him. Maybe he does it long distance in some way. Lures them."

"How? With a dog whistle? These are children we're talking about, Becker. They don't just break from a group and leave the mall. I mean, they might wander off, particularly boys, but not that far."

"How far would they wander?"

"What does that mean?"

"Don't get pissed off at me, I'm just trying to help. I admit I don't know much about kids any more. You're the expert on boys that age, it's a serious question. How far would they stray from the group? Let's say they saw something fascinating like … like what? What would fascinate your son?"

Karen blared her horn at the car in front of her that dared to be in the passing-lane doing less than eighty-five miles an hour. The car jerked back into the right-hand lane as if startled.

"At his age? Something that would pull him away from his friends? … A sports star, maybe? Michael Jordan? But forget that, if anyone that famous was at the mall, we'd know about it. And even then he wouldn't go without telling his friends and even then he wouldn't leave the mall itself …"

"But he might go far enough to separate himself from the group? I mean assuming for the moment he saw something that fascinating in the distance – never mind what that thing might be?"

"It's possible, I suppose, but at his age he lives for his

friends. It's just so unlikely that he wouldn't at least tell one of them what he saw ..."

"My point is, he wouldn't necessarily have to leave the mall by himself, would he? Or with Lamont for that matter."

"Then how does he get away?"

"Maybe he doesn't," Becker said.

"Shit!" For a second Becker feared she was going to slam on the brakes which at their speed would have meant disaster, but she held the car on line despite her agitation.

"Just a thought," Becker said. "I don't have much hope for it, but ..."

"You're saying he might still be in the mall somewhere?" "It wouldn't hurt to check. He could be under a counter, in a closet ..."

"Every shop there has to have a storage room of some kind. How much space does it take to hide a nine-year-old? Not much." Karen had the telephone in her hand, at the same time slowing and easing into the right-hand lane.

She continued to talk to Becker as she punched in the number of her office.

"What do you think, Lamont tucks them away somewhere until everyone clears out and then slips out with them at night?"

"I don't think that, no. But I do believe it should be checked out," he said.

Karen told her Malva in her office to wait, then turned her attention to Becker once more. "Why don't you think that?"

"How would he immobilise his victims for that long? That mall doesn't shut down until nine o'clock. He's got to keep the kid quiet for at least six hours."

"And then he leaves with the cleaning crew," Karen spoke into the telephone. "Malva, first, call the Chief of

Police in Bickford, tell him to search the mall thoroughly. He'll tell you he did, but I want him to go over it with a full body scrub, look inside every space at least ... oh ... say a foot and a half square. Tell him to start now, the entire mall, then you get as many men up there as we have to spare to help out. Put the arm on the State police to get their men over there, too. Tell him I want it done thoroughly, Malva, thor-ough-ly. I want the mall strip-searched, understand? The missing boy might still be there ... right ... then have Elias go to work on the cleaning crew that comes in at night. It must be a big one, the mall is huge. I want him to check the backgrounds of all of them to see if any of them worked at any of the other places where any of our victims went missing." She glanced at Becker. "Anything else?"

Becker screwed up his lips, thinking.

"I'll call you back, Malva," Karen said into the telephone. "I'm on my way home now, I'll be there by seven if you need me.

"It's no good, though, is it?" Karen said as soon as she hung up.

"You got to try," said Becker.

"If he drugged them to keep them quiet there's bound to be a fuss of some kind. If the drug takes effect immediately he'd have to carry them to the hiding place. If it has a delayed effect, the boys would struggle ... Unless they walked straight into the hiding place and he drugged them there. But how would they even know where the hiding place was? What is he, the Pied Piper? And why wouldn't someone notice a boy walking into their storage rooms or wherever? He might not use drugs; he could bind and gag them, but that's hardly an activity no one would notice – again, unless they walk right into his lair and it's big enough for both of them – it just doesn't work, does it?"

118

"Still, you have to check it out," said Becker.

"Of course." She banged the steering wheel with the flat of her palm, then wheeled the car into the passing-lane again, accelerating until Becker squirmed nervously in his seat.

"I thought for a second we might have something," she said.

"Could I make a request?" Becker asked.

"Of course. What?"

"Could you slow down?"

"Slow down?"

"The car. Could you slow down the car?"

Karen glanced at him and laughed. "Scared?"

"Spitless."

"I took the course in defensive driving, too, you know," she said, smiling. "Or is it that you don't trust a woman driver?"

Becker noted that she did not slow down. "I don't trust the speed," he said. "Where in hell is a cop when you need one?"

Karen looked at her watch. "I'll just make it by seven as it is," she said. "Close your eyes and think clean thoughts."

"I'm trying to remember my prayers," he said.

"I'm surprised you know any."

Becker's tone turned darker. "Oh, I used to pray a lot," he said. "A lot."

Karen noticed the change and let the topic drop. It was so easy to say the wrong thing with Becker. He could sail through the worst of incidents with his spirits up, joking and buoying those around him in the midst of horrors enough to depress anyone else, but when he looked inward, into what Karen thought of as the rat's nest of his personal memories and emotions, he could turn sorrowfully ironic in a second. Words took on a double meaning with him then, his frame of reference shifted and every sentence uttered by another became to him reference to his past.

Karen's sympathy for him at such times was matched by her growing impatience. The best cure, she had discovered, was to just be quiet. Becker did not enjoy the episodes, he did not relish self-pity, and he willed himself out of it as soon as he could. It was his resilience, in fact, that had most impressed Gold, the Bureau psychiatrist with whom Becker had spent so much time.

"He just refuses to be defeated," Gold had told Karen. "By his memories or his demons or anything else. Believe me, anyone else would have sunk into clinical depression or psychosis long since. They'd have been tipped over by a lot less than Becker's had to carry. The concept of the will is not in great favour in my business, but that's the best way I can think of to explain it. He can't prevent the flashes of sorrow, rage, pain, he can't prevent them from happening, but he seems to be able to shut them down almost immediately by the strength of his will. What do you have to remember most of all about Becker, Ms Crist, is that, above all else, John Becker wants to do the right thing. There is a certain kind of person he wants to be and he keeps willing himself to be that person, despite continual setbacks. We should all come as close to our goals, believe me. He's a remarkable man."

Remarkable in other ways, too, Karen thought. Ways that Gold knew nothing about. She reminded herself of that during the moments when his most overriding characteristic seemed to be that of a pain in the ass.

"Another thought," Becker said, already out of his funk. He tried to keep his eyes focused on the dashboard so he wouldn't have to watch the traffic that Karen continued to pass with undiminished speed.

"Go ahead."

"Have you done any investigation of the victims' backgrounds?"

"The usual, any relatives who might have taken the boys, any family enemies, that kind of thing."

"You might try to find out if there's any history of physical abuse prior to the kidnappings."

Karen looked at him sharply. "Why?"

"Studies show that women who have been sexually abused as children are more apt to be rape victims than those who have not. Right?"

"So?"

"So maybe Lamont is picking on those who have been preselected.'

"And he can tell in some way?"

"Maybe, I don't know."

"What are you doing, blaming the victim?" she demanded angrily.

Becker noticed that she slowed the car. "Some boys might make themselves more available."

"So they can be beaten to death? Jesus, Becker."

"I mean they might be more docile. I know I was an awfully good little boy."

"You, John?"

"I was so good it makes my teeth ache to think about it."

"Hard to believe."

"Trust me," Becker said dully. "I did everything I was told – but instantly."

Karen remembered that Gold had said that most of all Becker wanted desperately to be a good man. Still, it was difficult to reconcile the contradictory facts that this man, whose reputation within the Bureau for independence was matched only by his reputation for lack of tact, had ever been a child trying to curry favour with anyone.

"Why were you like that then, if you're not that way now?"

"Because I was under the impression that there were rules I could follow that would make me safe – if I could only figure out what they were. I assumed I was being beaten because I was bad and, believe me, I would have done anything to keep it from happening again. There wasn't anything I could do, but it took me a long time to realise it ... And you?"

"And me what?"

"Weren't you ... Wouldn't you do anything to keep it from happening again?"

"God damn you, Becker."

"Didn't you do exactly what you were told? You kept quiet, you didn't tell anyone, you were afraid what would happen to your family, you knew no one would believe you, anyway ..."

"God damn you! Leave me out of this. You don't know anything about me, nothing."

"Who was it, Karen? Your father, your brother, some 'uncle' ..."

"Just stop it!"

"It wasn't your fault," Becker said softly.

"I won't be linked with you, John. Stop trying to do it."

"You already are, it's nothing I'm doing, it's your past."

"You're just guessing, just flailing around in the dark. You want there to be some connection so you're making it up ..."

"I don't want that kind of connection. I don't wish it on anybody."

"You're doing it with me and I won't put up with it."

Becker studied the traffic for a moment, allowing Karen to cool down. He tried to estimate whether they had accelerated or slowed without looking at the speedometer. "What kind of child were you?" he asked after a time.

"I was a fucking tomboy, all right? I was a holy terror. I used to chew up the boys and spit them out again."

"What did you have against the boys?"

"They were jerks. Still are. Gold is better than this, isn't he?" Karen asked. "He must be."

"He's had more practice," Becker said.

"Why don't I just go to Gold when I have a psychological problem, then, all right? He doesn't have anything better to do than listen to agents whine about their parents, but you do, John. You've got a case to work on, and so do I, so let's keep it to that. OK?"

"This has to do with the case," Becker said.

"I don't have to do with the case. My history has nothing to do with it at all. And neither does the history of these boys. They are not asking to be kidnapped and tortured and killed. They are not wearing signs on their forehead saying "I am submissive, I have been abused before, come and get it"."

"You're sure of this?"

"Yes, I'm sure. I'm positive."

"Why?"

"How long has it been since you've been with a child, John? How long since you spent any time at all with one? Especially a boy."

"Not since I was one, I guess."

"That's what I thought," she said. "You're just working on theory, not reality."

"That's my exit," Becker said, glancing back as the sign for Clamden receded in the distance.

"I don't have time to take you home," Karen said. "I'll be late. And besides, it's time you met a real boy."

10

She danced above him, eyes flashing, smiling so hard it looked as if her face might rip. Her blonde hair flew out from her head as she moved as if even it were electrified by her excitement. To Bobby's bewildered eyes she looked like a creature from a Disney movie, all fierce animation and wild gesticulation. Like someone creating her own wind. Even her voice sounded like something from a movie, sped up beyond normal speed and crackling with agitation. He knew the words but could not fathom their meaning.

"We're going to have such a good time," Dee said. She had been saying it repeatedly since she and the man had brought him into the room.

"I know just what a boy like you likes," she said. "I know all about boys like you. Oh, we're going to have fun!"

She reached down, touched his cheek suddenly. Bobby flinched involuntarily although he had already been warned not to.

"Don't pull away from me," Dee said. She did not sound angry, but there was in her tone a hint of severity, masked and muffled by her good mood, but still detectable in the distance. Bobby held very still as she ran her fingers across his face.

"Think how that makes me feel," she continued. "You mustn't think only of yourself, you know. You mustn't be selfish. You must think of me, too. Think how Dee feels when you jerk away like that."

She smoothed the hair which habitually fell over his brow. "Well," she said, "you'll learn. Children are always selfish at first. They have to be taught. Especially boys."

She whirled away from him again. "Oh, I know all about boys. Don't I, Ash? Don't I know all about boys like him?"

Bobby thought the man she had called Ash was about to answer but she did not wait for him.

"I know all about them." This time she grabbed his toe and wiggled it. "All about them." Something in her tone suggested that she simultaneously chided and forgave him for mischief yet undone.

Dee rubbed his foot through the sheet for a moment, then uncovered his leg as far up as his knee. Bobby was naked under the sheet and he was afraid that she would lift the sheet further, revealing him completely, but he did not allow himself to squirm. As his feet were bound to the bed frame he knew he could not get away from her anyway, but he did not want to be accused of flinching again.

She seemed interested only in his feet. "Oh, look at these toes," she said with wonder, as if discovering something amazing on the ends of his feet. "Did you ever see such perfect toes, Ash? Just look at them."

Ash had been positioned by the door, leaning his back against it as if keeping outside forces from bursting in. Bobby wondered if his parents were out there now, waiting for the right moment to hurl themselves through the wood to rescue him. Maybe they were there with the police. Maybe they were there with guns and, and ... he couldn't think what else they might have but he was

125

pretty sure that the police arsenal was vast and deadly. He didn't want this man and woman shot. He didn't want anyone to hurt them. He just wanted to go home. To be untied and released from the bed, to have the gag taken from his mouth.

Ash came from the door and bent over Bobby's toes, regarding them as intently as if they were marvellous new growth in the garden, a biological marvel that was sprouting and stretching upwards right before his eyes.

Now was the time for the police to ram the door, Bobby thought. He was afraid to look in that direction for fear the man and woman would see him and realise their mistake, ruining the opportunity. But the door did not move, the police did not come.

All this attention to his toes made them itch with the desire to move but he didn't know if he was allowed to wriggle them or not.

Dee took his little toe between her fingers. "And this little piggie cried 'wee, wee, wee,' all the way home," she said, waggling his toe back and forth gently.

Ash laughed, glancing at Bobby to see if he enjoyed the moment, too. Urging the boy with his eyes to enjoy it.

Suddenly Dee bent forward and took Bobby's toes in her mouth. "Ummmm!' She moved her head back and forth as if in ecstasy over this mouth-watering delight. "Ummm-ummm!"

Ash laughed nervously and looked at the boy to judge his reaction.

Bobby whimpered despite himself. The warmth and wetness of the woman's mouth filled him with confusing feelings. Part of him liked it, part of him felt it was somehow wrong although no one had ever told him so. Maybe the part that was wrong was the part of him that responded to it.

Dee rolled her eyes up to look at him, her mouth still

on his toes, her face at bed level so that she regarded him across the entire length of his body.

There was something in her eyes that Bobby could not name but knew by instinct. A hint of promise. He felt a welter of reactions, but most powerful of all was embarrassment. This stranger should not be treating him in so condescendingly intimate a way. Even if he was kidnapped, even if he was tied and gagged and naked, he was not a baby to have his toes sucked. To be cooed over.

Dee pulled away from his toes with a loud smacking noise. "Better than candy," she said. "Sweeter than sugar."

She beamed at him, but Bobby did not respond. Without warning she pressed her thumbnail into the sole of his foot and ran it upwards along the muscle. Bobby's whole body jerked.

"Oh, he's ticklish," Dee said delightedly.

"He's ticklish," Ash said. As if they had discovered a wonderful secret about him.

Dee rang her thumb along the sole of his other foot and again Bobby's body spasmed on the bed.

"You see," she said triumphantly. "I told you I knew all about little boys. I know what you like."

She tickled the tops of his feet now with feathery soft fingers. Bobby writhed and tried to pull away while Dee and Ash laughed in the conspiratorial way of adults who thought they were giving pleasure to a child.

"Oh, we're going to have fun!" Dee cried.

"Untie him, Ash," Dee said excitedly. "And take that thing out of his mouth, for heaven's sake."

She made it sound as if the restraints were all Ash's idea.

"He's not going to do anything silly, are you, Tommy?" She leaned over him, a hand on either side of his body, smiling. Bobby smelled her breath which was clean and sweet with a faint hint of toothpaste. Then she came too close so that her face blurred and for a horrible moment he thought she was going to kiss him. Bobby squeezed his eyes closed in anticipation, but instead she rubbed her nose against his.

"Ummmm-ummm."

He could smell something on her skin, perfume or powder in a dose so small he could barely detect it. The scent reminded him of his mother who always used too much powder and had a familiar and mildly nauseating odour when she held Bobby too close. Dee smelled better, but she was still too close.

Ash removed the restraints from his feet first, then held him in place with a hand on Bobby's chest as he released the boy's body from bondage.

The gag was the last to go and just before ripping the tape from Bobby's face Ash leaned close and whispered, "Don't yell." He paused, waiting for a response from the boy. Bobby nodded his head.

"You promise?" Ash whispered. Bobby nodded again, his eyes wide in anticipation of being free. He had no idea of the passage of time but felt as if he had been tied and tickled and cooed over for hours. The tape came off so fast that Bobby gasped, but he didn't yell. Ash smiled and nodded his approval.

"Well, get up," Dee said. "Let's have a real look at you! Get up!"

"I'm naked," Bobby said in horror.

Dee laughed. "Oh, we don't care. He's shy, Ash. Isn't that sweet? He's shy."

She pulled the covers off and beckoned him with her hand. "Come on now, stand up."

Bobby clutched at the sheet but she pulled it away from him.

"Now don't be silly," she said. "It's just us. You can be naked in front of your family. Besides, how are we supposed to see you if you stay in that bed all day?"

Ash gently tugged at him and Bobby got to his feet, covering his groin with his hands. He felt his face burning with shame.

"Oh, Ash," Dee said, "look at him, will you just look at him. He's perfect, he's absolutely perfect. My perfect little boy."

She clapped her hands to her face and her eyes misted over. "Just perfect," she said softly. "My beautiful Tommy."

"I'm Bobby," Bobby said.

Ash touched Bobby's arm and shook his head violently from side to side. Bobby realised that the man was warning him against something, but he did not understand what.

Dee did not appear to notice. Tears were on her cheeks now even though she was still smiling at him. She touched his cheek with her fingertips with such softness it seemed she could not believe what she was seeing.

"My beautiful, perfect Tommy."

"I have to go," Bobby said.

Dee acted as if she didn't hear him. Bobby turned to Ash. "I have to go to the bathroom," he said, and as he said it he realised he had to go so badly he didn't think he could stand it.

"Well, of course!" Dee exclaimed, as if coming back to herself. With a sniff and a wipe of her hand, the tears were gone and her eyes were gleaming again.

"Why didn't you say so?" She reached for his hand but Bobby did not offer it. "Come on, I'll take you."

"I can go alone," he said, once more horrified at being treated like a baby.

"Come on," said Dee. Coaxing him, as if he were three years old. "Come on, I'll take you."

129

"I know where it is."

Dee steered him towards the bathroom with a hand on his back.

"Sooo modest," she said.

She held the door open for him, then followed him into the bathroom. "Go ahead," she said.

Bobby stood in front of the toilet, his hands still covering himself.

"I can't," he said. "You have to leave."

Dee squatted in front of him so that her face was on a level with his.

"Now you listen to me, young man. You see how we live. We don't have room enough for this kind of false modesty. It's not as if you have to perform in front of strangers. It's only me, you know. Now when I tell you to do a thing, I expect you to do it, and I expect you do to it right then, not an hour later when you decide. Is that clear?"

Bobby looked at her, speechless. He had to go so badly.

"And I won't have you shutting me out of your life, either," Dee continued. "You're not that old yet. Don't be in such a hurry to grow up. Now go ahead and do your business."

Bobby could see the man watching him from the other room. The woman wouldn't leave. He realised for the first time something of what his life was going to be like now... But he had to go so much.

For the first time since he had been grabbed in the car, he began to cry.

Bobby sat on one of the two chairs in the room, watching television. The big man sat on the floor with his back to the door, alternating his attention between Bobby and the flickering screen. The windows were closed. There was no way out of the room except right through Ash and Bobby could not think how to move him. He had been sitting in front of the door for hours, watching closely, even joining in as the woman had fluttered around Bobby, but not once had he left his position.

At intervals Ash would smile at something and point his finger towards the action on the screen, glancing at Bobby to see if he was appreciating it, too. Bobby knew that the man was trying to be friendly. There was a calm and gentle quality to him despite his size and appearance that led Bobby to think he was more to be trusted than the woman, Dee. She seemed to love him, but she was too familiar, she pushed too hard. She might be a nice lady, Bobby thought, if only she would relax a little bit. And listen to him. She never seemed to actually hear what he said, she acted as if she were always responding to a conversation he could not hear. Bobby was used to that quality in adults, of course. Many of them did it, but few with the ardour or intensity that Dee displayed. It had occurred to him that she might be insane, but the idea was too frightening to persist with. It was bad enough to be kidnapped, but as long as his kidnappers were reasonable people, he felt that it would be all right. It was clear they didn't want to hurt him. Why should they? If he could just figure out what it was they did want, he would give it to them ... But if they were insane, how could he ever figure them out? It was too horrible to contemplate. Bobby put the thought from his mind.

Bobby's eyes slipped closed and his head fell towards his chest. He bounded upright again immediately, blinking to regain control of his treasonous senses. From the bathroom he could hear the sounds of the woman puttering around, brushing her teeth, combing her hair, screwing and unscrewing the lids of creams and lotions. He had seen his mother go through the process many times and there was a certain comfort to knowing Dee was doing the same, familiar thing.

She hummed a tune to herself and as Bobby tried to remember what the song was, his eyes drooped and closed again.

And then Dee was in the room and she didn't look the least bit like his mother. A white nightgown was scooped low in front and trimmed with lace that only partly concealed the bulge of her breasts. Her legs were bare from the mid-thigh down and as she stood silhouetted against the backlighting of the bathroom Bobby could detect the outline of her body through the thin muslin.

Dee twirled once, holding her hands over her head like a ballerina. "Well?" she demanded. "How do I look?"

"You look beautiful, Dee," Ash said in a voice so thick with desire that Bobby turned to look at him.

"Thank you, thank you," she said. She executed a brief curtsy then turned her attention to Bobby. "Well?"

Bobby stared at her, fighting the tears that threatened him again. He felt his throat beginning to squeeze shut.

"Do I look all right?" she demanded.

"You look beautiful, Dee," Ash said again, this time for Bobby's benefit. He tried to use his eyes to tell the boy how to respond, but Bobby wasn't looking at him.

"You shush," she said to Ash. "Tommy? ... Don't you have anything to say to me, Tommy?"

"I'm Bobby," he said, forcing the words past an uncooperative tongue. He clutched the good-luck medal around his neck and squeezed it tightly.

A cloud of anger crossed Dee's face but quickly faded into disappointment. She pinched the nightgown in both hands and held it out wide from her body. It rode up even higher on her thighs.

"I went to a lot of trouble, you know," she said. "I wouldn't do this for just anybody. I wanted our first night together to be special."

"He thinks you look beautiful, don't you, Tommy?" Ash said.

"I'm talking to Tommy," Dee said.

"Bobby," said the boy, his voice so low he was barely audible.

"What? What did you say?"

Bobby looked frantically around the room, hoping desperately that he had missed what he sought before.

Dee stood right in front of him now, her body close to the chair. Bobby could see through the nightgown to the dark mounds of her breasts, the darker shape below. He hadn't allowed himself to look at these parts of his mother for years.

"What do you have to say to me after all the trouble I've gone to for you?" Dee asked.

Bobby's anxiety burst forth in an uncontrollable gasp. "Where am I going to sleep? There's only one bed!"

He began to cry, hating himself for it but unable to stop. Dee chuckled indulgently and pulled him to his feet so that he stood on the chair. His head was level with hers when she pulled his naked body into an embrace. He could feel her breasts pressing against his bare chest.

"You silly goose," she said. "Where do you think you're going to sleep? You're going to sleep in the bed. Is that what's bothering you, is that what's bothering my little boy? Why didn't you say so? You can always talk to me, you know. You can always, always, always say anything at all to me. And do you know why?"

She released him from the embrace but kept her hands on his shoulders and she leaned her face in close to his. "Do you know why you can say anything you want to me?"

Bobby shook his head to indicate he did not know.

"Because I love you, Tommy. That's why." She hugged him again, this time so hard it took his breath away. "Oooooh, I love you sooo much!"

Her whole body was pressed into his. Bobby tried to slip his hands over his groin so she wouldn't know that he was growing hard but he couldn't do it without touching her. He knew that if they saw he was stiff they would make fun of him and if they did that now he was certain he would never be able to stop crying.

"But now it's time for you to get some sleep, young man," Dee said. "Today was a special day so we let you stay up late, but enough is enough."

She lifted him on to the bed and pulled the sheet over him. Bobby didn't think she noticed his stiffness.

For a moment it looked as if everything was going to be all right. Bobby looked at the man by the door to see if he was coming to bed. Ash was watching Bobby and smiling, but he made no move to leave the door.

Dee noticed and laughed. "Did you think you were going to have to share the bed with him? No wonder you were upset. Don't worry about Ash, he never sleeps, do you Ash?"

"I never sleep," Ash said.

"He'll stay by that door all night making sure nobody comes in that we don't want in. That should make you feel nice and safe."

Dee sat on the bed beside him just as his mother did at home, tugging the covers up under his chin. Bobby tried to keep from looking at her breasts whose shape he could make out just above his face. Her breath was still sweet.

"Now we had a very exciting day together, didn't we? We had fun, didn't we?"

Bobby nodded.

"You're going to have to learn to talk more, honey. When I talk to you I want you to take part – but don't worry about that now. There are a lot of things you'll have to learn, but no more for tonight. You just close your eyes and go to sleep now."

Bobby dutifully closed his eyes. He felt her lean down to him. The kiss on his cheek was no harder to take than the ones from his mother.

"Aren't you forgetting to say something?" Dee whispered.

Bobby kept his eyes squeezed closed.

"Who do you love?" she asked.

He knew what she wanted but he also knew how much his mother would hate to hear him say it.

"Tommy? … Who do you love?"

He was so tired; if only they would leave him alone and let him sleep he could figure everything out tomorrow. Maybe tomorrow the police would come.

"Who do you love?"

"I love you, Dee," he said.

He could detect her pleasure without opening his eyes. Her weight lifted from the bed and he was alone at last. It was going to be all right, after all, he thought. He would have his own bed and tomorrow he would make them give him his clothes back and when he had a chance he would open the window and … he felt her pull the covers back on the other side of the bed, then sensed the change in balance as her body slipped on to the mattress. She wasn't touching him, but she was there, in his bed.

He opened his eyes and was looking directly into the eyes of Ash who remained at his position on the floor in front of the door. The huge man stared at Bobby with the face of longing of a dog made to stay behind while his master went away. Next to him, Dee still had not touched him, but Bobby could feel the heat of her body.

He grasped the medal around his neck, squeezed his eyes closed and vowed not to open them again until his parents burst through the door to save him.

11

Becker rose with his plate and carried it to the sink, prompting Karen to say, "I'll do the dishes, it won't take a minute. You two just go in the other room and relax."

"We've been relaxing all through dinner," Becker said. He returned to the table and picked up his glass, his silverware, the crumpled napkin. They had eaten in the kitchen and the trip from table to sink was only a few steps.

"Go on, go on," Karen protested. "I can do it quicker if you're out of here."

Becker looked at the sink which now held all of the plates, the cutlery, the serving dishes, the two cooking pots. All together it looked to him as if it would take something less than two minutes to rinse, scrape and stack everything in the dishwasher. It had taken little more than that to prepare the meal in the first place, a warmed-up conglomeration of a chicken and tomato ragout, rice, and a green salad. Karen cooked four entrees on the weekend and froze them for use later in the week, she had explained. On the fifth day she and the boy either went out to eat or ordered Chinese food delivered. She had not mentioned the weekend, but Becker knew that Jack's father frequently had the boy with him then. It was not hard to imagine Karen eating leftovers while standing over the sink when she was alone. It was the way Becker took most of his meals himself.

"Happy to help," Becker said.

"It's basically a one-person job," she said, standing with her back to the sink, protectively.

Becker understood that the object of the exercise was not to get the dishes done but to put him alone with the boy for a few minutes. Dutifully, he turned and walked to the living room where Karen's son was already sprawled on the floor in front of the television set.

"No television, Jack!" Karen called from the kitchen.

"Mom!"

"I mean it!"

Sullenly, Jack turned off the set.

"She's tough," Becker said.

Jack nodded his head in agreement and looked at an area in space about three feet to the side of Becker's head. After an initial stare of surprise when he first arrived at the door, Becker had noticed that the boy had never looked directly at him. Nor had he volunteered a word of conversation. On the few occasions when Becker had directed a question to him, Jack had frozen as if stunned by the need to come up with an answer. His shyness and embarrassment were so palpable that Becker changed his method of conversation. He worded his statements so that they could be agreed to or denied with a simple movement of the head. In that way he was able to string several sentences together, giving both the questions and voicing the answers himself with Jack registering some sort of involvement so that it appeared to be a dialogue. It certainly wasn't an exchange of ideas, but it wasn't silence, either. Neither of the participants were fooled, of course, but Becker hoped that Karen was. It seemed to be important to her that all should go well.

"Your mother's a good cook, don't you think? That

was a delicious, uh, stew thing, with the chicken and the tomatoes. If you eat like that every night, you're doing all right, Jack."

Jack kept his gaze fixed on empty space in Becker's general direction. An unhappy hint of a smile seemed frozen on his face. Becker realised it was the boy's approximation of politeness. He was being addressed by an adult, he clearly was expected to stand and take it, but liking it was out of the question.

Becker sought a way to end the child's discomfort as well as his own and conversation clearly was not the solution. The two of them sat for a minute in awkward silence, still playing a game neither of them understood.

"How's it going out there?" Karen called from the kitchen.

"Great!" said Becker. He pictured her standing by the door, ears straining to pick up every sound. The dishes must have been stacked in the dishwasher long since. He wondered how long she was going to put them both through this form of torture. And for what reason.

"Just a few more minutes," she said.

"Can I go to my room, Mom?" the boy called.

"You keep Mr Becker company," she called back. "I won't be long."

The boy's smile seemed to become even more firmly fixed, Becker thought. He wondered if the boy was really as close to tears as he looked.

"Can you find yesterday's newspaper for me, Jack?"

The boy looked at him directly for the first time. It was as if Becker had just pronounced him a free man. He darted out of the living room and into the kitchen. Becker heard a flurry of conversation between mother and son, and then the boy reappeared bearing the *New York Times*.

Poor kid thinks I'm going to read it and get off his case, Becker thought. No such luck.

"This is a famous trick," Becker said. "Performed originally by the wazir of Baghdad. Using the *Baghdad News*, I believe."

Becker separated the sections of the newspaper and laid them so they overlapped. He then rolled them diagonally into a long tube and proceeded to tear it halfway down from the top. The boy was watching, almost despite himself.

"A lot of your magicians will make coins disappear, but there's no trick to making money vanish, we all do it every day. And then where are we? Poorer." Drum roll, please, Becker thought.

"Or they'll pull a rabbit out of a hat. You've seen them do that, I imagine." Jack nodded. He seemed uncertain whether he wanted to participate in this affair or not. Becker kept tearing the paper into thin shreds, alternating each rip with a flourish of the hands as if every motion were special and magical.

"But what are you going to do with the rabbit when he's done? Did you ever have a rabbit as a pet, Jack?"

"No."

"A good thing, too. All they do is eat and poop."

Jack laughed.

"Eat and poop, eat and poop, eat and poop," Becker said.

Jack's shoulders shook and explosive sounds burst forth in his throat, where he tried to hold them.

Scatology, Becker thought. Works every time. Nothing funnier than bodily processes.

"And you know who would get stuck with the job of cleaning that rabbit's cage, don't you? You would, Jack. The rabbit would poop and you would scoop. Poop and scoop, poop and scoop. You know what that would make you, don't you?"

"What?"

"The pooper scooper. You be the pooper scooper."

"No, you be the pooper scooper," Jack said, grinning.

"Thanks very much, but not to worry. This is not going to turn into a rabbit."

Becker held the tube to his eye and looked through it at Jack. "You know what it looks like to me?"

"What?"

"A fart funnel."

Jack clamped his hand to his mouth, his eyes jumping gleefully. He looked to Becker like someone about to explode.

"Does your mother ever fart, Jack?"

"Sometimes."

"Well, when she does, you could look through this and say, 'I spy.' "

"Or ..."

"Or what?"

Jack took the newspaper tube from Becker's hand. He held it to his nose. "You could smell her," he said, sniffing loudly.

"What a fine idea, why didn't I think of that?"

Jack shifted the tube to his ear. "Or you could listen to her fart," he said happily.

"That's a good idea. Seek her out wherever she goes, listening, listening."

"You could hear her if she farts in the other room," Jack said, turning the tube towards the kitchen.

"Or under the covers," Becker said.

"You could hear her when she does it under the covers!" Jack agreed gleefully. "Or in the car, or in the kitchen, or ..." His imagination flagging, he looked to Becker for help.

"Or in the garage?" Becker offered.

Jack grunted, clearly disappointed.

Becker tried again. "Or when she farts in the soup."

Jack liked that one. "Or when she farts in the milk," he added.

"Now how is she going to fart in the milk?"

"She has to sit on the cow," Jack said, delighting himself with the sudden burst of inspiration.

Becker laughed aloud in appreciation then looked up to see Karen standing in the living room, glowering at them like naughty children. Jack saw her, too, and continued to laugh. Becker took the tube from Jack and put it to his ear and pointed it at Karen. Jack laughed harder.

"Cute," said Karen.

Becker looked at Jack, shrugged as if he couldn't hear anything, then handed the tube to the boy. Jack imitated Becker, leaning to listen to his mother.

"Nice influence, John."

"It's a magic trick," Becker said. He pulled from the centre of the tube and transformed the newspaper into a five-foot length of fringed pillar. "It's a eucalyptus tree," he said. "Or whatever suits your fancy."

"Real talent. Bedtime, Jack."

The boy exited promptly but returned after a moment and took the tube from Becker's hand.

"Good-night," he said.

"Good-night," said Becker. "Nice talking to you."

"Nice talking to you," the boy said. He paused for a fraction, seemed to consider saying more, then hurried out.

"Nice with the shit jokes," Karen said when she returned from putting her son to bed.

"I did my best."

"He thinks you're a scream. He was aiming that damned newspaper thing at me the whole time I was reading to him."

"He's a funny kid once he loosens up."

"He'd probably say the same about you."

141

"He doesn't see many adults, does he?"

"Adults? Or men?"

"Men, I guess."

"Well, his father, of course. I don't entertain much, if that's what you're driving at."

"I'm not driving at anything," Becker said. "I just meant that he seems very, very shy and I supposed it was because he isn't exposed to people like me very often. I mean friends of the family, social friends, that kind of thing. Uncles. Cousins."

"No uncles, no cousins. When you get home at seven and have to cook and feed your child and get him into bed by nine, you don't entertain a whole lot."

"No, I suppose not."

"The babysitter is here by eight in the morning and I leave to get to work by nine. Every other weekend, when Jack is with his father, I'm working, trying to catch up on what I would have done if I didn't have to be home by seven. On the weekends when Jack is with me, I devote myself to him."

"Um."

"What does that mean?"

"It sounds rather grim having someone devote herself to you."

"Jesus H. Christ, Becker, is there anything about me you do like? You criticise the way I raise my son, you make fun of my cooking ..."

"Your cooking?"

"I heard what you said about the ragout. 'That stew thing with the chicken and tomatoes'."

"That wasn't criticism," Becker protested. "I liked the stew."

"Then you mock me in front of Jack with all that farting business. I hate that word."

"We weren't mocking you ..."

142

"Farting in the soup is your idea of showing respect?"

"I was just trying to befriend him. I thought that's what you wanted."

"Why would I want that?"

"I'm not sure, but you certainly set us up that way. You were hiding in the kitchen for half an hour."

"I was doing the dishes, then I was cleaning up. I happen not to like a messy kitchen, if that's all right with you, although I gather it isn't, apparently nothing about me is all right with you. I'm sorry if you were subjected to such an ordeal."

"It wasn't an ordeal … What are you so mad about?"

"I'm sorry if you think I've deprived my son of an adult male role model which I happen to think he can get along without very well, thank you, especially considering the kind of role models that seem to be available."

"What are we talking about?"

"I don't know … Oh, it's just too hard, it's too damned hard."

"What?" Becker asked.

"Getting along."

"With me?"

"Who else are we talking about?"

"Sorry."

"Oh, don't look so woebegone. It's not just you, it's men. They're such a waste, I mean, really, John, you're all such a waste. You never say anything supportive, you don't seem to have a clue how hard I work or how difficult it is to raise a child by yourself and still hold down a full-time job and all I hear is criticism …"

"I think you're doing a terrific job at everything."

"I know what you think of me as a parent. You've made it equally clear you don't think I'm much of an agent, either …"

"You're a very good agent …"

"You think I'm a soup farter in everything I do ... Maybe I am ..."

"I think you seem to have lost your sense of humour a little bit ..."

"Not funny enough for you either," she said. "You see, everything I do falls short."

"I think ..."

She dropped heavily on to the sofa. "Who gives a shit what you think, Becker? What don't you just go home."

"I can't."

"Why not?"

"You drove me here. I don't have a car."

Karen slumped into the cushions, all the fight gone.

"Oh, why don't you stay then," she said. "I just don't have the energy to fight you."

"You were doing a pretty good job."

She dropped her head to the back of the sofa. Her face stared at the ceiling. "I am such a bitch sometimes."

Becker sat beside her on the sofa but she continued to stare upward.

"The hardest part is right at the end. The last fifteen, twenty minutes before I say good-night to him. I've had the whole day's work, the commute both ways, the hassle with a couple dozen agents who think they're a better man for the job than I am, fixing dinner, doing the dishes, cleaning up – I'm so damned tired, all I want to do is sit in front of the television and glaze over for an hour then collapse on my bed but instead I have to sit with him and read a story then go through this ritual of saying good-night in just the right way. If I'm impatient, he knows it. If I try to cut it short, he jumps on me for that. I've got to do it all just right or else do it over again, and he's watching me every step of the way to make sure I'm not faking it. Kids are so superstitious. Putting him to bed is absolutely the toughest part of the day – and yet it's my favourite part, too. I see so little of him and then for these few minutes we're completely alone together with no distractions, and I love him so much and he needs me like I'm his next breath. If I do and say everything just right, he'll feel safe and secure and he'll be able to sleep through the night – God, how can I ever be impatient about that? I am such a bitch. I'm not fit to be a mother."

"From what I've seen, you're a great mother."

"Do you really think so?"

"He's a nice kid, Karen. You're doing a good job."

"He's a great kid … And I'm doing a terrible job." She turned and looked directly at Becker. "John, he doesn't sleep. He's so afraid."

"Of what?"

"He can't tell me, or he won't tell me. Sometimes he talks about robbers getting into the house, but that's not it, it can't be that simple. Some nights he won't let me go, he grabs hold of me and just won't let me leave the room. He says he's afraid I'm going to die."

"What do you say to him?"

"I tell him I'm not going to die, what else can you say? Oh, I word it a little better than that, I tell him everyone dies eventually but it will be so long from now that he'll have his own grandchildren by then, blah-blah, but what can you really say? How can you promise anyone you won't die?"

"Is he worried because of your work?"

"My work? I'm not in any danger because of my work. Most of the time I'm in an office."

"Except for this case."

"Except for this case. But that doesn't mean I'm in danger."

"Does he know that?"

"I don't know what he knows. He won't tell me. But I've seen him, John. I've looked in and he's just lying there, my baby's just lying there in the dark with his eyes wide open. It kills me."

Becker took her hand. She allowed it but did not respond. Her hand lay in his palm as if it were dead.

"Why don't you leave the light on?" Becker asked.

"He has a night light."

"I mean the overhead light, the bedside light, the light in the hallway, every damned light in the house if that's what it takes."

"He's got to learn to sleep in the dark sometime, he can't grow up and keep the lights on ..."

"Why not?"

"... I'm not sure."

His thumb rode slowly back and forth across the top of her hand. "I don't know anything about kids," he said. "Nothing at all. But I know something about fear. If he's afraid of the dark, get rid of the dark. Maybe you'll figure out eventually what he's really afraid of – or maybe you won't. Maybe he'll learn to deal with it himself—or maybe he won't. But in the meantime ..."

"Turn on the lights."

"Right."

He took her hand in both of his and gently worked his thumbs into the muscles on each side of the palm. Karen sighed and closed her eyes. Becker worked on each of her fingers individually, lightly but insistently pulling one at a time, then insinuating his fingers between two of hers, letting them fall to the valleys then all the way out to the tips. Karen's lips parted and she moaned with a sound as light as her breath. When Becker finished one hand she gave him the other without opening her eyes.

"You have no idea how good that feels," she said.

"Yes, I do."

Her head lay all the way back on the sofa, her lips were still open and smiling now.

"Nobody just touches me any more," she said.

When Becker stopped massaging her hand, Karen slid all the way down on the sofa and lifted her feet into his lap.

"Please," she said, her eyes still closed. But Becker had already started massaging her feet.

Karen abandoned any pretence at decorum and moaned aloud. Becker ran a finger between her toes and she shivered.

"How can I ever repay you," she asked.

"It's my payment for dinner," he said.

"Dinner was never this good," she said. "I feel like I'm purring."

He pressed his thumb into the muscles of her foot and she stiffened, then relaxed.

"A lot of tension in your feet," he said.

"Who would ever have thought there was so much pleasure down there? Ohhhhh…. How did you learn how to do this?"

"I've had a varied life," Becker said. He ran his fingernails lightly across the smooth skin atop her foot. Karen gasped and tensed and relaxed and gasped again.

"That feels so good it almost hurts," she said.

"It does get confusing."

He worked on her feet for a long time, and after awhile they stopped talking. Karen simply lay back, eyes closed, and moaned openly while Becker massaged and caressed in turn, patiently and thoroughly.

Eventually he relinquished her feet and ran his hand slowly up the underside of her calf.

"I didn't shave my legs today," she said.

Becker didn't bother to answer. At the tender skin under her knee joint he smoothed his fingers like feathers and she gasped with pleasure.

He ran both hands halfway up her thigh, gripped

147

firmly, then slowly and with some pressure pulled his hands down the length of her thigh, her calf, across the foot and all the way off the toes.

"My God," Karen said. "Do you know what that feels like?"

"Yes," Becker said. He did the same with the other leg.

"I feel that everywhere," she said. "It may be better than sex."

"It is sex," Becker said.

He repeated the procedure, this time using his fingernails instead of the palms of his hands and going even slower. Karen groaned every inch of the way and arched her back.

"All this for dinner? I didn't even offer you dessert."

"I'm sure you will. You're too good a hostess not to."

"And you are a presumptuous male swine," she said lightly. She pressed her foot into his groin.

"You seem to be a little tense in spots yourself, John."

"It comes upon me at times."

"I'll let that one pass," she said. "Too easy."

Becker slid his hands all the way up her legs until his thumbs came to rest at the top of her inner thighs. He left his hands there, resting lightly with just a hint of pressure.

She opened her eyes and looked at him for the first time in minutes. "When did you know we were going to do this?"

"Right about when you did," Becker said.

"I didn't," she said.

Becker grinned at her.

"I didn't! ... I did not," she insisted. Becker continued to grin. "All right, I did."

"When?"

"Not until I saw you hanging from the mountain," she said. "Not a moment before that, I swear."

She slid her legs around his back and pulled him on to her. After a moment she stopped him with a touch and slipped out from under his body. "Pray he's asleep," she said.

Karen tiptoed to her son's room and peeked silently at his recumbent form. His eyes were closed and his breath came slowly and easily. She said a quick and indifferently directed prayer of thanks for small favours and returned to the living room.

Becker was not in the room but her bedroom door was ajar. She entered expecting to find him naked under the covers but when she saw him standing in the middle of the room with only his shoes off, she realised how much she had forgotten about the man. He was a deliciously slow and lingering lover, accomplishing in an hour what more energetic men would fail to achieve in ten minutes, and he relished every step of the process. So did she.

"He's asleep," she said. "We're in luck."

"I'm the lucky one."

He took her in his arms and kissed her, pressing against her from foot to face as if no amount of contact could be enough. The kiss was a form of seduction in itself. His lips explored hers languidly, almost shyly, but at the same time with a certainty of purpose. They seemed to Karen to be seeking out the proper join of his flesh and hers, and when they found it, his lips rested there on hers, pressing just firmly enough. She felt herself weaken and behind her closed eyes she had the sensation of a long, slow, very safe tumble through space. She loved to kiss and Becker was one of the few men she'd ever known who loved it as much as she did.

They seemed to kiss for hours. Karen knew that later the kisses would become hard, fierce, demanding, but not until they were both ready and could no longer restrain themselves. That was lust, this was love. Or at least it felt that way, she thought. For the moment it felt that way and for the moment that was more than enough.

149

Finally his hands began to move, stirring as if awakened from slumber. Slowly they traversed her back in opposite directions. One hand reached her neck, caressed her there, then moved upwards into her hair. Karen felt her whole scalp tingle with his touch. As earlier with her hands and feet, she became aware of a source of sensory pleasure she had long forgotten. She wanted it never to stop and, as if sensing her desire, Becker ran his fingertips to the top of her head, across her temples, gently down over her ears, then started back up again from the neck. Karen groaned against his lips. Once more she had the feeling that her mind was being released and tumbling languorously backwards. A swoon must feel like this, she thought.

Only when his fingers had stopped moving on her head and returned to her back did his other hand begin to explore. It slid slowly downwards, into the small of her back where it paused, as if seeking permission, before slipping on to the swell of her buttocks. It followed the curve of the buttock to where it met the leg then came up again until it reached the hip. His fingers spread across the hipbone and stretched until they stopped just short of the pubes.

Karen pulled his shirt from his belt and ran her hands up his back. He leaned away from her just far enough to insinuate one hand into the neck of her blouse. His fingers began the slow and tantalising descent to the rising mound of her breasts. Again he lingered for a long time, just beyond the breast, as if uncertain or not daring to continue. By the time his hand lowered still farther Karen's body was screaming for him to continue.

Later, when his lips replaced his fingers on her nipple and she emitted a shuddering sigh, Karen admitted to herself that she was overmatched. Becker seemed capable of giving her more pleasure and more excitement than she could stand. Certainly more than she could give in return. And much later, when he had finally removed all of her clothes and she had torn away the last of his and he eased her to the bed, she decided she was just a greedy bitch who was going to have to take all of this magnificent lovemaking and quit worrying about what she brought to it. It was not a hard decision.

They lay breathless for some time, as if stunned by what had happened. At the end they had both been howling and Karen had bitten into her pillow to stifle some of her loudest roars. The howls had turned to astounded laughter as they drifted down together, and then subsided altogether as they lay in each other's arms and panted against each other's skin.

"I'd forgotten what you were like," Karen said at last.

"Thanks," he said.

"I mean that as a compliment. I don't think you used to make love this way, did you? How can you possibly do it that way all the time?"

"I don't, normally." Becker said. "I happen to like you."

"I got that impression."

"Actually, I don't do it at all, lately. It's been a long time."

"I know."

"Is that in my file, too?"

"The Bureau isn't that interested in you, John ... It's been a long time for me, too ... Do you think that accounts for it?"

"For what?"

Karen buried her face in his chest and willed herself to shut up. There was a difference between complimenting him on his sexual performance – a blandishment she knew men required – and gushing like a schoolgirl who's just had her first orgasm.

151

After a pause, Becker said, "It is being duly noted that you didn't immediately say, 'I like you too.' "

"Do you want me to say that?"

"I'm just noting that you didn't."

Like you, Karen thought. Like you? I want to chain you to the bed and feed you oysters and clams, I want to have your magnificent knowing hands surgically implanted on to my flesh.

"I don't know if I like you or not," Karen said aloud. "But I obviously respond to you. Well, that's a bit of an understatement. I responded like a bitch in heat – and proud of it, let me add. As for liking you, I guess I don't not like you. But you're a hard man, John. Can we just live with that ambiguity for awhile?"

"It would be very adult of us," he said.

"Do you want to take back saying that you liked me?" Becker paused.

"You don't really get to take it back, you bastard," Karen said hurriedly. "It was a bogus offer."

"Oh, I don't want to take it back," he said. "I was thinking of clarifying the statement."

"Don't," Karen said and immediately regretted it.

"You're right. It speaks for itself. I was just going to gush for a while."

Gush! Karen thought. Rave on about my charms! But instead of saying it to him, she slid her hand from his chest to his abdomen and felt him react involuntarily to the tickle response.

"Can I ask you a question?" she asked after the silence had lengthened.

"Granted."

"Do you still see your ex-wife?"

"Cindi? Sometimes."

"I mean, do you see her?"

"We're divorced."

152

"I know. Still, it's not unheard of. You made no effort to get away from her, after all. You're still living in the same little town."

"Clamden's my home."

"I know. I'm just asking. Sometimes husbands think their rights continue after divorce, you know. Sometimes they keep coming around and try to resume relations."

"What did you do?" Becker asked.

"I didn't say it happened to me,' she said.

"How did you handle it?"

"With aplomb and diplomacy. I kicked him in the nuts. He didn't try again."

"The man's a quitter."

"I call him a fast learner. I only had to explain to him once."

"Amicable divorce, was it?" Becker asked.

"Do we have to talk about it in bed? Couldn't we discuss politics or something else cheerful?"

Becker spoke in a serious tone. "What did he do, Karen?" He felt her body tense against his.

"Let's drop it."

"I mean during the marriage," he said.

"I know what you mean." She rolled away, turning her back to him. "Let's not spoil the night, John."

"It would have made your life easier if you had given him more frequent visits, you could have had more free time without Jack, but you didn't. What went on?"

He put a hand on her shoulder in the dark and felt her tense against his touch.

"Was it something he did to you?"

"You've just ruined a great fuck," she said coldly.

"Or was it something he did to Jack?"

Karen started to get out of the bed but Becker held her. He put his arm across her belly and pulled her back so

153

she spooned against him. Her body was stiff but she did not struggle.

"Let go of me, Becker."

Becker held on to her and pressed his body against hers from behind. Karen grunted once and tried to jerk away but stopped when he tightened his grip. They both knew she was trained and skilled and could make a good battle of it if she chose to fight.

"What did he do to Jack, Karen?"

For a moment Becker thought she really was going to make a battle of it. Her muscles tightened as if she were going to spring. He would let her go if she really wanted to get away, of course, but he did not think she wanted to.

She was quiet for a moment and both of them were coiled and poised, but then she slowly relaxed. Becker continued to hold her tightly for both self-defence and support. If she was going to kick back into him, it would be when he eased up in response to her; but he sensed that she had given in and was releasing something from inside and his grip helped to show her he was there for her.

"He beat him," she said, her voice breaking with emotion. "The son-of-a-bitch beat my sweet little boy. I should have killed him, John, I should have killed him."

"No."

"I should have, I should have."

"When did it start?"

"When Jack was about four. Suddenly Carl seemed to blame Jack for everything that went wrong. Not just around the house, anything that went wrong in his life. And there were a lot of things going wrong in his life. Me, for one. I should never have got married in the first place. I'm too selfish."

"We're all too selfish," said Becker. "But we all do it."

"First it was just spankings, then worse, he started to hit him with things, belts, a hairbrush, usually when I wasn't around. I'd be at work and I'd come home and Jack would have a bruise and Carl would tell me he fell off his trike or tripped while running or … And Jack wouldn't deny it. He was so afraid of Carl he wouldn't even tell his own mother. What kind of mother does that make me?"

"Don't blame yourself. You weren't the one who was doing it."

"But I didn't stop it. I figured it out eventually, but even then I didn't stop it right away. Not as soon as I should have. Carl called it discipline and I just, somehow, I just couldn't believe he was doing it in the way he was doing it. I tried not to look it right in the face, John; I even told Jack to be careful and not enrage his father. I blamed Jack."

Karen stopped. She heard Becker's hard breathing behind her. He sounded as if he was engaged in a fight with himself that he would not win; but he made no comment.

"I'm not fit to have a son," Karen said. "I just could not admit to myself that it was happening. Even in court, even when we were fighting for custody, I couldn't bring myself to come right out and say it. I just couldn't believe it was happening to me. I don't deserve that wonderful little boy, John, but I'd die before I'd let him go live with his father. Nothing happens now on their weekends together. I check Jack as soon as he gets home. I've told Carl what I'll do to him if I even suspect anything. He knows I will."

"You said you couldn't believe it was happening to you, but you meant you couldn't believe it was happening to you again," said Becker. "Isn't that it?"

This time Karen was silent.

"Because it happened to you as a kid, didn't it, Karen?" She did not answer.

"I know it did, you told me about it ten years ago."

"I never said a word ..."

"No, you didn't talk about it, but you told me. I could tell by the way you reacted to my touch, the things you didn't feel comfortable with, all the things you didn't say when I told you about myself ... You don't have to admit it if that comforts you, but don't bother to deny it."

Karen continued to lie very still in his arms and the silence seemed to balloon around them and envelope the room. They could hear noises from outside – the wind against windows, the far distant cough of a car engine starting – but within the room it seemed to Karen that all sounds had ceased to exist. She could no longer hear Becker's breathing and was aware of her own only by the measureless rise and fall of her bosom. When she shifted her weight slightly, the groan of the mattress and the rustle of the sheets against her body seemed incredibly loud. In the new position, Becker's arm had ridden up from her abdomen so that it crossed her chest just below the first swelling of her breast. He still held her firmly and she was grateful now for the pressure and the sense of comfort it gave her. She wanted someone close if she had to confront the monsters of her past.

When Becker spoke his voice seemed so loud in the stillness that had come over them that Karen was momentarily startled.

"What else?" he asked.

"What?"

"Was there more? With Carl."

Her ex-husband's name sounded odd on Becker's lips and she realised she had not heard him speak it before. He had referred to him only as her husband, not by name, and the change seemed too abrupt, overly familiar. For a moment she resisted it, as if allowing someone else to use Carl's name was in itself a revelation of family secrets.

156

Her reaction was swiftly past, but it left her feeling slightly soiled.

"No," she said. "What do you mean?"

"Did he do anything else?"

"Isn't that enough?"

"It's too much, but it usually doesn't stop there. Violence creates its own appetite."

Karen wanted him to stop asking, she wanted to demand what made him such an expert. But she knew he was, she knew he understood it all better than anyone.

"He hit me, too," she said. Her throat was constricted and her voice so low she had to repeat herself. Even as she said it, she still found it hard to believe.

Becker grunted noncommittally, as if he had expected her statement and was waiting for the rest. There was a quality to his silences that Karen found compelling, as if she had to fill them. He seemed to know what came next but required the formalities to be observed by having her say it.

"It didn't happen that often," she said. "Any is too many, but it wasn't that often. The first time I couldn't believe it had happened, I couldn't believe he would dare to do it, that he would want to do it. It was still early in our marriage, I had convinced myself I was in love, we were in love, hell I wanted so much to be in love ..."

"To have someone love you," Becker interjected.

"Yes, I suppose, but to love someone else, too; I knew you were supposed to love someone else, that's what everyone said, so I convinced myself I loved Carl ... And then he was so repentant afterwards. He cried, he said he loved me, he adored me, he would never, never do it again ..."

"And you believed him."

"I wanted to. I made myself believe him. I was in a

157

marriage, I had to give that every chance, every effort, I couldn't just walk away because of one mistake."

Again Becker was silent and Karen felt she had to continue, had to find the explanation that would justify herself, that would win his approval.

"The second time was months later, he had been fine until then, we had had quarrels but he had controlled himself, I assumed that it really was only a one-time thing. But then he snapped, we weren't fighting about anything special, nothing particularly sensitive, he'd been drinking, not much, just a little, there seemed to be no provocation, then all of a sudden he was hitting me, hitting me and hitting me ... I wore pancake make-up the next day to hide the bruises at work, I was so ashamed. If anyone had asked what happened – no one asked."

"And you stayed with him."

"I was pregnant then, I had a child on the way – that was the curious thing, in the midst of his rage Carl had not hit me anywhere near the baby. In an odd way that seemed to show he cared about the baby, about us, about our future ... I don't know, I rationalised it a hundred ways ..."

"And you stayed."

"Yes, damn it, I stayed! Don't judge me, John, you don't know what it's like to be beaten by someone who's supposed to love you, it makes you feel so worthless, it makes you feel that you deserve it, it makes you feel it's your fault."

"I know," Becker said simply. There was no special pleading in his voice, just a statement. Karen realised there had not been any harshness in his tone before, either. The judgement was only in her mind. Becker was merely noting, just stating the obvious so they could get on to the next step as if the process had to be completed no matter what.

"I'm sorry," she said.

"It's all right."

"I did stay with him, you're right. I should have left him then, but it seemed so – so ludicrous that it was happening to me. I wasn't some welfare mother in the ghetto, I wasn't a hillbilly with trucks parked in the front yard. Carl was a professional, for God's sake. He was a radiologist. We weren't the kind of people this happened to. Plus, I was trained in self-defence. Even when it was happening, while he was hitting me, I told myself 'I can break this man in two'."

"It's not about self-defence, though," Becker said.

"No, not at first. But it got that way. When Jack was two years old Carl tried to beat me again. The baby was there in the room, watching, and maybe that's what gave me the courage, I don't know, but I realised right then that it was going to stop. I kneecapped him and broke his arm … He never touched me again."

"But he started on Jack."

"Not long after that, I think he must have, but I didn't know it."

Becker was silent.

"I swear to you, John, I did not know it. I did not. I did not know it."

Something broke within Karen and she began to cry, quietly at first, and then fully, sobbing, her body shaking with the effort. Becker pulled her even more tightly against her, covering her whole body with his own as she lay against him.

He let her cry until she had had enough, not trying to hush her or even comfort her beyond his close presence. When she was finished at last Karen felt as if she had returned from a distant place. Her grief had taken her out and away from the present and deep within herself, but now she was back, in a darkened bedroom, on her bed, with the wind pushing at the window panes and a strong man pressed against her from behind.

She could not say if the quality of the stillness changed when she stopped sniffling, or if the electric charge of the room had been that way all along and she had only become aware of it. Becker's body was warm against hers and his skin seemed alive in a way it had not when she was talking about herself. His flesh seemed to lie against her like a creature with a life of its own, as if poised to move whenever she chose. It was up to her entirely, she realised, and the thought gave her a sense of freedom and power.

She reached between her legs and touched him and felt him rise eagerly to her touch. They did not speak, they scarcely moved, then he was in her from behind and she was clamping the pillow to her mouth once more. This time it was direct and simple without foreplay or patience or tenderness, which was how both of them wanted it.

12

When Bobby awoke on the third day of his capture, he knew that he was being watched even before he opened his eyes. He could sense another face close to his, he could hear the hushed, too deliberate movements of someone trying to be quiet that did not make noise so much as they displaced space in a way that he could feel. He kept his eyes closed, pretending to sleep, clinging for a moment to the hope that the hovering someone might be his mother. Perhaps today when he opened his eyes the long nightmare would be over and he would be home in his own bed.

It could only be Dee leaning in close to him, studying him the way she did with that intense look of hers as if she were trying to memorise every detail of his face and body. Sometimes the look would take on tones of puzzlement as if she were trying to square his appearance with the image she had stored in her mind, but she would always come out of it, the wrinkle of skin between her eyebrows relaxing as she reconciled what she saw with what she wanted to see.

From the direction of the door, Bobby heard Ash repositioning himself, then the sibilant hush of Dee telling him to be quiet. "Don't wake him," she whispered. "He's asleep."

Ash made a noise in his throat, perhaps laughter, then

Bobby heard sudden sounds of movement from both of them, the door protesting in its frame as Ash pushed off of it, the sound of tiptoed steps, and just as quickly all was silent. Bobby held very still, listening, straining to hear them, but all sounds seemed to have been swallowed up. Had they gone? It seemed inconceivable that they would have left him alone at last, and yet ... nothing, he could hear nothing at all.

He tried to open his eyes just a slit, feeling the eyelids quiver as he eased them apart. He could make out only the sheet under his cheek, the carpet between the bed and the wall where his face was pointed. Pausing, not daring to hope, Bobby let his eyes open farther. He saw nothing before him but the motel wall, the sunlight streaming through the slats of the venetian blinds to make a pattern of lines on the floor. Ash was not by the door. Dee was not hovering over him.

He lifted his head, almost not daring to move. The room was empty, no sounds came from the bathroom whose door was open. Bobby sat upright in the bed, then slid his feet to the floor, still not daring to believe. He looked around the room again, wild-eyed.

"Dee?" he whispered. "Ash?"

There came a low, rumbling sound, like the growl of an animal and Bobby held his breath. It came again, a growl of something large and fierce and close and then Dee popped up from behind the bed, laughing, her hands over her head in a parody of a ravening beast.

"Grrrarrr!" she roared, still laughing. She swept upon Bobby, embraced him, lifted him.

"We fooled you! We fooled you, didn't we? Admit it, admit it! We fooled him, Ash!"

She bundled him in her arms and buried her face in his neck, kissing and growling. Ash sat up from the floor behind the bed, grinning proudly.

"We fooled you," Ash declared.

"Oh, look at him. You weren't really scared, were you? Were you scared, Tommy?"

Bobby pulled away from her, angry and embarrassed.

"We didn't mean to really scare you."

Dee hugged him again but he put his hands against her chest and pushed her away.

"Don't," she said.

Bobby ignored the warning in her tone and struggled against her grip.

"Don't pull away from me," she said.

Bobby tried to yank his arms free but she held him firmly in her grip.

"Let go!" he cried.

He kicked at her with his naked feet. His toes barely touched her shin.

"No!" Ash called, aghast.

Bobby didn't see the blow coming and he was shocked as much by its unexpectedness as its force. It had to have come from Dee, but when he looked at her with eyes filling with tears, both of her hands still gripped his arms.

"Don't ever pull away from me," she hissed. She lowered her face to his, her fingers squeezed his arms so tightly they hurt, but it was her look that frightened Bobby most. Something had happened behind her eyes, something that Bobby could see but not identify. It looked as if someone other than Dee was behind her eyes now. Someone or some thing, crouching behind the deep blue, glaring out at Bobby. Hating him.

"Never, never," she said, her voice still a hiss.

"Never," Ash said. He was on his feet now, shaking his head in warning to Bobby.

"I don't like it," Dee said.

Bobby sniffed. His nose was running, his eyes were

tearing and he was aware of a ringing in his ears, but he was still too stunned to cry.

"Do you understand?" Dee asked.

"Yes," said Ash, pumping his head up and down, urging Bobby to agree. "Yes."

"Do you?"

Bobby nodded. "Uh-huh."

"Imagine how it makes me feel, when you pull away," Dee said. Bobby noticed that the thing behind her eyes had slithered away and she was Dee again, a little wound up, a little too enthusiastic, but still a woman, still the same person he knew.

Bobby nodded in agreement once more.

"After all I do for you," she said. "When I love you so much and you pull away – it disappoints me."

She released his arms and Bobby saw how her grip had left white marks that only slowly became pink again.

"OK, case closed," she said, brightening once more. "No harm done, right, Ash?"

"No harm," said Ash.

"All right, Tommy? All done?" She smiled broadly. "I know you're sorry, I know you didn't mean to do it, but you must try very hard not to disappoint me. And I'll try very hard not to disappoint you. OK, sweetheart?"

She smiled at him, awaiting a response.

"Yes," said Bobby.

Her smile broadened even further. "You make me so happy!" she said.

She clasped him in her arms again. Her clothing was stiff with starch and scraped against his naked skin.

"Who do you love?" she asked.

"I love you, Dee," he said.

"I know you do, sweetheart. Just try not to let me down. It makes me feel so bad."

And then she was away from him, into the whirl of

164

activity that always seemed to accompany her. She swept into the bathroom, out again to her night table, gathering her things, perfecting her look. When she went out the door it was as if a wind had swept through the room and now was gone. Through the open door Bobby had a glimpse of the outdoors, a car parked in front of their room, a patch of grass that looked unnaturally green, a low hedge, a sampling of sky that hinted of rain. Then the door was closed and Ash was in front of it again.

"Don't disappoint her," Ash said.

"OK," Bobby said, dismissing it.

"No," Ash said, shaking his head, trying to convey to Bobby the seriousness of what he said. "You mustn't. You mustn't."

"Can I wear some clothes today?" Bobby asked.

Ash waggled his head in frustration. They never believed him when he tried to warn them. He was never able to make them understand ahead of time. Only Dee could make them understand, and then it was too late.

"No clothes yet," Ash said. "But listen, listen. Don't make her mad."

"I didn't do anything," Bobby said. "She just got mad on her own. It wasn't my fault."

"No," Ash said. "No." But it was no use. After the first day or two they were never really afraid of him anymore. No matter what he did they seemed to understand that he was not a threat. They obeyed him because they recognised he could force them to do whatever he wanted, but they didn't take him seriously. They knew how stupid he was, Ash realised, and as a result they never really credited what he tried to tell them. He knew he was stupid, but he also knew that he understood things they would never believe until it no longer mattered if they believed them or not.

"Maybe tomorrow you'll get clothes," he said.

"Really?" Bobby was excited.

"Maybe she'll take you out."

"Out? Out of here? You mean tomorrow we can leave the room?"

"Don't disappoint her," Ash said.

"I won't. I won't. You mean we'll leave the room, Ash?"

"She's going to want to show you off," Ash said. "She's very proud of you."

"Really? Do you mean it?"

Ash wanted to tell him not to get so excited. He wanted to explain that Bobby was safest at this stage, before Dee's expectations got too high. Before she loved him too much.

"You mustn't disappoint her," Ash said.

"I won't. Stop saying that. I'll be good."

"You have to be so good," Ash said. "So good."

The old fool was dispensing towels again. Like clockwork, as soon as the woman's car appeared, George jumped up from his chair and grabbed the towels. Reggie thought he looked like his damned chair was rigged. Like the gas station where you ran over a rubber hose and the bell rang, only here there was no bell, just a shot of adrenalin straight into the old fool's ass. Reggie watched him hovering around the office until "Dee" came home, pretending to work, pretending he knew how to read the books and count the figures. And all for a younger woman's smile.

Reggie watched with growing anger as he scurried out the door, holding the towels with one hand, patting his hairs into place atop his pate with the other. It was enough to make her spit. If he didn't look so damned ludicrous it would be sad, but as it was it was pathetic. Just pathetic.

The woman, of course, greeted him like a long-lost friend. Good old George, her personal laundryman, grinning and patting himself like a gigolo. If they had gigolos that age. Reggie looked at "Dee" waiting by the car, containers of take-out food stacked on top. She was very careful not to give George a peek inside the room, Reggie noticed. She would take the towels, smile and chatter away for a bit while George stood there and drooled, then, as he finally turned and walked away–and he usually wouldn't have sense enough to do that until Reggie stepped out of the office on to the porch – then, and only then, when George's back was turned, would she knock on her door and, when it was opened a crack, slip inside with the towels and the take-out food.

There was something suspicious going on in cabin six, and no doubt about it. George was too besotted to see it, of course, and there was no point in trying to convince him, but Reggie didn't need his help to find out what was afoot. She had been a motel owner for seven years and nobody's fool for long before that.

She left George safely watching a re-run of a sitcom that featured a famously stupid blonde with a chest that Reggie considered indecent and an equally famous vacuous young man who worked obviously hard at his acting. As long as the blonde was on the screen, which was most of the time, George would never know that Reggie was gone. Not that it mattered if he did know, she thought. She had a perfect right, after all.

She slipped out of the office door and paused for a moment on the front porch. The cabins stood in pools of light from their own outdoor lamps. Some of the lights were out and the guests already retired for the evening. Some of the cabins stood empty, unrented and dark. Cabin six was alight.

Reggie stepped off the porch and walked to the edge of the illumination that came from her own porch light. A few steps beyond it and she moved in darkness, which was the way she wanted it. She knew the way well enough, there were no surprises between here and cabin six, even though her eyes had not yet adjusted to the night. Reggie caught herself tiptoeing even though she was forty yards away from the cabin. She had no reason to sneak, she told herself. It was her motel, her property, her livelihood, and she had every right in the world to know what was going on in any one of her cabins. Especially when it was something undeniably fishy. Unconsciously she slipped back into her stealthy mode after a few steps.

When Reggie was halfway there, the light on cabin six went out with a suddenness that startled her. The transition from light to dark was so abrupt she thought she could almost hear a snap. A body came out of the cabin and opened the door of the car parked in front of the building. The interior light of the car showed Reggie that it was the woman, Dee, and then the car light, too, went off.

Reggie froze where she was, covered by a blanket of darkness that lay between the office and the cabin. She was certain that Dee did not see her watching. Reggie could only make out Dee's shape without the cabin light because she knew where to look. Dee hurried to the cabin. There was a brief glimpse of pale blue-green light from the television set in the cabin and Reggie had the impression of someone very large scurrying from the cabin and into the car. He seemed to be carrying something, but Reggie had no idea what it was. He was into the back seat of the car in an instant and the cabin door was closed even before that. Another shape hurried through the dark towards the car and Reggie knew it was Dee again.

Car doors slammed, the engine roared to life, but still there were no lights. Dee drove with her headlights off across the curved gravel drive. As it approached the road the car came under the light from the RESTAWHILE sign that stood beside the highway and Reggie could see Dee behind the wheel, but there was no sign of anyone else in the car. The car's headlights came on as the car pulled on to the highway and Dee was lighted again by the sweep of oncoming beams, but still there was no indication of another soul in the car.

Reggie waited until Dee's automobile was off, heading towards town, then she waited a minute longer, forcing herself to count to sixty to make sure the woman didn't remember something and come sweeping back. Finally, her heart beating faster, Reggie turned towards cabin six again. The woman had claimed her husband had trouble with his eyes which might account for the strange, un-lighted, dash into the car, but it certainly wouldn't have made him invisible. Why would a man run into the backseat of a car and flop down out of sight immediately? Reggie could not think of any legitimate reason for such behaviour.

With a glance back at the highway, Reggie fumbled through her keys, selected the right one and opened the door to cabin six.

It smelled funny, she realised immediately. Heavy, musky, stale. Not like unwashed bodies, she thought, not that exactly, but more like something that you couldn't wash away. It wasn't sex either, which was what Reggie had expected. There was a milky cast to the odour, and something sharp and acrid that she could not identify.

She eased the door closed behind her before turning on the interior light because even though she had a perfect right to be where she was, there was no need to advertise her presence.

The bedspread was missing, she saw that immediately. Some guests removed it on purpose and stored it on the shelf in the closet where it was intended to go, but most never bothered and slept with it over them, piling a blanket on top of the spread if it got cold. But, of course no one was cold now. Reggie felt her skin prickling as if she were about to break into a sweat just from the exertion of walking here from the office. The spread was nowhere to be found, which was all the reason Reggie would require to get rid of George's little favourite. Even he could not argue against theft of motel property. Sneaking off with a towel was one thing, and certainly a major nuisance, but an entire bedspread was another matter entirely.

It did not take long for Reggie to inventory the room. There was evidence enough of the "husband". A shirt of his hung in the closet, an old fashioned razor with two-sided blades was beside the sink. Even George used a disposable cartridge razor these days. The woman's cosmetics were strewn throughout the bathroom, atop the sink, on the top of the toilet tank, some spilling on to the floor. Reggie had known she would be a sloven. Three toothbrushes stood upright in the motel's bathroom glass. Two adult-size models with slanted heads and one children's size, baby blue. Wasn't she just too cute to bear, Reggie thought. Her little teeth were just too delicate for an adult brush. It was enough to make you sick. The woman's nightgown hung on the back of the bathroom door. Reggie flicked it with a finger, disgusted by the frilliness of it. She could just picture the harlot flitting around the room in her lacey nightie, her face painted like a whore's, her child's toothbrush in her mouth. She probably talked baby talk, too, Reggie thought. George would like that, of course. He wasn't many years removed from a second childhood himself.

Reggie returned to the closet, a doorless recess with a

170

shelf above and a single metal bar below. The woman had four pairs of shoes in there, the man had none, which meant he was wearing his only pair now. There were no trousers hanging in the closet, either. They had been in the cabin more than three weeks now, Reggie calculated, and the only change of clothes she could see for the man was that one forlorn looking shirt. She knew other men who would live like that if their women allowed it. Not George. The old fool had more clothes than Reggie did. A peacock, he thought he was a peacock. Reggie snorted at the image, but in fact she felt rather fondly towards George at that moment. Despite his age he tried to maintain a certain standard of appearance. She was grateful for it, too, although she made fun of his passion for colour co-ordination, more often than she applauded it.

The woman had a number of outfits hanging on the motel's unremovable hangers. Two wire hangers held freshly laundered garments still wrapped in see-through plastic. A single suitcase lay atop the motel's collapsable canvas-ribbed stand. Reggie opened it and rummaged quickly through the collection of women's underthings. Again, everything was Dee's. Her husband seemed to live only with the clothes on his back.

Except for the spreading cosmetics, the belongings of the room's occupants seemed surprisingly well contained. Things looked as if they could all be swept into the suitcase in less than a minute. Reggie resolved to not let them fall behind in their rent by so much as a day. They could bolt and be out of here before she could stop them if she so much as blinked in her vigilance.

She pulled the sheet back on the bed then gasped as she heard the noise at the door.

Ash covered the boy like a shell, his great body hunched over the smaller one, concealing and protecting it both

171

at once. Bobby could feel the man's form against his but his weight did not crush him as it so easily could have. There was no sense of threat. He knew that Ash would not harm him so he did not struggle against the bed-spread that surrounded him, or the hovering presence of the big man himself. Bobby lay still, waiting for the moment to pass. He no longer questioned the things that happened to him but tried to flow with them, offering the least resistance possible.

Once they were well away from the motel Ash sat up in the back seat and took the bedspread off the boy who rose slowly, blinking, at first not daring to believe he was seeing the real, familiar world flashing past the car windows.

Bobby looked at Ash for confirmation, and the big man smiled gleefully. The boy could sense Dee's jubilation without even glancing at the front seat. Her excitement poured off her in waves, as palpable as heat. She had twisted the rear-view mirror so that she could watch his reaction. Bobby could see her eye, part of her nose. The arch of her eyebrow told him without question of her mood. She was exhilarated by their outing and Bobby knew she expected him to be the same.

"Well? What do you think?" Dee asked.

"This is great," Bobby said. He looked out the window and tried to act as if all the passing scene of auto-body shops and fast-food restaurants were brass rings on the merry-go-round. He was careful not to look directly into Dee's eyes in the mirror. She was much too quick to tell when he was feigning interest. Ash was easier to fool and Bobby played him as a foil for his enthusiasm.

"Look," he cried, tugging Ash's arm. "Burger King!"
Ash nodded approval.

"Do you like Burger King, Ash?"

"I like Burger King."

"Can we eat there, Dee?"

"Is it a good one?" Dee asked.

"Yeah, it's great. They have great french fries."

"Let's go somewhere new," Dee said. Bobby noticed a change in her tone. A darker, more calculating note. He knew by now that she was never so excited that she stopped thinking. He had made a mistake in letting her know he had been there before. She would find a place where there was no chance that he would be recognised. They passed a familiar billboard for mattresses, a shop selling wicker furniture where his mother sometimes made them stop, the State patrol building where Bobby's father always slowed as he passed. They were going the wrong way. They were going away from home.

The sudden loss of hope infused his face despite his efforts and Dee saw it immediately.

"You don't like it," she announced.

"What? Yes, I do? I like it." Bobby was not certain what he was supposed to like.

"No, you don't." Her voice was flat, the excitement gone completely.

Ash gripped Bobby's arm and squeezed, shaking his head in warning.

"I do like it!" Bobby said, hearing the desperation in his voice.

"You're not having fun."

"Yes, I am. I am."

"We can just turn around right now and go home."

"No, Dee, please ..."

"If what I give you isn't good enough for you, then we'll just do without."

"It is good enough. Honest, it really is."

"I just thought you'd enjoy going out to eat for a change," she said, her voice now full of self-pity. "Naturally I want to show you off, what's wrong with that?"

"Nothing ..."

"But I don't want to show off an ungrateful little boy."

"He wants to go," Ash said.

"I do, I do."

"Well ..."

"I think it's great! It's fun being out here. It's fun being with you and Ash."

"Well ..."

"I don't care where we eat. Whatever you want. You choose."

"I did have someplace special in mind," Dee said.

"Great!"

"Well ..."

She kept on driving and did not wheel the car around and head back to the motel as Bobby had feared, but her enthusiasm was gone entirely. The face that he could see in the mirror was now hurt, sullen and wary. Disappointed.

They drove for half an hour and eventually Dee's mood lightened and she began to talk again, but without the buoyancy of before. Ash seemed genuinely delighted by their outing and he studied the passing scene with interest. His face was close to the window, his nose nearly pressing against the glass. He reminded Bobby of a dog.

Bobby began to relax. He was out of the motel room. They had allowed him to wear his clothes for the first time since the kidnapping. They were not taking him home, but he was going out. Out meant a chance. Ash could not block every exit now that they were outside the room. There would be people around them if they ever stopped the car. He could yell for help, he could outwit Ash – he knew he could outsmart him – and run. Maybe a policeman would be there. Maybe someone who knew him. Maybe his parents.

*

174

Dee selected a large McDonald's that featured a lighted outdoor playground. Despite the lateness of the hour there were a few young children running around the slides and see-saws. Harried mothers, taking a break from a long ride, stood nearby, watching their kids and hoping that this burst of energy would tire them sufficiently that they would sleep the rest of the way to their destinations.

Bobby and Ash ate in the car, consuming the food that Dee had brought them while she joined the mothers by the playground. Bobby devoured his dinner ravenously, deciding on the first scent of fried hamburger to postpone his plans until his hunger was assuaged.

"She's talking about you," Ash said.

Bobby looked up from his paper cup of french fries to see Dee chatting with two women. Her manner was very animated and she gesticulated frequently. He recognised the mood, it was the one that he feared most, the one in which she was the most unpredictable.

"How do you know?"

"She's bragging about you," Ash said. There was ketchup on Ash's chin and Bobby involuntarily wiped his own face. "She's very proud of you."

Bobby saw Dee pointing towards the car. Her face was beaming. She seemed so happy. He had never understood what there was about him that made her so happy.

Dee waved at them and Ash waved back.

"Wave," he said under his breath. "Wave happy."

Bobby waggled his hand and smiled. Dee waved more energetically and said something to the woman with her. They, too, waved at the car as if impelled to do so by Dee's energy alone.

Then Dee's wave turned into a sign of beckoning and Bobby heard Ash suck in his breath.

"She wants us," Bobby said.

He felt Ash's huge hand grip his leg.

"Be careful," Ash said.

"Sure."

"No, no. Be careful."

Bobby started to open the door but Ash held him back. "Tommy," he said, "Don't run."

Bobby feigned innocence. "What do you mean?"

Ash looked into his eyes, pleading. "Don't run."

"She wants us," Bobby said. "Better let me go, Ash, or Dee'll get mad at you."

"Please," Ash said.

"I'm not going to run," Bobby said. "Why would I run?"

"Don't disappoint her," Ash said, his tone imploring.

Ash kept a hand on the boy and slid across the seat to exit through the same door. They were out of the car and Dee was gesturing frantically.

"Come here, Tommy! Come here!"

Bobby started towards her and felt Ash's grip tighten again. The big man leaned down, his face close to Bobby's. Bobby could see the whiskers already sprouting from Ash's cheeks even though he had shaved earlier. Several longer hairs, black and wiry, rode the crest of his cheekbones, permanently untrimmed.

"Please, Bobby," Ash whispered. It was the first time Bobby had heard his real name used since he had been taken. "Please don't run away."

Bobby stared at Ash for a moment as the depth and sincerity of the big man's plea finally sunk in. At last he nodded and Ash released him. Bobby walked towards the women where Dee continued to beckon and urge him on like a puppy.

"Here he is, here's my darling boy," Dee exclaimed. "Isn't he beautiful?"

The women leaned over and clucked approvingly,

regarding him as Dee did, as if he were much younger, as young as their own children playing behind them.

"I'm so proud of him," Dee said, embracing him. She pulled him against her bosom, kissed the top of his head again and again.

"Why don't you go play with the other children now, darling?" she said. Bobby knew it was not a request.

He walked into the sand-covered enclosure and looked at it contemptuously. It was all too young for him. She thought he was a baby. He could barely fit on the slide, his weight on one end of the see-saw would keep any of the other children suspended in the air all night.

Dee had turned her attention back to the other mothers. They spoke of something and Dee burst into laughter, dragging them with her, puzzled by her energy, intimidated by her enthusiasm.

Ash hovered in the middle distance, watching, his attention roving back and forth between Dee and Bobby. Dee had not introduced him, had made no mention of him whatsoever to the women and they glanced at him now with misgivings, a hulking man, shabbily dressed. There was something not quite right about him, they could see that, a certain slowness of movement, the look of lagging comprehension on his face. Since, he, too, came with a child, they were not prepared to declare him dangerous but both women instinctively shifted their bodies, keeping themselves between Ash and their children.

Bobby found himself in a cage. The playground was fenced in, a safe place for two- and three- and four-year-olds to be contained while their parents consumed McDonald's fare. There was nowhere to go but back through the gate by which he had entered. He could try to scale the fence which came only to eye level, but he was certain Ash would get to him before he reached the top. Whom he could he yell to? The women with Dee?

He sat disconsolately on the swing, nudging himself back and forth with his toes.

"Is that your daddy?" One of the children stood next to Bobby, a girl with a runny nose. Bobby guessed her to be five years old. Hopelessly young, a generation away from understanding.

"No," Bobby said, following the girl's finger as it pointed at Ash. "I'm being kidnapped."

"My daddy's in the bathroom."

"That's not my mother, either," Bobby said. "See that woman?" He was careful to indicate Dee only by looking at her. He did not point. "She stole me from my real mommy and daddy."

"Oh." Bobby studied the little girl for comprehension. "Will you push me?"

Dee was not looking at him at the moment. Her head was tipped skyward in laughter, she was touching the arm of one of the women.

"I'll push you if you'll do something for me, all right?"

The girl nodded her head.

"You have to promise," Bobby said.

The girl wiped her nose with her finger.

"Do you promise?"

"Uh-huh."

"When we leave, tell your mommy that my name is Bobby Reynolds and I've been kidnapped."

The girl sniffed, then ran her entire forearm under her nose.

"If you promise to do that, I'll push you as high as you want," Bobby said. He glanced at Ash who was watching him curiously.

The girl turned and started to trot towards her mother.

"Not now!" Bobby cried. He grabbed at the girl and caught her arm, but the women had already seen the motion and turned to watch. "Not now," Bobby whispered, but the girl was still straining towards her mother, pulling against him.

"What is it?" said the girl's mother, moving towards the fence.

Bobby released the girl's arm, but too late. For a moment the child stood midway between Bobby and her mother, her arm still in the air behind her as if suspended by a wire. She sensed the air of tension both in front of and behind her, everyone waiting to see what she would do. The girl did not know what to do, nor what was expected, nor why the air was suddenly filled with stress. In doubt, she did what always worked. She began to whimper.

"He hurt my arm," the girl said.

"No, I didn't," Bobby said quickly, but it was already too late.

"I'm sure he didn't mean to," the mother said, but she was through the gate, reaching for her daughter.

"He did," the girl insisted.

Then Dee was upon him, wrenching him out of the canvas bucket of the swing seat, jerking him on to his feet.

"What are you thinking of?" she demanded.

"He didn't mean to," said the mother, trying to placate Dee when she saw the fury in her face.

Dee clamped her hand on the back of Bobby's neck, squeezing and propelling him forward so fast he stumbled.

"How dare you do this," she said. "How dare you do this to me."

They were across the parking lot in a flash, Bobby being pushed head first by the stony grip on his neck.

Ash had the rear door open and he slid in instantly next to Bobby, one arm around the boy's shoulder to keep him from bolting out the other side.

"It's all right, really." The other mother had pursued

them halfway to the car, but Dee did not even glance at her. "Please don't hurt him," the mother said. The doors were slammed and the car was in motion before she could speak again.

Dee drove without seeming to look at the road, her eyes were so fixedly boring at Bobby in the mirror.

"This is the thanks I get," she said. Bobby could see her nostril in the glass. It was flared in anger. "This is my reward for all I've done for you."

"He didn't run," Ash said, but was ignored.

"Imagine how I felt," Dee was saying. "Did you ever once consider how your behaviour makes me feel? I was talking to my friends, I was telling them what a good boy I have, how proud I am of you, and then you do this …"

"I didn't do anything," Bobby said.

"But you never once considered my feelings, did you? Not for a second."

They raced through the night. Bobby could hear the wind screaming through a crack where the window glass met the door frame.

"I'm sorry, Dee," he said.

"It's a little late for that, isn't it? I'm very disappointed in you," Dee said.

Bobby felt Ash sigh deeply as if he were shuddering.

Dee said nothing more all the way home, but every time Bobby looked her eyes were glaring at him in the mirror.

Reggie turned towards the door as it swung in sharply.

"What the hell are you doing in here?" George demanded.

"I have a right to be here," she said, furious with herself for having reacted with fear.

"I promised her we'd stay out," George said.

"How'd you even know I was here, anyway?" she

180

demanded. There was no place for her to direct her anger other than at George.

"I saw you leave," George said. He was talking to her but his eyes were scanning the room. He had promised not to come in, but it was still his property, too, after all.

"Are you spying on me?"

"Don't flatter yourself," he said. "I told her we wouldn't come in here. What if her husband had been in here?"

"I saw them leave," Reggie said. "She stole the bed-spread."

"Who?"

"What do you mean, 'who'? Your girlfriend, that's who."

"She's not my girlfriend."

"Uh-huh."

"And what makes you think she stole it, anyway?"

George had come all the way into the room and closed the door behind him. He touched the bed as if to confirm the evidence of his eyes.

"It's not here, that's what."

"Doesn't mean she stole it."

"Why don't you see if you can find it then?" George gave her a look from under his brows. He hated her tone of voice. He had told her a few thousand times not to speak to him like that, but he might as well have saved his breath. The only way she was going to realise he meant it was when he went out to get the mail and didn't come back. Which might be at any time now, if she kept this up.

"Just because I can't find it doesn't mean she stole it," he said. He snapped off the television set.

"I'd like to know what it does mean," Reggie said.

"I'm sure she's got a perfectly good explanation."

"That's right. Defend her."

"She hasn't done anything wrong. The only one's done anything wrong is you by breaking your word and coming in here."

"I never gave her my word. That was your bright idea. The only thing I'd give her is a piece of my mind."

"Careful, you don't have much to spare."

George had manoeuvred behind Reggie and was now herding her towards the door. He held his arms out to the side as if shooing chickens. Reggie resisted the urge to hit him.

"If she stole it, out she goes," Reggie said. "I won't tolerate theft. Out she goes."

"Out you go," he said, still driving her towards the door.

"It's the one thing I won't put up with," Reggie said. "I won't put up with a thief."

"I'll talk to her about it," George said. "It's a misunderstanding. Don't worry, I'll talk to her."

"I'll bet you will." She stood in the doorway, just to make a point. He wasn't pushing her out, she had chosen to leave and would make her exit when she wanted to. He stopped just short of her, careful not to put a hand on her.

"Of course, I'll have to explain how I know the bedspread's gone," he said. "Then I'll have to apologise for you."

"Don't you dare. Don't you dare apologise for me to that woman!" Reggie cried.

"Guess I'll have to," George said.

"I forbid it!"

"Fair is fair, and right is right." George rose up on his toes slightly as he made his pronouncement. He had been taller than Reggie earlier in their lives together but it seemed to him that she had somehow outgrown him lately.

"If you apologise to her, that is the last straw," Reggie declared. "I am not joking with you, George. So much as a hint of apology and I have had it."

He rocked up on his toes again and then he smiled. It was the smile that convinced Reggie, the smugness of it that made her want to paste him right on the nose. That woman was gone, Reggie vowed silently. She was out of here as of now, no matter how long it took to actually arrange the eviction.

Reggie intended to stay up until they came home, no matter how long it took. She wanted to be there to intercept them between car and cabin. She would face down 'Dee' and her so-called husband this very night, let them understand she knew about the theft and that they were to be gone as soon as they could pack. Never mind that they still had a week's rent paid in advance, the theft negated all that.

Her intention was to stay awake – but her body had its own plans. After a time even the anger she felt was insufficient to keep her eyes open. She drifted off, woke, and drifted again and woke once more. She tried to focus her eyes on a hairline crack in the ceiling plaster. If a car pulled into the drive she would see the lights sweep across the ceiling and be out of bed and to the door before the car came to a halt. Reggie fell asleep and dreamed she was watching the ceiling.

Dee killed the headlights as soon as they turned into the motel drive. She unlocked the door to the cabin and held it open as Ash struggled out of the backseat holding his bundle, then rushed into the sanctuary of the room.

Dee spoke for the first time since leaving McDonald's as she strode to the closet and removed the garment from the laundry on the rack.

"We'll see," Dee said. "Now we'll see who misbehaves."

By the time Dee had the wire hanger in her hand Ash had uncovered Bobby and handed him a pillow.

"Bite on it," he whispered. He began hurriedly to unbutton Bobby's shirt.

"What? What's she going to do?" Bobby asked. His eyes were wide with fear. He was afraid to turn and look at Dee who stood behind him, still muttering, and instead kept his eyes glued to Ash's face for a clue as to what was to befall him. There was nothing in Ash's face to give him hope.

"Don't yell," Ash whispered. His voice had the same imploring intensity as when he had urged Bobby not to run. "Don't make any noise at all."

He unbuttoned Bobby's pants and pulled them down then lifted the pillow to Bobby's mouth.

"Bite," he said and Bobby clamped his mouth on to the pillow.

The first blow fell almost immediately across his back. The boy gasped as much from surprise as from the pain. Ash immediately positioned the pillow in front of Bobby's mouth again.

"No noise," he hissed. The wire struck again and Bobby's cry was muffled by the pillow.

There was a brief pause as Dee snapped on the television, then the blows came steadily.

Bobby squirmed and tried to pull away, but Ash gripped him by the arms and held him in place.

"Don't make her mad," he whispered.

"Now we'll see," Dee said. "Now we'll see. Now we'll see."

She beat him in rhythm with her voice, but Bobby soon ceased to make sense of her words. Her only real message was pain.

13

Karen awoke to music and it took her a moment to figure out where it was coming from. The sound was muted and faint and the strumming of acoustic guitar gave her a fleeting sense of being serenaded from outside her window. Then she realised it was coming from Jack's room. He was up and playing his favourite tape of children's songs. She glanced at the red numerals on the clock radio, the two dots separating the hours and the minutes blinking methodically. It was too early for her to be up; but not too early for Jack. She could never understand how he functioned so well on so little sleep, nor how he seemed to awake fully refreshed and smiling while she had to claw her way into consciousness.

Remembering that she was not alone in the bed, she rolled her head to look at Becker but his side of the bed was empty. His clothes, which he had tossed on the chair the night before, were gone. The son-of-a-bitch has slipped out on me, she thought. Not so much as a good-bye, no farewell kiss. Just grab his socks and go. How typical, how sneakily, self-centredly, inconsiderately typical. They were all sons-of-bitches, so it wasn't her fault that she kept picking bad ones. There were no good ones.

Karen washed her face and brushed her teeth and when she was certain she could muster a cheerful smile for her son, she went in to see him. Becker was sitting on the floor making another newspaper tree and Jack, still dressed in his airplane pyjamas, was dancing around the room in a bounding gavotte that included frequent leaps on and off his bed.

"You still here?" Karen said. She was surprised by the tightness in her voice.

Becker held the newspaper over his head. "By popular request," he said.

"Stop jumping on your bed," she said to Jack.

"I was just showing him," Jack said. He pointed at Becker as if to clarify any doubt.

"You know you're not supposed to jump on your bed. Now stop it."

Although she had not raised her voice, Jack stopped in mid-bounce and stepped carefully to the floor.

"I forgot," he said lamely.

"How long have you been up?" she asked Becker.

"A couple of hours. I got up when I heard the fax machine working."

"You can't hear the fax machine from my bedroom."

"*You* can't hear the fax machine," he corrected her.

"What did it say?"

"It's not my place to be reading your faxes," he said.

"What did it say?"

"The first one was a report on the detailed search of the mall."

"And?"

"Nothing. He wasn't hidden there and they found no indication that he ever was."

"And the second fax?"

"It's a printout of all the delinquencies at hotels, motels and monthly rental homes within a thirty-five mile radius of Stamford within forty-eight hours of the time the boy was found. It's six pages long."

"What boy?" Jack asked.

"No one, honey. How about you getting dressed now."

"He said a boy was found," Jack insisted. "Was a boy lost?"

"Not really. Now you get dressed, Mr Becker and Mommy have a little work to do."

"How did he get lost?"

"Jack …"

Becker kneeled in front of the boy.

"He got lost because children do sometimes," Becker said, "but the reason he stayed lost so long was that he didn't do what he should have done. Do you know what he should have done when he got lost?"

"What?"

"He should have yelled," Becker said. "He should have yelled and screamed and made as much noise as he could so that the people looking for him could find him. There were a lot of people trying to find the boy, including your mommy. Your mommy is a very good finder, did you know that, Jack?"

Jack shook his head uncertainly. He was not certain of his mother's finding abilities but he was fascinated to learn.

"Well, she is. Your mommy is very, very good at it. But even she couldn't find the lost boy because she didn't know where to look because he didn't make enough noise. He should have made all the noise he possibly could and he should have kept doing it until he was found. The worst thing to do if you ever get lost is to keep quiet about it. If you're in trouble of any kind, you be sure to call for help. OK?"

"OK … But what happened to him?"

"He finally got found," Becker said.

"Did you find him, Mommy?"

"Not personally, sweetheart."

"The people who work for your mommy found him," Becker said. "The boy is safe at home now, and your mommy gets a lot of the credit for that."

Jack smiled. He was not sure that he completely understood, but the sense of pride he felt about his mother was clear enough.

"You're a pretty good liar," Karen said to Becker when they were alone in the kitchen. "I thought you prided yourself on telling the truth."

"When the truth is appropriate," Becker said. "If a lie is called for, I can usually manage."

"So how do I know if you're telling me the truth?" she asked.

"Why not assume I'm telling you the truth until you see my nose grow?"

"I think it's safer to assume you're lying until I see your nose shrink ... but thanks for the plug with Jack."

"You deserve it."

"It's nice to have your kid think you're good at what you do – even if he doesn't know what it is."

As Karen drove them towards the mall in Bickford, Becker went through the printout that had come in by fax.

"You check my logic as I go along," Becker said. "First we can eliminate the women from the list, right?"

"As devil's advocate, why?"

"Women almost never commit serial murders, one. Two, the upper body strength required to pitch the victim out the window of a moving car while driving it at the same time would make her some kind of steroid-huge iron-pumping giant. That's the kind of person who would have been noticed in the mall or museum. Women like that are certain to get a stare from every man in the place."

"Women would notice her, too. All right, eliminate the women from the list."

They were silent for a few moments as Becker went through the six pages and struck off the names that were obviously women. He circled those given names that were just initials for further investigation.

"You're very good with him," Karen said.

"Thanks."

"I didn't think you would be."

Becker looked up from the list and studied her profile. "Why?"

She shrugged. "No practice, maybe. I don't know. It just took me sort of by surprise."

"Do you think I'm some kind of monster?" He sounded hurt.

"I know you're not a monster, John. Forget the remark, I didn't mean anything by it. Some people are good with kids and some aren't, that's all I meant."

"We eliminate all those who stayed less than a week before skipping out."

"Why?"

"We assume Lamont was holed up with the victim, which is far safer than moving around periodically. Something went wrong, he killed the victim and fled. Remember, he kept all these kids for at least six weeks, right?"

"Except for one."

"Which makes it very unlikely he was going to a new location every week. That's too many transfers in and out of the car, too many times to check in, too many things to go wrong."

"OK," Karen said. "Check them off."

Becker moved slowly over the names, calculating dates.

"He likes you," Karen said.

"Good, I like him, too."

Karen flashed her headlights at a car in the passing-lane in front of her. The driver remained blissfully unaware. At the first opportunity Karen swung past him on the right, then into the left lane again. She jabbed her finger to the right, trying to tell the driver to get over but she could tell in her mirror that he had barely even noticed her.

"How do you know he likes me?" Becker asked.

"He told me," she said. She looked at Becker whose eyes had not left the list on his lap.

"He's a good boy," he said.

"He's a wonderful boy."

"That, too. I meant he's well-behaved."

"Oh. Well, mostly. He has his bad moments."

"He told me he's going to sleep-over camp this summer," Becker said. He drew his pen through a line and went on to the next.

"Next week," Karen said. "Did he sound ... how did he sound when he told you about it?"

"Excited. He's looking forward to it."

"Really? Excited? It's his first time away from home. He's very ambivalent about it."

"Didn't sound that way. How are you?"

"Ambivalent," she admitted. "He's so young. He's never been away, he doesn't even like to go to sleep-overs at his friends' houses."

"So why is he going to camp?"

Karen paused. "He says he wants to but ... I'm not sure how much of it is because I pushed him into it. I tried not to, I tried to stay neutral but maybe the way I worded it, maybe ... The idea of two whole weeks without any responsibilities to anyone but myself, it's like heaven. I mean, I'll miss him like crazy, I know that, but to just come home after work and vegetate – it's been ten years.

I wanted him to go, I wanted him to want to go ... And he is so quick to anticipate what he thinks I want. When he actually does do something wrong, which is not very often, if he spills his milk, for instance, he gets this look on his face as if he's going to be shot. It makes me feel like a monster. The other day he put his dinner dishes in the dishwasher without scraping them and he was so apologetic. I don't know, is it normal? Am I doing it all wrong? Do all parents worry about how they're raising their kids, or is it just single mothers? ... Or is it just me?"

"It looks to me like you're doing fine."

"You think?"

"I think you've got a hard job and you're doing a terrific job of it."

Karen glanced at him to judge the sincerity of his remark but Becker was intent on the readout. "I'm going to delete hotels, anyplace where he would have to negotiate a lobby and an elevator with the boy. Too risky. Also any rented rooms in a private home without a separate entrance. Same reason. Agreed?"

"Right," she said. Becker had already begun to whittle at the list. "For a minute this morning I thought you'd gone."

"I thought you seemed a little pissed-off to see me," Becker said. "Was that because I was still around?"

"No. I got pissed because I thought you'd skipped off without saying goodbye and when I saw you in Jack's room, you got some of the residue. Sorry."

"Why would I skip out?"

"Men do."

"Do they?"

"In my experience."

"You've had a tough history," he said.

"I've had a history. I'm a woman. That's basically the only kind we have."

"Nice that you're not bitter, though," he said.

"Screw you."

"Horrors. I'm on duty."

Karen glided the car into the right lane in preparation for the turn off to Bickford.

"Anyway, thank you," she said.

Becker looked at her in surprise.

"Are you really serious?"

"Not just for staying, but the way you did it. Being so nice to Jack, not acting like you were doing me any favours, being so patient and listening to me – and everything."

"Are we really such shitheels?" Becker asked.

"Given the chance," she said. "Most men, yeah."

"Why do women put up with us?"

"It's in our saintly nature. Besides, what's the alternative? If a woman waits for a really good man to come along, she'll die single and horny as hell ... the single part's not so bad."

Becker laughed and folded the printout on his lap.

"So anyway," she continued. "Thanks for being decent."

"You make it sound as if you're not going to see me again," Becker said.

"I didn't know how you felt ... if you wanted, to, or what. I kind of Shanghaied you last night."

Becker touched her hand where it rested on the steering wheel. "If I didn't make that clear last night, I guess I'll just have to try harder."

Karen thought for a moment about the sexual marathon of the night before and laughed. "Then I guess I'll just have to put up with it," she said. They lapsed into silence, both feeling slightly embarrassed and uncertain of the next move, as Karen guided them on to the exit ramp.

"The boy who didn't last as long as the others," Becker

said. For a second it seemed jarringly out of context to Karen.

"Ricky Stine," she said. "Taken from his schoolyard in Newburgh."

"Right. Didn't you say he was hyperactive?"

"That's right."

"Do you suppose that's why he didn't last as long? Lamont lost patience with him?"

"Or maybe he was harder to control. That goes with your theory that he is trying to pick the docile ones."

"And maybe it's their docility that keeps them alive," Becker said.

"Alive longer," Karen amended. "Not alive."

"Maybe alive long enough this time," he said. "Lamont is out there somewhere within thirty miles of us. We've got to get a list of every place a single male transient could be staying within a thirty-mile radius of Bickford. If we find any names on that list that match the ones on this one ..." He tapped the printout on his lap. "We'd have a place to start, at least."

"Why do you think he's that close? Why wouldn't he go as far as possible?"

"For one thing, he doesn't. He stays within a four-State area. Whether because there's something that keeps him here or whether it's just familiar territory, I don't know. But he does stay. Every body was found within fifty miles of the town where it was snatched. You can't always find a right spot and time on the highway to throw something out, you need a little leeway. I'm guessing ten to twenty miles. If it's longer, that means he started well within the thirty miles, which is even better. The point is, his pattern is not to snatch a kid and then go hundreds of miles and live with him for a month. He takes them and goes immediately to ground. That means he's already made a nest where he feels secure before he takes them."

"You think he's still here then?" She made a vague semicircular sweep of her hand.

"Well, yes, depending how you define 'here'. A circle with a thirty-mile radius covers an awful lot of territory."

"Tell me about it. You see how long it took to compile that list for Stamford, and that was six months ago."

"We need help," Becker said. "The Bureau doesn't begin to have enough people to do it fast enough. We have to get the State and local people working on it."

Karen snorted. "To us it's a serial killer. To them it's a local matter of one missing child. We'll be asking them to expend God knows how many man hours on what could very well be a wild-goose chase ..."

"Cops are used to chasing wild geese," Becker said.

"Their own geese. Now we want them to chase ours. We want them to undertake a major search because one boy – for most of them a boy who's not from their own town or jurisdiction – has been missing for a few days."

"A week," said Becker.

"Do you think you can do that?" she asked.

"Me?" Becker asked. "No, I couldn't hope to do that. I don't have the skills. I tend to alienate people, I'm too sure of myself. I could never convince them to do it ... But you could."

"Thanks a lot."

"A pleasure."

"Any bright ideas as to how I go about it?"

"No," said Becker. "But you'd better hurry. At the rate Lamont is escalating his hunger, I'd say Bobby Reynolds has two weeks left. Three at the outside – if he's very, very docile."

Karen stood outside the conference room in the Radisson Hotel in Bickford, slowly tearing the tissue she held in her hands to little pieces. The deputy chief of the Connecticut State police and the heads or representatives of two dozen local police forces were waiting inside along with as many FBI men from the New York and New England districts as she could command, beg, borrow or scrape. Getting them all together with only two days' notice had taken all the authority and good will that her position in the Bureau could muster. And that was the easy part.

Getting them all to do something was not a problem. They would make a token of assistance simply for the asking. What Karen needed, however, was a dedicated effort. Fast and concentrated and thorough. And this from men who resisted, on principle, the very idea, much less the practice, of being told what to do by the federal law enforcement agency. Men who would resist for reasons of turf and professional pride if the directions came from a seasoned agent, would resist even more fiercely if it came from a woman.

"A young and beautiful woman at that," Becker reminded her. He stood next to Karen outside the conference room. Karen had noted that her nervousness only seemed to amuse him.

"They'll hate me," she said.

"That is not the average man's reaction to a young and beautiful woman. Believe me, these guys are very average. You start at an advantage."

"Are you nuts? I'm walking into a nest of male chauvinists. I've got as much advantage as a kitten in a dog kennel."

"One thing's for sure, you'll have their attention," Becker said, grinning. "Come on, how bad can it be? You command a couple dozen men all the time."

"I'm their boss. When I talk to them they pay attention, they don't sit around and grab at their nuts. I don't

195

have to stand in front of them and convince them of what to do. I tell them."

"Probably not the best approach to take here," Becker said.

"Thanks for the advice."

Becker took her by the hand and removed the decimated tissue. "Makes you look nervous," he said.

"No shit. Wouldn't want to give the wrong impression ... I hate talking to groups. I'm not so bad one-on-one ..."

"Not bad at all."

She cast him a dark glance. His amusement was getting very hard to take. "... but I hate – hell, I fear talking to groups. Especially a room full of cops."

"I think you're supposed to imagine them all sitting there naked. That's supposed to make them less intimidating and to relax you."

"You want me to imagine a roomful of overweight, balding, middle-aged cops? That's disgusting. You try imagining that, I'll come up with my own nightmares."

"As a middle-aged cop myself, I rise to say, how unkind," said Becker.

"I don't mean you. For one thing, you're not overweight. You're not balding. You're certainly not disgusting."

"Sounds like damning with faint praise to me."

"Christ, John, I'm in the middle of a crisis here, I can't cater to your ego right now."

"You've got a law degree, don't you? You had to do a lot of talking to earn that."

"And I hated every second of it. Why do you think I went into the Bureau?"

"A thirst for justice and social equality?"

"This isn't funny! I hate it! Why don't you stop being a fucking wit and help me?"

"All right," Becker said. "I'll talk to them."

He started towards the conference room. Karen caught him by the arm and yanked.

"I'll do it," she said angrily. "I said I hated it, I didn't say I couldn't do it." She started towards the door, then paused with her hand on the handle.

"And I know that was a ploy," she said. "Trying to shame me into it."

"I know you know."

"It didn't work. I'm not so easily manipulated."

"Never thought you were," he said.

"Just so you know," she said. She glanced up and down the corridor to be sure they were alone, then she put her hand briefly in his crotch. "For luck," she said, grinning. She entered the room with Becker's laughter sounding behind her.

Karen strode into the conference room and listened to the quality of the conversational drone change as the men caught sight of her. When she took the podium the drone rose to a quizzical buzz.

"Thank you all for coming," she said. Her voice caught in her throat and she cleared it, cursing herself for a coward. "I am Karen Crist, Deputy First Assistant for Kidnapping for the Bureau out of New York."

They had stopped their murmuring and were looking at her now with curiosity and scepticism. Waiting for me to step on my own tongue, she thought.

The deputy chief of the Connecticut State police sat in the front row in a uniform so crispy starched and ironed that it appeared to be made of fresh cardboard. Next to him slouched the chief of one of the local forces, a fat, ageing, balding man whose belly slopped over his belt like so much run away bread-dough yeasting beyond the rising bowl. As she watched, the chief unconsciously tugged at his crotch.

197

"Assholes of the world united," Karen thought to herself and wondered if she were in the right profession.

She did not allow the doubts to linger, however. Looking up from the chief at the assembled waiting faces, she began.

"How many of you have children?" she asked.

14

Bobby awoke to find himself in the bathtub with Ash kneeling beside him on the bathroom floor. The big man was gently cradling the boy's head in one hand, holding it above the surface of the water while the boy's naked body stretched full length in the tub.

"It's all right," Ash said when he saw the boy's eyelids flutter. Bobby awoke in fright and confusion.

"You're all right," Ash said. "Everything's all right." Bobby tried to sit up and the pain struck him hard. Ash was ready and he had his free hand over Bobby's mouth before the scream could emerge. Bobby could taste the plastic of Ash's glove.

"Shhh, shhh," Ash said gently. "It will go away."

"It hurts," the boy said. His forehead was wrinkled with an effort to control it. He did not need Ash to be any more specific to realise that noise would bring Dee into the room, her face wild with fury. He remembered the beating now and each cut and welt upon his back seemed to be throbbing as if he were being struck again. No, not that badly, Bobby thought. Nothing had ever hurt as much as being struck the first time. He remembered the beating, Dee's insane rhythmic chanting, her grunts of effort, the nonstop rain of lashes. He did not recall passing out, had no recollection of Ash holding him in his arms, carrying him to the bathroom, easing him into the tepid water.

"It hurts," he said again, looking into Ash's face for comfort, or sympathy, or understanding. He saw all three as well as a brute acceptance of things as they were.

"It will go away," Ash said. "I promise."

He eased Bobby back down into the water and began to rub him all over with a bar of soap in his gloved hand. Dee had told him to always wash a cut before applying disinfectant and he was thorough in his work. Bobby winced and gasped and moaned when the wounds were touched, but he did not cry out. He's a good one, Ash thought. Dee would like this one better than some. She would let him last longer than some. As for Ash, he loved them all.

"Where is she now?" Bobby asked quietly.

"She's asleep," Ash said. "She was very sad. You made her very sad, Tommy."

"I didn't run," Bobby said.

"I know. That was good. But you made her sad anyway."

"I didn't mean to."

Ash shrugged philosophically. "Sometimes we just do."

Bobby looked at the water. Ash had opened the drain and let the faucet run as he scrubbed Bobby. The water had maintained the same level but the colour had gradually changed. It was just barely pink now, in another minute or two it would be clear.

Ash touched the medallion on Bobby's chest. "What is it?"

"It's a good-luck charm," Bobby explained. He lifted the medallion and looked at it, then turned it to Ash, who studied the face of John F. Kennedy stamped on the silver coin. Someone had punched a hole in the half dollar and threaded a cheap dimestore chain through it. The coin still shone brightly after all the years but the chain had turned a tarnished shade of brown.

"What's it for?"

"It's for good luck," Bobby said.

"What does it do?"

"It gives me good luck," Bobby said.

"How?"

"I don't know, it just does. Nothing bad can happen to me as long as I wear it. That's why I never take it off."

Ash held the coin gingerly between gloved finger and thumb, trying to imagine what bad things it had warded off for Bobby. For a moment Ash wondered if the boy was teasing him, but he seemed utterly convinced of his good fortune.

"You should get one, Ash," Bobby said.

"Would it work for me?"

"Not this one, this one only works for me."

Ash nodded solemnly, as if he understood.

"But you could get one for yourself," Bobby explained. "I could help you find one if you want."

"OK."

Bobby took the coin from Ash's fingers and put it back in its proper place on his chest. Ash regarded the coin with new respect.

"That's sure a nice ..." Ash groped for the proper word.

"Good-luck charm," Bobby offered.

"Good-luck charm," Ash repeated. "That's sure a nice good-luck charm."

"It's the best. It's never let me down. I found a five-dollar bill on the sidewalk once."

"Really?"

"Honest. Just lying there."

"I wish I had one."

"We'll get you one," Bobby said.

"Then I'll be as lucky as you," Ash said.

"Maybe," Bobby said. "It depends on how good your charm is."

Ash stood the boy in the tub and let the water continue to run as he poured disinfectant over his back and legs. Bobby bit down on a wadded washcloth but the pain was mild compared to all that had gone before, scarcely more than a sting.

"How come you wear those silly gloves in the water?" Bobby asked.

"Dee says," Ash replied.

"How come though?"

"Dee knows all about these things. She says it's for everybody's safety."

Afterwards Ash wrapped a towel around the boy and used another to dry the boy's hair. They stayed in the bathroom to keep from waking Dee. They could hear her make noises now and again in the agitation of her dreams.

"How come you never sleep," Bobby asked.

"I can't."

"Don't you get tired?"

"Sure. I get tired all the time but I can't let myself go to sleep because of what happens."

"What happens?"

Ash looked away. He wished the conversation had never started.

"What happens when you go to sleep, Ash?"

Ash shook his head stubbornly.

"Do you have bad dreams?"

"I don't have dreams. I don't sleep."

"Because I have bad dreams sometimes," Bobby said. "But I sleep anyway. I don't have them all the time, just sometimes, and besides, they're not really real."

"I don't have bad dreams."

"Then what is it?"

"I don't want to tell you."

"Oh, come on, Ash. I tell you things, don't I?"

"Yes …"

"I won't tell anyone else, I promise."

"Dee knows," Ash said. As far as he was concerned, there was no one else in their world to tell.

"Well then. If she knows, why can't I?"

"I kill people," Ash said in a rush.

"You don't either."

"I do. When I go to sleep I do."

"You don't either."

"Uh-huh."

"If you're asleep, how do you know?"

"Dee told me," Ash said.

"How does she know?"

"Everyone knows," Ash said. "I'm famous."

"You're not either."

"I fell asleep a long time ago and killed my family."

"How?"

"When I woke up, they were all dead."

"Your whole family?"

"My mother and father and sister and brother."

"You couldn't kill them," Bobby insisted. "You were just a little boy."

"No, I wasn't. I was sixteen. I was big. I wasn't old enough to be tried as an adult, though. Dee says I was lucky 'cause if I was any older they would have cooked me."

"Cooked you! They wouldn't do that, no one would do that."

"That's what Dee says. She said I was lucky I didn't fry."

"They don't fry people," Bobby said uncertainly.

"She said they would have fried me but I was too young

203

so they sent me to the hospital instead. That's where Dee found me."

"Were you sick?"

"They said I was sick to kill my family."

"You're not sick, Ash."

"I don't always understand things the way I should."

"I know. But you're not sick. I think you're nice."

Ash smiled brightly, revealing his teeth. Two of them were jagged and darkened at the roots and Ash hid them behind his hand as he continued to smile.

"I think you're nice, too," Ash said.

"Was Dee sick, too?"

"Dee isn't sick," Ash said hastily, the smile vanishing. "She has a controllable condition. She has pills. We both have pills. I'm controllable, too ... Sometimes Dee doesn't take her pills. But I always take mine."

"Why was she in the hospital if she wasn't sick?"

"It was a special hospital for people like me. You wouldn't go there if you was just sick. Dee worked there."

"You love Dee, don't you?" Bobby asked.

"Of course," Ash said, amazed by the question.

"I don't," Bobby said. Ash gasped and put his finger to his mouth. "She's mean."

"Dee loves you, Tommy. She loves you. Of all the boys in the world she could have had, she chose you."

"That's just something she told you."

"It's true. She picked you, Tommy."

"My name is Bobby."

"I know. But pretend, OK?"

"Why do I have to?"

"Because Dee wants you to be Tommy." The big man shrugged at the obvious inevitability of it all.

"She hates me," Bobby said.

"She loves you. She really does. I know."

"Why did she hit me so much?"

Ash stared at the closed door for a moment, trying to recall the right answer. "Well, that's because it's for your own good. There are some things children have to be taught and that's the best way."

"You wouldn't ever hit me, would you, Ash?"

Ash was stung by the suggestion. "Oh, no. I wouldn't hurt you, Tommy."

"I would never hit you, Ash."

Bobby leaned against the big man and felt Ash's arm move awkwardly around his shoulders.

"I wouldn't ever hurt you," Ash said. "I promise."

"Then why does Dee?"

"It's her job as a parent." Ash spoke slowly, trying hard to say it all correctly. "A parent owes her child discipline, which teaches it what its boundaries are. It's one of the ways for a mother to show her boy she loves him enough to do the right thing for him." He nodded, pleased that he had got it right.

"She's not my mother. Why doesn't she do it to her own boy?"

"They took her boy away from her," Ash said.

"Who did?"

"It was so unfair," Ash explained. "She was so, so sad. She almost died, she was so sad when they took her Tommy."

"What did you do?"

"I wasn't there. She told me about it."

"Why did they take him?"

Ash studied the door again. He realised he had never asked the question himself.

"They just did," he said finally.

They fell into a silence. Bobby leaned more fully against Ash, taking comfort from the man's size and warmth. He felt a security with the man's arm on his shoulders not unlike the sense of invulnerability he got when he cloaked himself in his special blanket at home. He had long ago dubbed the blanket bullet-proof and in times of stress he would wrap it around himself and peer out, immune to the dangers of the outside world. He tried to burrow into Ash now, seeking the same safe haven. The big man pulled him tightly into his body with the arm on his shoulders and with his other hand rubbed Bobby's head.

"How did you kill your family?" Bobby asked after a time.

Ash seemed prepared for the question, as if he, too, had been thinking about it.

"I stabbed my mother and father while they were asleep and I smothered my brother and sister," he said matter-of-factly.

Bobby thought for a moment. He finally said the only response he could think of. "You shouldn't have done that."

"I know. That's why I never sleep."

"You wouldn't do it again, now that you're grown up, would you?"

"I take my pills and I never sleep," Ash said.

"I know, but even if, let's say you forgot your pills, you still wouldn't kill anybody else, would you, Ash?"

Ash turned his head away from the boy and studied the crack where the floor tiles joined the wall.

"Would you, Ash?" the boy insisted. "You wouldn't, would you?"

Ash's silence grew. Bobby felt the uneasy quality of hesitation in the big man. It seemed to transmit itself directly through his body into the boy's own.

Bobby tried to look at his friend but Ash turned his head away, hiding his face.

The door opened abruptly and Dee stood there, her eyes bright and shining.

"There he is!" she cried. "There's my darling boy!"

*

George stood in the motel driveway chatting with the State trooper as if he were a long-lost friend. Reggie watched from the office window until her curiosity got the best of her and she stepped on to the porch. George turned his back slightly, subtly keeping her from the conversation. As if it were some kind of clubby man's thing, she thought. Both George and the trooper had a foot propped up on the squad car's front bumper. The trooper had both hands tucked into his broad gun belt and George had stuck his in his hip pockets. They looked to Reggie as if they were trying to emulate a scene from a western movie, two old pardners in the saloon with their boots resting on the brass rail.

George looked annoyed when she approached them but Reggie was certain she detected relief in the trooper's face. I'll bet George has talked the man's ear half off by now, she thought. Posing like some macho jerk, as if he had anything in common with a cop. Pathetic, she thought. Little boys to the end, all of them.

The trooper dropped his foot as she neared them and came to a rough approximation of attention. He dipped his head in greeting.

"Ma'am."

"Ah, Reggie," George exuded. As if he hadn't seen her all the time. "Officer here's asking for our help."

"He's certainly come to the right man," Reggie said, scarcely able to keep the sarcasm from her voice.

"I told him I'd do all I could," George said.

Poor trooper then, Reggie thought. He's no help around here, I'd like to see how he could help anyone else.

"We're looking for a man," the trooper said. "I was just telling your husband, he's a big man, unusually strong, probably well developed as if he'd been pumping iron."

George was already shaking his head negatively as if

each descriptive phrase merely served to put the suspect further away from the motel.

"He'd be alone," the trooper said. His attention had drifted from Reggie, back to George.

"Nawp," said George, studying the ground now as if could see the man's face in the gravel.

"Or might have a boy with him."

"Nawp," said George.

"How old a boy?" Reggie asked. The trooper looked at her reluctantly.

"Doesn't matter," George said. "No boys here."

"Nine years old," said the trooper. "Have you had any boys here in the last two weeks?"

"Nawp," said George, shaking his head.

"I couldn't say for sure," Reggie said.

"We haven't had any," George said. "I'd know it."

"Not necessarily, dear," Reggie said sweetly. She paused until she had the trooper's full attention. He removed his dark glasses for the first time. His eyes were a pale brown. Reggie decided he was cute in a traditional sort of way, but not impressive.

"How's that?" the trooper asked.

"I'd know it," George said. "We haven't had any." But he had lost the trooper to Reggie.

"Sometimes they come in at night, no reservations, just pull in. If that one's asleep ..." she indicated George with a move of her head that said he was often sleeping, "... I don't always go out to the cabin with them. I just give them a key. If they're early risers they just drop the key in the slot when they get up and off they go. They could have kids with them."

"Nawp."

"How would you know? They could have a whole orphanage with them. The only way to know is when you clean up the next day."

"You'd know then?"

"Kids are messy, they leave their own traces. You might know. They leave things behind, candy wrappers, comic books ..."

George scoffed. "Lots of people eat candy." He looked directly at the trooper, trying to grab his focus, grinning dismissively about his wife's maunderings.

"So you're saying you might have had a single man with a young boy here in the past two weeks?"

"I'm saying we could have and not know it."

"You wouldn't want to take that to court," George chuckled. "It's not proof."

"I'm sorry," Reggie said, smiling. "Did you want proof, officer?"

"No ma'am, that's not necessary. We just need some information."

"If I'm not being helpful, I'll just let you keep dealing with my husband, he can handle it, can't you, George?"

"You bet."

"I just run the place, is all. I check them in, I check them out. I oversee the rooms, the cleaning ..."

"You're being very helpful," the trooper said. "Do you have any single males staying here now?"

"We always have single men," George said. "That's most of our business. Travellers, salesmen, we get them all the time."

"We have three at the moment, to be precise," Reggie said. "Cabin two checked in yesterday afternoon and is leaving tomorrow."

"Did you see him check in?"

"Yes, I did."

"Was he alone?"

"He was. He was also short and rather heavy. I don't think he's ever lifted a weight in his life."

"We think the man we're looking for would have been here for at least a week already."

"Cabin one is a single man ..."

"He's too old," George said impatiently.

"Too old for what?"

"For whatever the trooper wants him for. He's close to seventy if he's a day."

Reggie looked at the trooper, her eyebrows raised.

"That's probably older than we're looking for," the trooper admitted. There was a trace of apology in his voice but Reggie was not going to accept it immediately.

"Maybe if we knew what he did we could be more help," she said.

"He can't tell you that," George said.

"Right now we just want him for questioning," the trooper said.

"What did I say?" George gloated. "They never tell you. They're not allowed."

"You said that you had another single man here?" the trooper asked.

"Cabin four," George said quickly, trying to regain the initiative. "He's an ugly duck. Mean looking. Sullen, you know? Doesn't like to talk. I'd say he might be your man but he doesn't have a kid with him."

"I have no trouble talking to cabin four," Reggie said. "I find him rather pleasant. I don't think he's what you want at all, officer."

The trooper tried to hide his impatience. He had half a dozen more motels to hit before the day was over, including a Ramada and a Howard Johnson's, both of which seemed more likely to be productive than this tiny operation.

"How long has this gentleman been staying here?" the trooper asked.

"A couple days," said George. "He slinks in and out at

strange hours, I've got no idea what he's doing but I don't like the looks of it."

"He's been here three days precisely," Reggie said. "He's leaving Thursday and he's visiting his daughter who just had a baby girl and doesn't have a spare room to put him up. The daughter's name is Gweneth."

"He doesn't care," George said. "He doesn't care what the baby's name is, either. Try to stay relevant."

"The baby's name is Kendra. I don't know where they got that one. People just seem to make names up these days."

"She doesn't know how police business works," George confided to the trooper.

"Well, like I said, we think this man has probably been checked in for at least a week already."

"That would be cabin six," Reggie said.

"Have you listened to anything the man's been saying?" George demanded. "Have you heard a single word?"

"Cabin six has been here eight days. They don't want to let us in to clean the room …"

"Really?" The trooper showed real interest for the first time.

"It's a woman," George said. "Cabin six is a woman."

"And a man," Reggie added. "A big man."

"You've never seen him." George turned to the trooper. "She's never seen him, he's sick, well, not sick, he has this vision problem so they have to keep the shades down and the door closed all the time which is why they don't want us in to clean the room …"

"I have seen him," Reggie said. "It was night and it was dark but I saw him getting into the car. He looked huge."

"But he's definitely with a woman?"

"A very nice woman," George said.

"He only goes out at night," Reggie said. "Like he's a vampire or something."

The trooper replaced his dark glasses.

"Well …"

"And they may have a boy in there with them," Reggie said.

"I just have to apologise for her …" George started. The trooper held up a hand to quiet him.

"How's that?"

"They might have an elephant in there with them," George scoffed, "but she hasn't actually seen it."

"Why do you say they might have a boy with them?" the trooper asked. When Reggie hesitated he removed his glasses once more and smiled at her. He was better looking than she had first realised, Reggie thought.

"There was a child's toothbrush in the bathroom," Reggie said.

George erupted with scorn. "A toothbrush? That's it? Did they have any boy's clothes? Any comic books, any kid's shoes, any anything? I got to apologise to you, officer. She just doesn't have a clue."

"He wasn't there so he was wearing his clothes," Reggie said uncertainly. She could tell by the trooper's face that it wasn't enough.

"The only clothes he had? I don't think so."

The trooper replaced the glasses and started for the car door.

"I don't believe the man we're looking for would be travelling with a woman," he said. "If you wouldn't mind just giving me the names of those single men you've got, we'll run them through the computer."

George escorted the trooper to the office to find the names of the registered guests but Reggie did not accompany them. She had crossed her arms over her chest and was standing her ground in the courtyard, studying cabin six. She was still there when the trooper returned, opened his car door and slid behind the wheel.

"Well, if you should happen to get a single male, powerfully built, with a nine- or ten-year-old boy with him, give us a call, will you?"

"You bet," said George. "First thing. Should we ask for you personally?"

"That won't be necessary," the trooper said, groaning inwardly at the thought. "Just call the State police and they'll send a detective to check things out. OK?"

"You bet."

As the trooper drove off he tried to imagine how many calls they would get answering that description. He was glad he wasn't going anywhere with his son this weekend. Half the divorced fathers in the state were going to be investigated if they had the misfortune to sleep overnight with their children. It wouldn't make any difference to someone like these motel owners if the child was a boy or a girl, either, he thought. The switchboard would be ringing off the wall with a description that vague. This was worse than a wild-goose chase. This was a needle in a pin factory.

"He seemed a little slow to be much of a cop," George said to Reggie as the patrol car pulled away. "Nice guy, but not too bright."

"They don't pick them because they're bright," Reggie said. Her eyes were still on cabin six as if she could see through the walls. "You don't see many college professors driving around in squad cars and asking questions."

"He was bright enough to know the difference between a woman and a man," George scoffed. "They never go after women for this kind of thing."

"What kind of thing is it?"

"Whatever it is," George said, his voice rising defensively. "Obviously something dangerous. Obviously something violent. They're after a big hulk, right? Women don't commit violent crimes ... They get you in

213

other ways." He waited for Reggie to rise to the bait, but she was ignoring him.

"They needle and nag you to death," he said, watching for her reaction. She continued to study Dee's cabin. It wasn't nearly as much fun if she didn't fight back. George kept at it but without much enthusiasm. "They get illogical and silly. That'll drive you nuts in the long run, believe me. That'll kill you just as dead as a slug in the head if you have to put up with it long enough. It's amazing I'm still on my feet at all."

"What about the toothbrush then?" she asked suddenly, still not looking at him.

George laughed cruelly. She had the mind of a child. A girl child. "I don't know," he laughed.

"What are they doing with a child's toothbrush?" she demanded. She turned abruptly to glare at him as if he owed her an explanation. "Answer me that, if you're so smart."

She had been listening to him, he realised with relief. It troubled him when she genuinely paid no attention to him, it made him feel alone and foolish. She could pretend to ignore him as much as she wanted as long as he knew she was really listening to him. It was when she truly shut him out that he couldn't stand it.

"I don't know, maybe she has sensitive teeth."

"Oh, for heaven's sake." Although she had thought that at first herself, it now seemed a woefully weak explanation.

"They don't have anything else that belongs to a child," he said.

"And why does the husband go out only after dark?"

"You know why."

"I know what she's told you," Reggie said.

"That's good enough for me," said George.

"I know it's good enough for you. But you'd believe anything your girlfriend told you."

214

"She's not my girlfriend."

"Not for lack of trying on your part," she said.

"Might as well talk to the trees," he said. He turned back towards the office. "Might as well howl at the wind. Just trying to explain things to you has given me a sore throat," he said. He put his hand on his neck and coughed exploratorily. "It really is sore," he said. "I'm going in ... You coming?"

"You're not getting a cold, are you?" She would have to nurse him for a week. He was such a baby when he was sick.

"I need some of that tea and honey and lemon juice you make," he said.

As if she had a special recipe, she thought. It was just tea and honey and lemon juice, as simple as that, and for forty years he'd acted like it was a magic potion that only she could make. So he wouldn't have to. So he could lie back and moan and fill a paper bag with used tissues and act like he was paralysed. As if he needed much of an excuse.

"I'll make you some," she sighed.

As they walked towards the office, George put his arm over her shoulders and Reggie allowed it to stay that way.

Dee felt wonderful. Her head was swimming with plans and notions. There didn't seem to be anything she couldn't aspire to, nothing she couldn't accomplish. The world was her oyster, and she already had the pearl. He stood before her now for inspection, his hair newly washed and slicked down so that the parting looked as if it had been drawn with a ruler, his ears cleaned, his teeth brushed and smelling of mint.

"Hands," she said and Bobby held out his hands, finger-nails up while Ash hovered nervously behind him. The boy's skin was softly pink and still slightly wrinkled from

215

his bath. The nails were clean and the cuticles were pushed back to show neat half moons of white. He had started to chew his fingers last week but Dee had quickly put a stop to that. No boy of hers was going into the world with his fingers always around his mouth, his nails bitten off; it reflected so badly on her. As if she didn't know enough to break him of his bad habits. As if any boy of hers had any troubles to make him gnaw at himself in the first place.

"Oh, Tommy, aren't you the handsomest little man?" she crowed. "Aren't you just my perfect, perfect little boy?"

She fell to her knees and drew him to her in an embrace. She hugged as she believed in doing all things, fully and energetically. Dee hated it when people held back from her, when loved ones tried to pull away or didn't give of themselves as freely as she did. She had been forced to have a little talk with Tommy about that, too, but he understood her now. His little arms went around her back and squeezed her tight until Dee determined it was enough.

She pulled away suddenly and squinted at him, her head tilted to one side. "Aren't you forgetting something?"

Ash held his breath and Bobby's eyes widened with fright. His mouth fell open.

"Who do you love?"

"I love you, Dee," Bobby said quickly. "I love you."

"Did you see his face, Ash? What a scared little rabbit you looked like, Tommy. As if you had anything in the world to be scared about. Don't you know that Ash and I will always be here to take care of you?"

Bobby cried from relief as much as fright. He thought he had made another mistake, he thought she was going to punish him again. It came like that, so swiftly, mysteriously, like a hurricane that roared at him out of a blue sky. He tried so hard to please her, to give her exactly what she wanted, but still the raging storms came no matter what he did, and they came more frequently and more violently all the time.

He forced a smile on his lips but he couldn't stop the tears which came spontaneously, nor the running of his nose. He tried to sniff so she wouldn't hear; she hated when he was messy and sloppy and trouble.

"I know you will," he said, pushing his smile even wider.

But this time she found his tears endearing. She kissed them from his cheeks, cooing as his mother had done in the past that seemed so long ago. He could never predict her and never be sure he had placated her. He was safe only after she had used the wire on him, when he lay in the tub with Ash tending to him, for Dee always slept then, falling on to the bed with exhaustion. And sadness, Ash said. Disappointment and sadness that Bobby had caused. For he knew he had brought it on himself. He understood very little else about it, but he knew it was his own fault.

Dee was on her feet again, pulsing with the need to be on the go.

"Well, let's get you dressed," she said. "We're going out."

As Dee pulled on his shorts, held his trouser legs for him to step into, buttoned his shirt, Bobby tried desperately to control his fear. Things were always worse when they returned from a trip. Her expectations were higher when they were in the presence of other people; her plunge into despair and disappointment more precipitous, the beating more savage.

As Dee worked his socks on to his feet, Bobby looked down at the place in her hair where her scalp showed through the part and the dark roots grew before they turned to blonde. Behind her, Ash stood, smiling encouragement, but Bobby could see that he, too, was nervous as his big friend rubbed the palms of his hands against his thighs.

Ash could set Dee off, too, and his nervousness was a bad sign. Dee missed nothing, Bobby was convinced. Ash thought she could read his mind and Bobby was not sure she could not. She certainly picked up on the slightest thing and Ash's nerves could cause her to turn on Bobby as surely as any mistake of his own. When the atmosphere was not right, Dee looked for a cause and the cause was always the boy.

She finished tying his shoes and looked up.

"What wrong?" she demanded.

"Nothing, Dee."

"You don't look very excited about going out."

"I am! I really am!"

"I plan these treats for you, you know. It's not easy for me to work and take care of our home and turn right around and go out again. But I'm willing to do it for you."

"Thank you, Dee."

"All I ask is a little appreciation and some proper behaviour."

"Yes, Dee. I'll be good."

"I know you will. You're my perfect little angel. I know you won't let me down … And don't you look handsome? Doesn't he look handsome, Ash?"

"He's so handsome."

Dee winked conspiratorially at Bobby. "As if he would know. Who's handsome, Ash?"

"Tommy is handsome."

"Who else?"

"Cary Grant is handsome. Gregory Peck is handsome. Robert Taylor is handsome."

Dee chuckled, still enlisting Bobby on her side. Bobby smiled uncertainly.

"Well, you've got those right," she said, then, to Bobby, "all those old movies. And who's the handsomest of them all?"

"Gregory Peck."

"Almost right."

"Cary Grant?"

"The handsomest of them all is our own Tommy," Dee said. She lifted Bobby's hand over his head like a champion.

Ash grinned and applauded. "I know," he said.

Dee was at the door. "I'll get the car," she said.

Ash moved Bobby with him into the bathroom, out of the line of sight from the door.

"And don't muss his hair."

Dee was gone. Bobby stood passively as Ash removed the spread from the bed. They did not speak because there seemed to be nothing to say. With Bobby wrapped in the bedspread and cradled in his arms, Ash turned off the light and rushed into the darkness outside. The television continued to flicker in the empty room.

Reggie felt awful, as if she had scarcely enough energy left to breathe, and yet she couldn't sleep. The cold had raced through her throat and head and settled into her lungs with such vehemence that she thought she had received not only her share of the illness but George's share as well. He had whined for a day, drunk his tea with lemon and honey then passed the germs on to her as he did so many other things, leaving her with all the work, confident that she would deal with it. She was up with the cough half the night, hacking fruitlessly against a phlegm that would not loosen. George had turned to the sofa as a bed, determined to get his night's rest despite

Reggie's discomfort, so Reggie was upstairs in bed alone, propped up on several pillows into a semirecubent position, drowsing between outbursts from her chest.

At that hour there was little to do besides look out the window at the night. Her eyes hurt too much to read, her brain rejected television. She watched the stars, trying to find the constellations her father had pointed out to her decades ago when the nights were darker and stars larger and more brilliant. And she watched cabin six. Because she could, she had but to turn her head to the side to see it; and because she wanted to.

She saw the woman come out of the cabin and into the car. It was the same drill as before. She came from the light to the dark, opened the car, turned off the interior lights, then returned to the door of the cabin. When it opened again the interior lights were off but the bluish-green brilliance of the television set was enough to reveal the shape of a man, a huge man, as he rushed into the car. He seemed as big as a bear with a chest as large as two men's yet he vanished into the car like a wraith. Again the woman drove towards the highway with her headlights off and again when she came within the light of the road sign, only her silhouette was visible in the car.

It was the third time Reggie had seen it happen and it was exactly the same each time. Two nights ago, on her second sleepless night in bed, Reggie had seen the car return. She saw the sweep of the headlights as the car turned in off the highway and then sudden darkness once more as the lights were extinguished. Only the woman was visible in the road-sign light but when the cabin door was opened, Reggie could see the shape of the bear-man again in the television glow, scurrying into the room like a frightened animal.

Only a fool such as George would believe that nothing strange was going on in there. She had joked with the trooper about vampires, but there was something just as sinister afoot, no doubt about it. And when she was well again, she would find out exactly what it was.

Reggie was seized by a spasm of coughing that brought tears to her eyes. When it released her, she slumped back against the pillows. She would wait until they returned. She would watch the pattern repeat itself, try to measure the dimensions of the bear-man. When she reported things to the State police she wanted to be very precise. She wanted no scoffing about "proof," this time. She would wait; she would be awake anyway.

15

Becker slept for an hour then woke, as fully alert as if he had slept the night through. He didn't move when he woke, just opened his eyes and lay still, listening, assessing his environment. As always he had a reaction to the darkness, a quick, involuntary flinch of the nervous system that he grasped and controlled before it could escalate into fear. There was no reason for fright, he told himself, no cause for alarm. His heart was pounding and his skin tingled with the rush of adrenalin, but he forced himself to lie still and listen.

"He told himself the time was now, not then. The demons of the dark lay in his past – or in his soul – but not here within this room. It was an ordinary night in his adult life, he told himself. The nocturnal noises could all be accounted for, the other breath came from the woman beside him. There was no tread upon the stair. His tormentors were long since dead, the feet that trod so heavily as they descended into the cellar had ceased to move years ago. His only torment now came from within, he reminded himself, and it required no racing heart to deal with it. There was no way to flee it in any event.

He continued to lie very still and to listen to Karen's breathing. He was accustomed to jolting awake like this, sometimes soaked in his own sweat; he was used to the struggle to control himself, his reason straining against instinct and the unwarranted alarms of his subconscious. In recent years his reason had always won the battle and in time his mind would be in command of his body. Anxiety remained with him always in the dark, but Becker was well used to anxiety, he regarded it as an almost pleasant companion compared to what lay in wait to take its place.

Karen's breath was loud, slightly irregular, the breathing of a dreamer. Becker rolled his head to the side to look at her. She was facing him, her mouth open slightly, her hair falling across her face so that it moved slightly with each exhalation. She had kicked off the single sheet they used in the summer heat and her T-shirt had ridden up her body, revealing her bare legs and stomach which looked ghostly pale in the night. She needed more time off from work, Becker thought. She needed to spend some time in the sun to get some colour in her skin, but he knew she would take no vacation as long as Lamont was on the loose.

He could understand her obsession, it was the way he approached a case as well, but Becker could not remember a case that had yielded so little, so slowly. After weeks of grinding, they seemed no closer to a solution that when they had started, and the fault, Becker thought, was his. Either they were missing something or they were working on false assumptions to begin with. In most cases of serial murder the hardest part was the initial discovery that a number of murders were related. Or, as was more often the case, that any murders had been committed at all. Frequently a serial killer was a hoarder of bodies as well. Dyce had dissected and boiled the bodies and stored the skeletons under his kitchen floor. Leon Brade had used the hair of his victims to stuff the crocheted pillows he kept in his grandmother's house. In those cases, to discover one body was to discover most of them and after that it was a simple man-hunt with Becker after a fleeing quarry. The hunt might take longer or shorter, but once the quarry was identified it was a straightforward if painstaking business. The motive and methods of the deaths were almost irrelevant, an afterthought to be dealt with at a trial, but not essential matters in the chase. With Lamont there were bodies in plenty, but not so much as a scent of the quarry.

They must be looking in the wrong places, Becker thought. Maybe the killer's method that Becker had hypothesised was all wrong and all the time and effort that had been spun off it was just so much waste.

Becker eased out of the bed as softly as he could. Karen's breathing and position did not change. His wife, Cindi, had slept as lightly as a cat, often waking if he so much as tossed in bed. Often he would come joltingly awake as he had just now, doing nothing more than opening his eyes, and her warm hand would slide across his chest to comfort him. As if she were connected to him in some psychic way that he could not understand. Becker tried to shake off the thought. He did not want to start thinking about Cindi now, not as he slipped out of Karen's bed. If he started to dwell on Cindi he could be at it all night.

He felt along the floor until he found his underpants. Becker and Karen had made love upon going to bed – as they had every night – and had fallen asleep immediately afterwards. Becker's clothes were scattered across the room wherever Karen had removed and discarded them.

Wearing his shorts, he slipped silently out of the bedroom and into the living room. Still moving in the darkness, Becker went to the window and looked out at the night sky. The moon was the thinnest silver but the stars seemed to be at their brightest. Becker stepped on to the porch and studied them. Stargazing had become an obsolete activity to all but astronomers, he thought, and what a shame. If one could get far enough away from city lights the night sky still twinkled and shone with as much fascination as it had millennia ago, night-time's eternal treat for the sleepless. When on a mountain climbing foray, Becker would lie for hours watching the slowly wending parade of the heavens. Although human nature seemed to Becker to be getting ever more perverse, heavenly nature remained the same, beautiful, impossibly distant, and available to anyone who would take the trouble to look.

Checking first that no neighbours were about, Becker stepped on to the lawn and looked at the house. The grass was cool and damp against his naked feet. A faint breeze blew the warm night air against his skin. Becker walked to an elm that grew close to the sidewalk. Standing in the shelter of the tree so that he was all but invisible to anyone looking from either the street or the house, Becker studied the window where the light shone from Jack's room.

To steal a child, he thought. To want someone else's child badly enough to steal him. To change forever the boy's life, his parents' lives, the lives of his siblings, his grandparents, the widening skein of lives connected with the family. To take the risk each time of being caught and then to tire of the prize that had already cost so much in human suffering. To abuse the child to the point of death – and then to kill him and discard him as so much rubbish, to toss him aside like one more bundle of roadside litter.

It made no sense of course, but sense was hardly the point. What it lacked for Becker was the emotional linkage that was necessary for him to follow the killer's tortured route. There seemed no handles for Becker to grasp the killer's mind. In other cases Becker had always managed to find a way to grip the thoughts of the madman. He had been forced to go deep within himself to uncover the murderous impulse in his own soul in order to do it, the price had always been high, but he had always done it. The intuitive connection had always given him the scent of the killer and allowed Becker to follow him. Even when the trail had gone cold, Becker had always had the image of the killer in his mind because, at least for a moment of chilling introspection, he had been able to step into the killer's skin.

As he had told Karen, it was neither trick nor magic, but an act of courage and honesty that allowed him to look at himself without disguise or hypocrisy. But in this case it had abandoned him. He knew only what it was to be Lamont's victim, not Lamont. There was something wrong, something hidden in the crime, or in Lamont, that Becker could not find within himself.

Becker stared at Jack's window. He imagined himself standing here now with the heart of a monster. But a human monster, a child who had grown to adulthood and become a monster, twisted and shaped that way by someone or something, or a thousand insistent somethings, so that now he stood as misshappen within as a gothic gargoyle. Becker imagined that he had come to take the boy who slept within that house before him. To slip within the room, past the sleeping parents, to lift the child from his bed and seal away into the night. Why? To what end? Becker knew the ultimate end, of course, the child must die, but killing him was not the point. The point lay in the six weeks of living. And it was not sexual. That was the most bizarre aspect to Becker. It did not conform with anything he knew or had intuited about the other monsters who came before this one. Sex was always a part of it.

Then forget the part he did not understand, he decided. Start with what he knew, let that draw him into the rest. First to steal the child. Experience that. Feel what Lamont feels when he sees the victim, sense the excitement, the dread, the irrepressible urge.

Becker stared at the light in Jack's window until it seemed to narrow and focus itself. The light became a tunnel in the darkness, the only way to move, the only way to get where he needed to go. Silently, Becker approached the tunnel of light.

Like his mother, Jack had kicked off the sheet and lay exposed upon the bed. He wore shortie pajamas with a fire engine motif. The walls of room were papered with athletes in action, kicking, catching, running, vaulting, and posters of football players adorned the walls. Jack looked even smaller and sweeter by comparison. He seemed to lie in a pool of innocence within his room, his little boy's limbs and sleeping face in sharp contrast with the hard-edged adults upon the walls.

As he peered through the window at such sweet guilelessness, Becker tried to feel the urge to violate it, the raging, irresistible compulsion to have it, to seize the innocence and make it his own by devouring it.

The boy moved slightly in his sleep, rolling towards the window. It was, if there is such a thing, the face of an angel and the monster at the window had to have it. Not because he hated it, for who could hate an angel? But because he loved it. The monster loved his victims. Lamont stole the boys because he loved them. It had to start from love, Becker felt. Only later did something go wrong and turn that love into an emotion that ended in death. But now, seeing the boy for the first time, the sense of love was close to awe. The desire to possess the boy was enormous, it made his body ache with hope. The monster turned from the window and started towards the door.

Karen was dreaming that someone was breaking into the house and then she was suddenly awake and aware that the exterior door was sighing shut against its pneumatic stopper. She was out of bed and had her service automatic in her hand before she remembered that Becker was with her. When she saw his side of the bed was empty she realised he had already heard the noise and responded.

She came around the door in a crouch, her weapon extended and held in both hands. Pausing for her heart to quiet, she moved forward into the darkened house, stopping every few feet to listen.

The living room was empty, and the kitchen. The light from Jack's room was on and it pulled her towards it like a beacon. Outside her son's room she paused again, her skin tingling with anxiety. She could hear the boy, moaning slightly as if in a dream, but she was aware of something else, another presence in the room.

Karen stepped into the doorway and saw a naked man leaning over her son.

"Don't touch him, get your hands off him!" she said. Her voice was as menacing as a growl in the dark.

"I wasn't," Becker said. He turned his head slowly, very slowly, to face Karen.

Karen saw who he was now but her position did not change, her hands held the pistol steady and pointed at the centre of his torso.

"Stand away," she said. Her voice was still like the rasp of a file on metal.

Becker moved two steps from the bed and slowly lifted his hands above his head.

Karen looked at Jack who tossed slightly in his sleep. He was obviously all right, undisturbed. She looked again at Becker, taking time enough now to really look at him. For the first time she realised he was wearing shorts. In her initial panicked glance she had thought he was completely naked. The look on his face was wary, watchful, but not guilty.

Karen lowered the gun. "Come out," she said, her voice now a whisper. She was immensely relieved that they had not awakened Jack. It would have been some sight to see, her mother waving a gun at her near-naked lover who was standing over his bed. How many years of therapy would be needed for that one, she thought.

Becker followed Karen into the living room, his hands still over his head.

"Stop that," she said. She turned on a lamp and sat in the overstuffed chair opposite the sofa, the gun in her lap, no longer pointing at him.

Becker lowered his hands and sat on the sofa. Karen glanced at him and then away. His face was a mask of grinning irony. It did little to hide the hurt in his eyes.

"I thought ..." she started. She could not say what she thought.

"You thought I was going to abuse him," Becker said.

"I heard someone come in the house, it's, what time is it, it's three in the morning. I thought you were a burglar."

"You knew it was me."

"Christ, Becker, it's three o'clock in the morning ..."

"You saw I wasn't in bed, you knew it was me."

"Coming in and out of the house in the middle of the night? Why would I think it was you? There's a naked man leaning over my son ..."

"And you knew it was me and you thought ..."

"I reacted, I just reacted, I didn't think anything ..."

"You're still thinking it. I don't blame you, I'd be thinking the same thing."

229

"I wasn't …" she said weakly.

"The world seems to be full of it these days. We're swimming in it, it comes from everywhere, priests and fathers and boyfriends and baby-sitters … Paranoia seems very justified."

"I know you, John, I know you wouldn't …"

"How? How do you know?"

"Because I know you."

Becker laughed. Cruelly, Karen thought.

"Nobody knows anybody that well. Including their shrink."

Karen paused. The automatic felt cool and heavy on her bare leg. They faced each other in silence across the width of the room. "What are you trying to say?" she asked.

"I'm saying you were right to react the way you did. As it happens, you were wrong in what you thought, but you were right to think that way."

"You don't mind that I thought – just for a second – that you were going to … ?"

"I mind intensely," Becker said. "I just don't blame you for it."

Karen paused again. She did not want to ask the obvious question but she knew she had to. When she did it would change her relationship with Becker, if it had not already been irretrievably altered. Not his answer but simply the fact that she asked, for within the question was the implicit demand for an alibi, an inescapable assumption of lack of trust.

Still, she had to ask the question. "What were you doing?"

Becker was silent for a long time. Karen watched him absorb the question and its implication and the pain that it caused him.

"Working," he said at last.

When he did not elaborate she asked, "Did you go outside?"

"Yes."

"Dressed like that?"

Becker looked at himself as if assessing his costume.

"Yeah."

She saw his jaw was set, he would be volunteering nothing.

"I don't want to interrogate you, John."

"Fine."

"But I don't understand."

"You wouldn't if I explained, either," he said.

"You were working?"

"Uh-huh."

She found it hard to look him in the face. He looked like a boy accused of lying by his parents for the first time, pained by the accusation, resigned that he would not be believed and saddened by the loss of innocence. What was lacking was the recognition that he had come within a breath of having been shot. He was, she concluded, the strangest man she had ever loved; maybe the strangest she had ever known, but also the most interesting.

"I'd like to go back to bed," she said.

They both lay awake the rest of the night, side by side but not touching, each pretending to be asleep.

As dawn approached Karen asked softly, "What did you learn?"

Becker answered as readily as if they had been talking for hours. "He loves them," he said. "Lamont loves those boys."

16

They drove in a different direction again. It was their fifth
trip away from the motel and Dee had chosen a different
route each time, leaving Bobby confused and without a
mental map of where they were or where they were going.
In time, of course, usually within a half hour or forty-five
minutes, they would come to an area whose dimensions
were familiar even if the particulars were not. They were
still in America, after all, and the fast-food chains and
the franchised shops were the same everywhere.

Ash coaxed Bobby into taking one more bite. The boy
had had no appetite for days and Ash ministered to him
like a nurse, trying to keep his delinquency from Dee's
attention.

"You have to eat some," Ash said.

"I did," Bobby said.

"That wasn't even a bite. Eat this much, just this
much." Ash tore off a small portion of the burger, removed the bun and lettuce, scraped off the condiments
with his finger. He held the piece of meat before Bobby's
mouth like a mother bird with a nestling.

Bobby shook his head, his lips closed. Ash glanced
anxiously through the car window. Dee had found a
single mother inside the hamburger restaurant and had
struck up a conversation by admiring the woman's two

children. Now she was pointing outside, towards Bobby, her face gleaming with pride. The other mother looked out politely.

"Wave," Ash said, lifting Bobby's arm. "Smile."

The boy managed an ugly grimace, trying to smile while battling the onset of tears. Bobby wept all the time now, often with no provocation, and it was all Ash could do to keep him from doing it in Dee's presence. Ash waggled the boy's arm at the elbow and his hand flapped loosely. There was nothing he could do about the smile, but from the distance Dee seemed not to notice. She sat in the booth with the other woman, her head tossed back in laughter. She reached across the table and tousled the hair of the children while the mother regarded her uncertainly.

"You know how she'll be if you don't eat," Ash said, putting the morsel to Bobby's lips once more.

The boy opened his mouth and chewed weakly. At least he still cares, Ash thought. At least he can still be frightened. When he stopped caring at all, it would all be over. Ash would help him then. He had tried to help the boy all along but he was never able to do enough. Only at the end could he really help.

Ash put the rest of the burger in his own mouth and ate it so that Dee would not know how little Bobby had consumed. He slurped at the milk in Bobby's cup, draining most of it, then carefully wiped the boy's face clean. Dee did not tolerate messiness. Not with Tommy. She would abide it with Ash, but Tommy reflected on her personally.

"Be sure to tell her how much fun you're having," Ash said. Inside the restaurant, Dee had stood up. She looked again towards the car, then bent and hugged both of the children who submitted reluctantly. With a smile and a gesture of the hand she left the mother and the children.

Ash could see the mother looking at her children, then following Dee out of the restaurant with her eyes. She said something to the children and they responded animatedly.

Dee strode across the parking lot joyfully, rising up on the balls of her feet with every step as if on springs. Her eyes were alight and her smile split her face from ear to ear. She started talking as soon as she made eye contact with Ash, while she was still in the lot, before he could hear her through the closed windows.

Ash nudged Bobby, making him turn to face her.

"Be happy," Ash said.

Dee swept into the car like a wind, smelling of mint and excitement. "She liked you, so did her kids, she said you were so cute." She kissed Bobby on the cheek and Ash noted with relief that the boy did not pull away or resist her at all.

"Did you eat your supper?"

"He ate it all, Dee," Ash said.

"What a good boy!"

"I'm having a wonderful time," Bobby said.

"Are you, darling? Is my sweet boy having a good time?"

"I like coming here with you."

"Oh, and I like coming here with you." She embraced him, squeezing him against her so hard Ash heard him grunt.

"I tell you what, I think you deserve a treat. Would you like that? Would you like a treat?"

"Yes, please."

"Then here we go, one treat coming up for my angel boy." She hugged him again. Her face was turned towards Ash, but her eyes did not focus on him. She had not looked at Ash since she entered the car.

"Who do you love?" she asked.

"I love you, Dee."

She started the car and pulled out of the parking lot. "And I love you, Tommy," she said. "I love you so much."

She put her hand on Bobby's knee and left it there as she drove. Ash watched the boy carefully. He was not smiling, he was not weeping. He seemed to be somewhere else entirely.

The clerk's name was Carelle and she worked evenings and hated it because she wanted to be home with her own children instead of selling clothes to other peoples'. Her two sons were at home now with Carelle's mother who fed them and talked to them and put them to bed the way her mother had done with Carelle. Being raised by a grandmother did not seem unusual to Carelle, but nonetheless she resented it for her sons because it deprived her of the pleasure of seeing those two fine boys as much as she wanted to. Still, working evenings allowed her to be home to get them off to school at an hour when her mother had already left for her day job, and her mother was home in time so they weren't alone more than an hour after school. The family needed the two salaries to get by, but not leaving the boys alone was the main thing. She didn't want them just sitting there staring at the television the way so many did, or, far worse, she didn't want them out on the street where you could learn so many ways to shorten your life.

She didn't see her own boys as much as she wanted, but she certainly knew what a healthy boy looked like, and this boy wasn't it. He stood about fifteen feet away by the rack of short-sleeve shirts that were marked down by twenty per cent, standing with a man who looked to Carelle like her idea of a caveman that somebody had stuck into jeans and given a quick shave and haircut. The boy was pale in a way no white boy should be in mid-summer, there were black bags under his eyes and even the areas above the eyes looked as if they'd been daubed with coal. The eyes themselves were dead. They weren't staring, they weren't looking around the way any normal boy's eyes would be doing, they were just – there. Stuck in his head as if somebody had placed them on the face but forgot to turn them on. The boy stood there like it was all he had the strength for, like some creature Carelle had seen in the movies, one of the living dead or one of Dracula's victims. As if all his blood had been drained out, she thought. And skinny? The boy was not healthy.

His mother, on the other hand, would not hold still. The woman jabbered like she was on the hustle, she talked so fast Carelle would have held on to her purse with both hands if it wasn't locked away in the back room. Or like she was on speed, more like it. Carelle didn't much like looking the customers directly in the eye, but she didn't miss much, either. This woman's pupils weren't dilated, but her eyes had a gleam in them that looked weird to Carelle.

And she didn't know anything about kids' sizes, either. She was trying to dress the boy in clothes that would ride him like tent. Asking for a ten-twelve for that poor little thing.

"You talking about that boy?" Carelle asked, moving her head towards the boy.

"That's him, that's my Tommy. Isn't he beautiful?"

"He's a beautiful boy," Carelle said without enthusiasm.

"Isn't he beautiful?" The woman waved at the boy as if he was all the way across the store, not just a few steps away. The boy waved back and put some kind of look on his face that was maybe a smile. The caveman just stood

236

there with his paw on the boy's shoulder, like he was holding him upright.

"Yes, ma'am. He sure is." Carelle thought of her own boys with their bouncing energy, their eager eyes. "But he can't wear no size ten-twelve."

"Of course he can," the woman said. "I measured him myself."

"Yes, ma'am, I'm sure you did, but I can tell without measuring him he ain't no ten. He too skinny for a ten."

"Skinny? My boy is not skinny." The woman sounded horrified, as if the thought had never occurred to her. Carelle wondered what the woman saw when she looked at the boy. Couldn't be the same thing Carelle saw.

"Didn't mean skinny," she said. "Just thin. He be thin."

The woman was studying the boy now, looking at him as if she had never seen him before. Carelle could see her face twisting all up in a dangerous looking way.

"He's only as thin as he should be," the woman said.

"Yes, ma'am."

"He's thin the way a boy ought to be." He face did not look as if she were convinced.

"That's probably it," Carelle said.

The woman took a step towards the boy who jerked backwards as if he were about to be hit. When she turned to face Carelle again the woman's face was blushing red. It wasn't shame, Carelle thought. It was pure anger, but it wasn't directed at Carelle. It seemed to Carelle that the woman was mad at the boy.

"I'll just see if we have a ten in that colour," Carelle said.

Her supervisor was behind the woman, suddenly. Carelle had noticed Ellen moving in her direction a while ago, then she had lost track of her while watching the woman and the boy. Normally Carelle knew exactly

237

where her supervisor was at all times, because most of the time it was right behind her, peering over her shoulder as if she couldn't be trusted. This time, however, Carelle was glad to see her, let her take a little heat off the crazy woman who looked like she was about to explode. Ellen was good at dealing with the white customers, they seemed to think she understood them better than Carelle did.

"Is there a problem?" Ellen asked, folding her hands together in front of her, the way she did, like she was holding on to a knife that was sticking out of her chest. Like it pained her but she was going to go right on ahead and do a good job anyway, just keep smiling, never mind her.

"Wants a ten-twelve for that boy," Carelle said, her voice falling into a mumble the way it did when there was trouble coming. "Getting her a ten-twelve, that what she wants, but he ain't no ten."

The supervisor was about to speak sharply to Carelle when she noticed the boy.

"I think I should know his size, after all," the customer was saying. She talked on and on, an edge of something to her voice, a franticness, something close to hysteria, but Ellen listened with only half an ear. She stepped closer to the boy and the boy and the huge man with him stepped away from her. This went beyond business, this wasn't about selling another shirt. This boy was deathly ill, and anyone could see it.

Ellen looked from the boy to Carelle who was watching her from under her brows, then to the customer who had stopped talking abruptly.

"This boy needs a doctor," Ellen said, surprising herself with the effrontery but feeling compelled to speak.

The man and the boy had already turned and were walking away swiftly, the man's big hand in the middle of the boy's back, propelling him.

238

"Oh, really?" the customer said. "Thank you so much for your opinion, but I think I know what my boy needs."

The customer stormed off, a look on her face that was ready to kill. Ellen watched them go, sensing Carelle moving up beside her.

"You right about that much," Carelle said.

It was the first moment of solidarity Ellen could remember having felt with the clerk.

"Well, any fool could see it," Ellen said.

"That's what I mean," Carelle said.

Reggie saw the headlights hit her ceiling then vanish, then heard the crunch of tyres on gravel. She lifted herself on her elbow and peered out the window in time to see the darkened car, wraith-like, come to a halt outside cabin six. The monster with the legs of a man and the body of two people hurried from the car and into the cabin, his form lighted briefly by the flicker from the television set.

Reggie watched the cabin for several minutes before easing herself back down on the bed, trying to divine its secret from the noises of the night. She was feeling better. Tomorrow she would be able to get out of bed, she was sure of it. There would be so much work to do, so much that George had left undone, or done wrong, but she had never minded hard work, thank goodness. And when her work was done, she would pay another visit to cabin six, but this time when someone was there. Whatever their dirty secret was, she would find it out and clean it up.

Dee moved in her sleep and touched Bobby and he was immediately wide awake. Almost as soon as he was aware of where he was he was weeping. Dee liked to fall asleep on her side with Bobby spooned in behind her, one of his arms over her body. Later, when she slept, he could roll away and try to find sleep in his own position, a pillow clutched to his chest, his legs tucked into it, but if she stirred in the night or became aware of his absence, she would moan and reach out for him, demanding some touch and reassurance of his closeness before drifting into unconsciousness once more.

He wept silently, the pillow pressed against his face. Moving as slowly as he could, he rolled to his other side, away from Dee, so that he could face Ash who sat against the door, watching television with the volume turned down. Just seeing his big friend was a comfort to Bobby and sometimes they whispered to each other in the night while Dee slept. Sometimes they would giggle at the sounds she made in her sleep, the little puffs and snorts and sighs that made it seem as if she were having a conversation with her dreams. Occasionally she would emit anguished cries and sit up, startled and sweating, eyes rolling in terror. She would cling to Bobby then as he clung to his pillow until the terror passed. He would have to tell her again and again that he loved her and that he would never let anyone hurt her, never, never, never.

But mostly she slept through the night as if exhausted by the ebullience of her days. Bobby and Ash could whisper together then and the big man would tell him the stories from the television. Bobby could not get out of bed to watch with him because that was not allowed, but he could listen to Ash's stumbling, garbled versions and construct his own movies in his mind to distract him from his life. Eventually, holding very still so as not to awaken the pain, Bobby would fall asleep again, lulled by his friend's voice.

This night Bobby saw something he had never seen before. Ash sat in his usual position facing the television, back against the door, but his head had fallen forward on to his chest and to one side. The big man was asleep.

"Ash," Bobby whispered. "Ash."

The sight of his sleeping friend frightened him. Ash was his one constant, a presence he could rely on to be there at any time, day or night. Dee came and went, capricious and wilful as a storm, but Ash was always there, always the same, friendly, solicitous, concerned. Loving. Even when Dee savaged Bobby, purging her furious demons on his back and legs, it was Ash who held him still so he would not squirm, Ash who spoke into his ear as the lashes fell, telling him to be brave, be strong, hang on, hang on, hang on, and when the beatings stopped it was Ash's arms Bobby collapsed into, Ash who soothed him, bathed him, fed him, cared for him. Seeing him asleep was seeing him transmogrified into a different creature, a person with failings and weaknesses. A man whose strength was gone.

"Ash," he hissed. "Wake up. You said you'd kill people if you went to sleep. Ash! Ash!"

The big man slept on, his head rising and falling with each surge of his chest. Bobby watched him, fighting back the fear. If Ash killed someone because he slept, who would it be? Would he kill Dee? The thought thrilled him. Dee dead. His tormentor gone, her body still and rolled under the bed, out of sight. No longer touching him, embracing him, kissing him, hurting him, hurting him, hurting him. And then the guilt swept over him. Dee loved him, she said so. Ash said so. At times Bobby believed it himself. It was like wishing his mother dead.

He had not thought of his mother in some time now, it was almost as if she had ceased to exist. He had long since given up the hope that his father would burst through the door, that his mother would take him in her arms and make the pain subside. He had a new family now, strange and more violent than his first one, but still his. He depended on them as he had on the other for food, shelter, identity. Without them, he was alone.

His tears had dried but he began to weep once more now that he realised his new position. For the first time since he had followed Dee through the mall so long ago, he was alone.

It did not occur to Bobby to try to run away. He almost never thought about escape anymore. Like his parents, it had become a memory without reality.

He wept and held himself still and prayed for Ash to wake up.

Reggie was on her feet again and yelling at him and George was planning a trip to Arizona. Just pick up and go. Buy a mule and hike out to the mountains or desert or whatever was out there, and live by himself for awhile. He wasn't too old for a sleeping bag. He could eat beans out of a can and do as well as Reggie's cooking, and he wasn't too old to get a companion, either. She seemed to have forgotten that, she seemed to have lost sight of the fact that he was a very attractive man who could get another woman in the time it took to change his shirt. She had definitely forgotten who she was dealing with when she was dealing with George – but now was not the best time to remind her. Reggie was always mad as a wet hen after she got over being sick. She found fault with everything, especially George, and he had learned long ago that the best way to deal with it was to make himself scarce. If she thought everything was in such an awful mess, let her straighten it up herself. Maybe it would tire her out enough to calm her down.

While she was ripping through the kitchen, bitching about his housekeeping prowess, George slipped outside and hurried towards the stand of trees that divided the motel property from the lot belonging to the neighbour,

242

a small firm that sold and serviced business machines. The trees ran only three deep but George thought of them as his woods. If he was very still and Reggie wasn't searching for him very hard, he could stand in the shade of the spruce and feel as if he were somewhere else, somewhere in a different time when the forests enveloped everything and domesticity was nothing more than a temporary growth in a clearing, no more substantial, nor demanding of a man's time and consideration, than a squirrel's nest in a tree, doomed for disintegration in a year or two. George could shelter in the security of his woods and peer at the doings of the motel like something divorced from himself and his concern, as superior in philosophy and dignity as an Indian looking bemusedly at the first scratchings of the Pilgrims.

After a time, still leaning against his favourite tree where the bark was worn smooth from seven years of accommodating his shoulder, George saw Reggie come out of the office and head for cabin six as directly as if she were going to put out a fire. Dee's car was gone which meant that Reggie was going into the cabin again, or, if the husband was there, to confront him. In direct contradiction of George's order. In flagrant breach of his promise to Dee. Which left George with two alternatives. He could assert his authority and rush over there right now, grab Reggie by the scruff of the neck and drag her away before she did any damage – or he could not be a witness and therefore remain ignorant of her open defiance. George turned and walked into the parking lot of the business machines firm to see what they were up to these days.

Reggie had the appropriate key in her hand when she knocked on the door. She was in no mood for excuses or delays, one way or the other she was going in and she was

243

going to have some explanations. And if the answers didn't satisfy her then "Dee" and whoever was in there with her were history, she didn't care how much they had paid in advance.

In truth, things being what they were these days, it was very difficult to evict someone unless they were in flagrant violation of the law. If the cops weren't prepared to arrest them and haul them off, and the tenants understood their rights, it was a long and costly procedure to have them evicted. Most tenants had no clue to their rights, of course, and Reggie was prepared to rely on a combination of Dee's ignorance and her own self-righteous anger to get the woman out.

She rapped once on the door, then listened. It was hard to make out anything specific above the noise of the television set, but she thought she heard the sound of scuttling and whispered voices.

She rapped again, then put her key into the lock. The door opened three inches then was held by the chain, but it was enough for Reggie to hear clearly the panicked noises of someone in the bathroom. Guilty, she thought. The noises sounded guilty, as if Reggie had caught the monster "husband" in the midst of some filthy act. She did not want to think what.

"Open the door. This is the owner," she said firmly. It was important not to give the man time to think or he might come up with some courage that right now she had scared clean out of him.

"I know you're in there," she said. She could see the opening of the door but not into the bathroom itself. A dark-green plastic leaf bag lay on the floor just outside the bathroom. Reggie wondered what size garbage these people could have. Although some people used bags like that for suitcases these days. People with children.

The box of plastic gloves was still atop the dresser.

What on earth did they use those for? She shuddered to think. Everything she saw fed her outrage. She didn't know what was going on, but whatever it was, she didn't like it.

"Open this door or I'm coming in," she called. In truth she had no way to get in short of a hacksaw to cut the chain and she thought, not for the first time, that all the locks in the motel needed to be changed to ones that she could control. But for the expense, she would have done that job long ago. If George were the least bit handy, he could have done it. Even then he would have complained, of course. Siding with the tenants, as per usual. Babbling on about privacy and tenants' rights. George and his precious privacy. Nobody needed privacy unless they had something to hide, Reggie thought. Thinking of George only made her angrier and she pounded on the door.

"Right now!" she demanded, and, as if on command, the man stepped out of the bathroom and faced her.

At the first knock Ash was off the floor from his station by the door and into the bathroom in three strides, bundling Bobby in his arms like a loose package of so many sticks of wood, his hand clamped over the boy's mouth. His shoulder brushed the plastic garbage bag that Dee had brought home from work and it fluttered from the dresser to the floor.

The woman was yelling and Ash was panicked, but he knew what to do, Dee had taught him, he had done it before. He was to stay out of sight, simply stay out of sight until Dee returned. She would take care of it, she always knew how to take care of everything. Ash just had to hide with the boy until she came home.

Ash stood in the bathroom, clutching Bobby tightly to him, as if for protection. Everything was going to be all right, he whispered to the boy. Or he thought he was whispering but then wasn't sure if he wasn't just doing it in his mind. Bobby's eyes were staring at him over Ash's hand clamped over his mouth. As the boy wasted away his eyes seemed to grow bigger and bigger and now they looked enormous. And frightened.

The woman was yelling again. Ash made sure he spoke aloud this time as he whispered, "Don't be afraid, this will be OK, she'll go away and Dee will come back and take care of us." Bobby's eyes seemed to show understanding and Ash did his best to smile.

Then it was the woman again. Threatening to come in! Ash didn't know what to do, but he knew for a certainty that he couldn't allow her to come into the room. No one had ever actually come into the room before. When they came to the door Ash had just taken the boys and hidden until they left – but if she came in ... He could not let her in. It could not happen. He must not let it happen.

Ash placed Bobby in the empty bathtub.

"Don't make any noise," he said.

Bobby nodded his head. His eyes seemed to fill his face.

"Please, Bobby. Please, please, please. No noise, no noise."

Bobby squeezed his good-luck medal. He looked as frightened as Ash felt.

Ash closed the shower curtain, leaving the boy standing in the tub, the medal held in front of him as if to ward off witches. The big man left the bathroom, carefully closed the door behind him, then turned to face the woman who was yelling at him. He could see only one of her eyes peering through the crack of the outside door.

"Open this door, please," she said, but the "please" sounded like a threat.

Ash stared at her, uncertain what to do.

"Hurry up, now," Reggie insisted. "I'm the owner, let me in." The big man just stood there, staring at her. Reggie could not believe his size nor the kind of bovine stupidity on his face. It was like looking into the eyes of an ox.

"What?" he said finally, the sound rumbling up as if from some cavernous depth through a passage seldom used.

"What?" she repeated. "Well the bedspread, for one thing. Where is the bedspread?"

He swivelled his big head slowly towards the bed. To Reggie's chagrin the spread was there upon the bed where it belonged. Now they were trying to play tricks on her. It had been gone, she knew it.

"You're not allowed to take that out of the room, you know."

He was looking at her again, his movements slow and studied, as if he were moving under water. Reggie thought he must be on drugs. One thing was certain, this man was nobody's husband. Certainly not "Dee's". Certainly not that sharp, sly, energetic young woman's husband. She would just as likely be married to a steer in a feedlot. And if he wasn't her husband, then "Dee" was lying to them. Reggie didn't know what the woman's relationship was with this huge oaf, and she wasn't sure she wanted to know, but it wasn't marriage and that meant she was lying and if she was lying about one thing, she was probably lying about everything.

Reggie pushed at the door in annoyance, jolting it against the chain. The man was startled. As if I could force it open, Reggie thought. Just as stupid as he looks. And one thing was obvious, he was frightened by the thought of her coming in. Not just resistant; he was scared.

"What are you hiding in there?"

"Nobody," Ash said. He shook his head from side to side to demonstrate his innocence.

Reggie squinted her eyes, studying the giant. Nobody? Why not nothing?

"You let me in right this instant."

"I'm sick," Ash said.

"I have a right to come in there and I insist that you open this door right now."

"I'm sick," he repeated.

"I can call the police if I have to," she said. "Is that what you want me to do?"

Ash closed the door in her face and sat with his back against it while his mind raced in panic.

Bobby heard the woman's voice angrily haranguing Ash and he pulled back farther from the shower curtain until the coldness of the wall tiles against his back startled him. At first he knew only that his friend was in some kind of trouble. The hostility in her tone was unmistakable and it pained and frightened the boy to hear someone treating his friend that way. There was another fear, less well defined, that seemed to hover in the air, intensified in the seclusion of the bathroom, grew stronger still in the enclosed space of the tub behind the curtain. He had felt it in the first flurried moment following the initial knock on the door, felt it when Ash swept him into his arms, felt it when the big man pleaded – needlessly – for Bobby to remain quiet. It was a fear that was transmitted to him directly from Ash, but one that he harboured on his own, as well, and only now, trying to hear Ash speaking to the woman, did Bobby understand what the fear was. He was afraid of getting caught, of being found out. Ash's fear, Dee's fear, was Bobby's own. He crouched in the corner of the tub, as far from the door, and discovery, as he could get.

*

248

From his vantage point among the trees George could hear Reggie squawking at someone in cabin six, really going at it with the kind of rage she normally reserved for George himself. He had taken his stroll through the neighbour's parking lot, making a return loop when he heard his wife's voice rising in the distance. He re-entered his woods just to the side of cabin six. He moved closer to the cabin now, careful to keep out of Reggie's sight. He did not want to risk having that outrage turned directly at him. It was dangerous enough to witness it from a safe distance, a man could get hit with a stray invective even while hiding behind a tree.

George saw the door shut in her face. And then the volume really turned up. She used her key and pushed with all her weight against the door but something was blocking it now. Whatever it was, if it had ears, George figured it would be deaf in a few seconds. Or it would wish it was.

Ash felt the woman pounding and kicking the door, each blow causing the wood to shudder and sending reverberations into his back, but she had no chance to force the door open against his weight. Her fury was obvious and vocal, but Ash did not know what else to do. Until Dee returned from work, he would keep the door closed. It was his only plan.

In the bathtub, Bobby strained to hear the drama in the other room. It was mostly the woman, but occasionally Ash would speak in his slower, lower tones. He could not understand what Ash was saying but the woman's angry, high-pitched voice came through the door clearly. She demanded to know what Ash was hiding and only slowly did it come to Bobby that she was referring to him. He was the thing being hidden. It was not simply that he was

249

hiding in the way that Ash and Dee were hiding. He himself was the thing being hidden. It seemed like such a long time since Bobby had thought of himself that way. For weeks he had been a part of the family, sharing their excitements and their anxieties. Their situation had become his reality and although he had not actually forgotten the world before he came to this room, it had ceased to have any reality for him.

Now, dimly at first and then with a building, accelerating, roaring clarity, his old world came back to Bobby. A surge of nostalgia and homesickness swept through him with such power that he cried out involuntarily. The homesickness was followed by an emotion that had died even earlier – hope. There was a life beyond the door of the cabin, there was a world outside of Dee and Ash and the voice of the woman yelling at the door was his connection with it. Bobby's body trembled with the rush of emotion, a longing ache so strong it felt like fear. He stepped out of the tub just as the outside door closed and the woman's voice was temporarily stilled. Easing the bathroom door open, Bobby put his ear to the crack. He could hear her this way. She was pounding on the door, still yelling but with her voice now muted by the thickness of the wood. But she was still there, still trying to get in. There was still hope. Bobby clutched his good-luck medal and squeezed his eyes shut as he willed the woman to batter the door down, to come charging in with police and weapons, to find him in the bathroom, to rescue him and carry him back to his own home, his real home. The possibility seemed so real, so palpably close, that Bobby began to cry. His crying was intermingled with exclamations of laughter as spasms of excitement racked him.

Ash heard the strange gurgling sounds coming from the bathroom and wondered if the boy was sick. The woman on the other side of the door was weakening, there were longer pauses between efforts to force her way in, the righteousness of her demands sounded less convinced, but now Ash was confronted by this new phenomenon coming from the bathroom. He couldn't leave the door to see what was wrong with Tommy, he knew that, however strong his urge to do so. He hoped the boy was all right. It was so unlike him to make noise of any kind. He barely spoke above a whisper these days and his cries when Dee beat him were all properly muted by the pillow as Ash had taught him. This was one of the very best behaved of all the Tommys they had and Ash thought he loved him more than any of them. He hoped nothing was wrong with him.

The voice was gone! Bobby could no longer hear her. He silenced himself, holding his breath, but she was gone. Bobby burst from the bathroom, screaming.

"Help!" he cried, running towards the door. "I'm in here, I'm in here, help me!"

Ash stared, stunned, as the naked boy ran straight at him, then tried to run through him, over him.

Bobby threw himself at the door, clawing at the chain that held it closed, calling and calling.

"I'm in here! It's me, it's me! Help me, help me!"

Ash stood, lifting Bobby as he rose, pulling him from the door as he continued to cry out for help. He sought the boy's mouth with his big hand as the boy called out "Please, please," sobbing now. His face was wet with tears and mucus and as Ash silenced him and hugged his body to control him, Bobby struggled with a strength and desperation he had never shown before.

Ash knew it could not last long and shortly Bobby quit fighting and sagged against Ash's body. Ash sat on the bed, his back against the headboard, and held Bobby against his chest.

251

"You promised to be quiet," Ash said.

Bobby muttered something against Ash's hand.

"You promised," Ash said.

He looked down at the boy's naked body held against his own. So pathetically thin, the flesh so close to the bone. So near the end.

"Dee will be so disappointed," Ash said.

The boy muttered something and twisted his head in Ash's hand. Ash knew he was begging Ash not to tell. But Ash had to tell.

"I have to," he said aloud.

There wasn't any way he could lie to Dee, and that meant there wasn't any way he could protect Bobby. Except one. There was always one way.

"Who do you love?" Ash asked. He did not remove his hand from Bobby's mouth, but he knew the answer was "You. I love you, Ash."

"I love you, Tommy," Ash said. Then he added his real name. "I love you, Bobby." Ash never forgot their real names. Dee never wanted to know them, but Ash never forgot. He wondered why that was.

Ash reached behind him and pulled a pillow away from the head board. They would have to move again, now.

George watched Reggie storm back towards the office. So mad, he didn't want to be within half a mile of her at the moment. Let her take her anger out on the cops or whoever she called – and she was certainly going to call someone, there was no chance she would just let this insult to her authority slide by unchallenged. If she found George she might well insist that he go over to cabin six and deal with it, but just what she expected him to do short of blowing the door open with a shotgun, George had no idea.

He waited until Reggie had reached the office before

he moved, sliding deeper into the woods and then back towards the neighbour's parking lot. As he went, he thought he heard a sound coming from cabin six. It was brief and terrifying, but then it was over. It had been so quick, so unpleasant in its implications, that George convinced himself he had not heard it at all.

17

Jack rode in the back seat of the car along with a rolled-up sleeping bag, a security blanket and a shopping bag full of books. The books had all been read before, which was why they were selected to come along to camp; they were proven favourites. A steamer trunk of clothing was in the boot of the car, enough to sustain him without laundry for two weeks. Becker suspected that in fact the boy would probably make do with the same pair of jeans and perhaps two of the twelve T-shirts provided. Becker had helped prepare Jack for the adventure, using a laundry pen to inscribe the boy's name in the collars of his shirts; the elastic of his shorts.

"In case your shorts run off by themselves and get lost, the police will know where they belong," Becker had said to the boy at the time. Jack had laughed at the notion of his shorts wandering off on their own.

Karen was less amused. "No one's going to get lost," she said sharply. "Everything's going to be fine. This is a very safe camp with excellent counsellors."

"Counsellors have to sleep sometime," Becker said. "Who knows what Jack's shorts will get up to then?"

"They might go off running all by themselves," Jack said, liking the idea. "They might go swimming ..."

Karen silenced them both with a glare. "Your shorts

254

are not going anywhere without you, and you are not going anywhere without a counsellor, is that clear?"

"I was just joking, Mom."

"I am aware of that."

"She's laughing on the inside," Becker said.

"I'm trying to impress certain notions of safe behaviour on Jack. You're not much help."

Becker hung his head, chastened. He looked at Jack under his brows and winked. Jack rolled his eyes in playful conspiracy against his mother.

Karen saw it all. "I think you're both a pair of baboons," she declared.

It was a cue too obvious to overlook. Becker made a monkey face at Jack who responded in kind. They were quickly walking like apes, scratching themselves, making hooting sounds. In the middle of their display Karen walked out of the room and shut herself in the bedroom.

"She's mad," said Jack.

"She's sad," said Becker. "But she doesn't want you to know it because she doesn't want you to be sad, too. She wants you to have a wonderful time at camp."

"OK," Jack said, uncertainly.

"OK what?"

"I'll have a wonderful time at camp."

"Good idea," said Becker. "That will make her very happy. The better time you have, the better she will feel."

"She doesn't act that way."

"That's because she's conflicted."

"What's that?"

"Conflicted? Screwed up. It's a grown-up thing, don't worry about it."

In the bedroom Becker tried to comfort Karen who was holding herself just on the teetering edge of crying without actually falling over into sobs and weeping. Her face would periodically turn bright red and puffy as if surely tears must flow, but then, with a physiological control Becker didn't understand but admired, she would step back from the precipice, her face would clear and the only residue would be a brighter, moist sheen to her eyes. It was as if she was reabsorbing the tears and having a really good cry inside.

"He's going to be fine," Becker said.

"How do you know?"

"He'll be perfectly safe."

"I know that."

"It will be a good experience for him,"

"I know that."

"It was your idea that he should go to camp."

"Christ, I know that, Becker."

She had been calling him Becker rather than John more frequently following the incident with the gun in Jack's bedroom. They continued to make love with passion and tenderness, but outside of the bed they circled each other warily.

"You want me to tell you something you don't know?" Becker asked.

"Only if it's something good."

"I don't know anything about this that you don't already know yourself."

"I know that," she said.

"Are you crying because you don't want him to go … ?"

"I'm not crying."

"Or are you crying because you do want him to go?"

"I'm crying because I'm a mother," she said.

She allowed him to hold her, but she held herself more tightly. His embrace offered comfort to neither of them.

Now, as they rode north on I-91 into Massachusetts, Karen see-sawed back and forth between a steely efficiency that concerned itself with time and distance and other details of the trip, and a moist sentimentality. If she had been in the back seat rather than behind the steering wheel, Becker felt certain she would have had Jack on her lap. It was probably why she had steadfastly refused Becker's offers to drive.

The car telephone emitted its muted ring.

"I should have turned it off," Karen said, reaching for it.

"I'm on my way to Jack's camp, Malva," she said, annoyed.

She listened for a moment, then said wearily to Becker, "There's another man in a motel with a boy."

Since Karen had enlisted the aid of the State and local police, the Bureau had been alerted to possible suspects at the rate of six per day. At her request, Karen had been informed of all of them and after they were investigated, she had been immediately informed of the results. On several occasions she had gone to the motels herself. They had discovered fathers and sons, fathers and daughters who were mistaken for boys, men and men, high-school students up to mischief, lovers up to privacy, even a mannish looking woman and her small dog. The effort had come to seem like an embarrassing waste of man hours.

"Where is it?" Becker asked.

"Spencer."

Becker glanced at the map which had their route to camp highlighted in red ink.

"It's on the way, about fifteen minutes from here," he said.

Karen sighed. "I'm on my way to camp," she said.

"We're forty-five minutes ahead of schedule," Becker said indifferently. "We can spend the time at a motel talking to a man and a midget ..."

"Or a ventriloquist and his dummy, or a woman with a small pony ..."

"Who has a pony?" Jack asked from the back seat, lifting his head from his book.

"I was just joking, sweetheart," Karen said.

"Or, we can spend the time waiting at camp for permission to leave," Becker said.

"Hang on," Karen said into the telephone. She looked at Becker with raised eyebrows.

"Whatever you want," Becker said. "It's your trip."

"My job, too," she said, then, into the phone, "Malva, give me directions to the motel. I'll take this one myself."

"Guess what," Becker said, turning to look at Jack in the backseat.

"What?"

"Not only do you get to go to camp today. You also get to watch a pair of supersleuths in action."

"Hey!"

"It's actually very boring," Karen warned.

"It's usually very boring," Becker said. "But then, you never know."

"Is there a pony involved?"

"No," said Karen. "Just a jackass." She thought a moment. "Or two," she added.

Another car followed them off the highway into the Restawhile driveway, going rather too fast for the situation. As Karen came to a stop in front of the office the other car moved quickly past and skidded to a halt in front of the farthest cabin. An elderly couple stepped out of the office, looking past Becker and Karen to the car in the distance. Becker saw a woman hurry from the car to the cabin door. She tried a key but the door would not open. She put her head to the crack of the door, said something, then stepped inside quickly as the door opened all the way.

Karen was trying to get the attention of the elderly

couple but having no luck. They seemed as engrossed in the distant scene as if it were the stuff of high drama. It was not until Karen produced her identification and announced that she was with the FBI that the woman seemed to notice her.

"You see," Reggie said to George triumphantly. "The FBI. I told you it was important."

"You really the FBI?" George asked.

Karen held her identification towards him but spoke to the woman. She could tell already that the woman was in charge.

"I understand that you responded to a State police request for information."

"Right there," Reggie said, pointing towards cabin six. "In six. Just what you're looking for."

"What did you understand we were looking for?" Karen asked.

"A man and a boy," Reggie said. "A big man, the trooper said. Isn't that right, George?"

George was studying the attractive young woman who claimed to be an FBI agent, trying not to stare while still getting an eye full. He seemed surprised to have been consulted.

"Ah, yeah. That's what the trooper said. A big man with a boy."

"Well, he's in there," Reggie said, pointing.

"In the bungalow where the woman just went?" Karen asked.

"She claims he's her husband, but don't you believe it," Reggie said. "He believes it, but don't pay any attention to him." She nodded her head contemptuously at George who was drifting towards the car in an effort to disassociate himself from his wife. He had hoped he could study the woman agent from that perspective without being noticed. Jack had rolled down the rear-window to hear the conversation and George winked at the boy, pretending not to hear the reference to himself.

"Did the State trooper mention that we were looking for a man and a boy alone?"

"That's your man in there, believe me. Take a look for yourself, he's as weird as they come."

Karen looked at Becker. Becker suppressed a grin.

"We think it's unlikely that the man we're looking for would be travelling with his wife," Becker said, his voice polite and formal.

"She's certainly not his wife," Reggie said. "I already told you that. Go look. Just go see for yourself. Something is going on in there."

"What sort of thing?"

"I'm happy to say I don't know. My mind doesn't work that way."

Becker glanced at George who was studying Karen's legs. He sensed Becker's eyes on him, looked up, grinned sheepishly.

"But it's something the police should look into," Reggie continued. She looked back and forth at Becker and Karen who were obviously reluctant to take any action. "Well, for heaven's sake, what did you come here for?"

"That's an excellent question," Karen said grimly. "Is the man there right now?"

"Unless he dug a tunnel he is. I've had an eye on that cabin ever since."

"Ever since what?"

"Ever since I saw him in it. You would too, if you'd seen him, believe me."

"Is the boy there now?"

For the first time, Reggie acted less than certain. "I'm pretty sure he might be," she said.

"But you're not completely sure?"

"Why don't we take a look and find out? He could be in the bathroom."

"I'm afraid I don't understand, ma'am. Did you see the boy in there earlier?"

"Not in so many words," said Reggie.

"You didn't see him in so many words?"

"I saw his toothbrush. I saw the way the man acted, he was hiding something, I saw him carrying something at night ..." She trailed off, losing steam as she was forced to voice her circumstantial case aloud.

"You mean you've never actually seen the boy in person?" Karen struggled to keep the annoyance from her tone.

"Not exactly ... but I don't have to see something to know it's there."

"Have you seen his clothing? ... His playthings? ... His books?"

"His toothbrush."

"Nothing else?"

"I've seen the man! That's enough!"

Becker turned to George and asked him if he had seen the boy. George put both hands in the air, palms open, disavowing any connection with the whole business.

"I haven't even seen the man," he said, not looking towards his wife.

"Why don't you just go see him," Reggie demanded, "instead of standing around, calling me a liar."

"Nobody's calling you a liar, ma'am," Karen said soothingly.

"Then why don't you go see the man for yourself and ask him? Don't rely on him." She indicated George with a gesture that was at once both designatory and dismissive. George grinned at Becker, inclining his head ever so slightly back at Reggie, trying to involve Becker in man's universal understanding of women.

"We'll just have a word with him, then," Karen said, turning towards the cabin.

"Ask him about the bedspread, let's hear him explain that," Reggie said, falling in step with Karen.

"I think it's best if we conduct the interview ourselves," Karen said.

"I know how to deal with him," Reggie said.

"I'm sure you do, but it's normal procedure for us to conduct an interview in private. I'm sure you would want the same consideration."

"If I'm not there, how will you know if he's lying?"

"We usually do this alone," Karen repeated. "If we need further confirmation, naturally we'll ask you."

"I can tell you everything you want to know," Reggie said, but she fell back, letting Karen and Becker proceed alone.

Karen leaned into the open rear-window of the car to speak to her son. "Just stay here," she said. "This shouldn't take very long."

"But ..."

"If there's a pony in that room, I promise I'll let you know," Becker said.

"This might be easier to take if I didn't get the impression it amuses the hell out of you," Karen said to Becker as they started towards the cabin. "You have a very strange sense of humour."

The woman came bustling out of the cabin before Karen and Becker were halfway there. She wore a starched white nurse's uniform, white stockings, white orthopaedic Oxford shoes. Contrasted to this snowy field, her eyes seemed to be blazing an unnatural blue. The blonde hair on her head had been piled into a bun to fit within a cap which she was not wearing at the moment and strands had fallen loose around her head, giving her a scattered look, even in repose.

But she was not in repose. She came at Karen and Becker with the zest of someone greeting old friends, eyes flashing happily, her toothy smile another element in white.

"Is she crazy, or what?" Dee asked merrily. "A nice old woman at heart, I'm sure, but alone too much, you know? You should talk to her husband about her, he'll give you an earful."

"I am Special Agent Crist with the Federal Bureau of Investigation ..." Karen said, pulling out her identification.

"Is that right? Good for you." She paused long enough to size up Becker from head to foot. "I'll bet you're special, too, aren't you?" And then to Karen, "Don't want to make him feel bad. He's trying his best."

Dee grinned at Becker to let him know she was teasing. There was a quality to everything she said that was so familiar in tone that Karen wondered fleetingly if they already knew each other.

Then Dee was past them, walking briskly towards the office, speaking over her shoulder and forcing them to follow.

"My husband has eye problems. You know what that's like. I didn't ask for much, just for him to be left alone during the day? Is that so much to ask for? I don't think so. Now the old lady has gone in there, scared the poor dear half to death, apparently scared herself to boot – well, you'll straighten this out, won't you. That's what makes you both special, isn't it? ... Oh, look! Oh!"

Dee veered towards Karen's car, gushing and exclaiming as if she had stumbled upon treasure.

"What's your name?"

"Jack Hollis," Jack said.

"You can call me Dee. And whose little boy are you?"

Jack pulled away slightly from the face coming at him through the rear-window and pointed at his mother.

263

"Oh, he's beautiful, he's just such a beautiful boy!" Dee said to Karen. "You are a very lucky momma."

"Yes, I know. Thank you."

"And you ..." Dee leaned into the car even farther. "You are so precious. I could just eat you up."

Jack tried to smile at the strange woman, at the same time edging away until he was stopped by the sleeping bag on the seat beside him.

"How would you like to come live with me?" Dee asked. "Would you like that, would you like to live with me for a while?"

Dee turned again to Karen. "Just for a little while? Can I have him?"

"Not right now, I'm afraid. He's going to camp today."

"Are you? Are you going to camp? Where are you going?"

"Camp Wasaknee," Jack said.

"You must be so excited ... You're not scared, are you? Don't be scared, there's nothing to be afraid of."

"I'm not scared."

"Good boy ... Oh, you're so beautiful."

Dee turned to Becker and Karen again. Her eyes had become teary, dimming the brilliant blue.

"You are so lucky," Dee said, touching Karen's arm. "You have no idea. Oh, I wish he were mine."

"He's a wonderful boy," Karen said.

"I hope you appreciate him," Dee said. "You shouldn't leave him locked in the back with the windows closed, by the way."

"I do know that, actually," Karen said quickly, offended. "And he's not locked in. And the window's open."

"It's hard to think of everything," Dee said, patronisingly. "Especially if you're a working mother and have to take him to work with you."

"I'm not taking him to work, we were on our way to

camp ..." Karen stopped, thinking her only hope for dignity was to remain silent.

"I'm sure you try your best," Dee said. She squeezed Karen's arm dismissively, then turned abruptly to Becker. Her tears seemed to have evaporated within a second.

"And just what are you contributing to all this?" Dee asked, smiling.

"Just standing around," Becker said.

"That's what they do best, isn't it?" Dee said to Karen.

Karen, still smarting from the implied criticism of her parenting skills, refused to be drawn into Dee's conspiracy. The woman was a reflexive flirt, Karen thought, turning on her overwrought charm for everyone she encountered, man or woman. It was heavy-handed as a club with women, but it seemed to work with men. She was annoyed to see Becker smiling as broadly as the woman.

"Well then, come on in and help me out," Dee said to Becker, and again she was on the move, skipping up the steps and into the office before Becker or Karen could react.

"She seems to have her own agenda," Becker said, still smiling.

"You find her funny, too?"

"I think she likes me, what do you think?" Becker said.

"I think she needs a valium."

"She's more fun than a midget, though."

Becker and Karen followed Dee towards the office and heard her already engaged in a shouting match with the woman owner before they reached the door.

"Is it too late to just turn and run?" Karen whispered.

Becker grinned sardonically and with a low sweeping bow, ushered Karen into the office before him.

Ash washed the boy meticulously, wearing the plastic gloves as Dee had taught him. He sat in the tub with the boy, holding his body with one arm and soaping and scrubbing with the other. Using one of Dee's nailfiles, he cleaned under Bobby's fingernails. He scoured the boy's ears, laved away the last of the tears, the scent of fear. When he had finished, Ash left the boy in the tub to let the water soak away the last traces of his earthly ordeal.

Ash dressed himself and waited impatiently for Dee to come home in response to his phone call. He was unable to lose himself in the television stories, his mind wandering again and again to the boy in the bathtub. He held Bobby's good-luck charm in his hand, squeezing it for luck, hoping that somehow it could change things. The boy had insisted that it had always worked for him, perhaps now it would work for Ash. He rubbed the coin between his thumb and finger, looking at the face of the man embossed on the metal, wondering who he was that he could bring such good fortune.

Ash was at the door when Dee arrived. She took in the situation in a glance and her voice was crisp and authoritarian. Ash had known she would be certain of exactly what to do.

"Put your gloves on and put him in the bag," Dee said. She peered through the drawn blinds at the small convocation outside the motel office. Reggie was talking and pointing at Dee's cabin.

"When I get everyone inside the office, you get that bag out of here, understand?"

"Yes, Dee."

"Get it to the edge of the highway, but out of sight, we don't want anyone finding it now. We'll pick it up tonight when we leave."

"Are we leaving for good?"

She gave him a harsh look. "Stop snivelling now, Ash. We have to act quickly. Put your gloves on and hurry up.

When I get them all into the office, you get out the door and into the woods as fast as you can with the bag. Got it?"

"Yes, Dee."

She looked at him again, holding him with her fiery eyes. "Who do you love?" she asked.

Ash smiled. "I love you, Dee."

Dee slipped out the door. Ash pulled on another pair of plastic gloves and picked up the trash bag from the floor and entered the bathroom. When he came out, holding the bag gently in both arms, he saw the good-luck charm lying where he had dropped it on the bed.

It did not seem right to keep it. Bobby had loved it so much. And maybe it would continue to bring him luck, Ash did not know. But it belonged to Bobby, no matter how much Ash wanted to keep it.

Ash undid the tie of the trash bag and gently placed the Kennedy half-dollar and its chain inside. He tied the bag once more then peeked through the blinds to watch the people outside the office. Dee was leaning into a car, then she was talking to a man and a woman whom Ash had never seen before, then she was moving rapidly into the office.

The man and woman talked to each other and Ash willed them to follow Dee. It worked, they went into the office, too, and Ash wondered if it had been Bobby's charm that made it happen. One last favour of good luck.

Ash picked up the bag in both arms and slipped out the door and into the woods that waited for him only a few steps away.

From the back seat of the car Jack saw the hulking man come out of the cabin and glance anxiously towards the office before hurrying into the thin stand of trees. The man was carrying a trash bag, but not as if it contained trash. He cradled it in his arms as if it were a treasure. Or a baby, Jack thought. A baby in a bag. Jack liked the sound of the phrase, the silliness of it. It was the kind of nonsensical notion that Becker liked to joke about with Jack. Poo on your shoe, baby in a bag. Jack vowed to remember and tell Becker but by the time he and his mother returned to the car, Jack had forgotten.

He watched the big man hurry through the trees, heading in the direction of the highway, the bag held delicately in front of him. The man disappeared for a minute behind a squat building that adjoined the motel property. When he came back, he no longer carried the bag.

The big man glanced furtively at the office again, and then rushed back into his room. To Jack, he looked exactly like someone playing hide and seek, except that he was an adult and, in Jack's experience, adults did not play games. The man never looked at the car, never noticed Jack, which did not surprise the boy at all. So many people never noticed kids, Jack thought. Like they didn't exist, or something. Like they were invisible. Or else they did notice and made a huge fuss, like the nurse who had come from the same cabin. Jack hoped she wouldn't make another pass at befriending him when she came out of the office. Given the choice, he would rather be ignored than made too much of, but, being a kid, he was never given the choice. When accosted by a gusher like the nurse, Jack tried to be polite and not withdraw because that made his mother proud, but inside he tried to make himself as small as possible, to pull his spirit into the tiniest ball and disappear.

Dee led them all out of the office, irrepressible and determined. Karen had given up trying to take control of the situation between Dee and Reggie. It was a mare's nest of charge and counter charge and of interest only to the participants. What surprised her was the continuing high spirits which Dee showed even after the shouting match with the motel owner. She marched along the drive towards her cabin with an impatient stride, looking back at the others to see why they were lagging behind.

Only a sense of duty forced Karen to play out the farce to its conclusion, a duty held not to the Bureau because this was clearly a tenant-owner dispute and of no concern to the FBI, but duty to herself not to appear a fool in public. She would look less foolish seeing this business to the end, going through the proper motions, than she would if she did what she wanted, which was to throw her hands in the air, declare it all a mistake and drive away. How much time did she waste in her life, she wondered, trying not to appear foolish? Becker did not seem to care, he freely acted the fool for Jack, and won Jack's affection in the process. If he were in charge of this operation, he would have cut and run already, she thought. He would flirt with the woman as much as amused him and then just leave, not caring about anyone else's opinion but his own. He would make a very poor woman, Karen thought.

Ash sat upon the edge of the bed, his eyes cast down towards the floor, his hands folded neatly in his lap. Like a pair of bear paws, thought Becker. The man's size was remarkable, but he was not in any way intimidating, he seemed as docile as a cow, and just about as bright. He was breathing heavily, as if he had just been running, or exercising. Becker tried to imagine spending all day, every day, in a room the size of the motel cabin. It was better than a prison cell, but not a great deal better. The battle against cabin fever must be a difficult one and the man's arms appeared pumped by regular, strenuous exercise. Becker imagined the man doing push-ups before the surprise visit by two FBI agents. A lifetime spent in a darkened room, hiding from the painful light, then two intrusions in the same day, the first from the landlady, contentious, aggressive, seeing kidnapped boys under the bed and in the shadows, and then two more authority figures, compelled by duty to ask questions and look stern. No wonder the man seemed stunned and dazed.

That did not explain the mud on his shoes, however.

Becker asked if he might use the bathroom and started for it without awaiting a reply. He squeezed past the nurse who seemed to be whirling and turning even as she stood still. Confinement would be hell for her, Becker thought. Why had she chosen to spend weeks at a time in a holding pen like this when the same rent money could probably have afforded a small house somewhere?

Dee made a show out of getting out of his way, arching her back and leaning into a wall that wasn't there, as if she stood in a narrow corridor with dimensions known only to her. Her breasts brushed against Becker and she touched his upper arm with her hand, as if to guide him past her.

Once in the bathroom, with the door closed, Becker could still feel the touch of the woman, the sensation of moving against the soft resistance of her breasts, the grip of her hand. There was something electric about the experience and it was there, he knew, because she wanted it to be there. The contact had been unnecessary, she had done it deliberately, and the result had been what she wanted, Becker realised. With the simplest of stratagems on her part, he was no longer thinking of her as just another person, but as a woman. As a woman to be desired.

Becker looked into the mirror and grinned at himself. You jerk, he thought. Despite the years, despite the experience, despite being very actively involved with another woman who was immensely satisfying sexually, he still had the indiscriminate sexual response of an adolescent. Huge and irredeemable jerk, he thought, and continued to grin at his reflection.

At first glance the bathroom was unremarkable. There was a clutter of feminine cosmetics and appliances for her, a razor that might have served both of them, a woman's hairbrush, a brassier hanging from the towel rod along with a moist towel that had been used recently. A few drops of water still clung to the shower curtain where it had been tucked into the tub, a few more that had spilled on to the floor had not yet evaporated. The man had obviously taken a bath or shower within the past hour or so since the woman had only just arrived at the motel at the same time as Becker and Karen. It seemed an odd time of the day for bathing, but then living a life indoors might well change your sense of time entirely, Becker thought. Except for the man's shoes, that is. He didn't get fresh dirt on the soles of his shoes by staying indoors. So he had taken a shower, gone outside and scuffed his shoes in the dirt, then come back inside. Or had he run outside and back in again, which would account for his breathing hard? And what difference did it make? Becker wasn't here to fathom the secrets of the man's life, he was looking for a boy, and there was no sign of a boy in the motel, and, indeed, scarcely any sign of the man except his physical presence. There was no comb – did he use the woman's? There was a tube of woman's cream for shaving her legs, but no shaving cream for him. Did he use hers? Did he use soap? It was as if the man had been slapped on to the relationship like an afterthought. As if the man were totally dependent on her for the simplest comfort.

Becker flushed the toilet to maintain the fiction that he had needed it and glanced into the waste-basket. There

271

were tissues blotted with lipstick, several bandaids that had been used and discarded – the man was a lousy shaver, and why not with nothing to soften his beard – and along the side of the basket, as if it were thrust into it rather than tossed, was the tip of something bright blue. Becker pulled it out and held up a child's toothbrush. The brush had been used, but not much, the bristles were still firm, the ends whole, unsplit by wear and tear. The old woman had been right about that much, Becker thought. There was a toothbrush – which could have been used by either the man or the woman, of course – but if a child had ever been in this room, he had left no other sign of his passing.

As he returned to the main room Becker realised that the old woman had been right about something else as well. There was definitely something weird afoot in this cabin, the occupants seemed as mismatched as possible, the passive, hulking dimwitted giant, the bright, animated, sexually radiant young woman. Ash was still sitting on the bed as Becker had last seen him, studying the floor. The woman was engaged in an animated but one-sided conversation with Karen who seemed beleaguered and seeking a fast way out. She wore the pained expression of someone forced to be polite for too long. As nearly as Becker could tell, the woman was talking about men and the impossibility of ever teaching them to be truly civilised. Her husband, for instance, was responsible for the sloppy housekeeping in the room. Alone all day, you'd think he could extend himself to tidy up, wouldn't you, she wanted to know. Becker thought that, all things considered, the big guy did pretty well in the housekeeping department. If Becker were cooped up all day in this cell, he'd be writing on the walls with the woman's lipstick. Or out kicking his feet in the dirt when the woman didn't know about it. Or maybe sitting on the edge of the bed with the woebegone look of a boy whose dog has just died, Becker thought. Living like this, he would have to be depressed.

Karen caught his eye with a frantic look and together they left the room, apologising for taking up their time, although the woman had appeared delighted by the diversion and the man had scarcely seemed to notice.

Dee followed them to their car where she once more leaned into the rear-window and gushed over Jack. She reached in and touched his cheek.

"You're precious," she said. "Just perfect."

Jack pulled back from her touch and Becker was reminded of an illustration from his childhood of the witch reaching into the cage to test whether Hansel was yet fat enough to cook. Hansel had held up a stick which the near-sighted crone had mistaken for his emaciated finger, Becker remembered. Jack had been forced to surrender his cheek.

Karen drove off with Dee still standing by the window.

"You take good care of my little boy, now," she called after them.

Becker could see her in the rear-view mirror, watching and waving for much too long.

"The woman is crazy," Karen said with relief to be away finally. "She had me confused with a long-lost friend. But if I ever had a friend like that, she wouldn't be my friend. Where does she get off, trying to tell me how to take care of my own son? Did you hear that? 'You mustn't leave him in the car with the windows up.' It was all I could do to keep from slamming her against the wall and reading her her rights."

"Got under your skin a little, did she?"

"And she didn't affect you, I suppose? I've never seen a grown man bat his eyelashes like that."

Becker laughed.

"What did you think of her, Jack?" Becker asked. "She acted like she wanted to eat you up."

"Gah," said Jack.

"She showed good taste in boys, though, to give her credit," Karen said. "I can't think of any boy I'd rather gobble up myself." She reached into the back seat and patted Jack. "You put up with it very politely. I'm proud of you."

"Strange taste in men, though," Becker said.

"Meaning you?"

"I was thinking of her 'husband'."

"One thing's certain," Karen said after they had regained the highway, "that is no average married couple."

"Certainly not average."

"Not married either," Karen said.

"How do you know?"

"Apart from the fact that he has one hanger in the closet and she has eight? That he has no other shoes? I don't know what there was in the bathroom but there was practically no sign whatever that he even lived there."

"Nothing in the bathroom, either," Becker said. "Except for two toothbrushes. And a child's toothbrush in the wastebasket."

"The old lady had that much right, at least."

"She had it all right," Becker said. "She said they were a strange couple, and she was right, she said the man was something spooky, and I'd have to agree with that, she said there was something odd going on in the room, and I'm certain that's true, although I'm not sure I know what it was."

"So she was right on all counts except the one we came for," Karen said.

"There's no law against being strange, however," Becker said.

"Or none we care to enforce," Karen said. "I don't

know what those two get up to together, but I'm sure it's in violation of some code or other."

"Flagrant weirdness," Becker volunteered.

"Worse than that. Something ... I don't know, unclean. I left feeling as if I wanted to wash, as if I have oil on my skin ... No sign of a child other than the toothbrush, I suppose?"

"None," said Becker. "But there was the toothbrush."

Karen grinned and shook her head.

"What?"

"Feminine secret," she said.

"Terrific."

"OK. I have a child's toothbrush, too. I use it to brush my eyebrows sometimes."

"You do?"

"You men have no idea what we go through, do you? I put hair spray on the brush then sort of comb them up so they don't go every which way."

Becker stared at her. Karen moved uneasily behind the wheel.

"*Some*-times," she said. "Only *some*-times."

Becker continued to look at her, exaggerating his bafflement.

"Stop it," she said sternly, after a moment. "So I think, in the absence of any other evidence, we can forget the toothbrush."

"I'll have to take your word for it," Becker said.

"We had to do it, though, right?" Karen said.

"Oh, sure, we had to check it out. And it wasn't a total waste of time."

"Why not?"

"Well, Jack gained an admirer."

"Great."

"And it got me thinking."

"You found that visit intellectually stimulating?"

"Well, it didn't make me start thinking about the Great Books. But the woman's nurse uniform did make me remember something. After the Bickford snatch I stood in on a couple of interviews. One of them was with a guy who made doughnuts. He said he had seen the outing of kids when they came to the mall."

"Yeah?"

"He said – I think he said – he saw the teachers, he saw the kids, he saw the school nurse. Did he say she was bringing up the rear? I don't remember, but I think so. I have that image in my head."

"Yes, so?"

"So does a uniformed nurse usually go along on every school outing?"

"I don't know. It seems like a good idea."

"It does. But does it happen? ... Jack? When your class takes a trip, does the school nurse usually go along? Does she wear a uniform?

Jack hesitated long enough for Karen to speak impatiently. "Jack, John asked you a question."

"I don't think I've even seen her in it," Jack said thoughtfully.

"You mean you've never seen her on an outing?"

"Oh, she doesn't go on those. Because what if someone at school gets sick? But I don't think I've ever seen her in a uniform. She just wears clothes at school."

Karen and Becker drove in silence for a moment, both thinking. Karen broke the silence as she reached for the phone.

"Of course that's just Jack's school," Karen said, punching in the phone numbers. "They might do it differently at other schools."

"Or a nurse just happened to be going in the same direction," Becker said.

"Just a coincidence," Karen said.

"Most likely."

"Probably ... Malva? Deputy Director Crist. I'm in my car. One, check with the principal of Bobby Reynold's school. See if a uniformed nurse went along on the outing to the mall on the day Bobby was ..." She glanced back at Jack. " ... when he went on the outing. Two, have Hemmings go through all the interview notes of the other Lamont cases and see if there are any mentions of nurses."

Karen paused, looked at Becker and arched an eyebrow.

"Do the malls have their own nurses?" Becker asked.

"And Malva, find out if the malls in question have uniformed nurses on duty ... That's right. I'll be in the car until around six. I want answers before then ... Thank you."

"Let's not get excited yet," Becker said as Karen returned the phone to its cradle.

"A, there are virtually no cases of women being involved in serial killings except the one in Florida.

"B, a woman could not have disposed of the bodies from a moving car with one hand."

"That would require a man with great strength."

"Or ... Christ, or two people. One driving, the other sitting in the back seat and using both hands. What's wrong with that?"

"Two people. Serials don't work in teams, they're loners."

"Although the Hillside Strangler was actually two people."

"And Braun and Rosenbloom committed those atrocities in New Haven."

"Yeah, for years."

"You had something to do with that case, didn't you?"

"Not enough ... So, it does happen."

"Not often, but it happens ... But never with a mixed couple, that I know of."

"It wouldn't have to be mixed. Sitting in the back seat, using two arms to lift. A woman could do that."

"Two women?"

"Why not? Just because we've never seen it?"

"The woman in Florida, she had another woman with her part of the time."

Becker took a deep breath and let it out slowly. "How much did you talk to that big guy in the motel?" he asked.

"Hardly at all."

"And why?"

"Because ... I'm stupid, I guess."

"No, you're not stupid, Karen. Why didn't you talk to him? Really."

"Because once the woman entered the picture, there didn't seem to be any point."

"Why no point?"

"What are you getting at?"

"Why no point in interviewing him?"

"Because a man and woman together didn't match our profile."

"And who gave us the profile?"

Karen paused.

"It's not your fault, John."

"Who came up with that profile?"

"Lots of us, all of us. It was a consensus long before you entered the case. This kind of thing is done by male loners ..."

"Who went out driving on the Merritt tossing bags out the window? Who convinced us all that it was, that it had to be a strong man, so we all stopped looking at or even considering anything else? Who was that genius, Karen?"

"John, we all agreed. I agreed. I'm still in charge of this case. If anything stupid was done, it's my responsibility."

"Your responsibility, maybe. My fault."

"Nobody's fault. And you were probably right. It probably is a lone male. Nothing has happened to change that."

Becker was silent.

"At least wait until we hear back from Malva before you beat up on yourself. There will be plenty of time for self-recrimination for all of us."

"After we get Jack installed at camp ..."

"Of course."

"We could just swing by the motel again ..."

"It's on the way," she said. "Do you have something specific in mind?"

"I'm going to ask that big guy for help in pulling my head out of my ass. I got it jammed up there so far this time I don't think I can get it out by myself." Becker glanced at Jack, then at Karen. "Sorry, for the anatomical reference," he said.

"What, because of Jack? He likes it. He thinks you're clever."

Becker turned and looked at the boy in the back seat. Jack was grinning behind his hand.

"Face it, Becker," Karen said. "You're a natural-born father figure."

"Every kid needs one," Becker said. "Whether he needs it or not."

"Oh, look," Karen exclaimed suddenly. "Look, Jack. There's your mountain."

Mt. Jefferson loomed abruptly alongside them, a sudden bulging disturbance in the landscape. Like most mountains in Massachussetts, Mt. Jefferson stopped ascending well short of the tree line and to the jaundiced eye accustomed to snow-topped Alps or Rockies it presented the aspect of an ambitious hill. To Jack, it seemed enormous.

"Your own mountain," Becker said. "How about that?"

"Are you looking, Jack? Do you see it?"

"I see it," Jack said. He wanted to add a note of impudence, telling his mother that he wasn't blind, but his throat was constricting and he found it easier not to say anything.

"You're going to love it there," Karen said. "It looks so fresh and clean, doesn't it?"

Becker, his eye on Jack as much as the mountain, noted the boy's rising discomfort. It was going to be a tearful parting. He glanced at Karen whose attention was exaggeratedly fixed outside the window.

All three of them stared at the mountain, keeping their thoughts to themselves, as they drove parallel to it for several miles, then began the slow and winding ascent to the camp.

18

Ash was surprised at how well Dee was responding to the loss of Tommy. Usually by now she would be inconsolably sad, sinking ever deeper into mourning until she was immobilised by her grief. It was normally his task to carry both of them into the car, first the garbage bag, then Dee who would slump in his arms as inertly as the boy's corpse. But this time she helped Ash pack, helped check the room to make sure they had left nothing behind. It was Dee who emptied the bathroom waste-basket into a paper bag for disposal later, Dee who double checked the drawers and under the bed to be sure nothing was left behind. It was Dee who decided to leave immediately, not waiting for dark as they usually did. And it was Dee who drove the car and waited while Ash retrieved the bag from the roadside ditch where he had stashed it, whereas before, she was always a crumpled heap on the back seat.

This time Ash sat in back, the trash bag cradled on his lap. It was all different and Ash did not feel comfortable with the change. It confused him, as any deviation from routine did, but it also deprived him of his chance to take care of Dee. She needed him only when she grieved, and then she needed him completely, he became her food and shelter. It was always a frightening time for Ash, but he liked himself in the role of provider and protector. He liked being able to care for Dee the way she cared for him the rest of the time.

But this time Dee was still very much in command, she was far more subdued than usual. She seemed to Ash to be angry rather than sad, but for once hers was a controlled anger. This one had the look of a passion that would not burn out in a flash, but would simmer and sustain itself below the level of fury, lasting a long time and Ash was frightened by it.

Dee drove with the map open on the steering wheel, weaving slightly as her eyes flicked back and forth from map to road. Whatever she was looking for was hard to find. She pulled the car off the highway and on to a rest stop and glared at the map for a moment in silence. "Ha!" she cried exultantly. "Got the bitch."

"What?"

"I know where she took him."

"Who?"

"My boy," she said, as if it were obvious. "My beautiful, precious, perfect little boy."

Ash looked down at the trash bag on his lap. He could feel the weight of the body pressing into his thighs.

"Get rid of that," Dee said. She waited until a van filled with teenagers pulled back on to the highway, leaving them alone at the rest area, then told Ash to get out of the car.

Ash carried the trash bag into the trees that separated the highway from the adjoining town. Through the leaves he could just make out the shape of a house fifty yards away. A dog barked in the distance. Ash hoped the dog would not disturb the bag. He laid it down then tried to cover it with fallen twigs and dead leaves, but the leaves and twigs slid off the smooth plastic. Ash always wished he could say something, he knew a prayer of some kind was in order, but he didn't know how to do it. He stood over the bag for a moment, looking around nervously, trying to muster a feeling of solemnity but nothing came to him except the urge to say goodbye. He bent over and patted the form within the bag. It was now as rigid as rock.

When he returned to the car, Dee was talking to herself, muttering in a low, menacing tone.

"Officious bitch … come into my home, asking questions … always questions, as if I don't know how … as if I'm not good enough … only they know how to do it, only their way is any good …"

Ash slid into the passenger's seat and snapped on his seat belt. Usually Dee would never start the car until he was safely buckled in but this time the engine was already idling and in gear before Ash had even leaned back in his seat. They were easing into traffic before the next car pulled into the rest area.

Karen was too quiet for the first several miles after they left Jack at camp. They had all weathered the initial hectic minutes bravely enough, getting Jack registered, installing him in his cabin and introducing him to his counsellors and the other two bewildered boys who had already arrived in the cabin. They had then walked him down the long hill to the lake where Jack was to have a swimming test that would determine his level of ability. It seemed to Becker to be a cruel and abrupt way to begin the two weeks, before the kids even knew the layout of the camp, but on the other hand it gave them something to worry about besides separation from their parents.

Jack revealed his nerves only by taking both Karen's and Becker's hands as they walked the rutted dirt path to the lake. As the boy's slim fingers slipped tentatively into his palm, Becker felt a surge of emotion so profound that he nearly yelled aloud with the shock. Karen noticed the change in his demeanour and saw him smiling in an unfamiliar, almost goofy way.

After weeks of seeing Jack daily, after sessions of rough-housing, story-telling, even a brief bout of counselling on how best to get along with his mother, it was the first time that he had voluntarily reached out to touch Becker. The hand in his seemed so small, so vulnerable, that Becker did not want to let it go. For the moment, he felt so wildly protective that he could not conceive of letting Jack go off on his own into a world as fraught with danger as summer camp. He wanted to bundle the boy in his arms and carry him back to the safety of the car. He wanted to take the swimming test for him, he wanted to speak to each of the counsellors to make sure they understood what a rare and excellent child they had with them, he wanted to corral all of the kids and threaten them with dire punishment if they ever spoke harshly to the boy, insulted him, excluded him. He felt, in brief, like a parent and it was a hugely strange and disorienting emotion.

As Becker looked at Karen, holding Jack's other hand, the warm glow he felt expanded to include her. He not only love this little boy; by extension he also loved the mother. More than loved her. He felt towards her the same protective urge he felt towards Jack. He would marry her, they would raise the child together and Becker would shield both of them from the world's perils, great and small.

Becker gazed at Karen over the boy's head. She looked back with a sour, pained expression.

As Jack released their hands and stepped up to the swimming counsellor, frightened but eager to have the ordeal behind him, Becker was overwhelmed by the boy's courage.

Becker put an arm possessively around Karen's waist. "Can he swim?"

Karen pretended to shift her weight and twisted, slipping away from Becker's arm.

"Not well. He's afraid of the water."

Becker heard the nervousness in her voice.

"I can teach him," he said.

"I'll teach him," she snapped, then tempered the remark by adding, "or they'll teach him here ... They're professionals."

Jack stood at the end of the dock, his little face turned attentively to the counsellor, listening to his instructions. He looked to Becker like a midget warrior being sent into battle.

"He's brave. I couldn't be that brave," Becker said.

Karen gave him a puzzled look.

Jack turned from the counsellor, took one look at the water and dived in, arms and legs flailing, landing on his stomach, his head and face arched backwards as if they could somehow avoid contact with the lake.

Becker gripped Karen's arm and they watched, both holding their breath, as Jack struggled across the roped-off area enclosed within the rectangular wooden dock. He swam the first lap like a startled spaniel, head out of the water, hands and feet paddling beneath the surface. The return lap was supposed to be done with a breaststroke and Jack attacked it gamely, using a stroke that looked little different from the first one. When he gained the dock again, he held on to it for a moment, puffing.

Becker and Karen watched the counsellor kneel down to talk with Jack, saw the boy nod his head to indicate that he was all right. After three deep breaths, Jack pushed off the dock into his version of the backstroke. His arms slapped at the water twice and then he sank beneath the surface. He was up again immediately, sputtering, arms still gyrating, then he sank again.

Becker started forward but Karen held him back.

"He's in trouble," Becker said.

"Don't shame him."

Jack had surfaced once more, still struggling. The counsellor was now walking parallel to the boy, holding a long, flexible pole, ready to intercede if needed, but, remarkably, he was not needed. Progressing by fits and starts, more under water than on the surface, Jack was gaining the far side. It looked to Becker like a form of medieval trial by drowning, testing not the boy's ability, but his tolerance for pain and terror.

Jack reached the dock at last, clinging to it with one hand, too tired to pull himself up, his face barely above the surface. The counsellor knelt again and conferred with Jack, determining if he was ready for the final lap required by the test. Even from a distance Becker could see the exhaustion in the boy's face.

"They're not going to make him go again," he said incredulously.

"Let Jack decide," Karen said.

"He can't possibly do it again," Becker said.

"It's up to him."

Becker fought an impulse to throw his hands in the air in surrender, to wave to the counsellor and let him know it was over. It was only Karen's steely control that made him stand where he was.

Jack turned to look at Karen and Becker, his mouth agape with the effort of breathing. Becker tried to smile, to let the boy know he had done enough, to give it up with honour. He was amazed to see Karen show a clenched fist of determination and encouragement.

"What will it prove?" he demanded.

"Whatever it proves," she said, not turning to face him. She nodded her head at Jack, tightened her lips, once again showed the fist.

Jack turned back to the counsellor, nodded, breathed

again, then launched himself for the final lap. It was meant to be swum with the sidestroke, but it was obvious that Jack had no idea how to perform the manoeuvre. After sinking once, he came up again on his belly and reverted to the dog paddle that had served him on the first lap. He inched across the area between docks, fighting for every advance, paying for it with a loss of vitality and buoyancy, sinking, then rising again with less and less strength each time. It seemed to Becker like an ordeal that would never end. He marvelled at his sudden vulnerability when it came to the boy, and was amazed at Karen's coolness. If this was what it was like to be a parent, he didn't know how anyone survived it.

When Jack gained the dock at last, he hung in the water for a full minute before accepting the counsellor's offer of assistance in getting out. After a hug and pat on the back from the counsellor who turned immediately to his next victim, Jack came towards Becker and Karen on wobbly legs, his face white, his nostrils pinched with fatigue. He was too tired to smile, but as his mother put her hand lightly on his shoulder and kissed his head, he looked into her face for confirmation of how he had done.

"Great job," Becker said, taking his lead from Karen and restraining his enthusiasm. He wanted to lift the boy to his shoulders and parade him in triumph. "Well done."

Jack continued to look to his mother for approval and Becker sensed a jab of jealousy.

"I cheated," Jack said, still gasping for breath.

"I know," Karen said.

"I didn't do the sidestroke," he said.

"I know."

"Hell, that's all right," Becker blurted. "You're only nine. You had to keep from drowning."

Karen stopped him with a frosty look.

Karen and Jack turned back towards the road leading up the hill to the cabin. She kept her arm lightly on his shoulder until the boy pulled away and stepped ahead of her, getting his strength back, his confidence now soaring. There would be no more holding of hands this day.

Becker trailed them both, feeling excluded and hurt, and angry with himself for feeling so.

They said goodbye at the cabin, Jack already restless and eager to have them gone. His bunkmates were talking about the swimming test and Jack wanted to join them. Karen's farewell was warm but brief, nothing to embarrass him in front of his new friends. Becker wanted to kneel and take the boy in his arms, to whisper wise last minute words of advice and encouragement, but in the end, merely shook his hand and said goodbye, Jack being already involved with the other boys.

When they reached the car, Becker saw that Karen's face was wet with tears although he had not heard a sound from her.

"What a wonderful kid," she said.

They sat in silence as they drove. Becker felt an overwhelming sympathy for her because he felt the same way, but he did not know how to express it to her in a manner that would help. They could be married while Jack was in camp, he thought, offering the boy a surprise when they came to rescue him in two weeks' time. Or would it be better to have the boy at the ceremony?

Becker looked again at her troubled profile and placed a reassuring hand on her thigh.

"It's hard, isn't it?" he said.

Karen looked at him as if startled that he could read her thoughts.

"It's just not going to work," she said.

"We'll make it."

She shook her head. "No."

"It's going to be tough, but it's only two weeks."

"Two weeks?"

"Before we get him back?"

"I'm talking about us, John. You and me. We just don't work together. It's not working out. It's nobody's fault."

Becker stared at her, trying to make sense of her words. They seemed to have torn right through his stomach and the rest of him was falling through the hole they had caused.

"You're trying your best," she said. "You always try your best at everything you do, I love that about you, but it's just too hard, it's asking too much of you to step into a situation where you have to deal with me and Jack both at the same time. I should never have expected you to be able to deal with it all. It's my fault."

It sounded to Becker very much as if she were saying it was his fault, and it still made no sense.

"I should have known better in the first place." She was talking rapidly now, the thoughts tumbling out. "You're a single man, single by nature, I know you've been married but look how that ended up – not that a failed marriage means you're a failure, I'm no one to suggest that – but you're a loner, John, you know that, you've said as much yourself. You have your own way of viewing the world, your own way of dealing with it. It works for you and that's fine, but it's not fair of me to expect you to toss that aside, you've spent a lifetime developing it, you shouldn't have to change just because something else is required when you're living with a woman and her child."

Becker stared numbly at her as she drove the car. He heard the words, understood the message, but couldn't penetrate the camouflage to discover the reason. There was a ringing in his ears, a hollow sound to Karen's voice that made everything seem unreal, otherworldly, as if he was watching the whole thing happening to somebody else. Some other poor uncomprehending schmuck was being dumped without just cause, not him.

"It's just the best thing all around," she was saying, and Becker realised he had not heard her for a few moments. He felt he must have missed something crucial, the causative link that would interpret everything else. He wondered if he should ask her to repeat herself. "And the timing is right, with Jack away. This way he won't have to watch anything messy, that doesn't do a child any good to have to listen to fighting and yelling. We'll just get it over with and when he comes home from camp everything will be as good as new. We really get along best by ourselves anyway, Jack and I. I know you tried, but I think he was getting conflicting signals. Kids like things simple."

Becker wondered if it was something about Jack. Was she jealous of Becker's attentions to the boy. Did she want Jack all to herself? Had Jack's hand in his at camp affected her as strongly as it had Becker, but in the wrong way? He thought there was an idea there that needed examination and he must get to it if the sinking in his stomach and the roaring in his ears ever stopped.

Karen glanced at Becker, the first time she had dared to really look at him since she began talking. He had slumped down in the seat, his eyes staring at the dashboard. Sullen, she thought. Lumpish and silent and not even troubling himself to talk back. He doesn't even care enough to argue. Male. So hopelessly male. And it was just as well; it made the job that much easier. Let him sulk, they were all good at that, it seemed to come naturally to them. Her ex-husband had been a master at it, jumping inside himself and battening down the hatches at the first sign of emotional distress. In his case he had always simply walked away, literally walked right out of the room rather than sit down and talk. Becker was a captive in the car now and couldn't walk, but she could see he was doing his equivalent of it.

"Do you have anything to say?" she asked, annoyed.

He took a long time to respond, as if summoned from a far place. When he spoke he did not look at her.

"Can I keep Jack?" he asked.

Reggie had watched the man and woman load their suitcases into the trunk, then hurried to the cabin as soon as the car was out of the driveway. As she had suspected, they were gone for good. The waste-baskets were empty, the room clean. Even the bed was made, the spread neatly in place and tucked in at the bottom with crisp hospital corners. Nothing had been defaced, nothing stolen. Reggie felt oddly cheated that they had left her nothing to complain about.

"They had four days of rent left," she explained to the two FBI agents who had returned minus the boy in the backseat. "But I figure they owe me that much for sheer aggravation."

"Nothing to justify a warrant then," the female agent said. She looked to the man for confirmation. He was hanging back, staring at the ground. He reminded Reggie of George and his hangdog look after he'd been scolded for something. Moping, aggrieved, and withdrawn. There and not there at the same time. Reggie felt a pang of sympathy for the officious young woman. Working with men was not worth the trouble most of the time. It was just easier to do things yourself.

"And you saw them leave, you say," the woman asked.

"That's right. Bold as brass, this time. Went out in broad daylight, and he wasn't wearing any sunglasses either, 'bad eyes' or not."

"Just the two of them? The man and the woman?"

"Who else."

"No sign of the child?"

"He could have been lying down on the back seat, of course."

"That's true," the woman said, clearly not believing Reggie. "But you said you watched them pack the car yourself. You would have noticed if a child got into the back seat, wouldn't you?"

"If I was looking right at that exact moment. I have other things to do, you know. I wasn't studying them or anything. They might have slipped several kids in that car while I was tending to business for all I know."

"That's true," the agent said again, and again clearly not believing it. "But you have no reason to suppose they did?"

Reggie looked briefly at George who seemed to be hiding a smirk. He wanted to be here for the excitement, of course, but would he help her? Not in this lifetime. Stand there dumb as a post when he might be of some assistance, then strut around when they were gone and tell any fool who would listen about how he helped in an FBI investigation. Helped who? Not his wife.

Reggie shrugged. "I may have been wrong about a child, I never actually saw him, I told you that the first time. I just saw a toothbrush, but that doesn't change the fact that something very strange was going on in that cabin."

The woman agent sighed. "No, it doesn't change that. They didn't leave a forwarding address or mention where they might be going?"

Reggie snorted. "They didn't even wave goodbye, but good riddance to bad rubbish, I say." She looked meaningfully at George who dropped his eyes to the ground and slumped his shoulders, just like the male agent. Like carbon copies of each other, Reggie thought. Lost causes, all of them.

"I guess that will be all, then," the woman said. She looked once more towards her male partner, but he had already turned on his heel and was heading back towards the car.

Reggie watched them drive off with a sense of disappointment. She had won her battle completely, she had gotten rid of that 'Dee' woman and her hideous 'husband' without any loss of property, and had even had the satisfaction of sic'ing the FBI on to them but still felt oddly cheated. Just what of, she could not have said. When she turned to speak to George, he had already slunk off.

The silence in the car was so thick that Karen felt as if it sloshed back and forth with each turn in the road like so much liquid. Becker would not even look at her and she could think of nothing to break the silence except to turn on the radio which seemed cold and insensitive. There seemed no point in even discussing the couple from the motel. They had no child with them and there was no reason to suspect them of anything and that was that. She did not blame them for leaving the motel so abruptly. After that kind of showdown with the owner, Karen felt she might well have done the same. Their only offence lay in being weird and in overtipping the proprietor with four days of prepaid rent. As for breaking off their relationship, it was clear that Becker had nothing to say, no defence, no argument. For all she could read into his attitude, apart from the insult of being the jilted party, he didn't seem to care at all.

The phone was a blessing when it rang. Karen snatched it up before the ring had ceased to echo in the car.

"Crist," she said, then listened for several moments.

Becker watched her listening the way an actor listens, with subtle exaggeration, pursing her lips, squinting with concentration, nodding her head in silent agreement. It was a small show she was putting on for his benefit, he realised, making it clear that she was a woman with more pressing things to do than deal with him. At one point she looked directly at him, smiled and shrugged as if to say, what could she do, she was a helpless captive of higher purposes.

Becker was grateful for her little pantomime, it gave them both an excuse to move away from the awkwardness and tension that rode between them like a hulking stranger. Any distraction would serve, and work was the best. They did not have to feign an interest there.

She moved the phone from her mouth and whispered "Malva" in Becker's direction, then nodded again, as if to reassure Malva she was still listening. Becker hoped the phone call would last for the rest of the ride home. He had been painfully aware of her intense scrutiny since she dropped the bombshell. Even during the perfunctory interrogation at the motel he knew she had been observing his every move and expression. Something was expected of him, Becker knew that, some display of rage, or sorrow, some deftly articulated show of emotion. She wanted a reaction. Women always wanted a reaction, but Becker could not give it to her. He responded to the pain as if he'd been kicked in the solar plexus. Paralysed by the sudden blow, gasping for breath, it was all he could do to curl himself around the pain and try to hang on. He had no strength left over to perform the dance she expected of him. It was for her, he imagined, a very unsatisfying jilting.

"Malva," she repeated when she hung up the phone at last. For the final moments of the call she had ceased her thespian antics and just held the receiver quietly to her ear. Becker wondered if Malva had not hung up long ago and Karen was trying to prolong the excuse to avoid him, no more eager to return to their strained silence than he was.

"Bobby Reynold's school says there was no school nurse on that outing and there never is. The Bickford mall does not have a nurse on duty. Hemmings has gone through the interview notes on two of the snatches besides Bickford so far. Nothing from one of them. At the other, in Peabody, a security guard mentioned having seen a nurse around the time of the boy's disappearance, but he wasn't sure if it was before or after. He remembered it because he said she was moving so quickly that he thought somebody must be injured somewhere. Then he said that right after the boy was discovered missing, a lot of people were moving around quickly. The interviewing agent asked the guard if there was anything particularly notable about the nurse and he said no, he thought he remembered her just because of the uniform."

"Does the Peabody mall have nurses on duty?"

"No, but they do have an eye clinic. The nurse there wears a uniform."

"Does the Bickford mall have an eye clinic?"

"I'll tell Malva to find out. What else?"

"We'll have to go through the list of sudden departures again and check for women this time, see if any names repeat."

"I'll put Hemmings on it after he finishes reviewing the notes."

Becker paused. Karen waited, then lifted the phone again. Becker stopped her with a gesture.

"If you wore a nurse's uniform with all that starch would you do it yourself? Wash it, starch it, iron it, whatever? The uniform on the nurse at the motel, you could cut your finger on the creases. Is that the kind of job a woman would do for herself?"

"You could, I suppose. I'm no expert on laundry, but if it was my uniform, I'd send it out, have it done professionally."

"So would I. Which means that if I had to leave town immediately, I might have left a uniform or two in a laundry somewhere, right?"

"If our theory is right and a boy has just been killed and you're packing up and leaving right away, you wouldn't wait around for the laundry to get done, that's true."

"We can check the possible cleaners by phone, no need to have a man go to each one personally. An unclaimed nurse's uniform shouldn't be that common an item."

"Hemmings," Karen said with a chuckle as she punched in the number on the telephone. Hemmings was a minor legend in the Bureau, one of the very few agents who actually preferred desk work to being in the field. Where most agents sought the solid satisfaction of an actual collar, Hemmings found his thrills in the slow sifting of details on paper. In an era when the computer had replaced the library and file cabinet, Hemmings was a throwback to the literary age, an archivist at heart. What made him a legend rather than a curiosity, however, was his appearance. Bald and hairless since birth, Hemmings began each day by donning a toupee and applying artificial eyebrows. Tagged 'Hairy' Hemmings by Bureau wags, the agent also affected facial hair of varying styles and lengths so that some days he sported a goatee, some days a pencil thin mustache, some days a full beard. He offered over the course of a year a kaleidoscopic variety of hair colours ranging from mouse to Irish red and Swedish blond. He was referred to by the agents as the man with a thousand disguises, none of them adequate. Above all, however, Hemmings was very good at his job. He worked the phones with the avidity of a teenaged girl and when it came to paper work it was rumoured than he could find a pattern in a pane of window-glass.

Becker shared Karen's small laugh at the expense of "Hairy" Hemmings. He found that his chest seemed lighter. The sense that his cheeks and ears were ablaze with humiliation had lessened. He still didn't want to look Karen in the eye, but he was able to feign levity.

She drummed her fingers on the steering wheel, waiting for Malva to answer. It wasn't much, but at least they were working.

19

Dee found them a motel outside of Hindsdale in the Berkshires. From the window Ash could see the mountains rising softly on all sides with the gentle curves of a woman's body. If he squinted he could imagine he was lying on the floor, looking up at Dee's naked body where she lay on the bed, one mountain being the rounded mound of her breast, another the swell of hip and thigh.

Dee was away, looking for work, and Ash was alone. The television was very disappointing, the mountains interfered with reception and there was no cable service. It was the least modern of all the many motels in which Dee and Ash had stayed together. Too far from the Berkshire Festival and Tanglewood to get the summer tourists, too remote from any sizeable city to attract travelling businessmen, located on too small a road to pull in even random travellers, the motel existed primarily on local trade, which meant high-schoolers looking for a place to drink after the prom, illicit lovers, home-owners whose bedrooms were being painted, or whose houses were being fumigated.

Fifty yards from the motel, without any line of demarcation, a car sat on cement blocks next to a pickup truck, spare parts scattered among the weedy lawn. Immediately beyond the autos was a ramshackle house with a line of washing hanging behind it. Two children played under the clothesline, screaming at each other with abandon as they slashed with sticks at each other's shins.

Behind the motel, parallel to the road, was the forest that surrounded all of man's incursions in this part of the country. Ash could not see from his side window just how close it was to the motel in the back, but he knew it was there, close by, a perfect home for bears. He imagined himself venturing into it some night, shuffling up the mountain amid the trees, smelling the trails of the other animals, hearing them scurry off at his approach. It pleased him to think of finding a cave high up the mountain, one known to other bears before him but never seen by man, where he could live on berries and fish and water from the high country streams. Dee could find him, of course, an eagle could go anywhere, but his lair would be too high and too steep for anyone else to dare. When winter came he would curl up amongst the leaves and sleep for months. No one would suffer because he slept because none would be within his reach.

Ash looked at the distant mountain with simple longing. Perhaps, if Dee brought no one home, she would let him seek the woods and mountains one night soon. But he knew she would bring someone home. And soon. She had taken no pills since Tommy left but had not crashed into her abyss of depression. There was a difference in her mood, however. It was no longer wide-ranging ebullience but seemed tempered and directed by a strain of hostility. Dee appeared to have found a target for her energies and was focusing on it in a way Ash had never seen before. When she got work, which never took her long, Ash expected her to bring someone home again. His chances to get into the woods were fading quickly.

Dee was successful at the third nursing home she tried.

As usual the manager looked at her as if she were a gift from heaven. In a business with a chronic shortage of qualified personnel, a young, attractive, white registered nurse with experience and the willingness to work in less than glamorous conditions on any shift and for low pay was even too much to pray for. And, of course, too good to be true. The manager understood that the woman was recently divorced and relocated, along with the implicit suggestion that this job would be temporary. How long could it be before someone like this found a better job or remarried or moved to a big city? Not very long, the manager thought, but however long it was, it was worth it. As usual, she asked Dee as few questions as possible and hired her on the spot.

Driving back to the motel, Dee formulated her plans. The situation was new for her. She had never had a specific target before, and thus had never really had a plan. Just a method. She had employed it when the circumstances seemed right and the need was overwhelming, but always with a strong element of randomness in the process. This time was different.

She felt a swelling sense of excitement. This time she would not only fulfill her irresistible need, she would also be performing an act of retribution. *Take* and it shall be taken from *you*, she thought triumphantly. There was a Biblical ring to it, and a Biblical fitness to what she would do as well. She would have her son back at long last, and those who had taken him away would suffer. Dee felt exceptionally good. The laughter bubbled in her chest and burst from her throat as she approached the motel. She was quickly laughing so hard she had to slow down to avoid swerving into the wrong lane.

She could see Ash's finger stuck between the slots of the room's venetian blind. He was gazing out at the mountains again, and exposing himself to discovery in

300

the process, but Dee could not be angry with him, she felt too good.

"Put on your hiking boots," she said as she opened the motel door. Ash sprang guiltily away from the window.

"Where are we going?"

"To the mountains, of course," Dee said. "I tried, but they won't come to us."

She was smiling so broadly that Ash's heart sank.

Becker wished he were a drinker. Rejection and sorrow seemed to call for burying one's nose in a glass of bourbon but Becker only found himself getting sleepy after the first drink and downright stupid if he forced himself to have the second. The sense of being out of control that alcohol caused frightened him far more than being unhappy, so he took his mourning sober.

"A little nip couldn't hurt," said Tee, tipping up a beer to prove his point. The police chief had brought over a cold six-pack on a mission of commiseration. Receiving no cooperation from his friend, Tee had undertaken the six-pack on his own. He was making impressive progress.

"It heartens the disconsolate," Tee said. "I read that somewhere. On a cereal box, I think."

"What heartens the disconsolate?" Becker asked.

Tee lifted the beer can. "Getting shit-faced."

"Are you disconsolate, Tee?"

"No, you are, but if you're not going to do it, somebody has to."

"That's what friends are for," Becker said.

"Is that what they're for? I always wondered. Well, it's a small sacrifice to make for a buddy. I know you'd do the same for me if I got dumped."

"What I will do is drive you home after you finish your sacrifice. It wouldn't look good if the chief got arrested for DWI."

Tee belched loudly, then tapped his chest with his fist, looking immensely pleased with himself.

"So why are these fine women dumping you all over the place?" he asked. "What do you do to them?"

Becker studied empty space for a moment before answering. "I think I make the mistake of falling in love with them," he said at last.

Becker's distress and confusion were so obvious that Tee shifted uncomfortably in his chair and examined the top of his beer can.

"I think in the beginning I'm a mystery to them and they find that intriguing and challenging. But once I fall in love with them, I'm not a mystery any more because I make an effort for them to really get to know me."

Tee wished Becker would not be quite so open about the whole business. He was not accustomed to being spoken to like this by another man. He didn't know how to respond. If Becker were a woman, there would be no problem, of course. Tee would already be on the sofa beside her, a comforting arm on her shoulder. A comforting arm on Becker's shoulder would make them both so uncomfortable that Tee could not imagine doing it.

"Once they get to know the real me, it scares them," Becker continued.

"You're not so scary," Tee said.

Becker looked at him directly. "You don't know the real me," he said in a tone that implied that Tee was much better off in ignorance.

Tee drank again, then broached a new subject. "So, you're retired again, or what?"

"She didn't think she could continue to work with me, under the circumstances."

Tee did not enquire what the circumstances were for fear of setting off further confessionals.

"Must be nice, sitting around, doing nothing."

"It sucks," Becker said.

"Well, except for that part it must be nice. You get awful broody when you're on a case, you know. On the other hand, look how bright and cheery you are now that you've got nothing to worry about."

"I haven't stopped thinking about it just because I'm not officially on the case," said Becker.

"Could have fooled me. You're just so carefree ..."

"A kid is going to be killed, Tee. We're going to find the body of Bobby Reynolds and then another kid will be taken and I know it as sure as I know you're sitting here, and there's not a goddamned thing I can do about it – except think."

"You ought to cultivate some bad habits ..."

"And every kid from here on is on my head. It's going to keep happening because I couldn't stop it from happening."

"It's not your fault, for Christ's sake ..."

"I fucked it, Tee. I just plain fucked it. I got off on the wrong foot because I was so sure it had to be a certain very specific kind of person. I thought I understood exactly who that person was and everything I did after that was wrong, and everything everyone else did was wrong, too, as a result of my being wrong and being sure I was right."

"What are you, Sherlock Holmes? You never fucked up before?"

Becker paused for a moment. "I always understood them before," he said.

"Understood who?"

"The killers. The animals. The monsters. Whatever you want to call them."

"What's to understand? They're shitheads."

"Spoken like a cop."

"You telling me they're not shitheads? You specialise in serial killers, no? You're the expert on psychos who

303

kill again and again and again, right? You're saying these people are not shitheads?"

Becker paused again. He fiddled briefly with his shoe lace.

"We're all shitheads, Tee. That's why I could always understand them."

"Maybe it's the beer," Tee said, "but it sounds to me as if you're lumping me in the same category as the shitheads, and I resent that."

"Maybe it's the beer," Becker agreed.

"Because I, personally, have never drained the blood out of people and boiled their bones, the way what's-his-name did. I have never grabbed a kid from a shopping mall and beaten him to death."

"They weren't beaten to death," Becker said. "They were beaten to dying. And then they were smothered."

"A nice distinction."

"A merciful one, maybe."

"You got a funny idea of mercy."

"You ever been beaten, Tee?"

"No."

"Beaten regularly, viciously, by someone you were dependent on for your food, your shelter, your life?"

"No."

"Beaten by somebody you loved and you didn't know what you had done to make them so angry at you?"

"I said no."

"Someone who kept reminding you that he loved you even while he was beating you? No? Then maybe you don't know if it was mercy or not."

"What are you pissed off at me about?"

"For that matter, have you ever killed anybody?"

"In Clamden? It's against the law." Tee chuckled, hoping Becker would join him, but Becker continued, his visage darkening steadily.

"What if you did, Tee? What if in the line of duty,

perfectly legitimately, you put a hole through some shithead and watched the life ooze out of him?"

"I guess I'd deal ..."

"And what if you found out, to your great surprise, it didn't bother you all that much? What if you discovered you even kind of liked it?"

Tee felt as if he was being hammered by the queries that were not questions. He wanted to be away, but the room seemed to have shrunk and the power of Becker's anger was pinning Tee to the chair.

"You didn't wish it, you hadn't planned on it, but suddenly there it was. Just an accident, a result of something else you were doing, but there it was. You liked killing the shithead. You liked it throughout your whole goddamned body and mind and soul, it gave you a thrill like nothing else could or ever had. What then, Tee?"

"I'd see a shrink pretty damned fast."

"Good thinking. What if you discovered that the shrink was fascinated by you but had no clue how to change you? What if half a dozen shrinks were powerless to erase that thrill that came to you in only one way?"

"Then I guess I'd have a problem."

Becker laughed, sharply, bitterly. "That would be correct," he said. "Now assume that you were, and are, an outstanding peace officer, sworn to uphold the law and preserve the Constitution. What if you were the fucking chief of police, but you had this little problem? Then suddenly you came upon a shithead who had a similar problem, had a tendency to thrill a little too much when he killed someone, you know, but with the difference that he wasn't an outstanding officer of the law and local chief of police so his chances to kill people legally were rather limited. So, lacking your own native strength of will and inbred desire to do good works, this shithead has taken to getting his thrills as best he can. Not always in the same

305

manly, straightforward way as yourself of course, not by just doing away with people in the course of duty, but in more inventive and leisurely ways more in keeping with his individual temperament and personality – such as slowly draining the blood out of his house guests as you mentioned or hanging them from the basement pipes to study anatomy before stuffing pillows with their hair or maybe just tying them up and practising all the positions in the Kama Sutra on their bodies before he feels called upon to get rid of them out of embarrassment over his excesses. See, whatever his peculiarities, he still suffers from essentially the same little problem that you have. Now, under those circumstances, and bearing in mind that you are the chief of fucking police and have an inherent tendency to consider yourself a human being despite your problem, don't you think you might make an effort to try to understand these shitheads? Since you have the same affliction and all. Like fellow stutterers, say. In terms of insight, you might be one step ahead of the average peace officer who not only doesn't stutter but also regards stutterers as different species altogether. What do you think?"

"It must be the beer," Tee said. "But I don't know what the fuck you're talking about ..."

"I thought we were discussing bad habits."

"... and tomorrow you're going to be glad I don't remember it, either." Tee tipped up the last of the six-pack of beers. He rose shakily to his feet. "A pleasure, as always," he said.

"I'm sorry," Becker said, suddenly contrite.

"Not at all."

"I had no right to dump that on you."

"Only glad I could help," said Tee. He clung to the chair to steady himself. "I live to serve. Besides, I've already forgotten what you said."

306

Becker drove Tee home and walked him to the door where Tee turned and dropped a heavy hand on Becker's shoulder.

"You're not nearly as big an asshole as you think you are," Tee said.

"How do you know?"

"Because if you were, I wouldn't enjoy drinking with you so much."

"I am awfully good company," Becker said. "It's one of my better qualities."

"And I didn't hear you stutter once all night, so what was that all about, anyway?"

Fumbling with his key, shushing Becker with a finger to his lips to keep from waking his wife, Tee stepped into his house in a half crouch.

Once inside, Tee drew himself erect and stopped staggering. He leaned against the door and sighed heavily with relief. It was not good, he thought, to know your friends too well. An awful lot of secrets were best kept that way.

Becker called Hemmings on his direct line, avoiding the switchboard and the resultant entry of the call in the log.

"You know officially I'm no longer on the case," Becker said.

"Back on the medical extension, I understand," Hemmings said cautiously. "Sorry to hear about that."

"Thank you." Becker wondered how much of the sarcasm he heard in Hemming's voice was his own imagination. Just how crazy did the agents think he was? Drooling, unable to tie his own shoe laces? Living on medication? Or just taking advantage of a good opportunity to get out while clinging to the pension rights. Or did they think about him at all?

"Just wanted to make sure you know my status,"

Becker continued. "I don't want you to end up with your ass in a ditch."

"I appreciate the thought. What can I do for you?" Hemmings asked.

"I was curious, Hairy. About the Reynolds case, and the others ..."

"Can't get it out of your mind, right?"

"Right, I'm afraid."

"Don't apologise. We're all obsessive/compulsive or we wouldn't be with the Bureau. What about it?"

"What have you turned up on the search for a nurse's uniform?"

"Well," Hemmings said, and Becker could detect in the single word the enthusiasm rising. A technician happy to complain about his problems. "I'm working only with a map and the yellow pages, you know. I started with the Arnell Wicker case because I figured since the Reynolds snatch is only three weeks old, any uniform might not even have come to the attention of the cleaners as unclaimed yet. The Wicker case is two years old. They would have noticed an unclaimed uniform by now if they are ever going to. So I started there and I'm working my way forward in time. I began with a ten-mile radius around the point of seizure, which was the Upper Saddle River mall and called every cleaner listed in the yellow pages in the towns within that circle. That's a little better than 314 square miles, you understand. A lot of cleaners. When that didn't produce anything, I increased the radius to twenty miles and started over. I don't know how quick your math is, Becker, but that increases the area to cover by another 942 square miles. You go to a thirty-mile radius and that's another 1,884 square miles and so forth out to the fifty-mile radius we figure is the maximum. That's a lot of phone calls."

"Good thing you got a Watts line," Becker said. Then,

in response to the silence, he added, "Must be a bitch."
Hemmings was not noted for his sense of humour.

"It's time consuming, what with one thing and another."

"Have you turned up anything yet?"

"One unclaimed uniform at a Royal Cleaners in Ramsey belonging to one Mrs. Howard Elston, R.N. Unfortunately, Mrs. Elston died three weeks before the Ramsey snatch so I don't think she's the one we're after."

"Are you still at it?"

"I haven't been told to stop," Hemmings said. "Yet."

"You know, it might be instructive to check the local hospitals and doctors' offices to see if any nurse turned up missing all of a sudden."

The phone was silent again. Becker thought at first that he had proposed a job of work huge enough to daunt even Hemmings.

"I think not," Hemmings said at last.

"Too much?"

"Wrong direction," Hemmings said. "I believe you are backing the wrong horse."

"Why?"

"I take it you haven't heard?"

"Hairy, I'm off the case. I haven't heard anything. What is it?"

"They found the Reynolds boy."

"Shit! God damn it! ... Where?"

"Off Route 84 in Connecticut between Bickford and Sandy Hook."

"Same m.o.?"

"No autopsy yet, they just found him this morning, but I gather it's the same. Beatings, trash bag, naked, so forth. But with a difference this time."

"What?"

"A print."

Becker caught his breath. "You said he was naked."

"Indeed. But there was a half-dollar in the bag this time. It had a hole in it, somebody was apparently wearing it as a medal. And on the half-dollar, so I am told, were a thumbprint and an index finger as clean and neat as you could ask for."

"Not the boy's, tell me it's not the boy's prints."

"I will do that. It is not the boy's."

"Have they traced it yet?"

"Oh, indeed. It popped up as fast as you please. There's an outstanding warrant on the man in Pennsylvania."

"Who is it?"

Hemmings paused.

"Don't tell me if you don't feel comfortable doing so," Becker said. "Don't jeopardise your job."

"You're on medical extension," Hemmings said.

"That's right."

"But still in the Bureau."

"Don't tell me if you're afraid to."

"Be good enough not to use reverse psychology on me, Becker. I may be in research but I'm not a cretin."

"Sorry, Hairy. But don't make me beg, for Christ's sake."

"His name is Taylor Ashford Jr. The warrant is for unlawful flight from the Pennsylvania State Correctional Facility where he was undergoing psychiatric treatment."

"A mental case."

"I think you could say that."

"What was he in for?"

"Apart from being crazy?"

"That's not a crime in itself. Do you know what he was in for?"

"You can't help yourself, can you, Becker? You know I pride myself on knowing things, so now you're challenging me to prove it."

"I asked you outright first."

"So you did. He was found not guilty by reason of insanity of murdering his father, his mother and his two siblings and was committed to an indefinite term in the bug house."

It was Becker's turn to be silent.

"So you see, it's likely that I'll be taken off the uniform chase as soon as Deputy Assistant Director Crist has the time to remember me at all."

20

Jack was already all the way down the hill and standing in line for the mess hall when he remembered he had promised to give the girl from the Algonquin cabin his copy of *Old Yeller*. He left the queue for dinner and started back up towards his cabin, running at first until he hit the steeper grade, then settling into a fast walk. Dinner was one of his favourite times at camp. The counsellors told stories and sang songs and put on skits and there was a feeling of camaraderie all around, even when the counsellors urged them to shout out the superiority of their own cabin over all the others. Jack didn't want to miss any of it, but he had promised the girl from the Algonquin cabin that she could borrow his copy of the book. He wasn't sure why he felt so obliged to fulfil his promise to a girl, except that she had said she would really like to read it. It seemed an easy enough way to make her happy – except for the climb up the hill.

The path was wide enough for a truck to get up and down with the food supplies but somehow when Jack walked it alone it seemed to narrow into nothing more than a rutted slice through the woods. When his whole cabin teemed down it together in the morning it was like a boulevard, pulsing with people and sounding with shouts and laughter. At those times he didn't feel any more in the woods than he would in a playground with too many trees. Traversing the path alone, however, made Jack aware of the primitive nature of the surrounding forest. There probably weren't any dangerous wild animals lurking among the trees, they had been told that often enough. There probably weren't bad men with axes and knives, either. One of the counsellors had assured them that bad men were restricted to the big cities and would be totally out of their element in the forest. Jack believed all of this because he had it directly from authority, and yet – there had been plenty of bad men in Sherwood Forest, just for example. And madmen who lived in the woods and preyed on children, not witches exactly, but … Jack was vague on the details, but his sense of anxiety was real enough. And there were all those ghost stories the older kids liked to tell at night. But here he was, making his way to the cabin alone, and the pride he felt in his courage more than outweighed his fears.

The nurse stepped in front of him as he reached the top of the hill. She appeared so suddenly that Jack wasn't sure where she had come from unless she had been standing behind a tree. He did not remember having seen a nurse in a uniform at the camp before. Her starched white dress and stockings and gleaming shoes seemed an intrusion into the rustic world of the camp.

"Your mother has been in an accident. I'll take you to her," the nurse said sternly. She turned immediately and walked towards the parking lot which was just visible past Jack's cabin.

Jack hesitated. He thought he knew the nurse, felt he had seen her somewhere before, but he didn't know where. He looked around for a counsellor to ask guidance. Was he allowed to leave the camp? Where was his mother? How hurt was she? It must be very serious for a nurse to come for him.

The nurse was well in front of him, walking quickly as if in a hurry. She turned once, looked at him, her face grim. It must be very, very serious.

"Come along now," she said sharply before turning once more on her heel and striding determinedly towards the parking lot.

Jack looked once more for someone to tell where he was going but there was no one so he hurried after the nurse. She walked as if she was going to leave without him if he fell behind, as if there was no time whatsoever to lose. She did not look back at him again.

At first Dee didn't know if Tommy was following her or not but she could not allow herself to worry about it. If they came, they came and if not then she could always try again another time. Sometimes they wouldn't follow because they didn't understand, but she could not risk stopping to explain. She would usually sweep past the tail end of a group, brushing them at a tangent, already on her path out of the mall and into the safety of the car. If she knocked her boy away from the group with her message and into the gravity of her own orbit, then she succeeded, but if she did not, she did not loiter to be noticed, she did not argue or discuss with them, and she did not stay close to them. Let them follow her, she would not walk with them, she would not hold their hands. She would not delay so they could seek advice or tell their teachers or siblings or guardians. They would come because they responded to crisis and command – or they would not. Often enough, they did. Because they were the right age to understand the summons of authority, because they were the right age to dare to trust their own judgement in following her without further approval, because they were the right age to love their mothers enough to be foolish for them. But most of all, Dee was convinced, they came because she wanted them. Because she needed them. Because, after all, they really belonged to her and in their hearts they knew it. They longed to be with her as much as she with them. If they followed, then they were meant for each other.

By the time she reached the parking lot, Dee knew that Jack was meant for her, too. She opened the back door of the car for him, still without looking back, and slid herself behind the wheel. There was no one else in the parking lot. No one else in sight anywhere. She could hear singing rising up from farther down the mountain.

The engine was started before Jack reached the car. When Dee heard the back door slam shut, she set the car in motion. In her rear-view mirror she saw the blanket rise suddenly and then descend, like the wing of a giant bird.

Becker was washing his solitary dinner dish when the phone rang. He had fried a chicken sausage and given some thought to adding a green pepper to the skillet and making a sauce. The plan had been to create a sausage and pepper submarine sandwich of the type he could buy at a pizza restaurant. In the end, however, it had seemed like entirely too much trouble to go to for only himself and he had ended up by eating the sausage by itself and calling it a meal. The dish wasn't even dirty since he had nibbled at the sausage while holding it over the skillet, but he washed it reflexively anyway. The idea of returning it unused to the cabinet was too depressing.

"It's Malva," said the voice on the phone and for a moment Becker thought excitedly that Karen was calling him. "Karen's son has disappeared."

Becker was still waiting for her to say that Deputy Assistant Director Crist wished to speak to him and at first the words made no sense. "What?"

"Director Crist's son has disappeared from camp," she said.

"Jack?" he asked stupidly.

"They noticed his absence about two hours ago. So far they're considering it just a local matter. They think he might have got lost in the woods."

"The lake," Becker said, voicing his first thought. He remembered Jack battling the water so bravely. So ineptly.

"Well ... He probably just wandered off."

"Of course."

"Children do that," Malva said.

"That's probably it," Becker agreed, trying to convince himself. He thought of Jack, his fear of the dark, his ambivalence about adventure. Just wandered off? Into the woods?

"I don't know that much about kids," he said.

"They do it all the time, I believe," Malva said. Becker could not remember if Malva had children of her own. Jack, wandering off by himself, gone for two hours so far? He could not make the connection with the act and the boy he knew.

"Where is she?" he asked.

"On her way to the camp."

"Did they think it was necessary for her to go to the camp?"

"I believe she thought it was necessary," Malva said.

"Of course. How can I help?"

"I think she needs somebody," Malva said.

"The closest task forces are in Albany and Boston," Becker said. "It would take at least a day ..."

"I don't mean help in finding him," Malva interrupted. "I don't know exactly what the status of your relationship is, but ... I think she could use someone now."

"I'm on my way right now," he said. "And Malva – thank you."

"She's a very special lady," Malva said.

"I know."

"But not always as brave as she pretends to be.

"Malva," Becker said, "none of us are as brave as we pretend to be."

He reached Wasaknee after the search had been halted because of darkness. Karen was installed in the camp office where a cot had been placed in a corner to serve as her bed for the night. When Becker stepped into the room she was conferring with the camp administrator, a middle-aged man, who looked mildly ridiculous in his ragged jeans shorts and camp T-shirt, and two local policemen who looked like brothers although they wore different name tags, both of them rail thin with faces that seemed to come to a point. All four listened attentively to Karen who was issuing orders. Becker noticed that she was wearing her FBI insignia on the outside of her jacket. He wondered at what point she had changed from worried mother to search coordinator. She glanced at Becker when he entered but did not miss a beat in her instructions. Her eyes showed no recognition of him, he was as routinely observed as if he were another counsellor stepping in to listen.

The two cops checked him out more thoroughly but they were clearly taking their lead from Karen now, and, if his presence didn't bother her, it didn't bother them, either.

Speaking calmly but with authority, Karen laid out the morning's search procedures for the three men. She explained the principle of grid exploration, defined the methods of communication, established the manners of coordination. The administrator nervously nodded agreement with every sentence she uttered and the cops appeared awed by the lovely young woman with the commanding presence and the impressive badge.

Becker had to admire the performance himself. To an uninformed observer there would be no indication that his detached executive was the mother of the missing boy. Except for the eyes, he thought. They looked as if they had sunken deep within her face, as if she had not slept for weeks. They were haggard eyes, and frantic, and revealed the price she was paying for her outward calm. Becker wanted to take her in his arms and kiss the eyes until he healed them, but instead he sat on the edge of one of the three desks in the office and watched.

She had a way of ending a meeting by simply changing her posture, signifying a dismissal by a move of her shoulders, the inclination of her head. The men filed out, the two cops again sliding their eyes over Becker as they left. In a community this small without a panoply of elected officials or a hierarchy more than one or two deep, Becker did not imagine that the police had to defer very often to anyone, but they left the office now like schoolchildren lucky to get away from the principal's office with nothing more severe than a good talking to. Karen had a way of not only taking command of men, but an even rarer trait of making them like it. Becker wondered that she was so plagued by self-doubts about her abilities.

Alone with Becker, Karen removed her suit jacket for the first time. He imagined her trekking through the woods that way, in a feminine twist on the popular stereotype of the FBI agent permanently encased in his suit and button-down collar. Of course she had come straight from the office, he realised, and had not had time to change clothes, but at the same time, the straight skirt and dark blue jacket made it easier for her to command respect than would have jean shorts and a T-shirt.

Her blouse was blotched with dark stains under both arms and across her stomach where it tucked into the skirt. She had been sweating profusely, he saw, and keeping it to herself. It was a warm day, but not that hot. It was nervous sweat, and when she stood next to him he could smell it, the sour odour of anxiety. Perspiration caused by physical exertion never smelled if it was fresh, but no deodorant made could mask the scent of fear.

He tried to hold her in his arms. She didn't resist but folded her arms in front of her so they rested on his chest, keeping her at a distance. Her body felt as tense as twisted steel.

"I hope he's got a broken leg," she hissed. "I swear to God I do. I pray that he's lying beside a rock with a broken leg."

"No ... shhh ..."

"Because if that isn't it, if it isn't just that he's not able to get back to us ..."

Becker tilted his chin so that her head fitted more closely to him. He rubbed her back and continued to shush her.

"If he's been snatched ..." She stopped, too filled with emotion to speak.

"He hasn't been snatched, he's just lost."

"How in hell did he get lost?"

"Kids do that," Becker said unconvincingly. "They wander off sometimes."

"Not Jack." She shook her head violently. "Not my Jack. He's too smart to do that. He'd blaze a trail, he'd take his bearings. He just wouldn't do it in the first place, you know what he's like. He wouldn't do it."

She was so tense her body was vibrating. Becker was surprised that she let him continue to hold her but she did not pull away. She seemed to need his presence even if she wouldn't give in to it.

319

"If he's been snatched …"

Becker slid a hand to the back of her neck. The cords there felt as if they were about to snap from the strain of holding her head on her shoulders.

"Better the lake," she said.

Becker rubbed her and murmured.

"I mean it. I prefer him drowning to being tortured by that fucking maniac."

"There's no reason to think that …"

"I feel it," she said.

"Just because the case is on your mind …"

"I feel it. So do you. Don't you. Jack wouldn't wander off, he wouldn't go into the lake by himself. He's too good a boy, too well behaved, too concerned about …" She pulled herself away from Becker and put her hands on his face. Her fingers felt icy cold and her eyes looked to Becker as they were peering towards him from hell itself.

"Our people in Pennsylvania are trying to dig up a photograph or at least a detailed physical description of this guy Ashford so we'll know what he looks like. When I find the fucking son-of-a-bitch, Ashford or Lamont or whoever he is, I am going to kill him myself."

"No …" Her fingers pressed into his cheeks, closing off whatever he would have said.

"Understand me, John, I am not discussing this, I am telling you. When we find him, I will kill him. I want you to just get out of the way and let me do it."

"You can't do that."

"You do," she spat.

Becker stepped back as if slapped across the face with the words. Karen was paying no attention to him, showed no sign that she had hurt him.

"Because he's mine," she said. "He's mine." Becker was not certain if she meant her son or Lamont.

Freed from Becker's arms, she began to pace, speaking to herself in a tone too low and garbled for him to understand.

Suddenly Karen stopped and teetered back and forth, all of the strain breaking through the mask and now revealing itself in her face as well as her eyes. She looked abruptly twenty years older and horribly weary. Her shoulders slumped, her head dropped and her eyes stared blankly in a kind of silent horror. Becker took a step towards her and she turned to look at him, as if seeing him for the first time. As their eyes met her face suddenly crumpled.

"I abused him," she said, but her voice caught on the word "abused" as if it were a live coal on her tongue.

Becker started to protest but she shook her head and repeated herself.

"I abused him," she said, clearly this time. "I hit him. I beat him."

"Who?"

"Jack. My Jack," and she began to weep, the tears flowing almost immediately as if they had been dammed up so long that finally they had to spill over whatever barrier was holding them back.

"Right after his father left us, right there in the middle of the mess, at the worst part. He did something, Jackie did something, I don't know what, it wasn't bad, he wasn't that naughty, just something, and I started to spank him and I couldn't stop, I just couldn't stop, I kept doing it and doing it. I don't know what happened to me, I just lost control, it seemed right ... I did it three different times. The last time I hit him so much he was bleeding. I made my Jack bleed, John!"

This time she sought his arms, pressing against him until the gun in her shoulder holster bit into his ribs.

She spoke into his shirt, her voice muffled by the cloth,

distorted by sobs. "Have I done this? Have I made him too passive? Is that why it happened?"

"No, no ..."

"That's your theory, isn't it? Lamont snatches the passive ones, the ones who don't shout or fight or ..."

"No, it isn't your ..."

"Isn't that what you wanted me to agree to? Didn't you keep banging at me about how I understood it all but wouldn't admit it? Didn't you say I shaped him this way, so he'd follow anybody?"

"For God's sake, Karen, you can't blame yourself for this. In the first place, we don't even know what's happened ..."

She tore away from him again. "I know."

She sank to the floor, wrapping her arms around herself as if to hold in the anguish, and began a high, wordless keen of grief and pain.

Becker watched her helplessly for a moment as she rocked back and forth, emitting a sound that sent chills through him. He knelt beside her, his arm around her and she turned to him abruptly, clutching his shirt and pulling his face towards hers. She pressed her lips against his with such force that she pushed him off balance.

"God damn it, help me, Becker! I can't make it till morning, I can't take it, I'm dying here, I'm dying."

She scrabbled at his belt buckle, then stood and turned off the only light in the room. Becker rose to his feet and she was back at him, clawing at his belt. She still wore her blouse and the shoulder holster but somehow between the light switch and Becker she had managed to remove her skirt and pantyhose.

"Help me, Christ, John, help me," she muttered. With his belt and zipper undone she pressed her lips against his again, then, frantically, attacked his mouth with her tongue. It was not a kiss, Becker knew, but another way of crying out in pain.

He tried to calm her, pulling away from her ravenous mouth and kissing her neck, running his hands down her arms, under the back of her blouse and pulling her body into his with gradually increasing pressure. She writhed against him, impatient, struggling, and the sour smell of her fear-sweat rose up strongly.

His hand moved up to cup her breast, teasingly soft and slow but she mashed into him rubbing wildly.

"Don't be gentle," she cried. "Not now!"

Becker tried to lower her to the floor but she shrugged him off and turned her back to him, pushing her hips back until her naked body pressed against his groin.

He took her from the rear, standing up, his pants at his knees while she braced her arms against the edge of the desk. She thrust harder than he did, growling low in her throat and grunting with every effort as they hammered at each other. He could not be too hard for her, or fast enough. Becker felt as if she were punishing herself, and using him as the instrument. It was the closest thing to being raped he would ever experience, he thought. When he had shuddered to a climax she simply straightened up and walked away, discarding him as if he were a tool that had served its purpose.

Half an hour later she took him again and then a third time an hour before sunrise with Becker half asleep and lying on his back. When she had finished her urgent actions and left him supine on the cot, she returned to the window where she had spent most of the night. Becker watched her staring into the night, looking first towards the lake, then at the woods, then back towards the lake, her heart being ripped apart by the two horrifyingly unacceptable possibilities.

21

Edgar Rapapport could not believe his luck. He had taken what looked on the map to be a shortcut between Springfield and Pittsfield and had ended up on a steadily narrowing back road that was threatening to become a cow path. He had been dawdling behind an ultra cautious Volvo for the better part of half an hour, aching to pass but being frustrated at every opportunity – and there were few on these hilly, winding roads – by oncoming traffic. There would seem to be no other cars on the road except the Volvo in front of him until they reached a brief section with dotted passing lines and then, out of no-where, would materialise another car, coming straight at him, pushing him back behind the Volvo. Meanwhile the road seemed to be shrinking in width with each passing mile.

His luck, however, was good, better than he could have hoped for, because when he was forced to stop at the only traffic light in a village at the base of a mountain, he saw her stopped opposite him, going the other way. It took him a moment to remember her name, but it was her, no question about it. He even remembered the dull green Dodge Charger; he had followed it from the mall to her motel.

She did not see him, did not even glance in his direction

when the light changed and she drove past him, less than twenty feet away. There was no mistaking her. Her face was stamped into Edgar's memory with all the force of major trauma. He remembered her pulling his clothes off, urging him to fuck her for all he was worth, then demanding more, taunting him, coming at him with a razor.

Dee, that was her name. Dee, the crazy lady, Dee the lunatic. And now, most important, Dee alone. Dee without her monster boyfriend.

Edgar made a u-turn in the intersection and followed her. He stayed well behind the Charger, trying to think through his options. What he wanted was to have her arrested. No, not just arrested, convicted, sent away and locked up. Let her know what he felt like in the trunk of his car, only for about five or six years. The problem was to arrange that without involving himself in any way that might get back to his wife. Or better yet, fuck her first, then get her arrested. Despite the brutal aftermath, Edgar still remembered the sex with Dee as the wildest, most exciting he had ever had. And she had obviously loved it, too. She couldn't get enough, in fact, which had been the problem. Edgar thought of ways of getting her alone and disarmed, then he would give her all the sex she could handle – but not when she wanted it, when he decided it was time for more. Chain her to the bedpost, something like that. He laughed at the thought, then realised it wasn't so outlandish after all. People did do things like that, he read about them. Did it willingly, that was the point. He had no intention of setting himself up for prosecution, he wasn't going to kidnap her, but she was just the kind of woman who might well be talked into it. She'd like it in the long run, no question. He was scheduled for one night in Pittsfield but he could stretch it to two.

Edgar pulled a little closer to the Charger so he could make out her head clearly. She was a good-looking woman. And sexy. Very sexy. Crazy, maybe, but as horny as Edgar himself. And alone now, thank God.

He wouldn't have to actually force her, he thought. She'd be willing enough once she understood it was in her own interest. All he had to do was threaten to call the cops on her, swear he would testify against her – how would she know that was a bluff? It wasn't force, just a little inducement to do what she loved doing anyway. Then get her into a motel without razor blades and the rest would take care of itself. He didn't really mean to tie her up – although that was an intriguing thought.

Edgar breathed deeply and tried to dismiss the whole fantasy. He was alone on the road far too much, the solitude was not good for the imagination. He was never as horny at home as he was when he was travelling, he never thought of tying up his wife. Nor, he was sure, did his wife, which was part of the problem. If Mimi showed a little more sense of adventure, hell, if she even seemed to want him, if it wasn't always Edgar who had to make the overtures, he probably wouldn't be in this condition in the first place. He remembered Dee on her hands and knees on the carpet, howling like a beast, Christ, there must be a way. Fuck her blind then get her arrested. Or just fuck her if that was all he could manage. But do it a lot, enough to make up for what she did. He almost rear-ended the Charger before he realised it had stopped at a railroad crossing. She looked in her rear-view mirror, he could see her eyes searching his face. Of course she remembered him, he thought, it was not the kind of night she'd forget. And since she knew he was there, he had to do something or just turn around and drive away. Amid flashing lights and clanging bells, a freight train surged past the crossing. Dee was going nowhere now. She was pinned between the train in front and Edgar's car behind her. She held his eyes in the mirror now and he saw her lips move. It was either get out of the car now or just look at her in the mirror then drive away and forget the whole thing.

Still not certain what he was going to say, Edgar walked to Dee's car. He leaned down with a big grin.

"Fancy meeting you here," he said.

"Small world," she said. The train was making so much noise he could barely hear her.

"Do you remember me?"

"Sure," she said with that mocking smile. Edgar remembered that smile. Sexy as hell, as if she were daring him to make the next move. "You're Lyle."

Edgar looked at the train for a moment, willing it to hurry past. Whatever he was going to say, he didn't want to have to shout it.

"Do you remember me?" she asked.

"Vaguely," said Edgar, trying to muster a copy of her derisive grin. "You're Dee."

"Good boy."

"I've been thinking about you, actually," Edgar said.

"Isn't that funny? I've been thinking about you, too."

"You want to go first?"

She looked up at him under lowered lashes. "I always prefer it if the man makes the first move," she said.

Edgar said, "That's not the way I remember it, but I don't mind. What I was thinking is, should I call the cops and tell them where to find you, or should I take you to the nearest motel and we can work something out together?"

"Do you have a phone in your car?" she asked.

"No."

"Then you can't make a phone call to the police from

here, anyway, can you? So you might as well go the nearest motel."

"I was hoping you'd say that."

"As a matter of fact, Lyle, the closest motel from here is mine."

"Oh, no," said Edgar. "We're not going to your motel."

"Why not? We could start working things out in five minutes."

"Because your gorilla boyfriend will be there."

"Oh, Ash isn't at the motel."

"He isn't, huh?"

"No."

"How do I know that?"

"I just told you. Don't you believe me?"

"Do you think I'm an idiot?"

"Yes, Lyle, I certainly do." She smiled so brightly at him that Edgar thought he had misunderstood her because of the noise of the train.

"I promise you Ash isn't at the motel," she said.

"Why should I believe that?"

"Because he's right here," she said. She took hold of his tie and pulled him towards her. For a second he thought she was going to kiss him but then he saw the movement in the back of the car. The whole seat seemed to rise up, then an arm flashed out. Edgar jerked away reflexively but Dee held him within the car by his necktie. He felt the crushing hand on his throat before he saw the face and enormous bulk of Ash emerge from under the blanket.

Jack heard the voices dimly, all sounds being muffled by the blanket and the body of the man on top of him. The motion of the car had stopped, there was a roar and a clanging which he knew to be a train crossing, then the

328

voice of a man and a woman talking above the clamour of the train. The man's body was not really on him, he felt no weight from it, just the shape of it, like a huge shell holding him down, or, oddly, protecting him.

Suddenly the shell was torn away as the body vaulted upwards. Jack saw light and lifted his head, blinking. He saw the man's arm stretching over the seat back, heard a man gargling dryly as if something was caught in his throat.

Jack saw the car door, clawed at the handle, then crawled out from under the blanket, out from under the man's body. The man seemed to have forgotten him. Then Jack was on the road and he began to run without seeing where he was going, just away, as fast as he could, off the road so the man and the nurse couldn't follow him. For a second he heard the gargling sound grow louder, more desperate, but then Jack had sprinted beyond the sound. He leaped into the shallow dry ditch next to the tracks and ran. The train slammed by him, dangerously close, and Jack recoiled, amazed that he hadn't noticed it before.

Almost at once he knew he had made a mistake. The ditch grew deeper, trapping him in its recesses. He had no choice but to continue straight ahead, climbing the bank to flatter ground would take him too long and he knew he had to flee as if hotly pursued even though he had not yet looked back to see if he was being chased. He didn't dare to look back, he knew that he would be paralysed by fear if he saw someone coming.

He could hear nothing; there was nothing to hear over the roar of the train. The wheels clattered against the steel rails and the cars swayed overhead as if they must surely topple into the ditch and crush him.

The ditch ran parallel to the tracks, around a curve, seeming to sink almost directly under the wheels of the train that never stopped and then it began to rise again, growing shallower by the step. At the end of it he could see first one, then the another house. Within a few steps he would be able to leap out of the ditch, into the adjoining field, then straight to the houses and people and safety.

He made the leap and felt something catch at his T-shirt. He hung on the lip of the ditch, teetering there, flailing his arms to keep his balance as something tried to pull him back down. He saw a girl in the backyard of a house staring at him from her swing set. She raised a hand tentatively, not certain if he was rotating his arms in a greeting.

Jack's weight was thrown to the side and he spun around, still atop the edge of the ditch. He ducked his head and found himself face to face with the nurse who was panting hard, her lips curled into a snarl. Jack pulled backwards and she peeled the T-shirt off his body like she was skinning a rabbit. Suddenly released, he stumbled and sat down abruptly, still looking straight at the nurse in the ditch. Before he could get up, she had him by the ankle. It occurred to him to yell as he was being dragged back into the ditch, but it seemed he needed all his breath to resist the nurse. Jack saw the girl on the swing watch in amazement as he disappeared, inch by inch, into the ditch. He managed to scream very briefly before he sank out of sight entirely and a hand clapped over his mouth.

The nurse was calling him "precious" and her "darling boy" as she dragged and carried him back to the car but Jack was too frightened to make any sense of her words. A huge man waited by the car, another man hanging limply from his hand. The big man looked puzzled, still clutching the other by the throat, holding him as if not quite certain what to do with him, like a toy rendered

330

useless now that the game was completed. Jack had seen a cat look like that, baffled and no longer interested, embarrassed to explain how the mouse had gotten in its mouth in the first place.

22

They ruled out the lake quickly enough. It was shallow and easily searched for a distance of forty feet out from the dock and the severity of the hills surrounding the lake elsewhere made entry any place other than the dock difficult. It seemed very unlikely that Jack, with his limited skills, would have, or even could have, swum farther from the shore.

The combined search party of Karen, Becker, Blocker and Reese – the two local policemen – and two dozen camp volunteers found no trace of Jack in the mountain forest and by mid-afternoon both Karen and the locals agreed it was time to summon the State police. She also summoned elements of the Bureau forces from both Albany and Boston who would not be able to reach them before the following morning.

Throughout the day Karen acted like a woman very much in control of herself as well as her circumstances while she ordered and organised the searches, conferred politely with Blocker and Reese, consulted Becker with the same diplomatic inclusion, made her decision and the phone calls. Becker saw no signs of either the frantic mother or the hysterical, guilt-ridden woman of the night before. She did not meet his eye directly all day long, but that was a clue to her inner turmoil that only he would recognise. To the world about her, she was a brisk professional set on accomplishing her task. He marvelled at her, at the strength she found in her work. Even her skirt and jacket looked as if they had been freshly pressed. It was only when close to her that he smelled the sour odour of her fear. She had showered first thing in the morning but the stench had already worked deeply into her clothes.

Following her decision to call in the State police, Karen pulled Becker aside, away from the local cops and the counsellors.

"I'm biased, John, so I need your perspective. If this were anybody else's child who was missing – would I have enough to declare it a snatch?"

"I'm biased, too," Becker said.

She waved his protest aside with a flick of her hand. No one else's concern could approach hers.

"Am I justified in thinking Jack has been kidnapped?" She faced him but her eyes roved somewhere over his shoulder.

"Does it matter? Do it anyway. He's your boy, who cares if it's technically justified or not?"

She grew very quiet and Becker watched the colour slowly drain from her face then gradually return. Her eyes stayed so steadfastly fixed in the distance that Becker turned to look. A squirrel climbed halfway up the trunk of a tree then appeared to notice the humans for the first time and skittered around to the other side. Becker studied the squirrel's antics for a moment, giving Karen time to recover herself. He wondered how many times this day she had gone through the same crisis, battling with all of her inner resources to fight off the powerful surge of despair.

"You are a very experienced agent," she said at last, her words measured too precisely. "For the record, I am asking if, in your opinion, I am justified in calling the State police into the case on suspicion of kidnapping. This is an official question. I would appreciate an official answer."

"What are you worried about, charges of abuse of power? Just go ahead and do it, if anyone questions you later, to hell them. It's Jack we're talking about."

"I am aware who we're talking about," she hissed.

"Sorry. But don't worry about it, everyone will understand."

For the first time she looked directly at him, her eyes burning with anger. "I don't give a fuck what they understand! I'm asking you a simple question. Stop being such a contentious bastard and just say yes."

"Yes, absolutely," Becker said. "You are fully justified in calling in the State police on suspicion of kidnapping. That makes it a federal case for the Bureau as well."

"Thank you," she said. "That wasn't so hard, was it? What did you have to be such a prick about it, for?"

"You're just upset ..." he said.

"No shit."

He reached for her shoulders but she pulled away and started towards the others.

"Do you want me to make one of the calls?" he asked.

"I called them both ten minutes ago," she said. "Now we have to decide what to do when they get here."

Blocker and Reese looked on as Karen spread maps of Massachusetts and the adjoining area of New York on the hood of one of their squad cars.

"At least it's less populated here than in New Jersey," Karen said. "That should help some." Her minor explosion at Becker had been contained. She was now the working professional again.

She turned to the two cops who were watching her with curiosity. "The State police should be here in a few minutes," she said. "Now you know how they are, they'll want to take over."

"Pretty much assholes," Blocker said. Reese nodded confirmation.

"Well, exactly," Karen agreed. "They'll want to push you guys right out of the case even though it's your case, your territory, your right to be involved."

Reese kept right on nodding agreement.

"Well, I hate that," she said. "I want to keep you involved, for my own benefit. You know the area better than anybody, you've been in on the case since the beginning. I want you on my team and I don't want any State cop pushing you aside."

Becker watched Karen's manipulations work their effect on the cops. He knew she would later apply much the same kind of flattery to the State people. It was good policy to keep everyone happy, but in the case of the local cops, he knew she had a further motive. It may have been true that they knew the area better, but it was also true that they were much easier to bend to her will than the State police. Karen was oiling them up now so that later she could twist them into whatever shape she needed. And coming from an attractive woman, this kind of blandishment was even easier to believe. Both cops harboured a secret hope that she really wanted them around because of her ardent desire to tear their clothes off. They were not fools enough to do anything about it, hoping as they did that this sort of passion would blossom spontaneously without any particular nurture on their part, but Karen was aware of their fantasies, perhaps more objectively than they were, and if she made a point of smiling at each of them as she appealed for their help, it seemed to Becker just good policework.

"So I think it's a good thing if we can get you actively

working before they get here, don't you?" She continued without waiting for their response. "What we'll need is a list of all the motels or houses for rent within a thirty minute drive. Any place a transient could get a room and have some degree of privacy. A boarding house with a separate entrance even. Any place this guy might have taken a child to hole up if he wasn't a local resident."

"Thirty minutes' drive?"

"It's not that far. It takes a good fifteen minutes just to wind down off this mountain, and there's a lot of empty territory around here. If thirty minutes isn't enough, we'll go farther out, but let's start with that."

Blocker said, "It's going to take us a little time to think about that."

"Well, yes. That's why I think you want to get started before the State guys show up."

"We can do more," Becker said when the cops had moved off to start their list.

"Tell me."

"I think we got lucky this time – I mean because of where Lamont – or Ashford, I still think of him as Lamont, I've been calling him that so long – because of where he chose to go. There aren't nearly as many places to hide in the first place and not many to run to."

"What do you mean?"

"We've spent a day walking through these woods. How many rabbits did you see?"

"Rabbits? None."

"And how many do you think live in there? Dozens? Hundreds? More? The reason we didn't see them is because they were just sitting still, hidden. But how many do you think we'd see if we went through there beating the bushes and getting them to run?"

"Go on."

"Lamont has made it to his hiding place. All he has to

do is stay very still and we won't find him unless we step directly on him. He's had practice at this, he chose his own spot, he's got the advantage. But if we can make him run, the advantage is ours. And this is the kind of country where we can do it. There aren't that many places to run to once he's flushed out of cover."

Karen studied the map, her mind racing. "How do we get him to run?"

"We've got to scare him, make him think we're coming right at him. That's the only thing that will make him break from his hiding place. Announce on the local radio and television that we're starting a house to house search, that we're concentrating on transient housing. Maybe he'll run."

"Maybe. But we couldn't possibly get the manpower to do a house to house unless we knew where he was."

"He doesn't know that. If he hears it on the radio he'll believe it. Why shouldn't he? Can he afford to take the chance?"

"So he runs. He's not a rabbit, he'll be in a car, he can go anywhere."

"We'll funnel him. Say the search starts along a line from here to here ..." Becker jabbed at two dots on the map. "He'll run this way. Once he's running we can funnel him even further. Look, there aren't that many roads through the mountains. Put a cop car at this intersection, another one here, and you force anyone trying to avoid the cops to Route 21. Put a roadblock ..." he studied the map for a second more, his forefinger hovering over it like a bee above a blossom. "... here. A real one, a full search of every car that goes through it. We can get enough men for that."

"There are ways to avoid it," Karen said.

"Yes, there are," Becker agreed. "If he's smart enough, if he knows the country, if he suspects a trap."

"Or he could be on the other side of the search line to begin with. He could ignore the bluff and stay where he is. He could turn north and head to Canada."

"In which case we're no worse off than we were. Look, Karen, it's not a great plan, but it is something positive, something we can do immediately. We have no time to lose."

Karen was silent, still staring at the map.

"Bobby Reynolds lasted only three weeks," Becker said. Karen winced. "Lamont is getting faster and faster. Jack may have ..."

"I know."

"Of course," he said. He put his hand on her back and but she stepped away from him.

"All right," she said.

"All you have to do is convince the State boys to go along," Becker said.

She snorted dismissively. "That I can do," she said.

As they started towards the others, she said "Do you know what really scares me?"

"What?"

"This is the first time you've admitted that it's Lamont."

Becker sighed. "I seem to hurt you no matter what I do," he said. "Every way I turn, I'm wrong. I'm sorry ..."

She slipped her hand into his and gave him a brief squeeze.

At least it was contact, Becker thought. She gave me that much at least.

In the camp office, after conferring with the State police, Becker and Karen settled in for the night in silence, Becker on the cot, Karen resuming her place at the window. A few hours before dawn she slipped on to the cot beside him, the two of them barely fitting on the

338

stretched canvas. He put his arms around her and waited to see what else she required, but it was all she needed.

"I don't know what else to do," she whispered, lost. "I've done everything I know how to do."

"We'll find him," Becker said.

"I know," she said. "And when we do, I'll kill him."

Becker was startled. He had meant they would find Jack. Just before dawn he awoke again and knew by the tremors of her body that she was crying, but she did not make a sound. When she got up at first light her eyes were dry but so red they looked painful. The bags under them extended downward almost to her cheeks, a spreading smudge of charcoal.

23

Ash found Dee's pills in her purse and painstakingly counted them on to the counter of the bathroom sink. She hadn't taken any in the longest time. He heard her voice from the other room, high, bright and animated as she told the new Tommy how lucky he really was that she had found him. Ash wondered if he could force Dee to take a pill. He had managed to do that in the past when she was in her sadness, lying inert in the back the car. He had been able then to put the pill far back on her tongue and hold her jaw closed until she swallowed. But that was when she was too weak to resist him.

He had never seen her this high, this long, and it frightened him. She was different this time, she seemed to need more, as if Tommy wasn't quite enough anymore. She was talking more and more about the workers who had taken her boy away, about how she had gotten him back just in time. In the past she had seldom talked about anything but the boy. Now she seemed as interested in revenge on the workers as the boy himself, and the change frightened Ash. He didn't dare to think it, but it seemed almost as if Dee wasn't really in control. And if she wasn't in control of things, where did that leave him? He knew he certainly wasn't.

If he tried to make her take a pill now, she would fight

him and he knew he couldn't fight back. He could never hurt Dee, no matter what. It wasn't even thinkable. He would hurt himself before he would ever hurt his Dee.

Ash returned to his position by the door, facing the television set which sat atop the dresser opposite the bed, the screen canted towards Ash. The new Tommy sat naked on the bed, covering himself with his hands as Dee talked to him. The boy looked frightened but Ash detected defiance in his face, too. He had already demonstrated his courage by running for freedom. Ash hoped he didn't try anything else that stupid because Dee seemed close enough to an explosion as it was, without provocation.

"Dee," Ash said, abruptly. "Look Dee."

He pointed to the television where a morning show had just been interrupted by a special report. The new Tommy's face filled the screen.

"It's Tommy," he said. That made her look and she turned the sound up immediately. "Look, Tommy, you're on television."

Jack's face was replaced by the image of Karen Crist, soberly intoning plans for a manhunt. Her face was so gaunt and drawn, her appearance on television so unexpected, that it took Jack a few seconds to be sure it was her.

"My mother," he said, amazed.

Dee stood close to the set, her face screwed up as if it gave off poison.

"The bitch," Dee said.

"That's my mother," Tommy said again.

Dee slapped him so hard he fell back on to the bed.

"That's the bitch who took you," she said. "Don't you ever call her your mother. She's not your mother, she's one of the case workers, she saw you, she saw how wonderful you are, how precious you are, and she wanted you for her own, so she made up all those lies about me so they'd help her steal you."

341

Karen's image was replaced by a map with a curved red line drawn across it and triangles like arrowheads pointing in the direction of advance. It looked like the chart of a military campaign.

"The bitch, the bitch, the bitch!"

Ash struggled to make sense of it all while Tommy slowly came upright on the bed again, holding his face where she had struck him. He had forgotten his modesty.

"She's coming," Dee said. "The bitch is coming, she's going to try to steal you away."

Dee hurled the suitcase on the bed and threw her clothes into it.

"Well, she's not going to do it. She won't get you again."

The regular programme had returned to the television screen and Dee snapped it off.

"Dress him," Dee spat at Ash. "We're leaving now."

Dee was packed in two minutes. She knelt in front of Jack who stood in the centre of the room, his pants on, his shoes untied.

"Don't you worry, I won't let her take you again." She took Jack's face in her hands. "You are so, so precious to me. I couldn't stand it if she took you away again. You couldn't stand it either, could you, Tommy? It would hurt you just as much as me. Don't you worry. She won't get you again. I'll see you dead first."

Dee stood and nodded and Ash lowered the bedspread over Jack like a net.

They drove west, away from the red line on the television map.

At a junction outside of Becket, two State police cars were parked perpendicularly across the highway, slowing the traffic as troopers peered into each passing car. Dee veered away from the troopers and headed northwest, into the mountains. She listened to the radio as she drove – something Ash had known her to do but rarely – and when another report of the manhunt was announced, she began to mutter darkly again about "the bitch." Ash could hear her from under the bedspread but he hoped that Tommy, covered by both the bedspread and Ash's body, could not.

A few miles later Dee shunted away from troopers at another junction, taking the only unobstructed road left open to her, straight into the eminence of Mt. Jefferson.

On the steepest grade, she rounded a turn and saw before her a long line of cars parked in the ascending lane. As she braked to a halt, muttering an obscenity, she could see the rear tail-lights of the car at the top of the road change from red to blank as the car inched forward. The shifting red made its way down hill like a slow wave as one after another the automobiles released their brakes and advanced one car length. By the time Dee moved forward, the line was solidly red once more and a beige Subaru station wagon had pulled into place behind her.

"Ash, can you hear me?"

"Yes, Dee," he said, his voice muffled by the bedspread over him.

"Listen carefully." She glanced in her rear-view mirror and saw the driver of the car behind her, a handsome, full-faced man with the look of Viking ancestors. He looked idly at Dee's car, then patiently at the line in front of him, the woods to either side.

"It's a roadblock," Dee said. "I want you to take Tommy and go straight into the woods. Do you understand?"

"Straight into the woods."

"Straight into the woods and back to the motel. Do you understand, Ash? I will meet you at the motel. We've been driving in a semi-circle so far. The motel is on the other side of the mountain. Can you do that, Ash?"

"Yes."

"And quickly, do it as fast as you can. I'm going to talk to the man behind us and when I tell you to go, I want you to get into the woods and out of sight as fast as you can go. All right?"

"All right, Dee."

"Good. Stay covered until I tell you, then run as fast as you can." She opened her car door, then hesistated.

"And Ash, you must not let them take Tommy away from you. They would make him suffer too much and I know you don't want that."

"I don't want him to suffer."

"Of course not. But they will make him suffer if they get hold of him again. If they're going to catch him, I want you to treat him the way you did your family. Do you understand?"

Ash was silent.

"Do you understand what to do, Ash?"

"Yes, Dee," he said, reluctantly.

"Good. Now when I tell you to run, you take Tommy and run into the woods and then over the mountain. All right?"

"All right."

"And who do you love?"

"I love you, Dee."

"I love you, too, Ash," she said as she left her car and walked back down the line.

Ash whispered to Tommy who lay beneath him, sheltered by Ash's bulk. "It won't hurt, I promise," Ash said. "I'm going to carry you, but it won't hurt."

Jack said nothing.

Dee smiled broadly as the driver of the Subaru rolled down his window to speak to her. The refrigerated air from the car feathered across her face like a north wind.

344

"I can't stick around for this nonsense, whatever it is," Dee said. "My kid's home alone, he's got a little flu."

"I'm sorry," the man said. Dee detected a faint European accent.

"It's nothing serious, but you know how we mothers are. We worry."

"Of course you do," he said sympathetically.

"So I'm going to turn around and go on back."

"Yes, of course."

"So if you wouldn't mind backing up a little so I can just swing around. You be careful, though. Somebody might be coming up behind you and we don't want anything to happen to you."

The driver smiled at her. "I'll be all right."

"Oh, that's what you all say," Dee said. "Then look what happens to you."

The driver was not quite sure what she meant, but she seemed so amused by him that he laughed.

Dee returned to her car and stood by the open door. When the driver of the Subaru turned to look over his shoulder while driving backwards, she shouted, "Now, Ash!' and the big man burst from the back seat, a large bedspread-covered bundle clutched in his arms. As he charged into the trees, bent over his burden, he looked like a parody of a football fullback running into the line with a football tucked into his belly.

Karen and Becker had set up a temporary headquarters with the State Patrol captain to monitor the radio reports coming in from the roadblocks as well as outside calls to the Bureau. The day started with good news.

"They found an old snapshot of Taylor Ashford," Karen told Becker. "They faxed it from Pennsylvania to Albany. The bad news is the agents left for here before the fax came in. Albany is faxing it to the Massachusetts

State Patrol and to the cop house in Becket. The bad news is the nearest State Patrol fax is forty-five minutes from here."

"And I'm not sure our fax works," volunteered Blocker. Karen had kept the two local cops, Blocker and Reese, with them to act as envoys or chauffeurs as the case demanded. "We don't use it that much," he added sheepishly.

"So, we'll have it in forty-five minutes," said Becker, sounding more philosophical than he felt. There was nothing to do but wait.

When the initial report from the roadblocks came in, Karen was the first to react.

"He may have been seen," Karen said matter-of-factly as she slid into Reese's police cruiser. Becker could tell she was trying not to get excited prematurely. "There's a call from a woman, the details are a little vague, I'm going to check it out."

"Keep in touch," Becker said.

Reese climbed behind the steering wheel, started the car then waited for Karen's order. Becker could see she had him trained already.

"No, you keep in touch," she said. "If you find him, remember, he's mine."

Becker grinned. "I'll remember, I don't want any part of him. I'm on medical extension, remember?"

"You remember."

"Good luck," he said.

"There's probably nothing to this," she said grimly. She nodded and the car shot forward.

Becker's call came a few minutes later. The caller was one of the patrolmen manning the roadblock on Winkler Road on Mt. Jefferson. "We have a motorist here," he said, "Mr Odd Ronning, who tells us he saw a man leave the line on Winkler Road and run into the woods. He says the man was carrying something wrapped in a blanket."

"I know him," said Blocker.

"Who?"

"Mr Ronning. Very smart guy. If he says he saw it, he saw it."

Becker grabbed Blocker and propelled him into the passenger seat of his squad car while Becker took the wheel.

"Tell them to hold him there," he called back to the Captain.

"Uh, technically, I should be driving," Blocker said.

Becker had the siren and lights going and was already taking a curve at a speed that made Blocker uneasy.

"We need you on the radio," Becker said. "I need two hands on the wheel."

"I see that," Blocker said.

"Call the roadblock on Winkler and tell them to hold all cars coming down the mountain."

"Down the mountain? I thought we were going up."

"We are. We're going up in the left-hand lane, the right one is full of cars being stopped by the roadblock."

"Right," said Blocker.

Becker waited to a count of three before he said, "Better do it now so we don't meet anyone coming down when we're going up."

"Right!" said Blocker, full understanding coming to him a little late. He reached for the radio as Becker squealed around a curve, into the left lane to pass a truck, then back into the right as an alarmed motorist in the oncoming traffic slammed on his brakes.

The name of the mailbox was 'Lynch' which Karen thought was grimly appropriate to her own frame of mind. An attractive honey blonde was waiting for them on her porch, a girl by her side. A large collie dog lay listlessly at the woman's feet. It lifted its head at the approach of strangers, then lay back down at a word from the woman.

"She a beauty, or what?" Reese asked under his breath. Karen glanced at him, wondering if his tone bespoke a relationship with the woman named Lynch, wishful thinking, or simple connoisseurship. To Karen's eye, both mother and daughter were beautiful.

"Hey, Peg," Reese said shyly, looking at the woman, then quickly away, and Karen realised it was wishful thinking. This woman had far too much natural dignity for a local cop to contend with.

"Astrid saw him," Peg said indicating the little girl peeking around from behind her. She spoke directly to Karen, cutting Reese out of the communication loop immediately. "She was playing in the backyard, yesterday. She told me right away, but I'm afraid I didn't give too much importance to it until I heard about the roadblock. Show them, honey."

The little girl had been standing behind her mother's skirt, but stepped forward now as if realising it was her turn on stage. She possessed her mother's colouring, the same bright eyes that twinkled with intelligence and barely restrained amusement. She led them directly to the back of the house and pointed towards the ditch that ran next to the railroad tracks.

"He came out of there," the girl said. "He climbed out then a hand cotched his leg and pulled him back in."

Karen shuddered at the image of the hand emerging from the ditch and grabbing ... She told herself it was not Jack. A boy playing with friends. Not her son. Someone else being caught and pulled into the ditch. Not Jack.

"Did you know the boy?"

"No."

"Did you ever see him before?" Karen asked. The little girl shook her head.

"What did he look like? Can you describe him?" She thought she would have to drag a description out of the girl, helping her every step of the way. Children were notoriously bad witnesses. But Astrid had either been rehearsed or she had a good eye for boys.

"He had brown hair and cut off jeans and a T-shirt," she said. "He was maybe a year older than me ... He was cute."

"The shirt ..." Peg started, then deferred to her daughter.

"And he was scared," Astrid continued. "He wasn't crying, but he was scared."

"Did you see who grabbed him?" Reese asked.

Astrid answered by speaking to Karen. She, too, seemed to know who was important.

"Just a hand," she said. "I just saw a hand."

"You can't see into the ditch from her angle," Peg said. She knelt to her daughter's height to demonstrate.

"Did you see anything on the T-shirt?" Karen asked.

"I'll show you," Peg said and turned to the swing set. "It was right here," she said, puzzled, then she muttered something and called "Erik!"

A second collie came around the corner of the house, a white cloth in his mouth.

"Come here," Peg said briskly.

"He's so dumb," the girl said.

After a brief tussle, the woman got the cloth from the dog's mouth. She stretched it out and displayed it to Karen. It was a plain white T-shirt, wet from saliva and torn from the dog's teeth.

Karen looked inside the collar and felt her knees buckle. She clung to Reese for support. The name written on the collar in laundry pencil was Jack's.

Karen's voice crackled over the radio as Becker began the long climb up Winkler Road, passing the string of stalled cars in the right lane.

"Anything yet?" she asked.

Becker took the radio microphone from Blocker's hand. "I'll be there in about two minutes. Where are you?"

"I'm with Officer Reese," she said. Becker wondered if she were driving the other police car, too. If so, Reese was in for a more frightening ride than the one he was giving Blocker. "We found Jack's T-shirt." Her voice was strained, as if every word cost her an effort. "We've been studying the map. If Lamont was in Becket yesterday and on Winkler Road today there's only one area he was likely to be coming from. We think he had to be staying some place along Route 37 unless he was out yesterday just driving around, which isn't likely. If whoever was driving the car on Winkler that he got out of turned around, chances are he's heading back to where he came from. It's probably the only safe spot he knows. We're going to check out the motels on 37. Reese tells me there are only three."

"How are you?" Becker asked.

Karen clicked off without answering but Becker thought he heard the bark of a sardonic laugh before the radio went dead. As they pulled to a stop at the road-block, Blocker said, "There are four," but Becker was already out of the car and moving.

"Ronning?"

The man from the Subaru station wagon extended a hand uncertainly. "Odd Ronning," he said.

Becker took the hand, using it to shake and simultaneously to pull the older man towards the police cruiser.

"Becker, FBI. Can you show me where the man went into the woods?"

"Of course," Ronning said, already being eased into the back seat. He exchanged nods with Blocker.

There was no place to turn the car around without time consuming manoeuvres so Becker put the car in reverse and went back down the mountain backwards.

"She was very charming," Ronning said.

"She?"

"But manipulative, you know? I had the feeling she didn't want me to see the man get out of the car."

"There was a woman driver?"

"Of course. Very attractive. Blonde, you know. Lovely smile."

"Christ," said Becker.

Blocker watched with growing anxiety as Becker wheeled the car backwards down the hill, his head out the window, the engine screaming in protest at speeds for which reverse gear was never intended. Neither Becker nor Ronning seemed aware that anything unusual was taking place.

"The man?" Becker asked.

"I didn't get much of a look. Nothing more than a glimpse, really. But he was very big, I'm sure of that."

"And you said he was carrying something?"

"He carried something against his chest and there was a blanket. I saw the end of it flapping halfway down his leg."

A good man, Becker thought. He wished he could exchange him for Blocker.

"Right here," said Ronning and Becker squealed to a halt. "The man ran in right about there," Ronning pointed.

"Could you tell which way he was headed?"

"Oh, up. Definitely up the mountain."

"And the woman left the line in her car and went back down the hill?"

"Yes. Of course."

Becker stood on the road and looked up the mountain. Visibility into the tree line was only a few feet and, from his angle, the top of the mountain could not be seen.

Becker took Blocker by the arm.

An angry motorist leaned out of his car and yelled, "What the hell is going on?" Becker ignored him.

"Get on the radio and ask for help, get at least three more men, then start up the mountain."

"What am I looking for?" Blocker demanded.

"What the hell are you guys doing?" the motorist called.

"Hey, shut up," Blocker said, then, to Becker, "How do we know this guy didn't just go into the woods to take a leak, waiting all this time in line ..."

"He took a blanket with him, maybe he went in for a picnic," Becker said. "Or maybe to take a nap. In that case it won't take long to find him, will it? Listen, Blocker, if this is Lamont, he's killed nearly a dozen people by now, including his own family. If you find him, do not assume he's hiding in the trees because he's modest about his bathroom habits. And do not try to engage him, either. Just get on your walkie-talkie and tell headquarters, then keep an eye on him, understand?"

"You never mentioned anything about his being a killer. I thought we were after a kidnapper." Blocker rubbed the handle of his service automatic nervously.

"Look, I know this is not the sort of thing you run across around here, but it's what you've got on your hands now. Just find him and keep a safe distance, nothing will happen to you."

"Where are you going to be?"

"I'm going to get behind him, if I can. Now call for help, please."

Becker stopped again as he was about to get in the car.

"What did you mean, 'there are four'?"

"What?"

"Earlier you said, 'There are four.' What were you talking about?"

"There are four motels on Route 37, not three."

"Doesn't Reese know that?"

"We usually don't consider the Melba Inn. I mean, when people ask us about a place to stay for the night, we send them to the other three. A tourist wouldn't be happy in the Melba."

"Tell her that," Becker said, then, "Never mind, I'll tell her."

Becker called Karen on the radio while squealing backwards down the mountain but got no response. He relayed the message to headquarters and asked them to pass it on. As he came to a stop, he wished they had more men. Karen should not be searching motels herself, she should be running the show. Not that she had much choice, Reese was hardly the calibre of man to trust with the job and all of the State Patrol men they had were manning roadblocks. The men from the Bureau had yet to show up and Becker wondered if, ironically, they hadn't been slowed by the traffic jams caused by the roadblocks.

Becker eased the cruiser off the road, into a drainage ditch and got out of the car. If he had judged properly and Lamont was going over the mountain to reach the only escape route on the other side, Becker now had the angle on him. If he hurried, he might be able to intercept Lamont before he started his downward leg.

Becker slipped into the woods and began to work upwards and around the mountain in a long spiral path.

The climb was steep but not arduous in the beginning and Ash was able to do it with Tommy still clutched in his arms. The closer he got to the top, however, the steeper the slope became and he was required to grab at trees and rocks to maintain his balance. He tried it one-handed for a time, but when he stumbled and fell directly on to the boy, Ash gave it up. He took the bedspread off and studied Tommy for injuries. The boy had only had the wind knocked out of him and he looked around now, wild-eyed, squinting at the first light in an hour but anxious to see where he was.

"We'll leave this here," Ash said, as much to himself as to the boy. He folded the bedspread carefully, then put it down atop a rock. He wanted to be able to tell Dee where he had left it so that they could come back and get it. They still had the blanket on the floor of the car, but she might want the spread as well. Dee was careful about not keeping things that did not belong to her.

He kept a hand on the boy's shoulder as he looked back down the mountain. There was not much to see through the fully leaved trees, but Ash could hear voices a long way away. Men were calling back and forth to each other, giving directions. He wondered if they were coming up the mountain after him. Dee had said to go fast. Ash got to his feet and pointed the boy up the mountain.

"You go first," he said. "I'll be behind you to catch you. Don't worry, you'll be safe."

Becker paused to catch his breath. He had been running when he could through the woods and up the increasing slope during his long spiral around the mountain. Now he was at the point he guessed to be opposite Lamont's ascending path on the other side. From here on it was straight up. If he had judged correctly, Lamont would be coming down on a route close enough to Becker's own that Becker would be able to see him, or at least hear him, when he crested the peak and started down. The peak itself was problematic at this juncture since Becker could see only a few yards ahead of himself through the trees.

Becker listened carefully, holding his breath a moment, trying to catch the sound of branches breaking, loosened rocks, heavy feet in the dead leaves and needles of the forest floor. Anyone coming from the top of the mountain would have to come the first third of the way down on the seat of his pants, clutching at handholds as he came. He would be as easy to hear as a small avalanche. If the man was not in a hurry, he could descend backwards, of course, picking his way carefully – and silently – but that would take time and Becker assumed Lamont was going to be travelling fast.

Hearing only the normal sounds of the woods, Becker started upwards, reaching for tree trunks and roots to propel himself forward up the ever increasing slope. He had dropped to his hands and knees, digging for handholds in the rocky forest soil when the trees abruptly fell away entirely and he faced a sheer wall of stone. Becker stopped, his breath thundering in his ears from the effort of his climb, trying to assess his situation.

He had reached the point of some geological accident where the steepness of the incline, the force of gravity and the effects of erosion had conspired to rip away part of the mountain face and leave a cliff as sheer as if it had been sliced from a cake by a giant sabre.

A few saplings had sprouted from crevices in the rock, jutting out at very shallow angles before curving almost perpendicularly and shooting directly skyward. Tufts of weeds and grass were scattered here and there upon the vertical face, and, most incongruously, several small clusters of flowers, their bouquets taunting anyone foolish enough to climb up after them; but for the most part, the escarpment was jagged reddish-brown rock, high and wide and forbidding, filling Becker's vision in either direction before it disappeared around the curve of the mountain.

Becker tried to estimate how long it would take to skirt the cliff and come around it on either side. Too long, either way, and worse, he had no way of telling which side Lamont would choose for his descent. If he struck off in the wrong direction, he could miss Lamont entirely.

As he pondered his choices, his breathing gradually subsided, and it was then that he heard the voice.

It was a high, piping, squeak of alarm, almost a squeal, shut off in the middle of its sound and followed by a man's deeper, startled tones. Looking in the direction of the sound, Becker saw a small shower of leaves and pebbles cascade the escarpment. Something, or someone, had come very close to tumbling over the edge. Still on his hands and knees at the end of the tree line, Becker watched as a man's head and upper torso appeared above the cliff edge. Becker drew silently back among the trees and observed the man as he peered downwards at the straight fall before him.

There was no mistaking him. It was the big man from the Restawhile motel. Becker remembered him sitting on the motel bed, looking stupid. Not nearly as stupid as I was, Becker thought. The man looked stupid now, too, his eyes searching the precipitous plunge as if hoping to see a magic staircase open before him. Another head appeared beside him. It was Jack, chastened by his near fall and crawling on his belly now to see what lay ahead. Both man and boy were panting heavily, sorely winded by their climb.

Jack's eyes glanced in Becker's direction then flickered away. Becker did not know if the boy had seen him or not, but if he had he had shown the presence of mind to keep quiet about it. Becker prayed that the boy could retain his poise for the next several minutes. His life might depend upon it.

It took Becker no time at all to make up his mind. He could not afford to guess which way to go and guess wrong, Jack would be lost and gone. He could not afford to wait and hope that Blocker had summoned help to back up Becker. There was no available help in the first place, not much chance Blocker had called for them in the second. To sit and wait was worse than guessing the wrong direction. If Becker stayed where he was, Lamont would evade him no matter which way he went. There was only one way to go, and it was forty feet straight up the cliff.

The big man turned away from the escarpment and looked back down the mountain in the direction of his pursuers. As Becker began his climb he could hear Lamont talking to the boy, but within seconds his ears were filled with the harshness of his own breathing as he hauled himself upward, hand over hand.

Ash could hear the men coming up the mountain, still calling to each other. Their voices were sounding winded now and they were stopping frequently to catch their breath. Ash had no choice but to wait until Tommy caught his breath, too. It was impossible for him to carry the boy along terrain this steep, he needed his cooperation.

"Are you ready?" Ash asked.

Jack breathed deeply, exaggerating his condition. "Not yet," he panted. "I'm so tired."

Ash looked uncertainly at the boy, then back down the mountain.

"OK," he said. "But hurry."

"I can't breathe," Jack panted. He was not certain if he had seen a man at the bottom of the cliff or not, but clearly there were men coming up the mountain behind them. Jack knew that running away would do him no good, the big man would catch him in a second and Jack was afraid of tumbling down the rocky slope. His only chance was to stall for time and he did not have to feign very much, he was genuinely exhausted. He resisted the urge to look back down the cliff to see if the man was really there.

From a distance of six inches the iron pyrite in the rocks looked fuzzily pink. Becker eased his way upward, his face close to the stone, his vision focused only as far away as his next handhold. Under normal circumstances, it was a climb he would never undertake without equipment. He needed a hammer and pitons to build himself a ladder in the rock, a safety rope to keep a slip from becoming a fatal fall to the bottom. But these were not normal circumstances. He climbed faster than he knew was safe, but the result of delay seemed worse than the danger of a fall.

There were no ledges to sit on, no rifts in the rock wide enough for him to secure himself, no place to rest, no grips firm enough for him to even lean out from the wall and look upwards. He could not plan his ascent any further than one set of holds at a time because he could see no further up with his face so close to stone. He could not hear anything over the sound of his own breathing. He dared not look down to see how far he had come, he could not look up to see how far he had to go. Fingers scrambling above him to find a ridge of rock that would hold his weight, toes seeking the tiny outcroppings his fingers had left, he inched his way upwards.

Becker tried to pause to ease his aching muscles, but it required more energy to hang there on three fingers and a toe than to keep moving upwards. Meanwhile, the part of his mind not concentrating on the climb was racing. If Lamont was the man from the motel, and Becker was convinced that he was, then the woman who was with him, the nurse, was involved too. His idea of searching for the uniform left in a laundry was not a bad one, after all. He remembered the motorist's description of the woman who had been driving the car from which Lamont emerged. 'Charming,' the man had called her. A woman who could make a man think she was charming after a few seconds of talk at a roadblock. The woman at the motel had worked like that, leaping into a conversation without preamble, as if she had known a man all her life. It had to be the same woman, and she conned us both, Becker realised. Diverted us both, took our minds off of our business almost immediately. She did it to me by flirting, Becker thought, remembering his sexual reaction to brushing against her in the motel room. And she distracted Karen by using Jack, by both flattering her and suggesting she was an unfit mother all at once. She put us both off balance and kept us there. Mentally, he cursed himself. Karen had to be told, she had to be warned who she was looking for – and how dangerous she was. But there was no way to do it now.

His left arm began to go into spasm, the biceps jerking wildly from the unremitting strain. Becker released the fingers of that hand, letting the arm hang at his side as he pressed closer to the rock, trying to merge with it so that he could cling with face and chest and hip.

"We have to go now," Ash said. He had been peering down the mountain toward his invisible pursuers for the last several minutes, his face thrust forward as if he could see them that much sooner.

"I can't," Jack said, still panting.

"We have to," Ash said.

"I'm too tired," Jack insisted, shaking his head, then dropping it between his knees. "I just can't. Honest."

Ash looked back down the mountain, bewildered. The climbers had become silent but he knew they were getting close.

"We have to," Ash repeated.

"Can't ..."

Ash grabbed Jack under the arm and pulled the boy to his feet. Jack sat again as if his legs could not hold him. With a trace of annoyance, Ash lifted the boy again and swung him around so that he rode piggy-back, leaving Ash's arms free. Ash took his first tentative steps along the crest of the mountain with the boy on his back.

Becker was falling, but his body hadn't submitted to gravity yet. He had reached the top, he could see it even with his face against the rock, the horizon hovering tauntingly just one more reach above him. But it was a reach he could not make. As he lifted his left foot to hip level to give himself the purchase to push up for the final grasp, the thin ridge of rock crumbled under his weight and his left leg swung down uselessly. His bloody fingers were barely holding on as it was and his feet had no way to move higher to relieve the weight. He hung two feet from safety, clinging to sheer stone with two fingers on one hand, three one the other and a toehold for his right foot that was more wish than security. There was no way to change position without falling, no way to ascend without plummeting down forty feet to the waiting granite below. His fingers began to dance with cramps, then his biceps. It was a matter of seconds, Becker realised, before the spasming of his own muscles jerked him right off the mountain.

It was then he saw the foot before his face. Lamont

stood above him along the crest, staring down, his mouth open in wonder.

"Who are you?" Lamont asked.

"Help me," Becker said.

"What are you doing?"

"I'm going to fall. Help me."

Jack's head appeared over the big man's shoulder and he gaped wide-eyed.

"Help him," Jack said.

"We have to go," said Lamont.

"Please!" Becker cried. His right foot slipped off its tiny ridge, forced back by the twist of his body as he looked straight up at Lamont. Both arms and fingers were jerking wildly.

Jack slid off Ash's back and reached down for Becker, but his arm was too short. Jack tugged at Ash's pant leg, imploring him to help. Slowly, uncertain what to do, Ash knelt and reached down and grabbed Becker's shirt collar. He pulled him upwards then caught one of his flailing arms and lifted him on to the crest of the mountain.

Becker sprawled forward on to the ground, his arms splayed out to either side. Still spasming, they flopped like landed fish.

"You hurt yourself," Ash said, looking at Becker's bleeding fingers.

"My arms," Becker moaned. "Rub my arms."

"We have to help him," Jack said. The boy began massaging one of Becker's twitching biceps.

"Harder," Becker said, gritting his teeth against the pain.

"We have to go," Ash said, but he took the other arm, watched what Jack was doing and imitated it.

"Harder, harder."

Becker's whole body began to jerk as the tension of the climb took its toll on his legs and his back as well as his hands and arms. The spasms rocked him, doubled him in pain, made him convulse so violently he threatened to roll back over the cliff.

Jack sat on his back, digging his hands into his biceps, then his leg. Ash followed the boy's lead, trying to bring the spasms under control.

A voice rang out from below them, startling in its clarity and closeness. The pursuers were coming on. Ash stared down the mountain. He still could not see them, but the nearness of the voices frightened him.

"We have to go," Ash said. He lifted Jack to his feet. "Come on, Tommy."

"Help me," Becker said, but the big man ignored him this time. Jack tried to pull away but Ash lifted him off the ground and held him to his chest.

"Taylor. Leave the boy with me," Becker said. He managed to flex the toes of both feet towards his body and gradually the cramps in his calves eased.

"She said to leave him with me, Taylor," Becker continued.

"Who said?" Ash asked, still holding Jack off the ground.

Becker struggled to remember the woman's name. He bent his wrists and forearms backwards, pronating them as far as he could to counteract the convulsing biceps muscles. The woman's name wouldn't come to him.

"It was Dee," Jack said quickly. "Dee said."

"Dee said?"

"That's right, it was Dee," Becker said. "She wanted you to give the boy to me."

Ash hesitated. Becker managed to bring himself to his hands and knees and move closer to the big man.

"She never told me," Ash said.

"You had already gone. I just spoke to her, she sent me to get the boy."

"That's right," Jack said. "Honest."

Ash tried to understand. Dee didn't trust anyone but Ash, he knew it, she told him all the time. She never let anyone else take care of the Tommies, never. Why would she want him to give Tommy to this man who was crawling towards him? She knew that Ash could take care of Tommy better than anybody.

"Dee said give him to me," Becker said again. He managed to crawl another step closer, willing his muscles to hold off, just hold off another minute. A few more feet and he would be close enough to get the man's leg. If he could just get him off balance, bring him down, he had some sort of a chance. But he couldn't do it as long as the man was holding Jack. He was too close to the edge, they could both go over if Becker made a lunge.

"Dee said." Jack struggled vainly in the man's arms. Becker was amazed at how calm the boy had remained. If he stayed that way, they had a chance.

"Give him to me, Taylor."

"How come you know my name?" Ash asked. No one had called him Taylor in years. Not since the hospital. His mother was the only one who had ever used his given name. His mother, and strangers.

"We've met. Dee introduced us." Becker inched closer.

Ash heard the voices calling to each other below. They were very close, now. He remembered what Dee had said. He was not to let them get Tommy back.

"I don't know you," Ash said.

"I'm a friend of Dee's," Becker said. He was almost there. Another foot and he could grab the man.

"You're a Lyle," Ash said contemptuously as he made up his mind. Dee said to kill the boy rather than let them take him back. Everyone would be better off that way.

Ash held Jack over the edge of the cliff and let him fall then began to run. Becker lunged forward and grabbed

Jack's leg. The boy's momentum yanked Becker closer to the edge and he came to a rest with his elbow over the void, the boy dangling in space at the end of Becker's right arm.

The spasm in his right biceps began again immediately and as Becker tried to grab Jack's free-swinging other leg, his left arm started to cramp, too. He caught Jack's trousers but the grip was too small for his fingers and they spasmed. He grabbed at Jack's ankle and the larger grip allowed him to hold on. Beyond that, there was nothing he could do. He had no leverage lying on his stomach and holding the boy at arm's length, and when he tried to wriggle backwards, his legs and back began to convulse.

The pain was so intense it forced Becker's eyes shut. He clenched his teeth and groaned as loud as he could, a forced keening sound as if he were lifting the world's heaviest weight. As his muscles jerked his whole body bucked and inched him towards the edge. They were both going over together unless he could do something, but he could not even dig in with his toes without his legs bouncing up again in agony.

He could hear the shouts of the police coming up the mountain but he had not the breath nor the control to call out. Even drawing a full breath would make him give up and give in to the pain.

"Scream, Jack," he said desperately through clenched teeth. "Scream."

24

The first two motels went quickly. Karen checked the registry first, then, with the manager's assistance, she and Reese visited each room that appeared even remotely suspicious. They worked fast but deliberately. After each of the first two motels, Karen radioed back to the headquarters to learn about Becker's progress. Each time she was informed that he was last seen backing the cruiser down the mountain at high speed.

The third motel caused a delay when the manager made a fuss about calling his superiors before authorising a search of the rooms. Frustrated, Karen walked off, leaving Reese to deal with the manager, and found a maid who was changing sheets. Karen flashed her badge, took the maid by the arm and proceeded to have her unlock every locked door on the first level of the motel. By the time Karen reached the second level, Reese appeared, grinning, with the manager in tow. Eager to appear to be in control, the manager assisted her with the remaining rooms himself.

Karen called the headquarters once more. They were still unable to raise Becker on the radio in the cruiser that he had commandeered from Blocker. Blocker himself had last reported in just before starting up the mountain with two patrolmen. Because of the mountains, the walkie-talkies were useful only for the men to communicate with each other, they could not reach headquarters with so weak a signal.

"He said to say there were four, though," the officer at headquarters said.

"Four what?"

"I don't know, he must have been jumping out of the car when he said it. All I got was "tell Reese there are four," then I couldn't raise him anymore."

Karen looked to Reese. "Four what? What does it mean?" Reese thrust his lower lip forward as he concentrated.

"Four motels?" he said at last.

"You mean there's another one?"

"That's all I can think he means."

"Is there another one, goddamn it?"

"Well ... sort of. There's the Eldba. But no one would stay there."

"Why not?"

"It's a dump. It's out of the way, it's off the road, no one goes there ..."

"That's exactly what he would want!"

"I didn't think you would be interested. There isn't even a manager there this time of day ..."

"Drive, damn it! Drive," she said. It took all of her control not to hit him.

"He doesn't even open the office half the time during the day," Reese said defensively. He could see the motel a quarter of a mile away. "The couple of regulars who live there don't need him and otherwise there just isn't any business until it gets dark. If someone happens to come by, they can call him at home – not that he's at home during the day, either. He works at the post office and is most likely out delivering mail ..."

The cop car slid into the driveway and Karen told Reese to begin at one end of the line of units while she started at the other. They would try the easy way first, and if that didn't work, Karen was prepared to get into the rooms anyway she could. She pounded on the first door and waited. From the general state of disrepair, it didn't look as if it would take much to spring a lock or two. If the door was locked from the inside with a dead bolt, they couldn't get in right away – but they would know someone was inside, too.

Dee opened the door to the officer as if she had been waiting for him.

"Thank God you're here," she said. "I've been calling and calling."

"What … ?"

"He's fallen, he hit his head, I can't wake him up!"

Reese looked around, saw no one but the frantic woman.

"In here," she said. "Hurry, please hurry!"

Reese followed her into the bathroom. She pulled back the shower curtain and revealed a man lying in the tub, fulling clothed. His eyes were wide and staring.

"Who … ?"

"My husband," Dee said. "He slipped, I can't wake him up, do something, do something, please."

The man's head was tilted crazily to one side as if his neck were broken. Reese stared at him, uncertainly, then to the woman who stood next to him, one hand behind her back. The guy looked to Reese as if he were beyond first aid, looked, in fact, as if he'd been dead a day or two.

"See if he has a pulse," the woman said frantically. "Please see, Lyle."

Reese didn't know why she called him Lyle, if he had heard her right. He didn't want to check the man's pulse, didn't want to touch an obvious corpse at all if he could help it, but he felt that he should give the appearance of trying to help before doing the obvious thing and calling the ambulance.

He leaned over the tub, reaching for the man's wrist. Dee made one swift pass with the razor blade across Reese's jugular vein then drove her knee into his ass, propelling him head first into the tub. His head hit porcelain. Dee continued the pressure with her knee while lifting on his belt, keeping him upside down and off balance.

Reese barely felt the slice across his throat, it was the banging of his head that enraged him. The crazy woman had him up on his toes, his face pressed on to the corpse so they were nose to nose. Reese tried to push up off the tub but she kicked him behind the knees so his leg went out from under him and he tipped further forward. Something hot and liquid gushed past his face and across his eyes but he didn't know what it was. He flailed backward with his right hand, reaching for his gun, but she grabbed his wrist and used his arm like a lever, pushing him still farther into the tub. His lips pressed against the corpse's mouth and Reese wrenched his head away and more steaming liquid poured into his face and he tasted blood. He was not even yet convinced that it was his own blood when his strength seemed to leave him entirely. As he slumped forward and fell atop the body in the tub, he was dimly aware that his throat had been cut. The slice was beginning to hurt. He reached for his neck and felt a moment of terror as the blood pumped over his fingers, and then he was gone.

Dee pushed Reese's feet into the tub so that the officer lay along the length of Edgar's body, then she drew the curtain closed. She rinsed the razor blade and put it on the sink, then picked it up again when she heard the sound from the other room.

The door was ajar and Karen called through it, "Officer Reese." She had completed her run of the units and was looking impatiently for Reese now so that she could begin the second phase.

"Reese? Are you in there?"

"Thank God you've come," came a frantic feminine voice. The voice sounded faintly familiar to Karen. She pushed the door open all the way and saw Dee rushing at her.

"I've been calling and calling,' Dee said. She grabbed Karen's sleeve and pulled her into the room, but she knew immediately that the agent had recognised her. There was no time to repeat the charade at the tub, so Dee turned and slashed at Karen's throat with the razor blade.

Karen jerked back instinctively. The blade cut her neck but missed the jugular and Karen managed to get her arm in the air to partially fend off the return swipe. Dee struck again, more wildly this time, and the blade sliced into Karen's scalp, then again, into the protective hand Karen had thrown before her face.

Karen recoiled then kicked out, her instep hitting Dee just above the knee. Dee staggered back, surprised by the pain. Karen dug inside her jacket for her gun when Dee lunged forward again. The razor slid across Karen's temple.

The butt of the gun was slippery in Karen's hand because of the blood on her palm and the weapon tumbled to the floor. Before she could reach for it, Dee was on her again, slashing wildly. Karen stepped to one side and kicked out again, knocking Dee back a few steps, but she kept coming.

Blood was flowing down Karen's face from her temple, clouding the vision in one eye. She tried to circle the other way, keeping her clear eye on Dee while swiping at the bloody one with her hand.

Dee was on her again, head lowered, her arms swinging around in a bear hug. Karen hit down with her balled fist into Dee's face, felt something crack, then hit her on the back of her neck with a karate chop. Dee's arms were around Karen's back and Karen felt the razor slash into her again and again like an animal's claws. Dee was working the blade upwards, searching for Karen's neck but with her own head lowered she could not reach quite high enough without releasing her hold on the agent.

The razor pierced Karen's jacket and tore down the length of her shoulder blade. Karen dragged Dee backwards, imprisoning the other's arms against the wall, but the pressure of their combined weight drove the blade deeper into Karen's flesh. The pain made Karen yell but she leaned into it, using her shoulders as a fulcrum as she brought her knee into Dee's stomach. She drove her heel into the instep of Dee's foot, then savagely brought the knee up again. Dee groaned and Karen drove the heels of both hands into the side of Dee's head at the ears.

She felt Dee's knees buckle and drove her knee into her once more and followed it with another chop to the back of the neck. Dee crumbled, sagging to the floor and Karen came off of the wall enough to release Dee's arms. The woman fell in a heap.

Karen tried to clear her eye of blood again and suddenly felt the razor rip across the tendons at the back of her knee. She tried to kick out but the leg was suddenly useless and Dee was rising, grinning. Her nose looked broken and was pouring blood and she had lost teeth but she was smiling, her eyes still glinting dementedly.

"You dirty bitch," she said, panting. "You'll never take him away from me again." She lifted the razor blade, now scarlet with Karen's blood, still gripping it lethally between her finger and thumb.

Karen's gun lay on the floor, ten feet away. Too far with two good legs, impossible with only one that worked. She cast wildly about for a weapon, saw the telephone on the table a few feet to her left. Karen lunged for it as Dee struck again. The razor caught her high on the forehead, ripped all the way across, then sliced the edge of her ear as Karen's momentum continued to carry her away. Her hand grasped the telephone, slipped momentarily because of the blood, then held and Karen swung it round with all of her strength, ripping it from the wall. Dee was rushing right into it, eager to get at Karen. The telephone caught her flush on the temple and she collapsed to the floor, sprawling on to her back.

Karen tried to walk across the room but her leg would not hold her and she hopped, fell, then crawled on hands and knees to her gun. She swivelled quickly, seated, her back against the door and lifted the gun with shaking arms towards Dee who lay where she had fallen, twitching slightly.

Gasping for breath, Karen lowered the gun to her lap and tried to assess her condition. She seemed to be bleeding everywhere. Her hands were cut, her legs, her arms. She could feel the pain of the spot in her shoulder where the razor had been driven deeply, but the rest of the cuts did not seem to hurt. But how they bled. The slice across her forehead was pouring blood now and she had to wipe her face with her sleeve to keep her vision.

Head wounds always bleed a lot, she reminded herself. You're not dying, you can still move, you can still think. But you need help.

Dee stirred and moaned and Karen lifted the gun to point at her. She needed the woman alive in order to find Jack. She had to get up, get help, get this woman under control and out of here. Where the hell was Reese?

The blood was in her eyes again and suddenly Karen

blacked out. She came to herself frantically, fearing she was blind. She clawed the blood from her eyes and scrabbled for the gun. It was still in her lap, the other woman was still across the room, but she was dragging herself against the wall, sitting up. The razor blade was still in her hand and Karen cursed herself for not taking it when she had the chance.

Karen pointed her service automatic at the woman. "You're under arrest," she said, realising how inadequate the words sounded.

Dee laughed, then swallowed some of her own blood and coughed.

"Where's my son?" Karen demanded.

"He's my boy, cunt."

"Where is he?"

"You'll never get him again, bitch. He's gone forever."

The roar of the automatic was deafening in the closed room and both women jerked in reaction. Dee turned her head and saw the hole in the wall a few inches from her head. Smiling, she looked again at Karen who sat across the room with her back to the door, the gun now pointed directly at Dee's body.

"Go ahead," Dee said. "Try again. We'll see who gets there first."

Holding the razor with surprising delicacy, her last three fingers off the blade, Dee sought her vein then drew the edge slowly and deliberately from just inside her elbow to her wrist. The line blossomed with blood.

Smiling at Karen as if proud of her handiwork, Dee put the razor in her left hand and expertly cut the length of the vein on her right arm. She dropped the razor at last and leaned back against the wall letting her arms hang straight down. She balled and released her fists to increase the blood flow.

"So where's that good-looking man you had with you

last time you visited me? What was his name, Lyle? He wanted me, you know. Did you know that?"

Karen pushed herself upright, her weight on her good leg. Her head swam and she had to wait a moment for it to clear before she opened the door and looked outside. There was no one in sight. Reese's cruiser was at the other end of the courtyard, impossibly far to drag herself and the other woman. The woman's car was right outside the door.

"Did you kill the cop?" Karen asked. She looked at Dee who was sitting placidly, observing the process with detachment as her life seeped out of her arms.

"Who, Lyle? You were better off with the good-looking one, believe me."

The phone lay on the floor close to Dee, the case smashed, the cord torn, useless.

Dragging her crippled leg, Karen crossed to where Dee sat and picked up the razor while holding the gun in the other woman's face. She sliced strips from the pillow case and tied hasty tourniquets on Dee's arms. Dee sat watching and grinning, as if it were happening to someone else.

"I can tell you're not real good at this, are you? Those won't work."

Dee's purse was on the bed. Karen found the car keys and put them between her teeth. Tucking the automatic in the skirt waist behind her back where Dee could not reach it, Karen started to drag the other woman across the room. She stopped after the first backward hop, mopping the blood from eyes and waiting for the dizziness to pass. I should have tried to stop my own bleeding first, she thought. But she wasn't dying, and the other woman surely would. The cuts in the veins had been surgical, the woman was a nurse and knew what she was doing, and she was probably right, the tourniquets wouldn't do the job.

Hopping backwards two or three times, stopping to wipe her eyes, then hopping again, Karen dragged Dee out of the room, across the mix of grass and gravel and up to the passenger door of the car. Dee was talking to herself now, mumbling in tones too low for Karen to understand. She grunted with the exertion of lifting the other woman, her good foot slipped and Karen fell to her knees. Dee's face was level with her own and she smiled at Karen beatifically. Her teeth were red with her own blood.

Karen folded Dee into the car by stages then hopped to the driver's side, using the car for support. She almost blacked out again as she opened the door, but she held on, fighting against her weakness. When it passed, she dropped behind the steering wheel, pulling her bad leg in with both hands.

She looked at Dee whose head was back against the seat, her mouth open slightly. Despite the tourniquets, blood dripped steadily from her fingertips on to the floor. From the corner of her eye, Karen saw a blanket in the back seat move, then a shape rose up rapidly, blanket fanning out like Dracula's cape, blotting her vision and falling upon her.

She was lifted straight over the seat, her arms pinned at her side, then she was on the floor of the car and encased, as if in a shell of flesh. She tried to struggle but she seemed to be held everywhere by a great weight that could crush her if it would, but merely restrained her so that she could not move.

"FBI," she tried to say, knowing it was pointless. The blood from her head wounds seemed to be pouring out of her now, filling her mouth and nose as well as her eyes. With the last of her strength she pushed up with her good leg, her arms, arching her back like a cat, trying to make a space for herself off the floor. The weight over her yielded that much, allowing her to position herself as she would, but not releasing her.

Karen froze in position, keeping the two feet of leeway for herself between her body and the floor. She could feel the man atop her positioning himself in the same way, accommodating her so as not to crush her while still imprisoning her.

"Dee?" Ash called. "Dee, are you all right?"

"I'm fine," Dee said weakly. "Where's my precious boy?" Karen tilted one shoulder down, trying to keep the man's body in place atop the other shoulder. He held his position. Fighting against the fainting sensation, she slowly arched her back forward while still thrusting upwards with her buttocks. Again the man atop her kept his position. She now had just room enough to slip one hand behind her back.

"I did what you told me," Ash said.

Karen felt the grip of the automatic with her straining fingers, slick with blood. She pulled it slowly from the waist of her skirt.

"You didn't let them take him away from me again?" Dee asked. Her voice was very faint, Karen could scarcely hear her.

"No," said Ash. "The men wanted to steal him but I didn't let them. I dropped him over the cliff."

Karen turned her wrist, pointing the barrel upwards, and pulled the trigger. She kept pulling until the noise stopped and the man's full weight fell upon her, crushing her against the floor. She felt blood soaking her body but she was no longer certain if it was his or hers. As she slipped into unconsciousness she thought she heard Jack's voice calling her, but she knew it was an illusion.

25

Becker lay in bed, waiting for her to return. Karen had heard a sound and had got out of bed to check on her son. Jack slept now in the living room, just outside of their bedroom door, and Karen would be out of bed at the slightest noise. Often as not she would find Jack lying awake. He would smile at her, seemingly untroubled, but his eyes looked as alert as if it were midday.

Sometimes Becker would be awakened in the middle of the night by their whispers as they lay in their separate beds, reaching out to each other for reassurance that the other was still there.

Karen came into the bedroom, limping with the walking cast on her leg. The scars on her head and hands were still red and angry, but healing. Becker had tried to assure Karen that they would not harm her appearance, that indeed, they merely added character to a face already beautiful. She had seemed a good deal less interested in the way she looked than he was, accepting the scars as a price she paid for the return of her son. He was certain she would have borne the loss of a limb with equal equanimity if it had brought Jack safely back to her.

She wriggled backwards into Becker, spooning against him. Since she got out of the hospital she had insisted on maintaining some physical contact with him throughout the night. Becker held her and drifted into sleep.

He was awakened by the shaking of her body. She was crying silently again, as she did every night. The first few nights in the hospital and at home she had been haunted with nightmares that shook her awake with dread. She dreamed of her battle with Dee, of Ash rising up from the back of the car like Satan himself, of suffocating in blood. But the nightmares had vanished with a speed that delighted the psychotherapists that the Bureau had assigned to her. The crying was a good sign, they told her. It was part of the mourning process, they said. Karen listened and nodded and said she was pleased they were pleased.

They told Becker that the nightmares were normal after such a trauma, the silent weeping was to be expected. She is suffering the natural reaction to having killed someone in the most gruelling and gruesome of circumstances, they said. They advised him to be patient with her, to provide her with a sense of security, to continue to reassure her that such grief was part of the healing process. In time she would be back to herself, they promised. All in good time.

Becker kissed the back of her neck. "It's all right," he said, as he had said for nights. "Go ahead and get it out. You should feel bad, it's natural, it will pass."

She twitched her head away from him angrily. "You know better than that," she whispered.

"It will pass," he said.

"That's not what I mean." She turned and took his face in her hands. In the light spilling in from the living room she could see him clearly. She looked straight into his eyes.

"What?" Becker asked.

For a long time he thought she wasn't going to answer